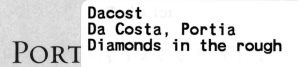

PORT

A Sund

2012 RITA

"Da Costa pens a highly titillating, tantalizing tale....
Not for the faint of heart, but Susan Johnson, Bertrice Small
and Brenda Joyce fans will savor the delicious fantasies within."
—*RT Book Reviews*

"It's been so brilliantly written that you forget that you're [not in]
Victorian England.... Excellent—can't wait to read the next installment."
—*Erotica For All* (U.K.)

"Portia Da Costa has an incredible talent for writing erotic romance.
She is particularly adept at creating dominant heroes
who push their lovers' limits hard, but fall in love so sweetly.
She fills the pages with an unparalleled level of eroticism that singes."
—*Romance Novel News*

"Forget about the rest and read the very best: Portia Da Costa."
—*Sensual Reads*

PORTIA DA COSTA

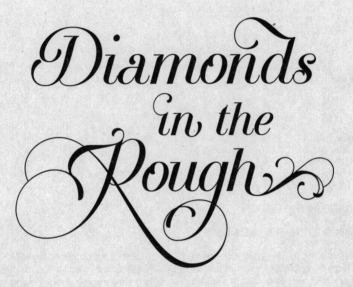

Diamonds
in the
Rough

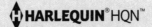

HARLEQUIN® HQN™

Recycling programs
for this product may
not exist in your area.

ISBN-13: 978-0-373-77811-9

DIAMONDS IN THE ROUGH

Printed in U.S.A.

HARLEQUIN®
www.Harlequin.com

Dedicated to Alice, a dear little feline friend.

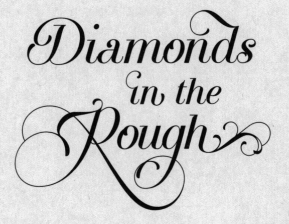

Diamonds in the Rough

❧ I ❧

A Flash of Black

Rayworth Court,
Summer 1891

Wilson Ruffington was bored, bored, bored.

I shouldn't have come here. I knew it would be tedious. These affairs always are.

He looked this way and that, up and down the landing. Rayworth Court was an ugly rambling pile, badly designed in the first place and made worse by haphazard additions. Even *he* was having trouble finding his way around, when usually he could create a floor plan of any building in his mind, hypothesizing from only a limited amount of data.

Frowning at a particularly hideous ancestral portrait, Wilson sighed. He'd come to this country house party for a change of scene, to shake off his ennui, but it wasn't working. He'd never been a great one for the social scene at the best of times, but in the past two months or so, since the split from Coraline, he'd barely even left his house at all. With his mistress gone, what was the point? Work, study, writing, building things and tinkering with things, devising more things to build and tinker with, all this had occupied him. Technical commissions and consultations and his intense intellectual schedule had neatly allowed him to avoid the fact that the first woman in seven years that he'd actually considered proposing to had deserted him. Jiggered off with barely a "by your leave" in order to marry a seventy-five-year-old Italian duke.

"Bitch!"

He spat out the word, but without any real fire. Did he even care anymore? It was only his trivial male ego that was affected by her departure. The greater part of him, the compartment of Wilson Ruffington that contained his intellect, simply trundled on as normal. His sexual appetite was a bit put out by her absence, and he certainly missed a regular diet of plentiful, vigorous and inventive fucking and other carnal activities. That lack, and his wounded pride, were the only things really getting his spirits down.

Stupid, stupid, stupid. To feel insulted and frustrated, and let it bother him.

I'll go home, back to my workroom and my workshop. The people here don't interest me at all, and the women are ninnies.

Feeling more cheerful already, Wilson whipped his notebook out of the pocket of his dressing gown and scribbled down a quick list of readily available chemicals and other ingredients. During a brief foray into the kitchen gardens at the back of the house he'd noted an interesting form of blight on some of the vegetable varieties. If he gave this formulation to the earl's head gardener, instructing the man to apply it as a soil dressing, it would at least go some way toward recompensing Lord Rayworth for his being such an abysmal guest.

Wilson closed his eyes and called up his imaginary floor plan, which worked this time. Left it was, then left again, and he'd find himself at the main staircase. Then up one floor and to his left again, and finally, the blessed sanctuary of his room. Perhaps he'd order up some tea, and some of that delicious plum cake he'd purloined from the kitchen when he'd passed through on his way in from the garden. He would instruct his man Teale to make arrangements for his departure, and while he waited, he'd lie in bed and think about a thorny problem with the submarine plans that was taxing him. The project was a government secret, so he'd brought no papers along, but he could do the calculations in his head. There had to be a way to make those damned flanges marry up correctly in such a confined space.

And if the submarine wouldn't behave, he might toss himself off instead, as a diversion.

Smiling, he opened his eyes again and turned to the left.

Only to swivel back instantly to his right.

What was that? A flash of black, barely glimpsed in the periphery of his vision, then gone again. He'd got the impression of a woman. A female in an inky-black gown, dashing purposefully along the landing at right angles to where he was standing. It'd been only a split second, but there was something…something familiar, and it grabbed at him. A fleeting recollection so astonishing that it made his heart leap.

No, surely not? Not *her*…

In stealth, he padded forward, sweeping back the panels of his open dressing gown, lest he create a flash of blue silk paisley that would attract *her* attention.

But if it wasn't who he imagined it might be, who was she, this swift and graceful figure, this dark, beguiling wraith, moving at speed? He'd seen no female guests wearing black thus far. It was all showy summer gowns, lace and muslin confections of the sort in which Coraline looked so fine. Unless a person was in mourning, black was an illogical choice for swanning around playing croquet, watching impromptu cricket games and admiring the rose garden, because it didn't reflect back the sun, and it made one hot. Even the dowager Lady Rayworth, she of the grim brow who'd frowned at his own sartorial choices, had been wearing light gray in response to the heat. All the fussing young belles were flouncing around in white or flower-sprigged pastels.

Wilson faltered. From somewhere in his memory storehouse, a compartment flipped open and the image of a white muslin frock rose up like a phantasmagoria, taking his breath away. White muslin against green willow. To his astonishment, his somnolent cock stiffened in his linen, firming so hard and so fast it made him grunt in pain.

Great God Almighty! Now there's a turnup.

At the corner's apex, Wilson flattened himself against the paneling and peered around the edge. He'd always enjoyed a spot of subterfuge, and hopefully, all this creeping around like an agent of secrecy might take his mind off his raging erection.

The woman in the black gown was standing with her back to him, trying the handle on a heavy, polished oak door. The hardware defied her, and as she twisted it this way and that, with prodigious force for one so slender, another memory escaped Wilson's capacious storehouse.

It must be you. Nobody else would attack like that. No lady, at least.

The inner photograph displayed another locked door, in another great country house, with another, or perhaps the very same, determined woman grappling to gain entrance. Wilson didn't know whether to laugh or curse. Both were appropriate.

What the hell are you *doing here?*

He'd seen no guest list, and made no inquiries. It'd been potluck. So there was nothing to say she couldn't be here.

Especially if her matchmaking mother had anything to do with anything.

Were parent and daughter both up to habits of old? The parent attempting to marry off the offspring; the child attempting to breach locked doors and gain access to dubious treasures. *Plus ça change...*

Or déjà vu, which I don't believe in.

Calculating the precise distance he could advance without being seen, Wilson leaned a little farther around the corner, and his heart skipped when he saw something he hadn't noticed before.

The mystery woman had been carrying a portfolio with her, what looked like a leather-bound sketchbook tied with ribbons. It was now lying on the carpet runner at her feet. She must have dropped it in order to apply two hands to the door handle.

Definitely you. Who else could it be?

There were too many similarities now for it not to be her, statistically. That slender female form was unmistakable, her shape indelibly branded into his memory. Likewise her glossy nut-brown hair, so thick and willful that it appeared ever in danger of escaping its coiffure. Even the black dress was right. Yes, she might well still be wearing mourning.

Do I want to see you?

Wilson braced himself. The last time he'd faced up to this determined cuss of a creature alone, just the two of them, it hadn't been a pleasant experience. In fact, it'd been a disaster, and peculiarly disturbing. The juxtaposition of hurling insults at each other and him developing a raging erection had unnerved him. And he didn't easily become unnerved. In fact, she was the only one in seven years who could make it so. Not even Coraline had produced quite the same effect.

Wilson debated turning away. There was no logic in court-ing unpleasantness. No advantage for either of them.

Oh, don't be a whining coward, man! You're not scared of her, are you? Ninny.

So he stayed where he was, watching, waiting for the right moment, waiting to see if she still had the nefarious skill he'd taught her once, that day long ago, when she'd wanted to get into a forbidden library and explore its exotic treasures.

Déjà vu indeed. The Earl of Rayworth was reputed to have a fine and very extensive collection of erotic books and scan-dalous works of art stashed away somewhere here at the court, a secret library of the proscribed and the profane. Wilson had a keen interest in all forms of esoterica, too, and the earl's hoard was said to include choice items from all over Europe and Asia, rich in words and pictures both divine and disgusting.

"Stupid, dratted, wretched, provoking thing!"

Wilson edged forward again, suddenly enjoying the sight of his quarry kicking out at the oak with a slender foot clad in a black boot of glace kid. The thump of footwear against door and her sudden yelp of pain sent his memory spinning back again, retrieving hot, wild cries that weren't stubborn or impatient in the slightest, but full of passion and joyous, sensual satisfaction.

About to wade into the fray, Wilson froze when a slender white hand reached up and prized first one substantial pin from her thickly coiled hair, then another. Crouching, her full skirt a black pool around her, the mysterious yet infinitely fa-miliar woman applied her makeshift picklocks to the source of her frustration.

If any last specks of doubt had lingered, they dissolved now. This was the final conclusive echo of the past.

Cracking the secret library's lock was precisely what he'd have done himself, and he always carried a set of picklocks and other miniature tools in his pockets. There were very often private cases in the many libraries he consulted, and he was too impatient to spend time parlaying with librarians who were overprotective of their scientific and literary treasures.

The graceful burglar beyond wasn't quite as accomplished at breaking into strongholds as he was, but he was the one who'd shown her how to do it, in that different mansion, and it seemed she hadn't lost the knack. After a few moments an audible click announced her success, and she straightened, her spine a shallow, exquisite arc as she reached up and jammed the pins back into her abundant hair, dislodging a few shiny, nut-brown strands in the process. The wayward tresses tumbled down against her neck, and absentmindedly she pushed at them. Wilson's hand flexed in a physical memory—of running his fingers through that lush, silky fall as she clung to him, gasping.

Without a backward look, the slim felon swooped down again to snatch up her leather binder, then opened the door and passed swiftly into the room beyond, her skirts gliding and floating as she swirled them out of the way to shut the door behind her.

Wilson sped forward, experiencing a mix of curiosity, irrational happiness and an uncharacteristic apprehension as he went. Would they argue like cat and dog again? Would it be the more recent bones of contention they scrapped over...or the older ones?

What's wrong with you, man? Surely you can meet her with equanimity? You've got the upper hand now.

How cold that sounded. He shook his head, focusing his attention on the moment rather than the larger picture of their tortuous familial complications.

With his fingers on the doorknob, he cocked his head, listening. What was she doing in there? Was she already perusing lewd Oriental etchings and obscene writings? He imagined her pale, narrow face flushing pink with the sly tickle of arousal.

Arousal? Good God, his own state was far more than a sly tickle now. He was up so hard that he was in agony, and if his hand could remember the touch of her, his damned cock had perfect recall. The throb in his rigid flesh was a direct conduit between past and present.

Stilling himself, Wilson set his ear against the thick door, but heard nothing. The only way to discover what she was up to was to throw open the door and surprise her. And quickly, because lurking here like a randy adolescent only laid him open to the danger of discovery. Not that he cared two pins for his reputation, but his presence would draw attention to hers, and she had enough problems already.

But even as Wilson prepared to make his move, a faint sound did issue through the thick door, and it wasn't the languorous female sighs for which his libido had been hoping.

What the devil is it?

A humming whir and an odd repetitive clacking noise were quickly followed by a delicious feminine chuckle.

Wilson turned the handle and pushed open the door to find his lady in black standing in front of a broad, leather-topped desk. On it stood what appeared to be a rather substantial but badly balanced praxinoscope, if he wasn't mistaken, and as she whipped around, she snatched her hand back and the thing slowed to a halt.

"Oh! It's you! I might have known."

2

Cousin Dearest

The familiar low, well-modulated voice expressed only mild surprise, as if Adela had been expecting him.

Wilson scowled, even though he'd not meant to. An expression of displeasure at this stage only gave her the advantage. But then, she had that already. She'd probably *known* he was here somewhere. That dratted mother of hers had probably dragged her here precisely for that reason.

"Indeed it is me, cousin dearest. And I assume you've been expecting me? I'll wager your mother, at least, knows I'm here."

A pair of large, fine brown eyes, almost exactly the rich walnut hue of her sliding, disarranged hair, glared back at him, stormy with suspicion. *She* didn't like their family situation any better than he. In fact, she had far more reason not to.

Adela didn't like *him,* either, and in his heart of hearts, he didn't blame her. He'd crushed her tender feelings underfoot on more than one occasion now. He had a God-given talent for saying the first stupid and often callous-sounding thing that came into his head, much to his self-disgust. Even if he didn't always mean it. Well, even if he didn't completely mean it.

"Indeed she does, *cousin* Wilson, indeed she does." Adela's emphasis on the word was a facetious rebuttal of any kind of endearment. They barely were cousins at all, when it came to it, their genealogy far more of a division than a bond. "Since Father died, one of her dearest wishes and perennial goals in life is to accidentally hurl the two of us together." Adela straightened her spine, almost visibly squaring her firm but narrow shoulders, as if ready to gird on a heavy suit of armor. "But what with our mourning, and your famously clever knack of ignoring and/or regretting our very existence, opportunities for collision have been like hen's teeth. When the countess took pity on us and invited us here, Mama nearly had an apoplexy, she was so thrilled to see you on the guest list."

"And what did you have?" Irrational anger made his tongue sharp. Her clear lack of pleasure in seeing him again was no surprise, but it still made him want to break something. At least she could have feigned a smile for form's sake.

And with a sweet, lush mouth like hers, even the faintest smile was a breathtaking phenomenon.

Dark eyes narrowed. "I experienced a distinct desire *not* to crash into you, yet now, despite my best efforts, here we are."

"You could have declined Rayworth's invitation." It would have been easy enough to claim some unspecified female malady.

Her stare was a basilisk's venomous dismissal, disdaining him, discarding him utterly. Did she feel no warmth at all? If not affection, then not even the slightest twinge of the baser, more animal emotions? "One can't cut off one's nose to spite one's face. I had hoped that I could avoid you as much as possible, while still accepting. It would have broken Mama's heart to deny her at least a shred of optimism. She'd rather live on hope than face the truth."

Adela was steely, but for a few fractions of a second, the way she bit her full, pink lower lip betrayed her. Likewise her narrow white hand twisting a fold of her gown. The contrast between the creamy pallor of her skin and the dull sheen of the black fabric was intoxicating. Unable to stop himself, Wilson imagined her in the kind of black satin boudoir garments that Coraline had so favored, and his wayward cock kicked again, hard, in his trousers.

Anger kicked, too, but not at his cousin. He actually felt enraged at the memory of Coraline for distracting him, as if she'd stepped into the room and interrupted this sparring match. Yet her presence seemed strangely indistinct.... He should have felt regret over his former mistress, but her image was blurred, like an inexpertly developed photograph.

The vision of his second cousin twice removed, however, was sharp as a razor. And despite the fact that the real woman was still scowling at him, the mental image of Adela Felicia Ruffington clad in a black corset trimmed with red lace and ribbons was delectable, and made him want to touch himself. And her.

Yes, you'd look very handsome in a few scraps of expensive frou-frou, Della. Very handsome indeed.

"You *should* be out in society, Della. Just because your mother's prepared to sacrifice you to me in order to save her fortunes and those of your butterfly sisters, that shouldn't stop you from having a little fun."

Adela drew in a slow deep breath, clearly sifting through a selection of sarcastic words with which to lash him. The action made her bosom lift, pushing her delicate curves against the confines of her hidden corset. Wilson's private fantasy of ribbons and black satin grew yet more agonizing in the area of his loins.

Adela was a slim woman, but she had a shape. A beautiful wood nymph's shape, and just once, for one blessed idyllic afternoon, he'd had his eager hands on it.

"Well, I thank you for your sage opinions on the subject of my welfare, Wilson." She inclined her head like some wily bird, assessing him. And not with favor. Wilson could see columns and tallies, and far too many negative ticks stacked up against him. Suddenly his own affected eccentricity, which usually secretly amused him, wasn't quite as satisfying anymore. He clenched his fists in the folds of his dressing gown, to stop his fingers from raking through his unruly hair in an effort to tidy it. He wished he'd made an effort to conform, and that he could change his lurid waistcoat for something more elegant and sober, and his silk dressing gown for a well-cut frock coat. His maverick attire did *not* find favor with his cousin. Her perfectly arched eyebrows spoke volumes.

"But for my part," she went on, her exquisite hauteur and proud deportment making her appear far more entitled to a deluxe life and aristocratic status than he'd ever be, "it's not the end of the world if the Ruffington assets go to you on the Old Curmudgeon's death. Grandfather has his reasons, and we'll make the best of the hand we've been dealt. Mama and the girls and I will manage, even if we have to take in washing. And if the worse did come to the worst, I can't believe that even *you* would throw us out on the street. Our *parasitical* status notwithstanding."

Will I never be allowed to forget that?

Certain ill-thought remarks, made on the occasion of their last meeting, were impossible to expunge. Adela still hated him for them, and he couldn't blame her. He had been nasty. With much on his mind at the time, a moment's lapse of con-

centration had led him to say vile things about Mrs. Ruffington, and all subsequent halfhearted attempts to retract had
only made things worse.

But being instructed—in a letter from her mother—that
he really ought to marry Adela, because the assets and riches
of her grandfather, Augustus Ruffington, Lord Millingford,
were rightfully hers, had made him see red. In cooler moments, he knew that the Old Curmudgeon was being callous
and cruel to his daughter-in-law and granddaughters. But
receiving this commandment while Coraline was being particularly capricious, and with memories of his own mother's
emotional manipulations still keen, Wilson had lashed out at
Adela when they'd encountered each other at the New Gal-
lery not long after.

No, calling her mother "a presumptuous, overbearing parasite with ridiculous notions of entitlement" had not endeared
him to Adela, making an already prickly relationship into a
veritable porcupine of resentment and enmity.

Still, he opened his mouth, not knowing how, but hoping
to make things better. "But that's not quite what I meant, and
you must admit I didn't say it to her face. I—"

His cousin raised a hand and silenced him before he could
get another word out.

My God, she's impressive. Wilson's cock lurched again, the
weight of desire almost making him double over.

"No, you fobbed her off with some pretentious taradiddle
of a reply. What was it…something about being 'married to
your work'?" Adela paused, her eyes narrowing, but still brilliant. "When we all know that your objection is to *me,* and
that you were already involved in a romantic liaison elsewhere.
How is the beauteous Coraline, by the way?"

For a hundredth of a second, Wilson reeled. Oh, how she
wielded the knife. "Still beauteous, as far as I know," he said,

affecting a nonchalance he didn't feel. "And please don't tell me you don't know she's split from me. I'm sure the jungle drums of society have thundered out all the juicy details."

"Ah, yes, her duke. How does it feel to be thrown over for a seventy-five-year-old in a bath chair?"

Wilson wasn't a violent man. In fact, strange as it seemed, considering his work for the War Office, he was a pacifist. But right now he wanted to box his cousin's ears.

"How does it feel to be out for upward of four seasons and not snare a husband?"

Adela remained impressive. Even more so now. Yet there was a flash of pain in her eyes, and he half expected her to demand, "Whose fault is that?"

And he half expected something else, too. The little gesture that more repercussions of his incautious tongue had initiated, the involuntary, yet graceful raising of her hand to her face, to shadow the slightly crooked bridge of her nose.

But she yielded to neither. She didn't even say, "Touché."

"I don't think I care to discuss these matters any further, Wilson. I came here to enjoy a pleasant weekend in the country, and I'd be grateful if you'd kindly leave me alone now to do just that."

No!

Irrationally, no, no, no! He couldn't leave. Not with fire in Adela's eyes and her blood up. Despite what she said and what he knew she felt, he'd never lusted for her harder than he did right now.

"Ah, but this is my pleasant weekend, too, Della. Can't you enjoy your explorations while I'm here? This room interests me. And it must interest you, too, or you wouldn't have employed the skills I taught you in order to gain entrance."

He wasn't lying when he said the room interested him. Under normal circumstances, he'd have been nose deep in one of the many, many choice volumes by now. But it was Adela he wanted to explore. After weeks of feeling sorry for himself, his cousin's delicate flower scent and her determination to spar fired him up, too. Good Lord, he even felt cheerful. His libido surged when she nibbled her soft lower lip again, as if the sound of her pet name, and his discovery of her breaking and entering rendered her vulnerable.

Yet her head was up and her voice was smooth. "I'll leave you to your studies and return later. You can be the one to explain how you gained entry without a key." Abandoning the forgotten praxinoscope, she swept past him, reaching for her leather binder where it lay on the desk.

With barely a conscious thought, Wilson grabbed for her shoulder as she moved by, his every instinct commanding that she stay. They hadn't seen each other in six months or so… and even then, when they'd flayed each other with insults, his blood had sung. More than that, it had been seven years since their fateful, carnal afternoon together. But he realized now he'd never forgotten a single second of it. While diverted by others, his memories of Adela had been haphazardly contained in one of his mental boxes, where he stored thoughts and notions for later review, or otherwise. But even during his bouts of exotic and protracted lovemaking with Coraline that box had still been there, radiant with golden, stolen moments once spent by a river with his distant cousin, its perturbations inchoate, but nagging.

Wilson held his breath. She *had* to stay, but she was struggling, shaking her arm wildly and jerking away from his grip. She even slapped him—hard—around the back and neck with her blessed leather portfolio.

You always were deliciously physical, cousin.

"Let me go, you insufferable oaf. Don't paw me." It was a low, controlled threat, not the squeal of a vexed miss. Resentment dripped from it. "You made it perfectly plain last time we conversed what you think of me, Wilson, *and* my family. Useless, you said, just sitting around waiting to be supported by a man or an inherited fortune, and myself, personally, neither accomplished nor beautiful enough to be worthy of either. Just as much a parasite as my mother."

"I didn't say that!"

Liar. Why was he denying his own bad behavior? He'd certainly implied she was no better than her mother, and just now, he'd attacked her with cutting words again. What was wrong with him? He couldn't even blame Coraline this afternoon, because his former mistress was so faint to him now he could barely picture her.

What would it be like to go back and expunge his thoughtlessness? To be a different man? A man free to take Adela's graceful body in his arms and gently comfort her. To kiss her and touch her… Maybe there was even some convenient river or brook nearby? A soft mossy bank where they could lie down and—

A sharp elbow gouging his ribs dissolved his wayward memories and urges. His grip loosened, and Adela raced for the door, clutching her leather folder while Wilson rubbed quickly at his rib cage, astonished at how viciously she'd jabbed him.

But he didn't box and run and practice a little-known Oriental fighting art for nothing. He had reflexes like a panther, and he shot across the room after his cousin, catching her at the door. He grabbed her again in a light hold that wouldn't hurt, but wouldn't yield, either. Why didn't he have the words to make her stay, without resorting to manhandling?

"Don't go, Della. I know our last meeting was somewhat disastrous, and I shouldn't have been so harsh…." He watched her face. Was she mellowing? "But let's put that behind us, shall we? And start again… Perhaps we can investigate this ingenious toy of yours?" He nodded at the praxinoscope. "And then perhaps select a few exciting volumes from this hoard together? It seems a shame not to, now we're here."

She was relenting. He was sure of it. Indecipherable emotions flickered in her gleaming eyes.

Adela's looks didn't conform to fashionable standards of beauty, and he was only too aware that, though she wouldn't admit it, certain imperfections troubled her. The slight crook in her nose troubled him, too, though not because it was unattractive. To him, it was piquant, almost provocative. It was only the little kink's provenance that irked his soul.

His fault. He couldn't be blamed for her chicken pox scars, though, even if Adela would probably have liked to pin them on him, too. The little pink marks were like a dusting of stars scattered across the apples of her cheeks that only accentuated the otherwise porcelain perfection of her skin.

But what female ever saw her flaws as assets? Adela was intelligent and pragmatic, but even the most sensible woman had vanity.

Her next words only confirmed that. "Well, if you'd stop gaping at my bent nose and my pockmarks, I might consider staying. But I'm not one of your scientific studies, you know."

"I'm not staring." More lies. He *was* staring. "It's just that it's, um, very pleasant to see you."

Good Lord, I sound like a gauche youth faced with his first woman.

His heart turned over and his hand went limp, freeing her again. Adela *was* his first woman, and he her first man. And whatever difficulties and conflict arose, that simple truth would forever be a bond between them.

"Well, it looks like staring to me." But Adela was the one staring now. She was gaping at him as if he'd gone stark mad. "And I don't care for it. I'm looking careworn and as washed out as whey at the moment." Her mouth pursed in a little moue of displeasure. "Black is the most unflattering of colors, and even though I know Papa wouldn't mind me abandoning it, thanks to the Old Curmudgeon and his grudges we don't have funds for colorful gowns at the moment." She fixed Wilson with an old-fashioned look, as if daring him to comment.

Black *did* suit her. Couldn't she see that? She looked superb in the inky hue, and was just trying to make him feel guilty. Again. "Don't be stupid, Della, you look exceptionally fine in black. It gives you a regal and very intriguing quality." It sounded fanciful and made-up, but by George it was the truth.

"You have a strange way of trying to butter me up, Wilson. It won't work." She gave him a stiff look, narrow of eye, but surprisingly, she stayed where she was.

"But I'm not trying to butter you up. It's the truth. You're a handsome woman." Her gleaming walnut-colored eyes widened. He saw her *wanting* to believe. "You're only being willful in denying it. If you don't believe me, I'll prove it to you."

Catching her again and spinning her toward him, he inclined his head and pressed his lips on hers. As hard as he could.

3

The Most Aggravating Man
in the World

The touch of Wilson's lips rocked Adela in her shoes. Seven years ago he'd done exactly this. Grabbed her and kissed her. Now it felt as if barely a second had passed between that kiss and this one, and just as before, all her resolution melted, lost in a heightened perception so intense it almost pained her.

Her cousin's mouth was like warm velvet moving against hers, infinitely teasing and tantalizing, and she could smell his shaving lotion and his soap, the notes of each one quite separately distinct. On his lips there was a very faint flavor of something sweet and spicy, plum cake perhaps. It was on his tongue when it traced the seam of her lips.

These impressions crowded into the space of a small, surprised fragment of a second, each one of them enough to rock her heart.

I should push you away. I should push you away and run like the wind. This is all wrong and it will only lead to trouble, no matter what Mama thinks.

Yet with this rationale in her mind, Adela still wound her arms around her outrageous cousin instead of thrusting him away. He was, and always had been, the most aggravating man in the world, but still she parted her lips for him, instead of clamping them shut and grabbing him by the ears to get him off her.

Oh, how she'd yearned for Wilson once, yearned for him with all her young heart and soul. But until a moment or two ago, she'd believed the urge done and dead, crushed by circumstances and Wilson himself. Now, it was patently obvious she'd been completely wrong about that. Her feelings for him were as alive and rambunctious as ever. The taste of his mouth and tongue thrilled her just as it had all those years ago. Sliding her free hand boldly beneath his dressing gown, she clasped his strong, lean back and pressed her body close to his, metaphorically waving adieu to her wits.

Ah! I'm not the only one with feelings alive and well, then....

His cock was hard, and it pressed against the curve of her belly, just beneath her corset, as hot and ungovernable as it had been those seven years ago. In the frozen moment of time that they stood together, his eager flesh seemed to twitch, calling to hers. Even though there were layers and layers of clothing between them.

Adela rocked her hips, the response like breathing. Wilson gasped, making a gruff sound in his throat, countering her action.

What was she doing? This was absurd. Unthinkable. In the space of a few fractious exchanges, he'd unmasked her. Compelled her to reveal her secret self, just by...just by *being Wilson!* Trying to back away, Adela shoved hard, her hand spread against his chest to dislodge him. No more blindly clinging and cleaving like a hysterical trollop. It was madness.

"Wilson! For heaven's sake, what are you doing? You can't

just grab me and kiss me as if you own me!" He seemed reluctant to let her go. His grip even tightened. But then he succumbed, fingers relaxing their hold on her arms. "Have some decorum. You're not a rutting dog!" Adela cried, jumping back a step.

"Decorum, eh? I'm not the one who threw her arms around me just now." Oh, that voice, that damned voice. It was familiar, thrilling, deep, its resonance playing across her senses like a bow across a violin. A narrow smirk curved her cousin's beautiful mouth with its sharply defined upper lip. "All I was hoping for was a chaste and cousinly peck on the cheek. I didn't expect to be manhandled."

You are an insufferable beast who should be thrashed and pummeled.

"It was just shock, cousin dearest. You kissed first and it surprised me. I wasn't quite in my right mind." She darted back farther, still clutching her portfolio of sketches. She had to get out of here. But just looking at him made it difficult to leave.

Her distant cousin Wilson Ruffington had always been an eccentric, and even his liaison with a notoriously fashionable French adventuress didn't appear to have tidied him up very much. In fact, he was more a wild man now. His thick, wavy black hair was longer than when she'd last seen him, curling around his ears and on his collar, tousled and yet shiny and clean.

Which summed him up, really. He was scruffy and fastidious. A puzzle in every possible respect.

Adela compressed her lips. Why, when he was so annoying and often hurtful, did he still make her want to smile? Her fingers just itched for her pencil, and in her mind she was already drawing him. Aggravating or no, he *was* a sight for sore eyes, tall, wiry, intriguing and stylish in a way that other men just weren't. Flagrantly bohemian, he still affected his dress-

ing gown during the daytime, as he'd done seven years ago at
Ruffington Hall. He'd swanned about in his robe then, much
to the consternation of the Old Curmudgeon—who'd called
him a nancy and told him to brace up—and it seemed he'd
not broken the habit. Today's example was a blue silk paisley
confection, and beneath it he wore an equally absurd waistcoat in a different pattern entirely. His trousers were thankfully quite normal, but he wore his white shirt sans neckwear
or even a collar, and a little open.

He was a ragamuffin prince, almost a comic opera figure,
drenched in a wayward male glamour. Beside him she was
the drabbest dark crow.

And yet…and yet the way Wilson was looking at her seemed
to say otherwise. His blue-gray eyes, so pale and all-seeing,
monitored every detail of her appearance even as she assessed
his. And they were hot. Searing, despite their icy color, their
devouring heat confirming what she'd felt at his groin.

How could he want her after what he'd said six months
ago? And the way he'd scrupulously avoided any chance of
being alone with her for seven years? He probably wanted any
woman, and Adela had simply blundered unawares into his
line of sight. Society talk—which she told herself was tedious
and uninteresting, yet followed avidly—said that he and the
famous Coraline had parted recently, so her randy cousin was
probably just missing his regular quota of carnal pleasures.

Adela narrowed her eyes back at him, imagining her head
clamped in place for a formal photograph. Wilson would *not*
make her back down and look away.

"I see you haven't improved your habits of dress yet, cousin."
She raked her glance from his toes to his shaggy head, school-
ing her face to not show the lustful feelings she couldn't suppress. Far from a lady in that respect, she must not allow him
to perceive her true nature, her dangerous secrets.

"I dress for rationality and comfort, Della, and to please myself. You should leave off your corsets and try it. You'd feel so much better.... Far less prone to fits of temper."

Ah ha! How little you know, Mr. Clever Boots.

At home, Adela *had* abandoned her corsets. She'd happily embraced a rational form of dress, inspired not only by Mrs. Wilde and other lady aesthetes, but also by some of her free-thinking friends at the Ladies' Sewing Circle. She'd joined the group just over a year ago, and found it a revelation, in ways she'd never have imagined. The loose, comfortable garments and lighter underclothing affected by some of the ladies were pure bliss after the restrictions of corsetry, and even better, through them she'd been introduced to a dressmaker whose charges were exceptionally reasonable. It was a lot less pricey to run up a lightly shaped "aesthetic" gown than it was to tailor a formal, fitted costume.

Adela was trussed up now only because Mama had insisted, even if it did mean that her only "presentable" gowns were those left over from mourning her father.

"Women wear corsets, Wilson. It's simply what we do. They're an aid to good posture and they create an elegant silhouette." Damn him, why did he provoke her to lie? And behave badly... Why did the way he looked at her make her suddenly long to rip the whole lot off, corsets, petticoats, drawers and all, just to make those silvery eyes pop wide? "And pray tell me what's so rational about the juxtaposition of *that* waistcoat with *that* dressing gown? It's sartorial chaos, an assault to the eyes and to the sensibilities of anyone with even the tiniest appreciation of good style."

"Ouch!" Wilson clutched dramatically at the offending waistcoat, even while his eyes still seemed to pierce her clothing and lasciviously view the body underneath. "But seriously, you don't need a corset, Della. You have immaculate posture and a perfect silhouette without one…and I should know, having seen it."

Curse the beast! Why had she ever even hoped that he wouldn't refer to their "incident"? Their tryst. It had changed her more radically than any other event in her life, but a thousand what-ifs made it far too painful to reflect on often. And she didn't want to discuss it or refer to it now. Not with the one other person on earth who knew it had ever occurred. Her closest friends from the Sewing Circle, Sofia and Beatrice, were aware that there *had* been a boy, in her youth… but Adela had revealed only the most oblique details. She'd never spoken of what still sang in her flesh….

"Well, I'd be grateful if you'd expunge that sight from your mind, Wilson, peerless as you claim it to be. The incident during which you saw it *never happened*. I thought we agreed to that?" She edged toward the door once more, then faltered, shocked by Wilson's expression. He'd winced, pain in his eyes and the taut, high lines of his cheekbones. It lasted only an instant, then disappeared again completely, eclipsed by a narrow, wolfish grin.

"I'm not sure I ever agreed to that, Della. But if you say it never happened, then it didn't…or did it?" Slowly, lasciviously, his tongue touched the center of his lower lip.

Her heart thundering like a runaway locomotive, Adela yearned to escape. But somehow her muscles just wouldn't work. Just the simple task of opening the door and exiting the room was a mountain to climb.

"Don't go, Della." His sharply angled face gentled, the look on it conciliatory if not precisely pleading. "Please stay a little while."

It was dangerous. *He* was dangerous. He was a colossal hazard to her peace of mind in a dozen different ways…and yet he was as irresistible to her as he'd been those seven years ago.

And retreat was cowardice, too, something she despised.

But what was better, a wise coward or a valiant fool? Despite his blandishments, Wilson's attention was most definitely straying perilously in the direction of her portfolio now and again, and if he saw its contents, she'd never hear the end of it for the rest of this weekend, at least. What he saw could become a weapon to wield against her almost indefinitely.

Wilson was shrewd. Brilliant, in fact. It wouldn't be an exaggeration to say he was probably a genius, one of the greatest minds in the empire. Yet even the simplest male thinker would probably be able to put two and two together, based on the evidence of her portfolio and her presence in this room. Her cousin was probably a hundred steps ahead of that already, portfolio as yet unseen.

Why, why, why did I bring it? I should have come only to look, not to compare, then sketched afterward in private. It's not as if I can't remember what I've seen....

But there were certain drawings reputed to be in the earl's collection, special items of which pastiches had been requested. It didn't do to disappoint her more discerning and extravagant customers.

Though Wilson would go to town on her having "customers" at all.

"So, will you stay...or scuttle off?" His pale eyes were narrowed again, as if he'd read everything passing through her mind. "Running away seems to be a habit of yours."

That did it. Adela's fingers tightened, ready to wallop him about the head with the portfolio, but in a massive effort of containment, she resisted.

"I will stay. Just for a little while. But only because *I* want to."

"Capital. Now let's inspect this toy of yours, shall we? It doesn't seem to be working very well." With a swift, tight, insultingly faux little smile, Wilson swept back to the desk and the praxinoscope that had amused her before his arrival, his silk dressing gown fluttering in his wake. He hadn't forgotten her portfolio, though, that was certain, and in one portion of his devious, extemporizing mind, he was no doubt still speculating on its contents with typical Wilson relish. Adela tightened her grip, just in case.

Watching him, she almost wished she'd powdered her cheeks a little, as Mama had begged her to do. The praxinoscope's picture strip was a risqué item, especially inflammatory in motion, and with her nemesis beside her a blush rose inevitably in Adela's face. She braced herself for the equally inevitable ribald comment.

But for Wilson the scientist, and tinkerer with all things mechanical, a close inspection of the mechanism proved irresistible, thankfully. Reaching under the drum, he probed for a moment, then lifted it clear. Removing the picture strip, he set it aside and turned the circular container over to study it closely before shifting his attention to the spindle on which it rode.

"Hmm…most interesting. Not a bad example. But obsolete, of course. The future of moving images is photographic, utilizing perforated celluloid film." For a moment he seemed apart from her, his mind turning over, sifting through possibilities in his grand passion for technological innovation. "There have been some exciting advances…. It's an area I'd take a crack at myself if I had the time, but there's a lot of trial and error involved." He was still frowning at the spindle, but Adela imagined him picturing other devices, assessing their flaws and strengths in fractions of moments. "I saw the Le Prince exhibit, and the work of Friese-Green…but there are still difficulties. Hand-cranking the camera makes it almost impossible to produce an entirely smooth result. The same with the method of projection…. I suspect the all-conquering Edison will prevail in the end. He mostly does…."

With his lower lip snagged between his teeth, Wilson appeared intent. He seemed completely focused on the job at hand, but who knew what was going on with him? When he set the drum on the desk, he reached into the pocket of his robe. Ah, the ever-present tool kit. She should have known he'd have it with him. Drawing out the leather pouch, small but containing a comprehensive selection of miniature tools, Wilson set to work without a heartbeat's hesitation. Utilizing several of the tiny appliances, and a few drops from a vial of oil, he made a number of swift but confident adjustments to the contraption's workings.

"Well, it's not exactly a miracle of the modern world nowadays…but Monsieur Reynard's mechanism still has its charms, I must admit."

Seconds later, Wilson reassembled it, then waggled his fingers—as if to say "jump to it"—indicating that Adela should pass the picture strip to him. Still keeping a firm hold on her precious drawings with her left hand, she complied, but her heart sank when Wilson glanced at her out of the corner of his eye. No matter how entranced he was with the praxinoscope, he certainly hadn't forgotten the portfolio, either.

Blessedly, he didn't remark on it, though, and got on with the job of setting the picture strip back in place. On a trial spin, the spinning mechanism worked perfectly, with just a smooth, swishing sound.

"Good Lord!" Wilson's dark eyebrows shot up and a smirk widened his handsome mouth as the drum whirled round and round, round and round.

The little scenario lasted barely seconds, but that was more than enough to get its point across. The colorful and surprisingly well-executed drawings depicted a red-faced, mustachioed gentleman of military demeanor in the process of spanking the bottom of a plump, brazen-eyed floozy wearing nothing but her stockings and what appeared to be a rather flashy diamond necklace. In a particularly piquant touch, the spanking colonel's manly member was poking proud and stiff out of the front of his trousers.

I must not look at Wilson. I must not look at Wilson.

Adela fixed her gaze firmly on the saucy show, and the repeated jerking and wriggling of the painted young woman and her rampant regimental beau. If Wilson was to look into her eyes right now, he'd know everything, her every dark secret, instantly. Then the whole scandalous farrago would be out in the open.

Yes, I might look like a drab, severe spinster, and a veteran of too many disastrous seasons…but I'm really just as much a libertine as Miss Spanked Bottom.

Nobody other than Sofia and Beatrice, and the boys at Sofia's private "establishment," were privy to Adela's hidden self-indulgence of her senses. Nor did more than a handful know that she earned her pin money as "Isis," one of London's most famous erotic artists, whose works were much sought after by the great and the broad-minded.

Wilson must never, ever know that she paid men to service her…or that she drew their naked bodies to pay her family's mounting bills.

The picture show circled on and on. The rude gentleman of the prominent member smacked the saucy young minx again and again. Wilson chuckled and leaned in closer, clearly entranced.

Adela waited for the worst. For the words that would say he'd worked it all out…and that she was damned.

"I do believe she's wearing the Ruffington diamonds while she takes her licks," he murmured, casting Adela a glance out of the corner of his eye. "She wouldn't by any chance be modeled on you, would she?"

Silently, Adela let out her held breath. It wasn't what she'd feared, but it still skimmed dangerously close to those shoals. Leaning closer, but not too close, she studied the painted necklace as best she could while the image still moved. It looked nothing like their family treasure, so why had Wilson made the comparison? He must have some ulterior motive, but as happened so often, his razor cheekbones supported an unrevealing mask.

"So, do you still find such activities titillating, Della?"

The taunting devil. That, at least, he did know.

During their shared summer visit at Ruffington Hall, all those years ago, they'd found other naughty treasures such as this. The Old Curmudgeon had his own clandestine collection of erotica, as so many of the nobility did, and after picking the library lock, she and Wilson had investigated it. Several very fine eighteenth-century etchings had made her blush like a peony, and had almost certainly ignited fires that they'd put out together, later, by the river.

Wilson didn't seem to notice that she hadn't answered him. "I was expecting to see dancing Harlequins or dogs doing tricks, not saucy libertines performing unspeakable acts of lewdness," he murmured.

"Well, you would be the one to know all about unspeakable acts of lewdness."

No! Why had she said that, of all things? Why did she let him goad her this way? Only ten or fifteen minutes in his company, and he'd already turned her into a complete nitwit again. Did his mighty brain act like a sponge and soak up all the intelligence in a room?

But it wasn't only her mentality he'd made deficient. Her body was still in a riot from that kiss. And it had been even before that. Wilson Ruffington could render her a madwoman with barely any effort at all, and the worst of it was, her senses adored it. Despite the potential for an almighty disaster, there was nothing she longed for more than his touch.

"Yes, I'm fully conversant with most acts of vile libertinage. How about you, cousin dear? How goes your sensual education these days? It must be a work still in progress, or why else would you be in here in the first place?" Wilson's voice was flippant, but there was an edge to it, as ominous as it was vague. His eyes were hard as he turned from the praxinoscope.

What's the matter? Have I touched a raw nerve? Surely you've not been thinking of me all this time, so it must be that *woman*.

"That woman" was the way Adela always referred to the famous beauty Coraline in her mind. She'd avidly gobbled up every tidbit of news about Wilson's association with the Frenchwoman, scanning the gossip columns and scurrilous rags like *Marriott's Monde*, all the while hating herself for paying any attention. Wilson's life was no longer her concern. Yet she'd still tortured herself, even purchasing a cabinet card of Coraline, then ripping it up, muttering over *that woman's* straight, exquisite nose and flawless, pearly complexion.

I'll bet you never aggravated her *enough to make her run blindly into the branch of a tree, did you?*

No, he'd probably murmured only sweet endearments and compliments to *that woman*, while they'd played exotic sensual games together. They'd have frolicked and indulged in spanking and other recherché practices. Adela ground her teeth, imagining them together, Coraline all flashing eyes, lush red lips and sublime, plump bosom, lust arcing between her and Wilson like the crackle from a demonstration of electrical power.

"Nothing to say?" Wilson's voice was harsh. Was he really hurt by his lover's desertion? "Don't tell me you haven't even thought about erotic pleasure since *I* touched you… I don't believe that for a minute."

Adela's fingers went white on the portfolio. Again came that urge to whack him, barreling through her like a giant rolling ball. She was normally even-tempered, scrupulously in control, but he turned her into a termagant. Emotions surged. Anger. Jealousy. Desire. Burning, fulminating desire, and a longing to murder him, to dispatch him by means of intense pleasure.

"I have some knowledge of erotic arts and pastimes." She hurled the comment at him, her chin up, her back straight.

"Really?" Wilson's eyes flashed. His grin was back. "Pray expatiate, cousin. Have you perhaps sampled the arts of flagellation?" He nodded to the now still 'scope, and the wriggling woman and rampant man, frozen in time. "I didn't even know you had a beau."

"One doesn't have to have a beau."

Oh, please, stupid woman, don't dig the hole even deeper!

Was Wilson closer now? It felt so, though she hadn't seen him move. All she was sure of was that she'd made the most tremendous error, the worst possible. By nature her cousin was inquisitive, investigative. He was a bloodhound after the faintest of scents, a Scotland Yard detective picking at the most obscure clue. "I simply read widely," she finished, praying he'd accept that, but waiting for his pounce.

"Hence your desire to breach this fortress." He gestured around the book-lined room, at its potential treasures. "To further that erotic education of yours." His tongue peeped out, just touching the center of his plush lower lip. "But there's a big difference between reading books and looking at pictures… and doing what we did together seven years ago."

Ah, now the knife goes right in! I should have run when he first arrived.

But running from Wilson had never been a successful strategy. Even if it would have allowed them the dance of polite avoidance during the rest of the weekend, instead of engaging in special combat, no holds barred.

"I was young, and I was a silly nincompoop." It was hard to keep her voice cool. She was *still* a silly nincompoop where this man was concerned. The more she argued with Wilson, the more her body told her in no uncertain terms what her last shreds of good sense pleaded she deny. The tips of her breasts ached against the rigid edge of her corset, and in the pit of her belly the surge of desire was like a pain.

"And I paid for it in more ways than one." Unable to help herself, she touched the bridge of her nose, where the tree branch had struck. It didn't hurt now, but it had been agonizing then, so blindingly intense that it had expunged the golden glow of lingering pleasure.

"I'm sorry." Before she could stop him, Wilson captured the hand that had touched her face, squeezing it gently. The apology was unspecific. It could have been for the tree, or for blunt words then or later, she didn't know.

How she wanted to hate him. She had plenty of reasons. What he'd said. What his infuriating arrogance had made her angry enough to do. The simple fact that he was a man, a Ruffington, and alive, and thus the future recipient of all her stubborn, misogynistic grandfather's wealth, as well as his title.

But none of this made any difference. Wilson's pale, glowing eyes and eccentric male beauty still muddled her. There was no way to remain rational and sensible when she was anywhere near him. He besieged her without even trying.

Run. Run now, her mind said.

Stay, for pity's sake, stay, said her body, singing with lust and energy.

Wilson's fingers were warm, the heat in them traveling through the point of contact and flowing around her like the glow from a jigger of brandy. She couldn't pull free. She no longer wanted to. And even if she did, she was hampered by the need to cling on hard to her portfolio.

What if I show him the wretched thing and be done with it? He'll find a way to see it, anyway. He's Wilson.

When Wilson kissed her fingertips, the thrill made her tremble.

"Well, it can't be helped now," she muttered, and his lips curved again as if he knew that was the most acknowledgment he would get of his scant apology.

Curse the man, he could *see* the effect he was having on her, and the only consolation was that effects worked both ways. When Adela stole a look at his groin, that was obvious.

Jigger of brandy? Surely she'd consumed a pint of it, but with just the intoxication and none of the detriments. To be desired so could turn any woman's head, not least of all hers.

Wilson laughed, following the direction of her glance, then nodded toward the portfolio. "So what's in this, then? More pictures of gentlemen's nether regions? That seemed to be what you were specializing in last time I saw your work."

With the words came another pounce. And prestidigitation this time. Wilson plucked the portfolio clean out of her hand, and Adela squeaked and tried to grab it back, without any luck. As he whirled away, his dressing gown billowed about him and he strode toward the desk. The praxinoscope had lost its allure now, and he shoved it aside and set down his prize.

Adela shot after him, her mind filled with the rudest insults. Confound his "sorry." It'd just been a trick to get under her guard. He was already picking at the ribbons securing the binder. "No! Don't! That's private. You have no business prying into people's belongings." She tugged at his sleeve, but he just went on, his long tapered fingertips easily conquering the fastenings. "Just because you're grandfather's heir doesn't give you any rights over me and my things. Leave that alone!"

Miraculously, he hesitated, the ribbons unfurled across the desk. He placed a hand over hers, on his shoulder, and his eyes were sly as silver ice as he regarded her sideways. "Why should I? Give me some incentive." His look made her blood run hot, then cold, then hot again, surging pell-mell through her veins. She wanted to kill him, but at the same time she wanted to lie down on the carpet and demand that he mount her. "Perhaps you could beg?"

Damn you! Damn you to damned damnation and back again, you despicable swine!

"Don't be absurd, Wilson. I'm simply going to ask you, as a gentleman, to observe my privacy." His warm hand was still over hers, transmitting messages of sultry seduction, addling her brain.

"But I'm not a gentleman. I've never claimed to be a gentleman." He prized her fingers off his arm and conveyed them to his lips again. The touch of his mouth minced her thoughts, leaving only urges. "Surely you of all people don't think I'm one?"

"No. I don't. Not anymore." For a brief time in their youth, he'd been a prince of the universe to her, its very center. But no longer. Not for years.

His mouth moved over her skin. Was that moisture she felt? Was the lascivious devil *licking* her? Her entire body shuddered, and only a titanic effort of will kept her from swaying. Instead of feeling Wilson's tongue against her palm, she seemed to feel its stroke, slow and lingering, between her legs....

She blinked, battling for control. Confused over how she'd come to this. Wilson pivoted on his heel and turned to her, still holding her hand. "How about we strike a bargain? You give me another kiss. A proper one, and a little dalliance with it… And I won't open this portfolio of yours and look at whatever it is you don't want me to see." His eyes were level, daring her to accept, their slow glint ever more disorientating.

Don't do it, Adela. Don't agree. You know him. You'll end up in even worse trouble. The drawings are precisely *what he thinks they might be….*

Why had she ever come in here in the first place? She had no need of Lord Rayworth's erotic treasures to inspire her; her imagination was sufficient. And her memory. Her mind was like a photographic plate, and she could develop anything she wanted on it. The ability to conjure images out of air was her great artistic gift.

Adela looked at Wilson's mouth, knowing she was lost. He was a blackguard, but he excited her more than any other man ever had or probably ever could do. She wanted those lips on hers again, and in other places, too. Zones they'd never actually explored in real life, but which cried out for him now. His eyes didn't look quite so silver currently; the pupils were huge, dark as a thunderhead, with a lightning-crack of promise in their depths, an intensity of desire that matched her own.

"What dalliance? What do you mean?" Oh, she was such a fool….

"Don't fret. Nothing too compromising, Della. Just a few pleasant moments, I promise…pleasure I *owe* you." He smiled at her, a very imp of mischief and devilment, exotic yet familiar.

She didn't trust him. She couldn't trust him. He'd been incorrigible seven years ago, and she had no reason to believe from their brief social meetings in the interim that he'd reformed even in the slightest degree.

"I don't believe you, Wilson. You'll take liberties. It's what you do." She tried to tug away, but couldn't. His knowledge of Oriental fighting arts meant he knew special arcane grips that were light yet unyielding. And even without them, his eyes would still have held her.

"But you liked liberties once, Della. In fact, you invited them." It was his turn to tug now, and as if drugged, she moved toward him. "Surely you've not forgotten what we shared? I promise I'll honor your secrets." He glanced at the portfolio, and the fingers of his free hand flexed. "All of them."

"You're a devious and manipulative man, Wilson," she hissed, and then flung herself at him, grabbing his warm face between her hands and kissing him hard on the lips.

Well, that's one way to distract him, the rational part of her brain observed coolly, while all the rest of her reveled in his taste.

But Wilson's soft grunt of triumph as she opened her mouth to him almost made her retreat again. She'd got him right where *he* wanted to be, and before she could react, his hands slid around her, gripping her tight. He was still scheming, but at least for the moment his hands were on her, not the portfolio. She let her own arms slide right around him, clinging close, her blood pounding and racing in her veins.

Oh, Lord, this is Wilson…. Wilson…

Everything always circled back to him. He'd made her what she was, a sensual woman with turbulent erotic appetites. Seven years ago, he'd turned a lever and set lust in motion, and even though they'd fallen out again almost as quickly as they'd clung together, she hadn't given up on the pleasures of the flesh.

Wilson Ruffington was the author, albeit unwitting, of a wicked secret life.

4

More Wicked than you Could Possibly Imagine

But there was no time to think of that moment of transformation now. In the perilous present, Wilson's tongue probed her mouth just as it had during their first hot kiss, the wicked muscular thrust aping that other thrust, that other wonderful hot, wet, hard intrusion. The possession she still wanted, and still wanted from *him*. Ignoring the murmuring voices of reason and tediously pervasive doubts about her reputation, she pressed her body against him as hard as she could, rocking her pelvis against his in a primal rhythm.

He was still hard, unyielding as the oak of the door and the desk and the mighty trees in the park beyond the window. She could feel the heat of him through all their layers of clothing.

"Oh, Della, my Della, how you still rouse me," he growled against her neck, his lips nibbling her skin just above the little collar of her gown. With one hand still gripping her bottom through her skirt and petticoats, he set the other to the task of unfastening the row of jet buttons down the front of her bodice. As ever, he was quicker and defter than any man had a right to be, but his manual dexterity had always matched his rare intelligence.

Adela tried not to think, because if she did, she'd deem herself too idiotic to be allowed to live. All that mattered was to feel and savor experience while she could. Her own hands ranged over what parts of Wilson she could reach, diving into his tousled, silky hair and stroking his strong back beneath the patterned fabric of his eccentric dressing gown. It was only fair that he should be revealed, just as she was, and as he rested her on the edge of the desk while he attacked her bodice, she snatched at his shirt and wrenched and pulled at his buttons.

"Yes!" Wilson paused in his efforts, dashed her hands away and ripped at his shirt himself, rending it open. It was a buttoned garment, unfastening all the way down in the new American style, and the little discs flew everywhere as he bared himself almost to the waist. Conveying her hand to his body, he pressed it against his skin and the wispy peppering of dark hair across the center of his chest.

When Adela dug her nails in, he laughed.

"You're a wicked woman, Della, though no doubt I deserve the punishment." Dashing her hand away again, he returned his attention to the front of her gown.

You do not know the half of it, cousin dear. I'm more wicked than you could possibly imagine. For a moment, Adela thought of other men, other chests.

Manipulating ribbons and buttons and hooks, Wilson managed to get at what he sought. She groaned when he wedged a hand inside the top of her corset by force and cupped her breast. She was slightly formed, and he cradled the entire curve, his thumb settling on her nipple as if he owned her very flesh. It might have been only yesterday when he'd last rubbed her this way and made her squirm. Instead of seven long years, during which lately she'd been compelled to seek other hands.

"You're beautiful…so beautiful." Given the length of the statement, and the long burning look he gave her, Adela almost believed him. Then reality returned, bringing with it her harsh little laugh. She *wasn't* beautiful, and he was a liar, an unrepentant sweet-talker of women. No doubt *that woman* demanded the tribute of pretty words and compliments as a right, but Adela Ruffington preferred the truth, unadorned.

"Don't insult me." She narrowed her eyes at him, even while she closed her hand over his. She wasn't lovely. She was flawed. But she still had needs, and as Wilson had stirred them, both then and now, it was his responsibility to assuage them.

"Don't start that again." He tightened his hand on her breast, his fingers and thumb ruthless. He trapped her nipple between them, creating a twinge of pain among the pleasure, a bright, intense shard that darted instantly from her breast to her belly. Between her legs, her sex pulsed in a warm ripple.

"Start what?"

His fingers twisted, lightly pinching. Pleasure-pain.

"Denying your beauty. I won't have it. You *are* lovely, and I'll punish you if you persist in denying it, believe me."

Adela could barely breathe. A threshold loomed before her, a line beyond which lay a delicious peril, the dark, sensual play only hinted at by the brash lovers in the praxinoscope reel. It wasn't an entirely unknown country to her, but she was almost certain Wilson wouldn't realize that.

The frolicsome pair in the moving pictures were far from the first she'd seen engage in a spanking game. She'd seen it in the flesh…and felt it, too.

"You can't order me what to feel, Wilson. Even if we'd been the most intimate of friends for the last seven years, I still wouldn't obey you."

They were a pair of mythical beasts head to head in a battle. Adela wouldn't give in, and she knew Wilson wouldn't, either. He had the upper hand at present, though—and it was on her breast, squeezing and plying wicked pleasure.

"Liars should be punished." His low, menacing voice made her wriggle just as much as his tormenting fingertips did. "And when you say you're not beautiful, you *are* lying."

"I'm not!"

"You are to me, and to any right-thinking man with even a scrap of discernment." He shot forward, grabbing the back of her neck with his free hand and jamming his mouth down on hers, tongue stabbing again for entrance. At the same time he pinched her nipple hard, making her gasp, and allowing him access between her lips.

Wilson kissed like a marauder, like a brigand, forcing her back against the edge of the desk, tweaking her nipple, plucking at it repeatedly as he thrust over and over with his tongue. Adela felt pins slipping from her half-collapsed chignon as his fingers held her head unrelentingly.

You're an animal, Wilson. A pirate. A wicked despoiler of women… Please don't stop.

Her jaw ached by the time he freed her and gazed into her eyes from the closest of quarters. His own eyes were as pale and silvery as ever around the periphery, but at the center his pupils were black and dilated with lust. "I'm going to punish you, Della," he breathed, the exhalation sweet and spicy against her face. "Just like that naughty little girlie in the praxinoscope reel. I'm going to smack your gorgeous bottom and make you squeal. And then you're going to damn well admit that you're lovely, do you hear me?"

"Do what the devil you want, Wilson, but I won't lie." She held his gaze, the pit of her belly trembling. Wicked urges rattled around inside her, wild and uncontained, despite his hold on her. She wanted to haul up her skirts and bare herself to him, challenging him to do his worst, inviting him to plunge into her as he'd once done, taking her breath away.

"Oh, I'll do what I want, don't you worry. But you *are* a liar."

Pausing only to give her tender nipple one last twist, he dragged his hand out of her bodice and grabbed hold of her skirts without further ado. Taking the voluminous layers of bombazine and flannel and cambric in an untidy grip, he hauled them up, tugging and bunching until he'd exposed her stockings and her garters and her drawers. The latter were old-fashioned; Adela had other calls upon her funds than the latest styles in pretty new unmentionables, and precious little to spend on presentable gowns to go over them. Wilson uttered a happy grunt when he discovered the split that gave him access to her body.

"Oh, I love these. All women should wear these convenient old things. It makes a man's job so much easier, especially when he's in a hurry."

Convenient or no, Adela was glad of her old split drawers when Wilson's fingertips reached their moist and trembling goal.

"I...I don't care. I don't dress for men," she gasped, "especially crude, grabbing ones like you." It was difficult to breathe, even to think. Unerringly, Wilson settled his middle finger on her clitoris and rolled it slowly and unctuously, like an oiled ball bearing. "I...oh, dear Lord...I thought you might have cultivated more sophisticated carnal manners by now, Wilson, but you dive straight in and paw madly, just the way you did at nineteen."

It was impossible not to squirm. Impossible not to rock on his hand, inciting more pleasure. Had he forgotten his threat to spank her? Adela hardly cared, as long as he caressed her like this first.

"More insults, eh, Della? On top of everything else. Time to spank you for disrespect and downright wickedness." There was laughter in his voice, but the needs of her body were Adela's one priority. All else fell by the wayside. Nothing mattered but Wilson holding her, and his finger flicking and circling. If he stopped, she might die, or at least scream blue murder.

Wilson stopped as if he'd heard her thoughts. He withdrew the divine finger. Adela let out a strangled cry and tried to jam her puss back onto his hand.

"Greedy Della. You like being toyed with, don't you? You like having me play with your plump little clitty, don't you?" His breath was hot against her neck, his whisper a zephyr drifting down over her throat and her exposed cleavage. Adela bit her lip, commanding herself not to speak or move, but a moan of need slipped the leash and her hips jerked.

"Answer me, Della. You like being played with, don't you? Just like some randy little maid in the pantry being interfered with by an importunate footman?" Wilson's mouth settled on her neck, in the hollow beneath her jaw, and he nipped her, his teeth sharp, the pressure measured to a fine degree. "Admit it, and when I've spanked your bottom, I'll fondle you between your legs until you spend."

"I don't need *you* for that, Wilson!" she hissed, every muscle straining with the effort of not reacting. "I'm perfectly capable of attending to myself, thank you. Every woman is."

"But not every woman has the wits or the sensuality to do it, Della. Most are too God-fearing or too afraid their mamas will find out that they're impure and degenerate."

"Well, I'm…I'm sorry for them, and I don't care two pins for what my mother thinks."

"Wicked, wicked Della. Lack of filial respect now. Whatever am I going to do with you?" His palm settled on her breast through her bodice again and gave it a quick, rough squeeze. "Come along, time to deal with your sins now."

Wilson Ruffington, you are the most towering hypocrite in the entire British Empire!

He was far more the sinner than she, despite her secret erotic life. He was self-indulgent and selfish. He cared nothing for the feelings of others, or for the observance of any kind of good or moral behavior. And yet right at this moment, she would allow him any liberty, anything at all, to assuage her needs.

"Lean over the desk. Show me your bottom."

Easier said than done. How typical of a man to forget about her corset only moments after he'd criticized her for wearing it. How would he like to wear it for a day, in the interests of scientific inquiry?

But one look in Wilson's eyes told her he'd not forgotten at all. He was an encyclopedia, all facts retained, and he was no doubt gauging how much the unremitting undergarment restricted her, and how its pressures might come to bear upon her body. A slight smile curved his lips, and when he maneuvered her into position, the lower edge of the stiffened garment dug into the pit of her belly, making her grunt aloud.

Wilson made a sound, too. A masculine purr of satisfaction.

The sensations were abominable. Wicked. Wonderful.

The lower border of her corset poked her in a sensitive zone, like an etheric hand bearing down on the very root of her clitoris. It made her want to sob, gasp for breath and wriggle against the desk—not to mention ignore every last atom of her pride, reach down to diddle herself and continue doing so until she had a shuddering, towering orgasm.

"Now then, let's see you." With cheerful efficiency, Wilson attacked her skirts again, dragging the whole lot of them upward, petticoats and all, in one haphazard mass. "Oh, very nice," he murmured, slipping a fingertip under her garter and the top of her stocking, and running it along the bare skin above.

Adela gnawed her knuckle. How much more of this could she stand? The pressure in her belly, and the dreadful tension in her sex, were playing havoc with her decorum. Not that she'd ever had much of that in the first place. Slowly, slipping into a sensual reverie, she began moving her hips rhythmically, and clenching her inner muscles. Perhaps she could trigger a crisis for herself and cheat her wicked cousin at his own game?

Deft fingers grasped the edges of the vent in her drawers and dragged it wide-open. The room was warm, but the cooler draft across her hindquarters made them quiver and flex. Adela let out a sob. She was exposed, ignominiously uncovered.

Adela Ruffington, you are the second most towering hypocrite in the entire British Empire!

The voice inside her, the spokesperson of her senses and her deepest urges, remonstrated with her. The exposure was intoxicating, her bare bottom a potent source of feminine power. She could almost taste Wilson's lust even without feeling the pressure of his cock. Her exposed rump was an object of veneration to him. He was no different from any other man in that respect. The professional boys at Sofia Chamfleur's house of pleasure all enjoyed ogling their clients' buttocks, even hers, which weren't particularly ample. With a secret grin, Adela clenched her interior muscles, both for her own pleasure and to make her flesh dance.

What do you think of that, dear cousin?

"Della! You wicked vixen," Wilson growled, laying his hands upon her bare behind like a greedy boy grabbing a brace of muffins. "You're sublime. You know that, don't you? So delectable, I've really got to punish you."

"Well, get on with it, then. Don't shilly-shally." Resting

on her elbows, Adela twisted around and glared at him, challenging him with her eyes, and with the smooth nakedness of her flesh.

"Very well. As you command, milady." The cry was hoarse as his hand came up in readiness.

Adela looked away again, bracing herself.

Wilson's palm crashed down on her left buttock, swift and hard.

Oh…oh…oh…

She let out a long, hiccupping groan, the cheek of her bottom flaming in less time than it took to acknowledge the impact. Her sex surged, the bump of the blow transmitted to her clitoris by the corset's edge pushing against her belly.

"Oh, please, please…" Was that a sob of desire or a wail of pain? She wasn't sure. Between the lips of her sex, fluid oozed and flesh rippled.

As Wilson landed a few more slaps, she lost the grip on herself, surging and rubbing her hips against the desk like a wild woman, moaning like a wanton. Her bottom tingled more and more with each blow.

"What do you want, Della? Tell me…give me the words."

The hand that had spanked now lay still across her simmering buttocks, spanning both cheeks. In an act of supreme provocation, one finger dipped into the groove between.

"Make me spend, you hideous plaguing monster. Make me spend right this instant, or I swear I'll do it myself!" Tugging at her skirts, she began to rummage beneath them. How long would it take for Wilson to galvanize himself into action? She couldn't wait on his whims.

Roughly, he dashed her hands away.

"No! Don't touch yourself. You'll take pleasure at my hand, or I'll tie your wrists together and leave you here, unsatisfied."

"You wouldn't dare!" She attacked her skirts anew in defiance.

"Try me," purred Wilson, effortlessly catching her wrists at the small of her back with one hand, then applying his other hand to the bundle of bombazine, flannel and cambric. Throwing the whole lot back up over her hips, he slid his fingers in between her legs, right into her sex. One long digit plunged into her vagina, up to the second knuckle.

Adela grunted. Wilson's fingers were narrow and elegant, the digits of a scientist and inventor, but the one inside her felt thick and intrusive. Was he surprised at how easily it breached her? For all he knew, she'd been chaste for seven years.

If only you knew what I know. What I've done and seen.

To confound him, she gripped him hard with her inner muscles, then bit back another cry as pleasure blossomed. It just needed his finger on her clitty to tip her over.

"If I release your hands, will you struggle?" He leaned over her, his voice low in her ear. "I'll make it worth your while not to."

Have you read my mind, you evil man?

It seemed he had. When she nodded her assent, beyond speech, he attacked her clothing, sneaking a hand under all the layers and beneath her belly, to seek the heart of the matter. A lot of tussling and burrowing was involved, but Wilson was nothing if not persistent. Within moments, his fingertips inveigled their way into the front split in her drawers, pushing straight at the wiry curls of her puss, searching for his target. As he did so, he twisted the finger inside her, crooking it against an area of sensitivity that made her grunt anew, rendered animal by sensations as disquieting as they were pleasurable. It was too much, too intense, too perverse, but even as tears of surprise formed in the corners of her eyes, she bore down, without the power to resist.

"I...I..."

Her voice failed her again, muffled by an agony of feeling. It plagued her far more than the heat in her bottom, yet seemed akin to it, as hot in its own way. As Wilson nudged and rocked her, low animal sounds broke from her throat, horrifyingly revealing.

"Good, eh?" he whispered, the middle finger of his other hand sliding around in the slick delta of her sex. The tip of it brushed her clitoris from the side, making her jerk and shift her hips to get more contact, but he slid it away again with a low, wicked laugh.

"I never realized that you might be such a voluptuary, Della... You don't seem to have any inhibitions. Do your friends and acquaintances know how randy you are?" Leaning over, he kissed the nape of her neck, his lips nestling against thick strands of hair that had broken free from her coiffure. "What would they say if they knew you let men stick their fingers inside you like this?"

"I don't know and I don't care!" Her voice ragged, she wriggled about, defying him, grabbing at the offending digit with her channel, using her hands to brace herself against the desk for more control. "I don't let many men stick their fingers inside me...and I've only let you do it because it pleases *me*. I wouldn't do it solely for your satisfaction."

Wilson let out a gasp. "You amaze me, Della, and sometime soon I will be asking you some very searching questions." He nudged against her, rubbing his groin against her haunch, where he'd spanked her. His cock was like stone where it pressed against the glowing, heated skin. "But in the meantime, be assured that touching you has always delighted me."

"Tumescence isn't satisfaction," she retorted. "As I know, right now, to my cost." She swirled her hips, then let out a sharp cry at the fierce sensations. "Now come on, Wilson, play the game. You made a bargain. Fulfill it!"

"Of course, my queen. As you command." His voice was silky and facetious, but it was his fingers, not his vocal cords, that concerned her. She groaned long and low as he obeyed her, settling a fingertip on her clitoris, then circling hard.

White flame danced behind Adela's eyelids, and her hands flailed like captured doves. Her sex convulsed in long, racking waves of pleasure, massaging Wilson's finger as her clitoris danced and pulsed. Dimly she heard a crash, and in a far part of her mind realized she'd knocked the wretched praxinoscope clean off the desk and undone all Wilson's good work with the tiny set of tools.

Her hips jerked and rocked as if a demon possessed her body. She'd not climaxed this hard in a long time, if ever, and her clash with Wilson only made the bliss more luscious. The hands of her cousin, also her enemy, were like an angel's.

The orgasm rose and waned, rose and waned, then rose again, but eventually, she was a spent, wrung-out rag. Slumped forward over the disordered desk, she quite forgot the firm restriction of her corset and the nakedness of her bottom, bared to the world. The door she'd opened with her hairpins remained unlocked, but she hadn't the energy to worry about it. If a servant or a fellow guest came along, it was the whim of fate. All that mattered was the soft, golden glow in her loins and buttocks, and the iron-hard cock still pressed against her thigh.

But it was Wilson's turn for pleasure now. Quid pro quo. Glow or not, she would have to rouse…and shock his senses.

5

Quid Pro Quo

There was no question of intercourse.

No matter how much she wanted to fuck Wilson, and how much her body—satiated or otherwise—cried out for him, it simply could not occur. And she had a shrewd suspicion he wouldn't even *ask* her to oblige.

Despite their thorny history, her cousin had never seemed to doubt her intelligence. Seven years ago they'd been a pair of blundering, clueless ingenues, but now they were both adults. And well informed, both with a clear idea of the results and repercussions of heedless rutting. Wilson might be arrogant, manipulative, impatient of those less brilliant than himself, but he wasn't an unfeeling beast. Which, it had to be said, some men in society were.

Wilson would never expect her to put herself in real jeopardy to satisfy his lust.

At Sofia Chamfleur's discreet establishment for women, devices of rubber were employed. French letters, which ensured there were no unfortunate consequences to secret pleasure.

Adela even possessed a small tin containing several of these essential and useful items herself, although thus far, she'd never contemplated needing them outside the walls of Sofia's quiet Hampstead mansion. Simply having them at all was a defiance. A secret way to thumb her nose at a society that seemed expressly fashioned for the advantage of men over women, despite a member of her own sex on the throne. They were a talisman of the freer life to which she aspired, and to some extent actively pursued.

But with no French letters about her person at the moment, she would have to take Wilson in hand if she planned to bring him off.

Finally managing to stir herself, Adela straightened up. The black swathes of her skirt dropped neatly into place, and apart from her unbuttoned bodice, she appeared decent.

Working on doing up her buttons, her fingers shook. Pleasurable aftershocks, and the heat in her rear made her fumble. Wilson's sharp, pale eyes followed her every tiny movement, and that didn't help, either. He was still close enough for her to feel his breath upon her, and leaning on the desk, with his hands in his trouser pockets, he made no attempt whatsoever to hide his erection. Ever contrary, he seemed to be flaunting it.

"I expect you want me to do something about that?" Adela nodded at the excitement in his trousers. No use prevaricating.

"That would be most pleasant. Most pleasant indeed." Wilson's voice was bland, but his face was more telling. A strange amalgam of a cool scientific, detachedly observing his own physical phenomenon…and infuriating masculine smugness. They were all like that, men. The handsome boys at Sofia's house were inordinately proud of their own equipage, even dedicated as they were to the service and pleasuring of women.

Something Wilson would readily discover if he reneged on their agreement and opened her portfolio.

There were sketches of Yuri and Clarence and Lionel—her three favorites—among her drawings, all in a blatant state of nudity and arousal. These works were destined for the pages of the journal *Divertissements,* or as commissions by private buyers, regular and wealthy patronesses of the beaux in question, all of whom had generous funds at their disposal.

This secret career as "Isis," the noted erotic artist, was how Adela had been clandestinely bridging the gap between the pittance allowed to her mother, herself and her sisters by her eccentric, misogynistic grandfather…and Mrs. Ruffington's social aspirations, and the maintenance of a standard of living to which she was accustomed. Adela might be frugal in respect of her own requirements, and young Marguerite was naturally wise, but Mama and Sybil hadn't a clue about money, except how to spend it.

Adela's art income was a necessity, and she couldn't jeopardize it by revealing its provenance to Wilson.

She decided on a direct frontal attack. The best way to distract even a polymath genius, if that genius was male. "I won't fuck you, so you can forget about that."

"I don't expect you to, Della. I wouldn't want to compromise you with a babe out of wedlock."

Adela looked sharply at him. He'd edged a few inches away from her now, but seemed to have retreated much farther than that. His voice was cold and his eyes looked angry. About to speak, Adela hesitated. What had caused the sudden reaction? Was it simple annoyance? Or pain? What?

"Hah, if Mama were here, she'd probably throw you bodily onto me thirty seconds after she'd finished screeching and wailing and having the vapors because you'd compromised me." Adela almost laughed. She could imagine such a thing really happening. "Anything to compel you to marry me. It *was* her primary goal in accepting this weekend's invitation."

"I don't doubt it. But she'll be disappointed, even if you aren't." Wilson's beautiful mouth thinned into a hard chilly line. It was as if they were right back to those days at Ruffington Hall, when he'd come out with all manner of blunt, apparently unfeeling utterances, sometimes, she suspected, purely for effect. "I don't plan to marry and I'll never be a father."

How can you be sure?

The question balanced on the tip of her tongue, but his silver-blue eyes kept her silent. Had he wanted to sire a child on his mistress, *that woman,* and been refused? Was that the true cause of their parting?

"Grandfather won't be pleased. He's pinning all his hopes on you, now that our line of the family has produced nothing but useless women who drain his resources."

"Not entirely useless. Not from my standpoint." Heat stirred in the silver now, like pale hot metal. Clearly, Wilson still possessed his youthful facility to shut away unpleasant thoughts as quickly as they'd occurred. He glanced down at the bulge in his trousers with a mercurial wink.

"You're atrocious. Indefensible." Yet Adela still found herself smiling, and drawn to him like iron to a magnet. She flicked her gaze to his groin, wondering, wondering. It was seven long years since she'd seen what lay behind that fine worsted, and no doubt the best quality woolen jersey of his undergarments, but she could still recall every particular detail. Her first ever sight of a man's rampant member. She'd drawn it from memory often enough.

Oh, dear. I'm weakening.

If Wilson hadn't been watching her like a raptor, she'd have clutched her hand to her bosom to calm her inner fluttering. He must *not* know how susceptible she was. She could accept his knowledge of her as a woman of physical needs, but her finer emotions must remain impenetrable.

And for that, she needed to quit this room as soon as possible. Which required that she dispatch Wilson to erotic oblivion as quickly as she was able, and then flee with her portfolio. To stay longer was to risk playing tricks with her mind, and making one afternoon seven years ago into yesterday. Her emotional equilibrium was a hard-won prize, and she wouldn't sacrifice it for a few moments of dalliance.

She could purchase her dalliances with no attendant complications. To tangle them with Wilson was to flirt with disaster....

WHY AM I TREMBLING? *This is Adela, not Coraline. She's a cautious spinster nowadays and probably as inept and fumbling as we both were seven years ago. She probably hasn't seen a cock since she last had her hands on mine.*

Used to the sophisticated caresses of Coraline, and before her, a very small number of experienced women, Wilson wasn't sure what to expect of Adela. Granted, she had a rather unexpected and tantalizing interest in erotica, but with no husband and no suitors that he was aware of, what practical experience could she have had since they'd last been together?

And yet she'd been responsive to *his* touch. And willing in a way that took his breath away. Her only resistance had been to *him,* not the pleasure. She'd actively courted his caresses... *and* the spanking.

As if she's used to them...

He dropped his hand to his crotch, ready to ply the buttons, but before he could, Adela dashed his fingers away. No dithering near-virgin would be so confident. His heart skipped and his cock throbbed heavily, even while the snake of suspicion stirred.

Where did all this confidence come from? Was there some secret swain in his cousin's life? He followed the doings of the Ruffington women, but there was no scandal attached to them, nothing of a risqué nature. They lived relatively quietly, and were certainly not a part of any set that he moved in. But to be this assured, Adela *must* have had her hand on a man in the past seven years, despite her lack of prospects.

"Come on, let's get this over with," she said crisply, attacking his fly without a hint of hesitation, as if she whipped some lucky fellow out of his trousers on a daily basis.

Wilson clamped his teeth together. Biting down on sudden, twisting jealousy while Adela made short work of his buttons, and then his linen within.

Who the devil has she been toying with? I'll have to investigate.

Then his resolution dissolved. Warm, assured fingers settled on his flesh and gripped him in a clever light hold, bringing his erect cock out into the cooler air.

No room for thought now. His universe contracted into just a hand and a cock, a woman's slender grasp caressing his aching flesh. Wilson groaned and braced himself against the desk. His knees seemed to turn to paper, and he could barely stand up. When Adela slid closer, and centered her finger and thumb above and below his glans, his hips bumped forward, pushing his eager loins at her.

"Oh, Della, Della…"

She took his breath away, stroking and teasing, delicately rolling the head of his cock and massaging the sensitive areas with all the skill of a practiced courtesan. Silky fluid flowed from his tip, and he shook his head and closed his eyes as she reached down into his drawers to cup his balls.

Oh, God, he was going to come any second. He wanted to shout, but he knew not what. This torment was too exquisite;

he needed more than just an instant's worth. He wanted it to last, to go on and on. Maybe forever.

Yet still, in one of his mental compartments he was still thinking, frantically thinking, thrashing around for explanations. How in heaven's name had Adela learned to handle a man like this? Even if she did have a sweetheart, she was no Coraline, no high demimondaine. Yet her touch spoke of a legion of enslaved lovers, discarded yet still begging her to return to them. The shadow of the woman he'd so recently considered marrying hovered over him, but he closed his eyes and compelled her back from whence she'd come, angry, yes, angry that Coraline had intruded at this moment. He didn't want to think of another woman when the woman he was with could do *that* with the tip of her finger.

Wilson bit down hard on his lower lip. He *had* to last, even if Adela was intent on driving him clean over the edge.

"What were you doing in here, Della? Surely you didn't pick the lock just to play with the praxinoscope?"

His voice was high and strangled, and he couldn't keep his hips still. They jerked convulsively, wafting forward, seeking more and more of the divine ministrations of his cousin, the unexpected love goddess.

"Oh, so you saw that...." Her fingertips teased and twirled. Wilson fought, fought hard for control. "I'd heard that the earl had a collection of erotica and I wanted to see it. The praxinoscope was simply an amusing bonus."

"But why would you want to see lewd drawings?" His fingers twitched, preparing to drag her hands off him before he screamed and howled. He wanted to close his own fingers around hers so she never, ever let go. "I would have thought that by now you'd have grown out of youthful curiosity.... It's not exactly a ladylike interest, is it, erotica?"

Adela's laugh was sharp and derisory. Her hand stilled.

"Good grief, you men. You're all the same. You have no comprehension of the inner life of a woman." She gave him a narrow look, one that made him feel small, even while he was rampant. "And I thought that you were different, Wilson. A man of vision…yet it seems you're just as narrow in your views of women as the rest of your sex." She started to pull away, but he caught her hands and held them on him.

"Please…please, don't stop, Della," he gasped. "I'm sorry. I was making unsupported assumptions. It's just…"

What the hell was she doing to his brain? He couldn't think straight. The compartments were all collapsing into one blind, yearning mess. Not even Coraline had ever done this.

"You can't imagine why a gently bred woman like me would continue to be interested in the life of the senses, eh? Someone as plain and dull as me?" Her dark eyes flashed, but blessedly, she began to caress him again, her fingers slow and taunting. "Someone with so little in the way of glamour and savoir faire to recommend her?"

"Oh, for pity's sake, Della, stop saying that. It's just willful. You aren't plain and dull. You're a handsome and alluring woman…I've always believed that. Why won't you believe *me?*" He gasped, the glittering jewel of release barely a breath away.

"Do you have a handkerchief?"

His eyes snapped open. *What?*

"A handkerchief, Wilson? Do you have one? Even someone who dresses as bizarrely as you can't be seen to be sporting semen stains, and it would be the height of bad manners to ejaculate all over the earl's fine furniture or carpeting."

Wilson almost choked with laughter. She was priceless. He fumbled in the pocket of his dressing gown and wrenched out a freshly laundered white handkerchief. Adela snatched it from him, shook it open and enrobed the tip of his cock in it.

Then she went to work on him in earnest. Stroking firmly, back and forth, back and forth, she slid her fingers up and down his length in a way that made him grunt, jerk his hips… and finally, in a savage rush, release his seed.

For a few seconds, Wilson was blind, deaf and dumb, existing only in a state of ragged bliss and pounding sensation. The moments lasted a century, yet also a micro pinpoint of time, then, reluctantly, he tumbled back into himself again, as if falling from a cliff high above. With some distaste, he observed his subsiding member wrapped up in the bundle of his own handkerchief.

With a spirit-crushing little moue, Adela withdrew her hands, relinquishing him as quickly as she'd grabbed him in the first place. Wilson watched her rub her fingers together as if anxious to wipe off his spoor.

"There, all done," she said briskly. "Everyone's satisfied. Now I must go, if you don't mind. It'll soon be time to dress for dinner, and with just one maid among four of us, that takes quite a while."

In the midst of stuffing himself back into his linen, and his handkerchief into his pocket, Wilson realized that she'd grabbed up her portfolio and was halfway to the door.

"Don't go. Stay just a minute. I have so many questions…." He fumbled with his buttons even as he shadowed her across the room. It was only by physically leaning on the door itself that he stopped her from quitting the room without another word.

Adela tapped her foot, pursed her lips, visibly desperate to be rid of him. Where was the languorous sybarite who'd charmed him barely moments ago? She seemed cool, detached, irritated.

Irritation flooded Wilson, too. Was he so repugnant to her that she regretted *everything*? Dash it, she'd enjoyed herself at the time. Not even the most accomplished actress could have faked those moans and the way she'd wriggled and thrashed. And she'd been wet, by God, silky wet. That simply could *not* be fabricated. If she denied her pleasure, she was an out-and-out liar. He grabbed the door handle and immobilized it. He'd have an answer from her if it killed him, and the un-yielding set of her mouth made him feel as stubborn and as mulish as she was.

"Why were you in here? What's in the portfolio that you're so protective of?" He fired the questions like bullets. To shock an answer from her. "Where did you learn to pleasure a man so exquisitely?"

Her glowing eyes widened, and she clasped the portfolio to her bosom. She was still calculating the probability of escaping the room, working out if she could get away with all her secrets intact. He could see her sharp mind ticking over, almost as cleverly as his. Was she weighing how much to reveal? Which of her secrets was the least critical and could be sacrificed?

Whatever were they, these things she hid?

Wilson almost gasped aloud when Adela snagged her lower lip with her strong white teeth. His cock—which he'd believed settled—kicked again, hard in his undergarment like a length of tropical wood, aching, aching, aching as if he'd never spent.

"Very well." Her chin came up. She almost seemed to grow in stature before his eyes, a martial Amazon, girding for battle. And yet what came next was frank and unequivocal. "In respect of your first demand…I came looking for inspiration for my art. Regarding the second, this portfolio—" she tapped her forefinger against it "—is full of that art. My erotic drawings, brought for comparison with classical interpretations." Her eyes met his, burning darkly, not exasperated as he'd first thought, but infinitely brazen. "And as to the third question? Well, I sell those drawings for a great deal of money, Wilson, and I use a portion of that money to purchase the services of gentlemen of pleasure."

What?

Wilson's mouth dropped open. He knew he looked a fool, but didn't care. He'd heard words, but they hadn't made sense.

"Now may I go? I'm rather fatigued and I plan to take a rest before dinner." When Adela shoved on his arm, Wilson stepped aside like an automaton, numbed. His hand slipped from the doorknob and she grasped the thing immediately, gave it a swift turn and wrenched open the door. Before he could speak, she'd swept right by him, her black skirts rustling as she went.

He was still frowning when she disappeared around the corner of the landing, a dark flash, gone again.

Gentlemen of pleasure?

There was no mental box he could seem to fit that in.

Wilson Ruffington couldn't frame a rational thought.

6

Why, oh Why, oh Why?

"Idiot! Nincompoop! Why, oh why, oh why?"

Adela hurtled into the bedroom she'd been assigned, flung herself and her portfolio on the bed and pummeled the mattress with her fists, gasping for breath. Her mind was a whirl and it was hard to breathe. Corsets weren't suited to wearing under pursuit…or in times of high stress and anxiety.

What have I done? I must be deranged. Gone quite mad.

Wilson had been on her tail within moments. He wasn't a man to be nonplussed for long. But in a stroke of blind luck, Adela had escaped him. She'd ducked into a water closet on the landing round the corner, and had been able to close and lock the door with barely a sound.

Thirty seconds later, there'd been a wild thumping on the panel.

"Della! Are you in there? Come out this instant. I want to talk to you."

Torn between silence and telling him to go and take a running jump into Lord Rayworth's lily pond, she'd had a sudden inspired flash. Adopting a strangled, amateur dramatics voice, she'd called out in the quavering tones of an elderly dowager, "Kindly go away and stop hammering on this door, young man! Such impertinence!"

Ten long seconds had ticked by in silence, but eventually his footsteps had retreated. A few minutes later, still half expecting him to pounce on her, Adela had inched open the door, and on finding the coast clear, run pell-mell for her room.

You've done it again, Wilson Ruffington! Addled my wits... No sooner do I set eyes on you than I turn into an imbecile and a wanton, and let slip the very last secret that anyone *should be privy to, least of all you.*

Still breathing hard, Adela sprang up and stomped back to the door to turn the key. If he didn't already know which room she'd been given, it wouldn't take Wilson long to find out, and she needed time alone...to assess the degree of damage she'd done.

If only Sofia or Beatrice were here! Adela could have opened her heart to either one, as both were women of emotional wisdom and experience, and she was confident they'd have words of advice for her. But neither of her two dearest friends moved in this particular set, and this new Wilson dilemma wasn't something she could discuss with anyone else. Neither her mother nor Sybil must ever know her darkest secrets, and though Marguerite was sensible and intelligent, she was simply too young to share matters of sex with.

Oh, it was all such a mess of complication. This situation had been difficult to begin with—Ruffingtons set at odds with each other by her grandfather, the damned Old Curmudgeon who had no time for women.

But now she'd made it insupportable with her own foolish actions.

A bag of nervous energy, Adela marched across to the window and looked out, although she hung back behind the curtains in case Wilson had taken it into his head to go outside. If he glanced up and saw her, he'd know which room was hers.

There was no sign of an eccentric figure with wild dark hair and a ridiculous dressing gown, but the gardens, the lush green lawns and the topiary were all very easy on the eye. The house itself was a bit of a sprawl, but outside all of nature was kept in order, groomed and harmonious. Some of the house party were out there on the lawn below her window, lounging in white painted garden chairs, consuming lemonade and engaging in small talk. Some sheltered beneath gaily striped umbrellas; others basked in the sun's rays. All appeared very innocent, relaxed in ambience, yet observing polite decorum.

But who's tupping whom in secret? Surely I'm not the only one who's been getting up to mischief.

Knowing something of house parties, Adela suspected there were any number of liaisons taking place beneath the conventional, convivial surface. But all looked normal and respectable out there, just as she'd planned to be before her encounter with Wilson. The only risks she took were confined to the discreet, luxurious confines of Sofia's pleasure house.

Until now. One look at Wilson and Adela had turned into a lunatic. Ten minutes in his company and one shouting match later, she'd been putty in his hands. And the one delicious orgasm he'd bestowed on her hadn't been nearly enough. Her body craved more. The very four-poster bed behind her seemed to cry out for his presence, and from the corner of her eye she seemed to see him lounging there against the pillows and the linens.

Damn you, you obnoxious beast, you've primed me like a pump and now I won't be satisfied without a torrent!

Struggling, Adela focused on the view from the window. Her sister Sybil was fluttering around with a croquet mallet and being coy, flapping her eyelashes at her adoring swain, Lord Framley. At least that little exercise was going as planned, and Mama was clearly thrilled. The besotted lad's aristocratic family was rolling in money, and so far nobody had raised any objection to him paying court to a virtually penniless young woman with no apparent prospects. If Sybil bagged him, it would alleviate a lot of worries.

Turning from Sybil, Adela frowned. There was another handsome male creating a source of disquiet. But in this case one she personally did not find attractive.

Her mother was flirting. Batting her eyelashes at Blair Devine, the young solicitor who she'd met at a small poetry soiree hosted by her old friend Lady Gresham. Adela wasn't quite sure how interested her mother was in poetry, but Mama had apparently struck up a conversation with Devine, who Lady Gresham declared was "indispensable" for the discreet handling of small legal matters, and now the fellow seemed to have attached himself to the Ruffingtons. Adela didn't begrudge her mother the pleasure of amusing male company, or a second chance of happiness for herself; after all, one of Papa's last wishes was that his widow not be lonely forever. It was just her choice of male companion Adela found dubious, and she'd been a little disquieted when Mama had engineered an invitation for her favorite to this house party—Blair Devine was just a smidgen too sleek, too attentive. He set Adela's teeth on edge, especially when he looked at *her* in a vaguely speculative fashion, too, as if debating whether to pursue her instead of her parent, and was trying to work out whether he could bring himself to court a rather plain spinster. Mama might be the older woman, but she'd been almost a child bride, a mother at seventeen, and she looked wonderful in black, mature yet vivacious.

What was the fellow up to? Dancing attendance on Mama.

Offering her more lemonade, even as Adela watched, and inducing almost as much eyelash batting as Sybil was currently indulging in. There was something not quite pukka about Devine's smooth, handsome style, even though he'd fit right in to the house party, and seemed to be on friendly terms already with a number of the other guests. His modus operandi wasn't obvious, or particularly flashy, but it, and the man himself still bothered her. She'd tried to be polite to him, nevertheless, for Mama's sake, as had her sisters. Sybil probably liked him, anyway, because she was amendable to all comers, especially good-looking young men, but Adela had sensed that Marguerite, their youngest, shared her own misgivings. The baby of the family was wise beyond her years, but luckily for her, a little too young for a potential match with Blair Devine.

Well, if you plan to direct your attentions to me eventually, sir, you can think again. I'd rather marry that accursed monster Wilson than you!

And back to Wilson again. Ever thus. Their cousin, both relative and nemesis. Mama swung wildly between poles where he was concerned. One day she heaped complaints upon him for being the unwitting recipient of their grandfather's riches and title, in the absence of a closer male relative. The next, she hinted and wheedled and schemed, still deluding herself, despite Adela's vociferous protests, that a marriage between her eldest daughter and the future Lord Millingford was both desirable and a strong possibility.

It will never occur, Mama. You would have done better to fling Sybil at him, or even Marguerite at a pinch. Not me.

But Sybil was interested only in dresses and hair ribbons and her handsome but rather dim Viscount Framley. She and Wilson were like two different species, who spoke different languages. Marguerite's astute intellect was something that

Wilson would probably admire, but she was still only thirteen years old.

Feeling as if her brain was whirling, Adela turned from the window again and began pulling what pins were left from her sorely disarranged coiffure. Her mother would most certainly have a "turn" if she discovered that Wilson had compromised her daughter, but she'd recover like lightning and be delirious with happiness if it meant there might be a marriage.

But I've been compromised these seven years, Mama. Much good it has done us.

Unable to settle, even though she was suddenly exhausted, Adela paced the room, touching familiar items brought from home as talismans: her hairbrush, a bottle of smelling salts, the little glass jar containing her favorite cold cream.

Curse the man, when he gave something, even the slightest hint, she always wanted more. Her body was racked with odd, unsettled sensations. Familiar ones. One she'd experienced within the hour. Ones she'd experienced, just as keenly, seven years ago.

Get out of my head, Wilson!

Impossible, though. He'd never left. Not really. The image she saw now was of the younger man, the provocative friend with whom she'd tramped through the willow wood at Ruffington Hall and taken that fateful dip in the river.

In those brief, halcyon days, Wilson had been simply a remote relative on a summer visit, one who just happened to be there at the same time as her family. He'd not been the heir to the family title then, not even close. With Papa still alive, and Mama young and healthy and eager for more offspring of their fond and uxorious union, a long-awaited brother for their three daughters had still been a strong possibility. And even with none forthcoming, another cousin, Henry, was next in line to be Lord Millingford.

But Adela had been fascinated, even enraptured by her blin-dingly brilliant cousin Wilson, by his beauty and his pecu-liarity both. On a hot day, they'd crept away from formal tea on the lawn, and the rather sedate and yawn-inducing tennis match being played by several of the guests.

And then her life as she'd known it had changed forever....

7

Seven Years Past

Ruffington Hall, Summer 1884

"Let's go and take a splash in the river, eh, Della? Are you game?" Wilson had said, those silver-blue eyes of his glinting. "At least it'll give you something new to draw." He grinned, nodding at the portfolio she was carrying, that she always carried. She'd refused to show him her work, but knew he was determined to see it.

"What do you mean?" Adela ignored his remark about the portfolio, concentrating on Wilson's challenge. She had a shrewd idea what he was really suggesting, with his "splash." Wilson liked to be as shocking as he was clever. Already half in love with him, she couldn't resist the challenge. She'd follow and to the devil with the consequences.

Low-hanging branches and ground-hugging brambles caught at her skirts as she trudged after Wilson through the wood, planning to catch hold of his dressing gown and slow him down if she could. She couldn't imagine why he wore it, except to promote his image as an eccentric academic. For her own part—despite her mama's frantic protests of impropriety—she'd left off her corset and her bustle and two of her petticoats. It was just too oppressive to be trussed up on a summer day, and being slight of build, she didn't think anybody but her mother would be aware of the deficiency. Her white garden dress with its pretty green sash was so comfortable with fewer layers beneath, and it was much easier to sit without all that stupid paraphernalia beneath her skirt.

Not that white was ideal for an arboreal expedition. Mud quickly caked both her hem and her shoes, but the exhilaration of defying all chaperonage, and the dizzy, delicious feeling she always experienced in Wilson's presence made it seem as if she were floating along the path behind him.

All she could think about was seeing him "splashing." All she could hope was that he'd strip off his clothing to do it. She'd grown impatient with anatomy treatises and classical statuary. She wanted to draw a real man at last. And more…

"Slow down, Wilson. This path's uneven and I'll trip if we keep up this absurd pace. We don't have to flee. Nobody noticed us leave, and I doubt that anyone's missed us yet."

Wilson stopped short and Adela cannoned into him. Just as she'd feared, she tripped and lost her footing.

Strong arms caught her and held her, quelling any unconscious urge to struggle. Wilson was wild and unpredictable, yet hugged close against his body like this, she still felt safe. His chest was warm and firm where she leaned against it, and on touching the fine lawn of his loose white shirt, she discovered he wore no undergarment beneath.

"Steady on, Della." There was a laugh in his voice, and it dawned on Adela that her touch had been more voracious than she'd realized. Nothing less than a fervent exploration of his musculature.

She shot back, nearly tripping again, but this time he caught her chastely by the arms. Her heart beat wildly and she wasn't sure what she wanted. Wilson's smug, twinkling eyes made her want to thump him with her fists, and yet do other things, too. Sensations surged through her body, ones she knew that a proper young woman must never admit to feeling.

But I'm not proper, and I'm not like other young women.

Or perhaps all her sex felt the same? And every woman was hiding passion beneath her layers and layers of petticoats?

"What is it, Della?" His silvery eyes narrowed, as if he were monitoring her very thoughts with his analytical scrutiny, but just as she was about to protest about his staring at her, he smiled and gave her a friendly little shake. "Come on, old thing. The river awaits and I'm dying for a dip. It's so hot!"

"If you're so hot, why are you wearing your dressing gown?" Adela aimed the question at his back as he turned and set off along the path again. Wilson just laughed and continued on ahead.

Between the trees, the glitter of sun on water was their goal, and the air felt fresher, less vegetal and moldy.

"Here we are," Wilson cried as they burst forth out of the trees and into a little dell that hugged the edge of the river. It was secret and idyllic, the sort of place where fairies might peep out from among the water plants. The sort of place where wonders might occur.

"How beautiful!" There was magic enough without the fairies, though. A palpable excitement in the air, despite the superficial tranquility, as if the flowing water itself was generating energy. "I never knew about this spot." It was true; she'd explored the grounds of Ruffington Hall before, escaping Mama, but never found this place. Trust Wilson to know it was here.

"Yes, it's special, isn't it?" His voice was quiet, and he

sounded wistful. But when she turned to him, he was looking at her, a challenging expression on his face.

"Well, I think I shall do a little sketching," Adela announced. She mustn't let her cousin rattle her. Best to go
calmly about her own business. But where to sit, wearing a
gown of white, without getting mud or dust or plant stains
upon it? She could hardly *stand* the whole time while she was
drawing.

Wilson whipped off his dressing gown in a whirl of silk
and set it down on the grass in a little patch of shade. "Better not to sit in full sunlight, Della. I've been reading some
studies into the effect of sunlight on human tissue, and I believe long exposure may prove harmful to delicate complex-
ions." He patted the robe, making it flat for her. "Your skin
is exceptionally smooth and fine, so you really should take
the best care of it. I could formulate an emollient preparation
for you, if you like?"

"Um…yes, thank you. That would be very kind.…"

This was typical Wilson. A pretty compliment combined
with scientific instruction. Or maybe he was just trying to
butter her up? So he could take liberties.

Ah, but you want that, don't you? The liberties…

The voice of wisdom jabbed at her. She knew what she
wanted, and knew she was a fool to want it. Yet still she
couldn't suppress her yearning. She caught her breath when
Wilson swiftly undid the buttons of his shirt, then whipped
the thing off over his head.

"Right then, it's a dip for me." Flinging his shirt away,
he revealed his bare chest and shoulders, so smooth and well
shaped. Adela's eyes skittered to the fastenings of his summer
flannel trousers, and she wondered what lay beneath them.
Was it drawers or just Wilson?

Her cousin laughed. As usual, he seemed to have guessed what she was thinking.

"You'll have to wait and see." Waggling his dark eyebrows at her, he threw himself down on the grass, just a foot or two away from her, and attacked the laces of his boots.

Adela applied herself to her portfolio, but even with the green bounty of the natural world around her, and a freshly sharpened pencil, the blank page remained unsullied. She was trying not to look at Wilson, and failing abjectly.

He flung away his boots and socks, then stood again. Turning directly toward her, in a blatant challenge, he slowly and teasingly unbuttoned his trousers and let them drop. Then laughed when Adela looked away.

Wilson *was* wearing drawers, but they were summer-weight ones, reaching only to his knees. Adela didn't get much chance to admire their style, though, because before she could protest, he was slipping them off, too. She turned resolutely away from him and studied a small white flower growing a few inches from where she was sitting, a bloom of delicate beauty and frailty.

"Not interested in human anatomy, then?"

The temptation to look at him had the force of the fast-flowing stream beside them, and all its inevitability. Her neck ached from the effort of not swiveling in his direction. "I'm very interested in anatomy, just not yours, Wilson. I'm fully conversant with the male form. I've studied many great works of art."

His laugh rang out, lusty and free. It was a happy sound, but it made her clench her teeth. She was always a source of amusement to him, and yet she couldn't stop seeking his company.

"Oh, Della, Della, Della… Don't you know that all the classical artists tend to err on the side of underestimation in certain male characteristics?"

"Don't be disgusting."

She was fighting, fighting, fighting now. Resisting what in her heart she knew she'd really come here for.

Fiddlesticks!

Trying not to seem at all concerned, she slowly turned in Wilson's direction. Only to find that he was already at the riverbank and wading in, his back to her.

Drat the man!

His shoulders, his back and his bottom were glorious, though. Before the latter disappeared beneath the water, she admired the firm, tight musculature of his buttocks and the way it moved, propelling him forward. The white flower was forgotten, and she began drawing as fast as she could, her pencil flying, inspired. It was always like this when she found a subject that really enchanted her. She could work quickly, almost at lightning speed, the result forming not only on the paper, but etched into her memory as if on a photographic plate, ready to be retrieved at any time, reworked and adapted.

This was her great gift, and she knew that even if she never saw her cousin's magnificent arse ever again, she would still be able to draw it over and over, whenever she wanted to.

It took but a few moments to complete the study. Naked Wilson, his firm backside, his well-shaped torso, his dark hair, silky and tousled down the back of his neck. Smiling, she flipped over the page and drew another impression, this time changing the angle, making the view more a profile. But she didn't attempt to portray his genitalia. Somehow it didn't seem right, in case she shortchanged him.

"Why don't you come on in, Della? The water's deliciously refreshing. A swim will do you good." He half turned, smiling at her over his bare shoulder. "Can you swim?"

"Indeed I can. I've bathed in the sea and I found it most

invigorating. And even with the heavy drag of my bathing dress, I quickly took to the strokes."

Wilson cocked his head to one side. He looked impressed. "Well, then, you'll find it even easier and much more pleasant if you swim naked."

"Wilson, you really do and say the most absurd things. I can't possibly take my clothes off in front of you. It's completely improper and I don't know why you would even suggest it."

Even as she spoke the words, she almost choked on her own hypocrisy. She'd come here to see, think and do improper things. That was her nature. She'd already left off half her underpinnings, knowing full well it was daring and scandalous and would give Mama an apoplectic fit if she ever found out.

"I don't think you care about propriety, Della," said Wilson, his voice low and challenging as he spun around in the flowing stream and approached the bank again.

I should turn. I should turn.

But Adela didn't. She watched the point where Wilson's body met the water, holding steady as his loins breached the surface and all was exposed to her.

She blinked. Well, it didn't seem as if *that* would go under one of those tiny fig leaves that adorned most classical statuary. Certainly not. His male appendage was sturdy, and had a cheeky, rather insolent look about it. Even as she stared, it gave a twitch, and she could swear it got plumper and longer.

Wilson gave a low chuckle as he stepped onto the bank. "I'm sorry. I've disappointed you, haven't I? You were expecting a weapon of massive proportions." Adela's heart nearly stopped when he reached down and casually fondled himself… something that seemed to make his flesh expand even before her eyes. "But in my defense, the water is quite cold, and that always has the effect of making the male member shrink in order to protect itself."

"It, um, looks perfectly adequate to me." Her pencil settled on the paper, and almost of its own accord began sketching in the missing manly parts of her second drawing, before swiftly moving on to another depiction, this time of Wilson's penis in magnificent isolation.

"Shall I pose for you?"

Adela's heart thudded hard. Yes, indeed, she did want him to pose for her, but there were other things she wanted, too. Things that obsessed her more than ever now. Not only did she want to draw, she wanted to touch, to caress and to explore. She wanted to feel the reality of a man's body, rather than just look at it and sketch it from a safe distance.

But if she told Wilson that, there would be no turning back. He was a man, and they were wont to make a yard of liberties out of an inch of compliance, because they couldn't help themselves. Adela wasn't sure if she wanted more than a foot.

And talking of inches, wasn't he was bigger down there than before?

"Yes…please. Perhaps you could lie down over there?" She pointed to a patch of flattish turf a safe distance away. It was shaded by branches that dipped low, toward the river, and the play of light and shadow would afford an interesting texture.

That's it. Concentrate on the technicalities. See him purely as a pleasing natural structure to be recorded.

Wilson shrugged and padded to the area she'd indicated. With a grace that nearly made her sigh aloud, he sank down and struck a pose, much like a modern Apollo taking his ease. Closing his eyes, he stretched back his arms, causing a stark tension in the muscles of his chest and abdomen. With one leg straight and one lifted, bent at the knee, he seemed to offer his manhood to her, its prominence magnified.

It's just a pleasing natural structure.

Adela's pencil raced again. She might never get another opportunity to draw a naked man from life. Even if she were lucky enough to find a husband soon, the gentleman in question might not want to lie around in the altogether to indulge her artistic whims.

Sketching almost without thinking, Adela frowned. No beaux were as yet on the horizon, and even if one hove into view, she wasn't sure she *wanted* one who hadn't got time to pose. From what she'd seen of her early marrying friends, marriage wasn't the entirely desirable state that women were led to believe it was. Adela wasn't at all excited by the idea of homemaking and entertaining and "supporting" her husband in all things. Or producing infant after infant. One or two would be a joy, and she was certainly very interested in the begetting side of the process, but her instincts were not at all maternal. Most people's children were rather tiresome.

As all this was passing through part of her mind, another segment was recording and reproducing Wilson's physique. And yet another portion was desperately wondering what his bare skin felt like to the touch, and how…how much bigger his penis was going to get. It was now eye-poppingly tumescent and pointing up at a robust angle.

"Yes, I'm afraid that can happen in the presence of beautiful women."

He'd done that trick again. Read the thoughts and notions going through her mind.

"Can you not control it?" Adela's pencil snapped. She was pressing on it too hard. Reaching into the portfolio and a little leather notch, she drew out a tiny knife and sharpened the point. The small activity was a respite. She had to concentrate in order not to cut her finger. While focusing on the blade she couldn't look at Wilson's burgeoning sex.

"Oh, I could if wanted to," he replied airily. "I could apply myself to the never-ending conundrum that is pi, or tax my brain with one or two little theorems that are interesting me at the moment, and that would probably result in a gradual collapse of the offending organ…." The sharpening was finished, and Adela looked up again, to find him grinning at her. "But I don't want to. It's rather pleasant to be aroused…. I like being reminded that I'm male, and animal, and that I'm lusty." Slowly, he ran a fingertip along his own length. "And I love the way it brings the roses to your cheeks."

Adela drew in a breath, to calm herself. The sight of him fondling his own flesh did hot and peculiar things to her. She wanted him to do far more than simply touch. She wanted to know what happened if he just kept stroking and stroking. Having inveigled her way into her grandfather's library—with Wilson's help—and perused certain volumes, *and* listened to racy talk from certain wild girls at the ladies' academy she'd attended…well, she was fully aware of what happened to men, and what they did with the result during the act of carnal congress.

But all that was purely theoretical. Actually observing the male phenomenon occur in front of her was making her quite giddy.

"Well, you might as well plunge back into the river to cool off, both yourself and your masculine appendage," she said as briskly as she could, hoping to sound clinical and detached. "I've seen quite enough for now. I can draw whatever I need to from memory henceforward."

"I rather like the idea of my erection being preserved forever in your mind's eye. Every time I look at you from now on, I'll be wondering if you're thinking about my cock."

"Don't be ridiculous. I'm drawing you as a life study, not thinking about your…your…"

"It's called my cock, Della, and in the interest of art, and of science, I think you should touch it to ascertain its texture. It'll assist you in your sketching."

Would she even be able to sketch anything now? He'd got her all in a fluster. She'd come here with daring activities in mind, but faced with the moment of truth, she found her natural fears had resurfaced. Not sure what to do, she stole another glance at Wilson, trying not to let her eyes roam in a southerly direction.

Her cousin had that sympathetic expression on his face again. So unlike his usual blunt and arrogant imperiousness, the armor of his exceptional mind. He gave her a little smile that could be construed as an apology. As if he felt remorse for unsettling her.

"Yes, I think a dip is a good idea." He rose, and Adela looked quickly away again. The way his cock bounced and swung made her face burn. "And for you, too, Della. If you like, I won't look until you're safely up to your chin in the water."

"I'm not sure." The water did look inviting, though, and it was such a warm day. Even in less underwear than usual, she felt oppressed, and envious of Wilson's total lack of modesty and the way it allowed him to do whatever he wanted.

"You'll enjoy it. Come on in." Wilson was already wading back into the stream, and Adela felt a sense of loss as he moved away from her. Devil that he might be, she wanted to be close.

"Perhaps I can keep my chemise and drawers on."

Wilson turned again, although fortunately, the organ that bothered her so much was now hidden beneath the surface. "Don't be silly. You don't want to go back to the house with soggy underpinnings, do you?"

Damn the man, he was back to goading again.

"Oh, very well, then!" Setting aside her portfolio, Adela

swiftly unfastened the buttons of her boots, kicked them off and then sprang to her feet. Her heart pounding, she attacked the buttons down the front of her garments next, trying not to be hampered by the shaking of her fingers. With a nod, Wilson turned away as she shed the bodice of her dress.

"You can watch if you want. I don't care!"

Why in heaven's name did I say that?

"Very tempting, but I think you deserve some privacy, cousin. I've teased you far too much already." With that, he waded out farther, his fine back disappearing beneath the water until only his head was showing. His shaggy black hair kissed the surface of the stream.

Infuriating beast!

Adela grappled with her clothing, muttering to herself. Wilson really was the most contrary creature she'd ever met, or could imagine meeting. He was so fickle, changing tack again and again, that she just didn't know where she stood with him.

Buttons and ribbons and garters defied her. She tugged and wrenched. Wilson didn't think that she dare unclothe herself before him, but she would show him. She would show him, indeed, show him everything. But she had to do it before her nerve failed her.

Though the day was warm, she shivered as she unveiled her skin. It was the strangest sensation to be naked in the open air. She'd only ever undressed to bathe before, in the privacy of her bedroom or the bathroom. Even when she'd swum in the sea, she'd disrobed in the safely of the bathing machine, and come out in a voluminous costume. Now, a light breeze flowed over her bare skin, like zephyr's caress. Her nipples had already firmed, but the sense of exposure made them tingle in a way that was half pain, half pleasure.

Out in the water, she saw Wilson turn his head. Was he looking at her even though he'd said he wouldn't? She wouldn't be at all surprised.... But she resisted the urge to try and cover herself with arms and hands. Let him see! Let him know she wasn't afraid of him! Padding across the turf, she made for the water's edge, her body still in conflict, incompatible compulsions at war. But still she managed to keep her arms at her side.

"Good grief!"

The flowing river *was* cold, despite the warm sunny day. The chill hit her like a blow, but she waded forward, clamping her jaws together to stop her teeth chattering.

"I did warn you it was cold," said Wilson, cutting through the water toward her as she sank to shoulder level, almost in a state of shock.

"I thought you were just claiming that to excuse the small size of your organ," she retorted, her voice half choked by the frigidity of the water.

"Touché," replied Wilson, up close now. Very close indeed. Adela glanced down and realized that the water was unexpectedly clear, like crystal, and she could see every detail of his body.

As he must be able to see every detail of hers. The devil, he'd known this all along. He was almost flaunting himself, swaying in the water, making his penis move slowly. It seemed to have acclimatized itself to the temperature and was quite sizable.

"Shall we swim a little…get out of our depth?"

I'm already way out of my depth.

Wilson reached out beneath the water and took her hand, leading her into the deepest part of the stream.

The flow was erratic, faster here, and for a moment she was afraid of something other than her randy cousin. When she'd indulged in sea bathing, it had been in a sheltered cove, noted for its lack of currents and breakers. This stretch of the river was actually far more active.

As if sensing her fears, Wilson tightened his hold on her hand, and immediately she felt safe again. Well, safe from drowning. Of other hazards, she wasn't so sure.

They swam around for a while, Wilson setting her free when she found her confidence, and Adela was quickly exhilarated by the sensations and the freedom. Water against her skin was even more seductive than air. It was like being embraced by cool silk that flowed everywhere, tantalizing her most sensitive zones. Her very soul seemed to open like a flower, subtly stimulated, not only by the water, but by the presence of her handsome, provocative companion with his probing silvery eyes and his strong, masculine body. She knew she would have to face up to both when they eventually left the stream again.

Invigorating as the swim was, Adela knew she couldn't stay in the river forever, so as she felt herself beginning to tire, she made for the bank. Not giving herself even a heartbeat's hesitation, she climbed out of the water, trying to move as elegantly as she could.

Once on the shore again, she felt the cool breeze lick her skin, and began to shiver, her teeth chattering.

Oh, fiddle, how on earth am I going to dry myself? She'd have to use her petticoats, but then they would be damp when she put them on. Wonderful as her dip had been, second thoughts rushed in, in abundance.

The slosh of water as Wilson emerged, too, made her turn around, even though she'd not planned to. His eyes narrowed, and she knew he'd seen her shivering.

"Sit down on my dressing gown. I'll dry you."

"But—"

"No buts. Don't be silly, woman."

Adela did as she was told, and the moment she was settled, Wilson snatched up his white shirt and began rubbing her vigorously with it, massaging her skin and stimulating the flow of blood as well as drying her.

The sensation was delicious, warming to the senses and unexpectedly relaxing. Adela almost purred as her circulation heated and surged.

"Better?"

"Blissful!" She said it without thought. It was true, too, but a second later, dangerously revealing. Here she was, being handled by a man, with only a layer of fine cotton between his fingers and her body—and Wilson didn't hold back; he was drying her everywhere. He rubbed the shirt over her breasts, the action slower and more circumspect, in respect of the more delicate nature of her anatomy there, but with his hands curved in a way that was cupping and caressing. Adela knew she should command him to stop, and tell him that she'd deal with those areas herself, thank you very much. But she couldn't. She liked it. She liked it a lot. Coming up on her knees, pretending to investigate her bedraggled hair, and her half-collapsed chignon, she invited him to take further liberties.

Wilson doubled up the cloth of the shirt, slipped it between her thighs and began to rub it gently back and forth.

Adela grabbed his shoulder. Their eyes met. The shirt moved slowly, but he was silently asking the question, *Shall I stop?*

This was scandalous. Forbidden. Beyond daring. Yet so heavenly that Adela could not resist. She dug her nails into Wilson's bare shoulder and let out a small, indistinct sound of assent.

The soft, slightly damp cloth molded to her sex, and she could feel his fingers through it. They sought and found her most sensitive spot, dividing her curls. He moved beside her to gain better purchase, his other hand settling on the small of her back. Adela bore down, rocking now, and moaning at the heavy, gathering sensation. She knew what it was. The books in her grandfather's library said very little about a woman's side of things, but her faster classmates at the ladies' collegiate had seemed to know all of it, and their racy talk fired her to experiment. The pleasure she'd experienced had been intense and shocking, and even though the whispers at the collegiate had implied it was a wicked sin, and perverse, Adela didn't think so. Something so lovely couldn't be all that bad.

And it wasn't bad now. It was wonderful. Even though she was taking the most enormous risk, letting her disreputable and infuriating cousin do it to her.

"Shall I stop?"

The words shocked her far more than Wilson's touch ever could. "No," she managed to reply, her voice cracking as she threw her arms around his neck, holding him in a death grip. Nothing was going to stop her reaching her goal, not even Wilson's conscience and second thoughts. She nearly throttled him when he withdrew his hand, but it was only to toss away the now redundant shirt. A breath later, his bare hand replaced it in the niche between her thighs.

The exquisite artistry of Wilson's fingertips rubbing and circling her clitoris was too much. She was too excited. Almost immediately her core began to ripple and clench, and, with breathless pleasure surging, she spent. Her arms tightened around him, and another time, she might have realized she was probably hurting him, but all she wanted now was to keep him and his divine hand closer than close. She buried her face in his neck to muffle her cry of release.

Her entire body was hot now, fired by her orgasm, but somehow what she'd felt still wasn't enough. There had been other matters discussed at the collegiate, and despite the dangers, Adela would not be denied. She wanted more.

Falling back onto Wilson's dressing gown, she hauled him down with her, feeling a triumphant rush of desire as his body pressed against hers. He was hard as iron, his member shoving against her belly.

This was uncharted territory, a world away from girlish dreams of romance, and her imaginings of what the matrimonial embrace might be like. This was darkness and danger on a brilliant summer's day, and the rebel in her reached out for the risks...and for Wilson's sturdy cock. He groaned as she folded her fingers around him. She wasn't quite sure what to do, but it seemed to her that a man was sensitive in this particular area, and to treat him like a pump handle might be more painful than pleasurable. With a light grip and a slow stroke, she began to caress him, half her mind still amazed at what was happening.

"Oh, Della, Della, you have the touch of a courtesan," he gasped, his hips pushing in time to her fondling. Adela faltered, doubting for a moment. Did she want to be compared to a light o' love? And what did Wilson know about courtesans, anyway?

"Oh, don't stop, darling girl, your caress feels wonderful. You have magical hands.... It must be the artist in you."

Flatterer.

She was glad to please him, though. He'd certainly pleased her, and she was all for fair play, for gratitude expressed. But it was more than that. The way Wilson's cock felt to her hand was intriguing, fascinating and delightful. It almost seemed like a discreet living entity of itself, rather than a part of him. It was the very essence of life, and of man.

He made strange noises. Rough groans and grunts, muttered words, some of them very crude, but raw and exciting.

The very sound of his voice was a reciprocal caress, stirring her without even touching her.

"That's it, Della...that's it...bring me off...." The words were harsh, but she sensed he was still trying to contain himself and not shock her or grab at the pleasures her flesh represented to him. Did he think she was afraid? Did he think she was cold and indifferent, now that she'd had her release? Well, he was wrong. Her appetite had only just begun to stir.

Adela pushed her body against Wilson's even as she played with his cock. She was on fire again, her belly alive with a gnawing hunger, and emptiness for which there was only one answer. It was madness to give in to the urge. Her rational mind knew that, but good sense and logic were being washed away by a force as inevitable as the flowing stream.

She took a firmer hold on Wilson's erection and, parting her legs, drew him to her, wiggling around until she was right beneath him, open and ready.

"Della! What are you doing? We can't do this!"

Adela's eyes shot open and she looked up into Wilson's. At their center they were black as night, giving lie to his words, just as his cock did. He wanted her, he hungered for her, but the learned man, versed in physiology and biology, was fighting to remain in control...and yet losing, in the same way her own wits were addled.

Yes, we can! I can't bear it if we don't!

She didn't speak. She wasn't capable of it. But she knew Wilson understood her completely.

"Oh, Della, Della," he gasped again, moving into position. "I adore you, you are...you are... Oh, God, Della, you are perfect...so perfect."

So are you! And so...big.

The head of Wilson's cock seemed to know its way to the very quick of her, and pressing against her entrance, it felt huge and hot and rounded. Much too big to enter, surely? He pushed a little harder, and then, clearly feeling the resistance, attempted to pull back.

"No! Don't you dare deny me!" As her hands clasped her cousin's firm bottom, Adela was stunned by the sound of her own voice. It was that of an entirely different woman, an Amazon, an imperious goddess, not to be gainsaid or thwarted.

Above her, Wilson blinked, as if he was just as astounded as she, then dark fire blazed in his eyes, the devil answering her.

"Very well," he growled, adjusting his position again, taking weight on his elbow and reaching down between them to nudge his cock to the sweetest spot with his fingers. His touch there again made Adela whimper, the sensation was so divinely lewd. She bucked her hips at him, interfering with his aim, yet unable to control her own body.

"Stay still! I don't want to hurt you."

"I don't care. Just do it! Just fuck me!"

Wilson's body jolted as if the sound of the forbidden word on her lips was a lash of raw energy. His hips jerked, shoving the rounded tip of his cock against her, right at her entrance. Adela's fingers tightened of their own accord on the firm rounds of his bottom, more to quell her own hesitation than to scotch his.

"Damn you, Della...I shouldn't do this!"

Her answer was to hurl her hips upward, not giving him any second chance. Wilson roared and thrust hard, his cock breaching her.

Adela let out a yelp at the sharp jag of pain. It hurt. It did hurt. But somehow the discomfort was unimportant in the face of her goal, and the almost instantaneous sensation of being filled and stretched and made whole as Wilson slid home. If he tried to hesitate again, it only lasted the merest hint of an instant. Once he was in her, she knew the point of return was a thing of the past.

Gasping, she held on to him hard, clutching his bottom, wrapping her legs around him. There was no question what she needed to do; her body just did it, as if naturally formed for this act and imbued with an ancient knowledge of it. There was still a sliver of pain as she hitched her hips up, pushing herself at him, but it seemed distant somehow, as if another woman were feeling it.

The real Adela could only exult in the sensation of being possessed, savoring the fullness within, the knowledge that Wilson's living body was inside hers.

They were both shaking, but whether it was from the cold water, excitement, fear, pleasure or happiness, Adela couldn't tell. She just held on to Wilson for dear life, catching her breath, absorbing the fact that she was no longer a virgin, and in her heart of hearts elated at the fact.

"Have I hurt you? Are you in pain?" Wilson's voice was raw. He hardly seemed able to force the words out, he sounded so taut.

"No," lied Adela, and the truth was, for such a momentous act, the discomfort was indeed strangely fleeting. All she felt now was a delicious gathering of tension, like the feelings when she touched herself—or when Wilson had touched her—but subtly and thrillingly different. The urge to move was like a living thing, and she surged against him.

"Are you sure? You cried out."

"I'm sure…yes, I'm sure." She wanted to command him to get on with the job, but that seemed too crude. Instinct told her men were as susceptible in these moments as women were, and if she gave him the sharp edge of her tongue in desperation, it might spoil his enjoyment. Well, at least that was what she thought might happen. With no practical experience of these matters, she could only guess, only surmise.

"What about you? Do you feel all right?" The question popped out, sounding so prosaic. She'd never expected to be having a conversation in the middle of her first carnal embrace, but she couldn't seem to help herself.

"Yes." His teeth were gritted.

"Very well...but...well, shouldn't you be moving or something?"

Wilson let out a low, despairing growl, his body as tense as wire, and still virtually motionless, apart from a fine trembling. "For God's sake, Della... I'm trying not to come. I don't want it all to be over before we even start. I'd like you to have some pleasure in this, too."

Adela frowned. The urge to caress him and kiss him and move against him was nearly killing her. She did adore Wilson, for all his foibles and high-handedness. She wanted to be a siren for him, a houri, a pleasure giver, too.

"But I've had some pleasure. I don't mind.... You should have your turn." Unable to contain herself, she clenched her inner muscles experimentally, embracing Wilson's member, and gasping at the jolt of sensation it gave her, too.

"Oh, Della, Della...please..." he groaned against her ear, "That feels too good.... Oh, my dear, you'll unman me if you do it again."

She did it again, almost groaning herself at the gathering, gathering, gathering sensation it induced. It was like standing on the edge of a precipice, almost there.

"Della! No!" To her horror, he tried to push away from her, to withdraw, but like a lioness, she clung harder, baring her teeth as she jammed her loins against his.

Even as she pushed against him, she felt the change. From resistance to hunger. Not exactly acquiescence, but a sudden opening of a pent-up dam, the transformation from tentative boy into man, ravenous and dominating. He thrust and thrust, smooth and deep, clutching her for purchase just as she held on to him, his thick cock pushing in, right to the hilt in a way that made his body knock against the sensitive button of her clitoris.

She was so close, so close. She strived, rocked, arched, her fingers flexing as she dug her nails into Wilson's buttocks. He grunted and winced, yet the action seemed to have a galvanic effect on him. His hips hammered, pounding, pounding.

Yes! Oh, yes!

But even as Adela clawed for the shimmering prize, the experience she could not have described in words, she was thwarted. With a great roar, Wilson wrenched himself away from her, his hips still working as he withdrew his cock, then thrust it against her hip, rubbing and jerking.

Shocked, Adela felt something warm and slippery against her skin. His seed, pumping out of him, anointing her. Emotions awhirl, she didn't know whether to be distraught or relieved. She knew why he'd done it, but the gnawing frustration and emptiness she felt pushed away all rationales and good sense. All her primal urges screamed in outrage and churning desire, harshly denied.

Wilson seemed shell-shocked for a moment, then literally shook himself, tossing his curly head, blinking furiously. Sliding to one side, he thrust his fingers between Adela's thighs, where he'd just been, and found her core.

"What are you doing?" she growled at him, trying to pull away, her heart in chaos.

"Finishing you. You didn't spend...."

"I don't need that!"

"You do!"

Still she tried to get away, but his fingers were too insistent, too clever, too surely focused on the zone of most exquisite sensation. With a sob, Adela subsided, grasping him again, arching and accepting on a primitive level what her rebellious spirit almost resented.

Gasping, she bent like a bow, pressing her sex to his hand. Her mouth went soft as he kissed her, his tongue thrusting into the warm interior just the way his cock had thrust into her body moments ago. He was trying to sweeten the experience, bring some tenderness to the act of finally dispatching her lust. She should be grateful, she knew that, but still, she hated him that moment as much as loved him.

Heat pooled in the pit of her belly, like syrup boiling and rolling. She might die, any second, if something didn't happen. Then that second ticked, and the thing did happen. She opened her mouth to scream with pleasure, but Wilson kissed harder, containing the sound, *increasing* the pleasure.

Adela jerked and rocked and bucked, her mind a white haze, her sex fluttering, pulsing, grabbing at emptiness, at the void where Wilson's cock should have been. Overcome, she called him a foul name she'd once heard a street urchin utter. She barely knew how she remembered it; it just came out, seemed right.

"I'm sorry," said Wilson some little time later, when Adela was lying on his dressing gown, curled up tight and trying not to think too hard about anything. Frowning, she rubbed at his seed where it had dried on her skin.

"For what?" she asked in a small voice. Wilson had sounded vaguely cross, and the slight coldness had sliced at her. This wasn't how she'd imagined the blissful aftermath of the sensual embrace might be. But then, of course, she'd always expected the embrace to come after marriage, and to have been shared with a husband who doted on her. Surely the expectation of most women?

"I shouldn't have taken advantage of you. I shouldn't have allowed myself to give in to your blandishments."

Adela shot up, sitting straight, then twisted toward him. All her uneasy languor had disintegrated. What on earth did he mean? She had a suspicion.

"What on earth are you talking about…'blandishments'? You seemed more than pleased by my willingness not so long ago. What are you trying to imply, Wilson? That I'm a weak and fleshly woman who can't control her own urges and I've… I've polluted you somehow?"

It was nonsense. She knew that. She knew he knew that. But inside her, sorrow for what was not had started to boil in a most peculiar way that destroyed her rationality.

"I'm sorry," he said again, looking a bit red along his elegant cheekbones, and as confused as she. "I chose my words poorly. I didn't mean…well, I don't know what I meant. I only know I should have been more responsible and more continent." He hauled his shaggy dark hair back from his brow and combed it with his fingers. "It's not that I didn't want you…or don't want you, Della. It's just that I should have resisted my urges, instead of encouraging yours. There might be consequences."

She knew what he meant, even though he'd pulled out. It was entirely possible that a little bit of his seed was still inside her. Doing what it did… And she wasn't going to show her naïveté by asking.

"Of course. I might be with child."

"Indeed."

Adela reached for her clothing, grabbing at her drawers. Somehow they'd got twisted up, and she wrenched at them, clenching her teeth. Then clenching them even harder when Wilson calmly took the garment out of her hand and un-twisted it. Without a word, he passed it back, and she turned away from him and wriggled into it, fumbling with the fastenings. Fortunately, she managed to get her chemise on the right way round.

Wilson was getting into his clothes, too, but without warning, he snapped at her. "How could you be so idiotic, Della? I'm just a stupid, weak, lickerish man, desperate to know what shagging a woman feels like…. You must have known I wouldn't be able to control myself. Yet still you threw yourself at me even when you knew you might become enceinte."

Adela stood up to get into her dress, crushing a delicate little wildflower under her foot, along with certain silly, girlish, romantic notions she'd only just realized she was harboring.

Had she wanted to snare Wilson that way? Many of her friends from the collegiate were betrothed. Some were even already married after a single season. She wasn't totally obsessed with the idea of becoming a bride, but she couldn't deny it had crossed her mind. And when it had crossed, Wilson had always been the theoretical groom. Buttoning her bodice, she heard again his words in her head: *Desperate to know what shagging a woman feels like….*

Like the mechanism of a clock ticking out the hour, it dawned on her.

She hadn't been the only virgin in the dell.

Stupid tears welled in her eyes, and she dashed them away surreptitiously. What should have been a quiet time of peace, after the sharing of a precious mutual gift, had devolved into an ugly blame-slinging contest.

But she still couldn't stop herself.

"Well, I'm sorry, Wilson. I was just a weak, lickerish woman. We *do* have urges, you know, just like you men. I was subject to the carnal itch, that's all, and I forgot myself for a moment and reached out for you as the convenient one to scratch it. Nothing more."

What in the world is wrong with me? When did I turn into such a shrew?

She glanced at Wilson and saw a look of horror on his face as his head popped out of the opening of his shirt, an expression of genuine pain. But then it was gone again, and his beautiful mouth thinned into a line that was almost ugly, if anything about Wilson could ever be considered thus.

"Well, that is gratifying, Adela. To know that my cock means nothing more than that to you. I never realized you were quite such a progressive." His eyes narrowed, hard and brittle as slate. "I will, of course, marry you if you are pregnant, despite the fact that my finer feelings mean so little to you."

Your feelings mean everything to me. Or at least they did....

"Well, I'm sure I'm not with child. I'm told that it's most unlikely the first time.... So I think you can breathe easy and count yourself lucky that you've probably escaped the horrible fate of marrying me. It's clear that you find the idea repugnant." She flopped down again, to pull on her boots, unable to look at him. The silly tears were threatening once more, and she would not show him them, she simply would not.

"I don't find you repugnant, Della. Not at all. That should have been obvious." She felt a jerk, and realized he was trying to retrieve his dressing gown from beneath her. Shake her off so casually, would he? "Although I am very averse to the idea of being trapped into marriage, and I've seen the way your mother's eyes dart from you to me when we're in the same room. It seems to me she sees me as a good catch for you."

"Don't be ridiculous." Adela leaped up, shamed to admit that her mother probably did feel that way, with three daughters who'd all need marrying off. And that in her own secret daydreams, Adela had supported Mama's hopes, even if she'd never informed her parent of the fact.

Wilson whipped up the robe and whirled into it in a way

she'd have thought dramatic and dashing in any other circumstances, even though it now bore some grass stains.

"Ah, but it's not ridiculous, is it? We're cousins, but not very close ones. Your mama is playing the odds. Hedging her bets. Three daughters and no son, and she's a woman of middle years...and if anything should happen to cousin Henry, well, you don't have to be a logician or any other kind of theorist to arrive at the obvious solution."

He was right. So right. Mama would have tried to marry her off to Henry, just in case, if he hadn't already been engaged elsewhere. Anything to ensure that Grandfather's wealth and title would come to her eldest daughter through marriage, if she herself couldn't produce a brother for Adela, Sybil and Marguerite.

"Of course you wanted me to scratch your itch, Della, but it served your mother's purpose, too. Did she put you up to it?"

Like a mighty wind, anger swirled inside her. How could he be so hateful? He was wrong, and Mama, for all her scheming, was not as devious as all that.

Without thinking, Adela fetched back her hand to strike him, but he caught it in a firm grip, meeting her glare. She thought he might kiss her in anger, to punish her somehow, and for a moment he seemed to let his guard down in readiness. Feeling the lapse, Adela jerked free, spun around and set off down the path leading back to the house, hurling the words *"You're disgusting!"* over her shoulder as she went.

Hurtling along, her eyes blurred with tears, she just wanted to get away from him, as fast as possible. She sped along on instinct, not even sure that she was going the way they'd come....

Then *bang!* Something thick and greenish-brown flew into her face with a crack, as if from out of nowhere. Pain exploded in the bridge of her nose and she saw stars as a hot rush of blood gushed from her nostrils and splattered crimson down the front of her gown. At the same time, she heard thudding footsteps approaching and a body bashing through the undergrowth.

Go away, Wilson, was her final thought as unconsciousness claimed her.

8

Mother and Daughter

Rayworth Court, 1891

Where the dickens was that girl?

Mrs. Amelia Ruffington glanced around, seeking a familiar figure, stubborn and slender, and clad in black. Not seeing her daughter Adela, Mrs. Ruffington shuddered. The sun was warm and pleasant, and the company convivial, but somehow, "mislaying" Adela like this, in these particular circumstances, always brought with it a dark, disquieting memory.

The horrid shock of fear and worry when she'd been sitting on a lawn, much like this one, drinking tea, much like this, and Wilson Ruffington had walked out from among a stand of trees, carrying Adela with her face and her dress covered in blood.

Horrible. Horrible. Horrible. A day of disaster. Poor, poor Adela. Suffering not just the pain and shock, but a permanent disfigurement, too. Her straight and elegant nose, so much like that of her handsome father's, had been badly broken. Not the best efforts of the finest surgeon the Ruffingtons could afford had been able to correct it, and Adela's nose remained crooked to this day.

But where was she now? And, for that matter, where was Wilson?

Mrs. Ruffington reached out, almost expecting tea, and found that she'd been drinking lemonade. Good grief, anxiety over Adela was quite taxing her wits. She took a sip and pulled a face. Not sweet enough. The robust tang of the lemons reminded her of Adela, too. Her willful yet still strangely lovable daughter, a strong personality, always challenging but never tedious.

Yes, Wilson was nowhere to be seen, either. Was there any chance the two of them might be together? Mrs. Ruffington's heart leaped. Might there still be a chance for those two, despite Adela's undisguised disdain and dislike of her cousin? It was a constantly perplexing puzzle. Until the day of the broken nose, Mrs. Ruffington had been so hopeful of a match between them, and her eldest off her hands at eighteen, despite her independent nature and worryingly radical outlook.

But then the accident had occurred, and all had changed. Adela had barely spoken to Wilson after she'd regained her senses, and had looked upon him with patent dislike, despite the fact that the young man had carried her all the way back to the house, having happened upon his cousin insensible, during one of his health walks.

A dark suspicion stirred, and Mrs. Ruffington quashed it. As she always did. It was nothing more than that. Nothing. Nothing.

And yet Adela's enmity toward her cousin remained, and the rather strange young man who'd once seemed quite smitten with her eldest daughter had seemed indifferent at best to her at every social encounter since.

Shaking off the less than pleasant thoughts, Amelia glanced around the happy group on the lawn, her heart warming at the sight of her pretty Sybil, so enchanting in one of her new summer frocks, smiling winsomely at Lord Framley. The young aristocrat was grinning back adoringly.

Ah, those two are so smitten!

There was the great hope for the fortunes of the Ruffington women, in the face of her father-in-law's cruelty and stinginess. A brilliant marriage into a high family with vast wealth would ensure the comfort and security of them all. And then it wouldn't matter if Adela persisted in her spinsterish ways, and didn't try to overcome her unfortunate nose, and less than perfect skin. She could remain unwed, while Sybil's new family supported the lot of them and covered their ever-mounting debts.

And that would mean the diamonds wouldn't have to be sold, after all.

"Are you well, Mrs. Ruffington? You look a little perturbed about something. May I get you some more lemonade? Some sugar biscuits, perhaps?"

Snapping away from her ever-present worries, Mrs. Ruffington looked up and smiled with pleasure, a flutter of feminine excitement in her breast. Even though still technically in mourning, she couldn't stop herself feeling this way at the attentions of a handsome younger man.

"Why, thank you, Mr. Devine. That's so kind…." She made a practiced gesture toward her glass, one of her most elegant, she thought, hoping that the amenable young solicitor would notice the delicacy of her wrists in her black lace mittens. "I was just wondering where my Adela had got to. It seems a shame that she's not out here enjoying this beautiful day with us."

Blair Devine beamed at her, inducing more flutters. He really was a most thoughtful man, and so clever, too. Mrs. Ruffington had been so pleased to meet him at her friend Violet's poetry evening and was impressed by his professional credentials as well as his good looks. She knew he'd done discreet services for a number of her acquaintances, and some of the suggestions he'd made about her own situation were very exciting. The possibilities he'd raised, though a little problematical in some aspects, that might eventually lead the way to a radical improvement in the fortunes of her daughters and herself. She hardly dare think about it all too deeply, though, in case it all came to naught.

"Don't worry. I'm sure she's taken herself off somewhere sketching," said Devine pleasantly, reaching for the jug of lemonade and replenishing Amelia's glass. He really did cut a fine figure in his dashing summer suit of pale linen. "She has such an exceptional talent, does Adela. So rare in a woman. I'm sure that artistic fervor must drive her to exercise it constantly. She's probably taken a walk in the rose garden, or even the arboretum, searching for suitable subjects."

Amelia smiled back at him. He was so handsome and agreeable, with his smooth, beautifully groomed brown hair and his fine eyes and his sympathetic expression. Was it wrong of her to find him so attractive, and to harbor what amounted to a tendre for him? It was much more sensible to encourage his interest in Adela. He seemed to respect and admire her eldest's accomplishments. Might that not lead to more ardent feelings?

If only Adela would do something with herself! A more becoming and fashionable hairstyle. A new gown or two…surely they could run to it, especially with the surprising amount of pin money she earned with her pretty drawings of pets and flowers? And, though God forbid they mention it to anyone, perhaps a little bit of powder for her cheeks? There was nothing to be done about her nose, but surely the aftereffects of a late affliction with chicken pox could be hidden? The little red marks were faint enough to be hidden by a very discreetly applied cosmetic.

And if Adela were to wear the Ruffington diamonds a bit more often, the gentlemen, in this case Mr. Devine, might be sufficiently dazzled by them to overlook their wearer's defects.

"Yes, perhaps you're right, Mr. Devine. My daughter is a most diligent artist. It's rare to see her without a pencil and her sketchbook. I'm sure she's somewhere about with them, hard at work." Amelia leaned forward, touching Blair Devine's linen-clad arm. "I'm so proud of her, you know. She's a splendid girl. Much sought after, but very particular…. Although I'm sure that it won't be too long before she finds a suitor to match her exacting standards."

"I'm sure any man would be proud of such an accomplished wife."

Amelia's excitement surged, along with a perplexed confusion. He seemed interested. Should she push? Encourage? Was all hope of Adela's landing Wilson gone?

How will I feel if my daughter marries the man that I admire?

Amelia forged a smile to match the one on Blair Devine's face.

SILLY OLD BAG. *Her eldest is more firmly on the shelf than any other spinster I've seen, yet still she parades her in front of any poor man who happens to cross her path.*

Blair Devine smiled, yet beneath the facade he had nothing but disdain for the anxious mother he was courting. Most fortune hunters would have thought that the Ruffington women, both mother and daughter, presented very lean pickings indeed, but to him, they represented a variety of promising possibilities.

At the very least, there were those famous diamonds. They

belonged to Amelia Ruffington, free and clear, given as a personal gift by her late husband and not part of the family estate. Blair had been delicately hinting that she might sell them, and that he could arrange for a set of very fine paste replacements to be made, and act as her discreet agent in the matter.

He didn't tell her that he knew he could get a very fine price for them indeed, and that his "commission" would exceed the sum she'd receive. This was a ruse that had worked well in a number of instances, with the ladies in question still none the wiser and happy to commend him to their friends. Amelia Ruffington was particularly gullible. Just look at her, preening and all of a tiz-woz. Making a needy, overweight widow feel as if she was desirable again only made her all the more malleable to his schemes.

But the Ruffington diamonds weren't the only prize.

By a combination of happy accident and a keen eye for what was advantageous to him, Blair Devine had developed some unusually nefarious contacts for a solicitor of superficially impeachable pedigree…and some even more unusual ways of acquiring income. Of late, blackmail and leverage had become increasingly lucrative. And ever more amusing, because people were always happy and grateful to deal with him, so sympathetic and discreet, acting as their agent in these grubby matters so they needn't soil their hands…never realizing that it was he who was the blackmailer!

Yes, there were always letters he hoped to acquire, and for a little while now, he'd been on the lookout to acquire a particular bundle. One day, over tea, Mrs. Ruffington had revealed a little worry of hers, a scandal narrowly avoided, that had involved the flighty Sybil, and certain indiscreet love notes. How it had pleased him to hear that these incriminating missives were still in existence, and he'd resolved to find a way to get his hands on them.

Such little bundles were always useful, either as leverage to be employed promptly, or tucked away for a rainy day, when they might be used to obtain even larger sums.

There were other documents, too, that he'd put out delicate feelers to acquire when he'd first begun to amass information about the Ruffington family. He wasn't the only young man of the law who was far from averse to twisting it, to a greater or lesser degree, if advantage were forthcoming, and a conversation at his club one evening had opened up the exciting possibility of an exchange of intelligence with a like-minded acquaintance.

Pretending to enjoy the languid afternoon, he watched the Ruffingtons and the rest of the party at their leisure, while he turned over his many schemes in his mind.

You're all such idiots. So many of you living beyond your means, and if you have the means, you haven't lifted a finger to deserve them.

He hated the aristocracy, especially its minor orders. By means of wills, bequests and inheritance, they kept the wealth all to themselves rather than spreading it about a bit. He'd been cheated out of family money himself; a good sum that had gone to a cousin who was already well-to-do, because a will had not been drawn out correctly. That was what had driven him to the law...to make it work for him, wherever he could, and so that he might know how to bend it judiciously.

But he'd get a tidy amount out of the Ruffingtons, one way or another. And there was the potential to ensure himself quite a fortune out of them, if the cards fell his way. It would even be worth wedding that stubborn, surly rationalist Adela in order to secure the greatest prize. Through her, there was a ready path to the millions of Lord Millingford, her grandfather, if all worked out and the most daring of his schemes were to materialize.

And in the dark, it might even be fun to fuck her now and again.

9

The Ruff Diamonds

Adela jerked upright, clutching her nose. It didn't hurt after all these years, but the moment of breaking it was as vivid as ever. Looking down, she half expected to see blood on her clothing.

Against the pin-sharp memory of making love with Wilson, she remembered very little about the return to her room afterward. Being tall, and wiry and strong, he'd easily been able to carry her part of the way, but when she'd come to her senses, halfway across the lawn, she'd struggled and kicked, and he'd had to put her down. The rest of the way had been half stagger, half trudge, her accepting his help with a dazed reluctance. And a growing antipathy. She knew now—and in her heart then—that the clash between her face and a tree branch wasn't Wilson's fault, but her half-swooning mind had buried the notion. Beyond rational thought, pain, disappointment and anger had forever linked themselves with her cousin.

Some days after the incident, her portfolio had been delivered to her, intact, in a carefully tied parcel. No note accompanied it, but the devious, elaborate knot fastening the package could only have been wrought by Wilson's hand. Adela had burnt the contents…beginning again.

The way the sunlight had moved round the room now made her glance at the small ormolu clock on the mantelpiece. Sometime during her reverie, she'd flung herself on the bed, but now she flew to her feet.

It was well past the time to dress for dinner, and she was still lolling about in her day dress, hair half up, half down, all disheveled. Coming from a somewhat depleted household, the Ruffington women had but one maid between them, and the way Mama was fussing at the moment, it meant Lizzie's time was mostly assigned to her. Sybil got next dibs, because of her beau, so Marguerite and Adela were having to fend mostly for themselves. Marguerite's youth meant she wore her hair loose and wasn't yet corseted, and Adela had developed ways of managing her own clothing, out of necessity.

But she was going to have to hurry now. The dinner gong was bound to ring any moment, because she could swear she'd heard the dressing one sound ages ago. There was no time now to turn the events of the past over and over again, in a pointless whirl, like the praxinoscope reel. There was plenty to fret about in the present, anyway, especially the ramifications of her interlude with Wilson, and the absurd liberties she'd allowed him to take.

"Allowed"? Encouraged, more like, you brainless twit!

Pushing the unsettling truth aside, she applied herself to the quickest possible quick-change act she could manage, grappling with her clothes and muttering and growling out the sort of curse words that would induce even more of a fainting fit in her parent. There was no water in her ewer or her basin, so she risked a quick dash to the bathroom at the end of the landing to fling a bit of cold water in the general direction of the most overheated portions of her body. Twisting to look at her posterior view, she was relieved to see her bottom was barely pink now. Wilson had a skilled hand nowadays. Had he got it from practice with *that woman?*

No time to worry about her now, though. Hurtling back to her room, and narrowly avoiding cannoning into several prompt guests on their way down to dinner, Adela squashed all thoughts of her cousin's fashionable ex-mistress. Coraline certainly wasn't a woman to compare oneself with when preparing to dine at a glamorous house party.

But Adela's usual clever ruses with her corset weren't so clever this time. She kept losing hold of the laces, and the hooks kept coming unhooked. If only she'd rung the bell, there might have been a maid free to attend her. Although it wasn't overly likely. She and her sisters were probably very low in the pecking order at such a large and fairly distinguished gathering.

You're so clever, Wilson. You should design something better and easier to put on than this. With the bow finally tied in front, she rested her hands on her lightly constrained waist, thankful she didn't have to pull it in all that far. *Or better yet, if you have such a low opinion of corsets, you should speak to some of your cronies in high places about making dress reform a law of the land for the good of British womankind.*

But had he really meant what he'd said about corseting? The sumptuous Coraline had been ferociously laced in her photograph, exhibiting lush, rounded bosoms almost overflowing her Worth gown, and the classic tiny waist, barely a hand span.

Just as Adela was fastening the tapes on her second layer of petticoats, an imperious knock came at the door, and before she could call out an answer, it was flung open and the second-oldest Ruffington girl sailed into the room. Sybil was already gowned, but her lovely golden hair was in almost as much disorder as Adela's. Clumps of it seemed to have been pinned up in a rather ham-fisted fashion, and the rest was still tumbled freely around her shoulders.

"Della, please, please help me with my hair. I'm having such a terrible time. Mama's got Lizzie, and Maggie's useless, and nobody answered the bell, and when I tried to do it on my own, it went all over the place."

Adela smiled. Sybil could be a self-absorbed little minx at times, but when she stopped to think, she was a kind-hearted girl. She also had looks that were hard to resist and impossible not to love. An innocent yet voluptuously gilded temptress, she resembled their plump and flaxen-haired mother rather than their late father, who'd been lean and limber and brown-haired, much like Adela and Marguerite.

"Come here, Syb, and don't get in such a state. I'm sure we can create something acceptable if you'll just keep still."

Sybil flew across the room, the satin of her white gown swishing. Despite the trials with her hair, her toilette was otherwise complete. Her smooth, creamy shoulders rose in gleaming magnificence from the low, boatlike neckline, making Adela frown. Surely a flighty eighteen-year-old shouldn't be showing so much flesh? As daughters they were now out of mourning for their father, but Sybil's display of cleavage was still excessive in Adela's opinion.

"Shouldn't you perhaps wear a fichu at your bosom, Syb? That gown exhibits rather more of you than it should, you know. What on earth will Mama say? She'll realize you've been tampering with the neckline."

"Oh, Della, you goose. It was Mama who instructed me to change it. She's determined that I should get Algernon to propose this weekend." Smiling and self-satisfied, Sybil reached out and angled the glass so she could admire herself. "She doesn't realize that he's already absolutely and completely devoted to me."

Oh, dear, what had Sybil been up to? Not having been out much in the two years since their father's death, they barely knew the young viscount. But Sybil must have worked fast to make such a huge impression at just one or two music recitals and relatively small soirees. The accent had probably been on "fast"....

"What do you mean, devoted? You hardly know him."

"Ah, but I do...." Sybil pressed her fingers to her pert, curvaceous bosom. "And he knows me. He drew me aside at the Wotheringtons' musical thing. Told me he'd never seen anyone as beautiful as me in his life. And..." She drew in a breath, making some kind of fichu or lace insert even more necessary. Something would have to be said to Mama about unsuitable garments for a naive young girl. "...that he'd die if I didn't hold out at least a small hope that one day he might have me."

"Sybil!"

"Ouch, that hurt!"

Adela's disquiet was now a tolling bell of alarm. Sybil had put herself in such danger before, playing with the affections of young men. There had been an incident with a precociously literate gardener's boy when she'd been barely sixteen. Fortunately, the matter had been put a stop to, without any harm done, but Adela was fearful of her sister's passionate, capricious nature.

It doesn't matter what happens to me. My secret can come out, and nothing will be spoiled, because nobody wants me, anyway. But you need to preserve your reputation, sweetheart.

Adela grasped her sibling's shoulders. "You haven't done anything silly, have you?" She glared at Sybil in the glass, trying to be the wise, authoritative older sister. Oh, the hypocrisy... "Tell me you haven't compromised yourself, please."

Not like me.

"Of course not. Don't make a fuss, Della. We've exchanged a few letters, that's all."

Letters? Oh, not letters again. That was worse than a few indiscreet kisses or caresses. Much worse. Letters were tangible and could get into the wrong hands.

"How many? You haven't written anything stupid, have you?"

Sybil beamed. "Oh, he writes so beautifully, Della...quite takes my breath away." She patted her bosom again, and Adela wondered if her sister did, in fact, have one of these epistles tucked down her corset. "He's perfectly lyrical."

"Well, I'm more concerned about what *you've* written. Remember the trouble we had with those notes you sent to Jimmy Roberts? If those had gone any further astray, you'd have been ruined, you fool. It was devilishly lucky that we found that he'd simply mislaid them, after all...and even luckier that he gave them all back when the foolishness ended."

Sybil shook her head, making the latest tress Adela had pinned into place come tumbling down again in a cascade of gold. "Don't worry, I've learned my lesson. I keep them safe, and Algernon keeps his safe, too. We're not children!"

Adela sighed. No, her sister was a grown woman, even if she didn't quite understand the ramifications of pursuing her passions and urges...and then writing about them.

And how could I of all people blame Sybil for her feelings, and her flirtations, and her courting of danger? You're not the one who lost her virginity to the first man who fancied it, are you, Syb? Or the woman who secretly purchases the services of handsome, well-formed young men to satisfy her passions.

She kissed the top of Sybil's head, then started again on her coiffeur. "Just promise me you'll be very careful, sweetheart, won't you? I couldn't bear it if anyone hurt you and made you unhappy." She attacked another long golden strand and secured it in place.

"I will, Della, I will…." Sybil's smile in the mirror was a little sheepish, but genuine and loving. "Don't worry, and thank you for caring about me the way you do. I know it can't be easy when you don't have a beau of your own." Her grin widened. "But I'm really looking out for all of us, you know, by snagging Algernon. If Grandpa won't give us more than a pittance, and you won't make an effort with Wilson, someone has to make sure we all have an income."

Is it so obvious, the enmity between Wilson and me? I thought I'd covered it up quite well.

"There's no effort to be made with Wilson. He and I don't have much in common, other than he's our remote cousin. We barely come into contact with each other." Adela fought the urge to stuff a hairpin slightly more forcibly than she should into Sybil's hair. Her younger sibling didn't mean to be tactless, but everything about Wilson was a delicate issue, especially now. "And anyway, if you're so concerned that Wilson's going to get all the Old Curmudgeon's money as well as the title, why don't *you* set your cap at him, Syb, instead of Algernon?"

Sybil tossed her head, making Adela tut. Her sister's hair was as thick and glossy as her own, and just as wayward. It needed a very firm hand. "Oh, I'm too much of an utter nitwit to interest Wilson. You and he *do* have things in common. You're very intelligent, Della, and artistic, and you know things. And he obviously prefers older women." To Sybil, seven years of seniority made Adela ancient. "It's obvious he admires you."

"I can't imagine how you can think that." Adela coiled up one gilded tress after another, securing them in place. "As I've said, we rarely if ever see him, and I'm sure he's still smarting from the loss of his, um, latest sweetheart."

"Oh, tish poo, he isn't! The fabulous Coraline threw him

over. He probably hates her for running off with some Italian duke who's even richer than he's going to be...." Sybil's pretty mouth thinned, and Adela had to hide her smile as her sister obviously switched tack. "Rich with *our* money. Oh, I hate Grandpapa! If only you'd been a boy, Della, we'd all be living in the lap of luxury.... If Mama had given him a grandson, he wouldn't have hated us all so, and he would *have* to keep us all in a grand manner."

Their perennial story...

"Well, I'm not a man, am I? And we have to do the best we can. So you'd better keep still and let me finish your hair. Then Algernon will be so overcome with love that he'll propose tonight and you won't have to write any more silly letters." She set the last thick tress in place, and began to primp and tease the small curls around Sybil's forehead. "And please tell me that you've burned those other ones." Her sister had cherished the bundle of love notes long after her misguided tendresse had been over. Adela had seen her reading them not long ago.

Sybil swung around, an outraged expression on her face. "I could never do that! Never!"

"But, Sybil—"

"I won't discuss it, Della. I won't. And if you'd ever enjoyed such a beautiful amour, you wouldn't destroy its mementos, either." Sybil was a mule when her mind was made up, and Adela could see her mentally dismissing the topic of the letters and moving on to the next order of business. She smiled into the mirror, patting Adela's handiwork and preening. "Perfect, Della.... It's absolutely perfect." Her head up, she touched her fingers to her throat. "Now, wearing the Ruff diamonds tonight I shall be completely irresistible!"

Another cause for concern. Had Mama brought the famous gems with her? It was foolhardy, not so much because they might be stolen, but because they were a treasure whose possession was a continuing matter of contention.

The Ruff diamonds, as everyone called the brilliant and famous gems, were Mama's own possession, a personal gift from Papa, on their wedding. But there had been some talk that the Old Curmudgeon insisted they belonged to him. Papa had purchased the parure for Mama himself, but as his income had derived solely from his father, the old fellow insisted that he'd paid for them, and that they were the Millingford Diamonds, not the Ruffington ones, thus creating yet another bone of contention. Mama was standing firm, though, which was possibly why she'd engaged that slinking weasel Blair Devine as her advisor.

"Do you think it's wise to wear them, Syb? We know they belong to Mama, but what if Wilson sides with Grandpa and decides they're part of *his* inheritance? Wouldn't it be better to keep them out of sight and mind?"

As if she'd not heard Adela speak, Sybil sprang up and began to turn this way and that before the pier glass in the corner of the room. Then, apparently satisfied that she was adorable, she spun around. "Wilson has never given the slightest indication that he's interested in the Ruff diamonds, has he? If he was going to claim them, surely he'd have asked for them for his French concubine, and now they've parted he doesn't need them, does he?" She winked and gave a smirk. "Or perhaps he might want them for somebody else?"

Adela gave her sister an old-fashioned look. "How many times do I have to tell you, Wilson has no interest in me whatsoever. And kindly govern your tongue. Mama would have one of her turns if she knew you were flinging words like *concubine* about, not to mention writing letters to young men again. She doesn't realize what a wicked little minx you still are. She thinks that you've mended your ways."

Hypocrite! Hypocrite! Hypocrite! If Mama found out about my *"ways" she'd probably expire!*

Sybil laughed, a joyous sound that made Adela smile despite her worries. She had learned to cover her own tracks with all the skill of an agent of the Crown, but Sybil was young and believed herself invincible.

"Well, then, if you're really not interested in impressing Wilson tonight, you won't need the diamonds, will you? Which means I can wear them to dazzle Algernon and make him my slave."

"Sybil!"

Her pretty sister flew across the room and hugged her. "I'm only being practical, Della. You know I'm thinking of all of us."

Adela pursed her lips, resigned. As ever, Sybil believed that her own immaculate complexion and pert button of a nose could save the day, whereas her sister's flaws rendered her powerless. Was she right?

"You don't have to carry the whole burden, though, my love. My drawings sell well to my friends of the Ladies' Sewing Circle, so we'll always have that income, too."

Sybil gave Adela a curious and unusually perceptive look. "They do seem to buy quite of lot of them, don't they? And yet you never show *us* what you sell…just the drawings you do for casual amusement. I'm beginning to think there's something a little fishy going on, Della, really I am."

Adela wriggled free. Maybe Sybil was far more astute than she gave her credit for? "There's nothing more outré than those studies of Mr. Kipper I showed you only last week. That's the sort of thing I sell…." Mr. Kipper was their cat, fondly pampered by the entire household. "Nothing untoward about those, was there? The ladies of the Sewing Circle are all particularly fond of their own pets, and like the drawings to remember them by…and also, well, other kinds of wildlife."

Pets and wildlife indeed. That wasn't all that far off the mark. A number of the ladies of the circle did have special pets among the pleasure boys, and some of the activities involved were most definitely wild. And in addition to her work for members of the circle, Adela had a growing roster of other clients, mostly brought to her by the good offices of her dear friend Sofia, who was at the center of a very racy set, most avid for erotic art in all forms. Unclothed studies of various handsome swains from Mme Chamfleur's private establishment were popular way beyond the Sewing Circle, and many ladies from the highest echelons of society had the work of "Isis" tucked discreetly in their handkerchief sachets or other clandestine hideaways. Adela's work had also graced the pages of many issues of *Divertissements* and other risqué journals in the last year, too. Women with generous allowances were eager to obtain such scandalous treasures to enhance their private entertainment, as were many gentlemen of a certain persuasion.

And Adela was more than glad of each and every sale.

Sketches of kittens and puppies would scarcely have paid for the satin ribbons on Sybil's latest gown, nor would they have paid for the elaborate creation their mother now swept in wearing. But Adela had managed to keep them all in a reasonable degree of comfort by supplementing the pittance grudgingly bestowed on them by her grandfather.

"Adela, what on earth do you think you're about?" Mrs. Ruffington cried, fluttering and bustling as only she knew how. The new dress—only nominally mourning, black but encrusted with ruffles and bows, and showing almost as much cleavage as her middle daughter's—rustled and swished as she swept forward, with both quiet Marguerite and their harried-looking maid, Lizzie, in her wake. "You're barely dressed yet, and the champagne reception commences in ten minutes."

"It won't take me but a moment, Mama."

Despite her claims, she was pressed for time, but the ever-efficient Lizzie darted forward and, with no need for instruction, began to help Adela into her gown with the quick deftness of much practice.

All the time, Mrs. Ruffington tutted and frowned. "I do wish you'd allow a little bust improvement, Adela." She pursed her lips at Adela's modest bosom in her black, square-necked gown. "You're so slightly built…. It's not really cheating, and the gentlemen do like to see a curvaceous form in a woman." She reached out and tweaked the discreetly trimmed neckline a little lower. "Ah…I wish we could have run to a new dress for you, too, my sweet. I'm sure Mme Gwendolynne would have extended our credit just a little further…. Black is so severe, especially on the young."

Adela smiled in an effort to placate her parent. It was the wrong time to get into an argument, at this late stage. A smiling set of Ruffington ladies would be much more likely to impress than four frowning faces and four mouths pinched and cross.

"Ah, but I think this gown flatters me very well, Mama. You've always said so." Surreptitiously, she undid the neckline tweaking. "And Lizzie does such a good job with my hair… and perhaps if I wore my nicest jet beads?" Lizzie was already at work, having launched into action the moment Adela had sat down, creating clever coils from its heavy, lustrous weight.

Mrs. Ruffington quirked her lips, her eyes narrowing. Mama wasn't quite as silly as she sometimes appeared to be, and Adela guessed that her parent, too, was wise to the fact that serene smiles all round would make a better impression on the menfolk downstairs. She advanced on Adela, then waggled her gloved fingers toward Marguerite, who was quietly following the conversation. "Perhaps you're right about the gown, Della my sweet. It *does* suit you…and it would make a perfect frame for you-know-what."

Marguerite flipped open the velvet case she'd been carrying. Adela had registered it peripherally, and had been waiting for the play of their trump card.

No matter how many times she saw their only assured birthright, Adela still drew a little breath. The famous Ruff diamonds were a wonder to behold, and even though she didn't set too much store by material wealth for herself, she loved their beauty and their exquisite rainbow fire.

Almost hypnotized, she reached out to touch them—even knowing that she wouldn't be the one to wear them.

The collet diamond necklace of exquisitely matched gems was held by many to be superior to a similar necklace owned by Her Majesty the Queen herself. Reposing in their blue velvet case, the jewels glittered like enormous crystal droplets, flashing an entire spectrum of radiance. Nestled to each side were a pair of matching pendant earrings, equally as fine.

Dear heaven, I'd love to wear them. But they'd look absurd on an ugly duck like me.

"If you wear them, and add a touch of powder here and there, perhaps people won't notice your little blemishes quite so much, my dear."

The sublime gems seemed to dim. No matter how many times Adela told herself that she didn't care a jot about her bent nose and her little scars, sometimes she did. Sometimes she wished she was pretty. Sometimes she prayed that she could reverse the course of time, live that day again…and not flee like an idiot from Wilson. If she hadn't argued with him, she might have been in a different place at a critical moment, and not caught a dose of chicken pox, either.

If. If. If.

If she'd been pretty enough, they might have been married by now, and Mama and her sisters secure and comfortable, despite the Old Curmudgeon's best efforts.

What would it be like to be married to Wilson? Would we be happy?

Would he love me?

Lost in her reverie, Adela reached out for the dazzling necklace and put it around her throat. Lizzie dashed around to her back and secured it without being asked. Adela had a feeling that the devoted servant wanted *her* to wear it, rather than her sister.

In front of the pier glass, Adela almost gasped. She'd tried on the Ruff diamonds before, but never with an evening gown. The effect was miraculous. The exquisite gems imparted an enchantment to her appearance, and with it a great swell of female confidence. Bathed in their radiance, she saw a simulation of beautiful. Her imperfections were barely noticeable, transformed into piquant features of distinction rather than defects.

Bathed in the strange effect, she seemed to see Wilson looking back at her out of the mirror, too. His pale eyes glittered like the stones, and yet she knew that it was she he sought to possess, not the diamonds. She imagined him standing behind her, his fingers spread at her throat, fondling the gems and the skin they lay against. In another flash, her gown and her undergarments disappeared, and his free hand roved her body, pressing her back against him as his erect member nudged the curve of her hip.

Stop that, Della, you nincompoop! That way lies madness.

She shook her head to clear her brain of the heated pictures. Her cousin might condescend to dally with her because he happened to be alone and bored, but nothing more than that.

He certainly didn't want any kind of responsibility for her, never in a million years.

"Adela, is anything wrong?" Marguerite's voice was sharp with concern. The youngest Ruffington was perceptive and watchful. "You look awfully queer. You've gone quite white."

Adela glanced around, meeting their faces. Her mother looked a little dazzled, too, as if her hopes of getting her eldest daughter off her hands had suddenly been revived by the beautiful treasure. Marguerite was frowning, worried. Sybil was also frowning, but for a different reason. Reaching around the back of her neck, Adela unfastened the catch.

"I'm perfectly well, Maggie…thank you. But these baubles are far too much for me. They're overpowering with my hair and coloring. They'll be shown off to much better advantage by Sybil…don't you think, Mama?"

Mrs. Ruffington looked perplexed. Mama loved all of them, and tried to avoid showing favoritism…but Sybil was by far her brightest star.

The bright star was grinning now, and she swept across the room to hug her sister. "Thank you," she whispered, and Adela knew that for all her frivolity, Sybil understood when a sacrifice was made.

"No, thank *you,* Sybil," she answered just as quietly, as she set about securing the diamonds around her sister's smooth white neck.

Yes, it'll be much easier not *to wear the diamonds. I can eat my dinner in peace without anybody in particular noticing me, and Sybil can dazzle and be enchanting for her viscount.*

Very rational. Eminent good sense. The old but well-loved string of jet beads felt familiar and comforting around Adela's throat as she followed her mother and her sisters down the grand staircase toward the reception salon.

And yet why, in the name of all that was sensible, did she

still want a certain person to make her the center of *his* attention?

Why did she *still* wish she could dazzle Wilson, diamonds or otherwise?

10

Under Scrutiny

The meal was interminable. Far too many courses, all horribly rich, with no attempt at balance on the palate whatsoever. Wilson had pushed his food around his plate, and sent back most of it untouched, wishing he was at home in his workshop in London, eating bread and cheese, with a glass of beer to wash it down.

The only consolation was that he wasn't the only one with a poor appetite tonight. Adela was sending her plates back barely touched, too.

Gentlemen of pleasure.

Wilson scowled. The mousse framboise turned to ashes in his mouth, and he laid down his spoon, finally abandoning all hope of feigning an appetite for his hostess's sake.

Had Della meant what she said? Did she pay for the sexual services of men? He stared across at her, sitting at the other side of the table and a few places down from him. She was talking quietly with a gentleman on her left, Sir Horace Blatchford, if Wilson wasn't mistaken. The fellow was paying close attention, and hanging on her words.

Where on earth do you get the notion that you're unattractive, cousin? The man's clearly besotted. Just because your idiotic mother tells you that you're flawed and not buxom enough… I'm sure your "gentlemen" all think you're adorable.

If Wilson had still been holding his spoon, he'd have smashed it down on the table and bent the blessed thing.

"What do you think of Rayworth Court, Mr. Ruffington? The gardens are most glorious at this time of year, aren't they?"

Jerked from his fulminating reverie, Wilson turned to the fat matron on his right and gave her a dazzling smile. From his early adulthood, in order to disguise his boredom as well as his natural shyness, Wilson had cultivated a method of making small talk without really engaging the higher functions of his brain. He could manufacture a pretty conversation without too much effort, and he now spun a few pleasantries for both the overeating Mrs. Something-or-other to his right, and the rather thinner and far more rabbity young woman on his left. If he'd been at all concerned, he would have been cynically amused, knowing he'd hoodwinked them with his simulation of rapt attention. But he wasn't.

There was only one thing on his mind.

Yet while the talk flowed over and around him, he attempted to concentrate on other matters. Such as deciding exactly why the design of his dessert fork had been all wrong—the weighting was poorly balanced, and he would have liked to have made a sketch of a better version, perhaps a whole suite of cutlery. When he was unable to work on one of his many official projects, he tended to fuel the racing engine of his mind with an endless parade of tinkering notions that might improve just about anything.

Tonight it was badly designed cutlery, the possible detriment to health of fatty foods, and playing conversational tricks on unwitting dinner guests. Anything to stop himself gawping at Adela and imagining her in bed with another man, moaning and writhing in ecstasy.

Perhaps you could get that clod Blatchford to service you? He looks keen enough, and it would be cheaper than paying for it!

And it seemed that his cousin also possessed some of his own talents. She was doing a sterling job of not revealing how little she was interested in her dinner companion. Sir Horace was beaming, and appeared to think he'd made a conquest, but to Wilson, tiny telltales screamed out.

The way she, too, toyed with her dessert fork. The hint of tension in her delicate jawline. A faint pulse beating at the base of her throat, adjacent to those dull black beads she wore. Her skin shone like satin there, like freshly poured cream against the edges of her gown, its gleam almost supernatural. Wilson wanted to touch her at that spot. He wanted to kiss her there, maybe go so far as to bite her just a little and show her she didn't need the embrace of a gigolo to stir her blood.

Adela's eyes snapped toward him, flashing. Had she heard his thoughts? He lifted his glass to her in a toast, and after a moment's hesitation, during which a complex melee of emotion crossed her face, she lifted her own glass infinitesimally in response.

When she looked away again, maintaining her facade of polite interest in her dinner companion, Wilson glanced down at the raspberry disaster on his plate, then rapidly back up again, toward his cousin.

Those dim black beads irritated him. She ought to be wearing the Ruff diamonds instead of that simpering miss, Sybil. The younger girl was too bland for such stones. It was like draping them around a blancmange such as the one he'd just mangled; she was a soft girl, and better suited to pearls or opals.

Adela was challenging, and uncompromising, and as complex and mysterious as the Earth's most unyielding form of carbon.

Wilson glowered, angrier than ever with her. Why hadn't she insisted on wearing the gems? Surely, as the oldest girl, she was more entitled to, if her mother chose not to sport them? For the first time in several hours, he thought of Coraline. She'd have demanded the diamonds as a right. She wouldn't have acquiesced and been satisfied with such a nondescript adornment as those jet beads.

But Adela wasn't Coraline. They were nothing alike, and the contrast made him angrier than ever. With himself. And her.

Why do I let women make me stupid?

He'd spent upward of a month fuming and sulking and what he'd assumed was pining for Coraline, and now, after a few moments of dalliance with his stubborn, dismissive cousin, all that time spent feeling sorry for himself was devalued. Pointless.

It's absurd. You make me feel as if I'm superficial and fickle, Della.

Maybe he was superficial? Maybe he was more fickle than any woman ever born? His appetite gone, all he could think of now was his jealousy. Of her, with her paid-for pleasure. Of her, being fucked, her legs open for another man. Of her, having an orgasm that *he* hadn't given her.

It was intolerable, but he wasn't going to just sit back and seethe about it. He was Wilson Ruffington, and his life was devoted to solving problems, and taking action, and deducing brilliant answers to every question he'd ever asked or been asked.

And he'd find a solution to the "Della problem," too… even if it killed him.

Why is he scowling at me so?

Adela scowled herself as she followed the other women into

the salon while the men settled to cigars and brandy in the dining room. She'd got a headache now and it was mainly Wilson's fault, although not entirely due to him.

Sybil and the likelihood of yet more incautious letters, the oily attentions that Mr. Devine was paying to her mother—these both pricked at Adela's peace of mind…or what was left of it after this afternoon's shenanigans with Wilson. Watching the interplay between various parties across the dining table had strung her nerves out tight, like violin strings, and Wilson's never-ending scrutiny had only jangled them and stretched them even tauter.

He'd stared throughout the entire meal, and somehow, he'd seemed to be staring even when he wasn't looking her way. For some reason, her necklace displeased him. Once or twice, he'd appeared to be frowning directly at it, his pale eyes filled with dislike. She could have understood it if she'd been wearing the Ruff diamonds, and he had decided that she, or Sybil, or Mama, weren't entitled to them. But what offense could her simple string of jet beads have caused him?

You're a very strange man, cousin, and you're turning this entire house party into an ordeal of strength.

Withdrawing with the other ladies was a respite, even if Adela did find the practice archaic and discriminatory. She'd take any odds that the men talked just as much nonsense over their brandy and cigars as the women did over their petits fours and coffee, but there was no way to find that out for herself.

The grand salon, where the ladies retired, was a beautiful room, furnished in an ornate, luxurious style with comfortable sofas and armchairs thoughtfully arranged in convenient conversation groups. Most of the womenfolk clustered in the vicinity of a rather fine grand piano, but Adela selected a spot on a chaise close to the wall, afforded a little privacy by a large potted palm. A few moments later, on being served her coffee, she was glad of her choice.

Miss Minnie Blankenship, who had rushed forward to claim the piano stool, was no musician and even less of a vocalist. Her selection of self-accompanied light arias by Messrs Gilbert and Sullivan were a stringent test for the eardrums.

Admiring the girl's pluck and unshakable self-belief, Adela still winced at a high C missed by a mile. A sip of indifferent coffee didn't help matters, and she sighed, wishing away the ever-increasing niggle of pain in her temple. She rubbed the spot with her gloved fingertips, a tactic that rarely worked, but at least made her feel she was doing something.

"Are you unwell?"

Adela jumped, almost tipping over her coffee cup, but Wilson swooped forward with uncanny speed and saved it.

"Do you have a headache?" His own brow was ruffled in a frown, but whether it was concern now, or just more displeasure, she couldn't tell. He looked as unimpressed with the coffee as she did when he sniffed the brew, then set her cup on a small table at her side.

"No, thank you, Wilson. I'm perfectly well." Adela dropped her hands into her lap and attempted a genial, social smile. Best to look calm and amenable. The appearance of Wilson, a man, in this enclave of matrons and virgins, was already causing quite a stir.

Her cousin flopped onto the chaise beside her. "Are you sure?" He was still frowning, but he spoke quietly, as if it had suddenly dawned on him he was out of place…and in jeopardy. As a well-set-up bachelor with an even larger fortune coming to him, he was most definitely a major catch despite his eccentricities. Some of the adjacent virgins and their mothers were just as much on the lookout as Mama was.

"Yes, thank you, Wilson. It's nothing." Minnie struck a particularly discordant note, and Adela winced as Wilson pulled a face. "It's just that I'm not much of a music lover."

"She's quite spectacular, isn't she?" He nodded in the direction of the chanteuse. "But one can't fault her for enthusiasm, I suppose."

Adela smiled. Despite everything, he, too, had tried to see something to admire in Minnie and her cacophony.

"Indeed. That's her talent, I think." Adela reached for her coffee once more and took a sip, for something to do with her hands. Wilson was staring again, his eyes not especially friendly.

"I admire your talents more," he said, his voice provocative as he stretched out his legs in front of him.

What was that supposed to mean? What talents? Almost certain he wasn't referring to her artistic prowess, Adela set aside her coffee and studied those long legs of his. Long, well-formed legs in surprisingly well-tailored trousers. He'd abandoned his most outré garb this evening, and looked almost sartorial. For Wilson. No dressing gown now, but he still hadn't submitted to a formal evening dress. Wilson's nod to conventional male elegance was an overlong frock coat somewhat in the Aesthetic style, its unusual shade of midnight-blue set off by the flashiest yet in his series of evermore flashy waistcoats. This latest example was elaborately embroidered, a Byzantine design in several shades of blue such as might have adorned the wall of a Moorish love palace. The base color was near black, and the pattern picked out in threads of silver gilt and gold. Adela had seen the older gentlemen of the party, and many of the ladies, sucking their teeth and tut-tutting at such "preciousness" in male apparel, but to her it was beautiful and suited him to a tee.

To further defy convention, her cousin wore a soft-collared shirt with a floppily tied foulard instead of white tie, and as usual, his shaggy hair had not formed a relationship with the Macassar oil bottle.

Having apparently given up waiting for a response, Wilson ruffled his tie, then trailed his fingertips down the brocade of his waistcoat. "Do you approve?" Were her eyes playing tricks, or did his touch linger momentarily in the vicinity of his nether regions?

Her cheeks hot, Adela snapped her eyes back to Wilson's and saw his were cool, yet dancing, giving off an aura of antagonistic excitement.

The fingers that caressed his waistcoat had caressed her, only hours ago. That palm had landed hard on her bottom.

"Well, yes, I believe I do," she replied, keeping her voice light. "That coat is a vast improvement on the dressing gown… although I do think you might at least have combed your hair for the occasion." She paused. His intense regard was giving her the jitters. "Is there something wrong with my appearance this evening that you object to? You've been scowling at me ever since you came down to dinner."

Wilson pursed his lips, and for a moment, almost appeared dismayed. Then his face hardened again. "You look splendid as always, Della."

Adela's heart lurched. He was an unflinchingly blunt man, not given to pretty compliments. He'd once said that social niceties were both hypocritical and boring. When he said something, it was always exactly what he meant, and being a woman often passed over because she failed to meet the most exacting standards of female beauty, she found herself touched by his statement. New Woman or no, pragmatist or not, she did like to hear nice things, even if they came from him.

"It's these dull beads," he went on, reaching out. For a moment, Adela thought he was going to wrench them from around her throat and scatter them over the carpet. But instead he just flicked at the strand contemptuously, his nails barely brushing against her skin. "You should be wearing the Ruff diamonds, Della, not these dreary mourning baubles. Only you can match their luster and magnificence…and you're the eldest Ruffington girl, so surely *you* should be wearing them, not Sybil."

Was that it? Was he so cross about the diamonds that he'd looked daggers at her all evening on their account? No, it wasn't that. Why was she trying to avoid the obvious issue? The real reason her cousin had scowled and been unable to mask his raw resentment.

And despite his espousal of total honesty, Wilson was currently lying and avoiding the issue just as much as she was. He was jealous. Jealous of her "gentlemen of pleasure," furious about the very idea of them without even knowing whether she was fibbing to him or not. Perhaps he hated the idea that she might even *consider* such men?

"The diamonds belong to Mama, and it's up to her who wears them. I have no special rights." How long were they going to dance around the real thorn in Wilson's paw? "Although I thought you might claim the diamonds as part of *your* bequest, Wilson. I half expect Grandpa to initiate litigation to acquire them any day."

Wilson let out a bark of laughter, causing one or two ladies in the vicinity to look around. "What do I want with diamonds? I've no interest in any of the Ruffington assets. I've got plenty of money of my own…and I certainly don't want the stupid title, either." He sounded dismissive and vaguely bitter.

Against her will, Adela bridled. She remembered seeing a porcupine raise its quills in threat when she'd recently visited to the Zoological Gardens in Regent's Park, and she imagined herself the little mammal, affronted. "And of course *I* do?" She flung the question at him. "You think that's all we're interested in, somehow getting our hands on Grandfather's wealth, and maybe his title if we could find a way to twist the law? To you we're just useless parasites, sitting around bewailing the fact someone else is going to end up with the money we think should be ours?"

"I never said that!" snarled Wilson, his eyes flashing. He looked vaguely guilty, too, and Adela felt a small stab of triumph. "Well, perhaps I did say something like that, but I never meant it. I was probably distracted at the time…."

Forgetting the room and the women around them, Adela watched, hypnotized, as Wilson closed his eyes and raised his long fingertips, pressed together, to his lips. He was attempting to master strong emotion through sheer force of will, as she often did herself. Seen in him, it was exciting, and made her want to goad him, to test that mastery.

"I'm sorry," he said in a low voice. "What I said about you, and your mother and your sisters, was churlish and thoughtless. I take it back." He seemed about to reach for her hand, then thought better of it. His face hardened again. Had he lost his battle?

Adela didn't know whether to press him and goad him into admitting the source of his ill humor, or instead to try a more gentle tack and reach a rapprochement. It wasn't fair to Mama, or to their hosts, to make an embarrassing scene, and she was just formulating a conciliatory comment when the double doors to the salon were thrown open and the rest of the gentlemen began to amble in, noisy in their bonhomie and the effects of fine brandy. Adela wrinkled her nose. A powerful smell of tobacco drifted around the army of males that passed by her, and she was glad that as far as she knew Wilson had no fondness for smoking.

The arrival of the men coincided with a change of entertainment. Minnie was dragged firmly away from the piano by her frowning father, and another young lady, unknown to Adela, took her place. A far more accomplished musician, this one. The newcomer launched into a piece by Schubert, played lightly and with skill.

"That's better," observed Wilson, disquietingly bland. "Now that *is* talent, wouldn't you agree?"

"Absolutely. She's very accomplished. I wish I could play so well." Adela had taken lessons, as most well-brought-up young women did, but her aptitude was minimal and she'd soon abandoned it and returned to her first love, drawing.

"You don't need to play the piano, cousin. You have gifts that far exceed a modest battering of the ivories." Adela opened her mouth, not really knowing what she was about to say, but Wilson held up a hand. "Don't deny it." His lips curved, his expression mutable. She couldn't tell whether he was taunting, or genuine. "I should like to see what's in that portfolio of yours, Della. You managed to distract me this afternoon, in a way that was undeniably pleasant." His long, thick eyelashes flickered. "But I'm determined to discover your secrets… artistic and otherwise."

Curse you, Wilson. One single moment of behaving like a human being and you're back to your tricks again. I don't owe you any allegiance or responsibility.

"This afternoon was an aberration. A mistake…. I've been overwrought about various matters lately, and I acted, and spoke, very foolishly." She kept her voice low, too. People were close by, and at least two or three eager mothers were still eyeing Wilson as a potential stallion for their young fillies. "And if you have any chivalry in you, cousin, you'll forget it, too."

Wilson's eyes were almost metallic, with sparks in their pale silver-blue depths. He wasn't going to take the bait that she'd offered in jest, to annoy him. He was a razor and could always detect lies.

He shrugged his shoulders. Was he going to let her off, after all? She noticed absently, with her artist's eye, how powerful those shoulders were beneath the fine dark cloth of his coat. He'd filled out since they'd last been close enough and spent time enough in each other's company to quantify such things. He'd gained muscle, become fully a man, leaving the last vestiges of his adolescence behind him.

Coffee was being brought around to some of the gentlemen now, and Wilson took a cup, accepting a tiny dash of cream but no sugar. He sipped the brew and grimaced, then put the cup down very precisely on the occasional table at his side. With a sensation that an ax was about to fall, Adela glanced around the room again. The headache was nagging as if some demon imp were stabbing repeatedly at her temple, exacerbated by the cigar smoke, the brilliance of the salon's many gas lamps and the elevated level of chatter since the menfolk had returned.

"So, are there drawings of these 'gentlemen of pleasure' in your portfolio? Naked studies of them…and their accoutrements…the way you once drew me?"

The stabbing imp was Wilson now, and his implement a rapier, going straight for the jugular.

II

The Very Molecules
of the Night

"That's none of your business, Wilson." Her brown eyes were steady and cool, dismissive. "It's enough that you know I draw erotic subjects. The identity of my models is none of your concern."

But it is *my concern. Everything about you is my concern.*

Wilson almost laughed. He was being childish about this most adult of topics. But he couldn't disengage his feelings. They had him by the throat, and as a man of rationality and cool logic, that appalled him.

The thought of Adela with another man—other *men*—turned his blood molten. He'd always been an equable and, in the main, pacifistic man, abhorring unnecessary violence both in personal matters and on behalf of the nation. But right now, he wanted to seek out these so called "gentlemen of pleasure" of hers and inflict on them all the harm of which he was capable. His fists clenched, ready to box, ready to strike.

"I should like to know who these men are. And what it is about them that you find so alluring."

She didn't quite gasp. It was just a little huff of air, let out in obvious exasperation. "Why will you not let this topic alone? I…I was exaggerating. To distract you. You wouldn't have let me leave that room otherwise."

Her face was blushing a delicate pink, the hue enchanting. She blushed like that in the throes of passion, just as she had this afternoon. He pictured that face, glowing against a white pillow as she lay in his bed, sprawled on tangled sheets, her slender limbs slack with repletion. It was a gorgeous image, and he hardened instantly. He'd already become semierect, simply from being in her vicinity.

Her mouth was an angry line now, but he imagined it bruised from kissing. Kissing him, not some anonymous, purchased swain. Ire boiled up again, more acidic and fulminating than before. *Who'd* been kissing her? *Who'd* been touching her and fucking her? Somebody had, and he wanted to destroy him.

Oh, why could he not contain this anger? There seemed to be no mental box that would hold it, and worse, it was dragging out other feelings, other hurts in its wake.

"I don't believe you, Della," he growled, and a woman not too far away turned from her brainless conversation about some acquaintance she didn't like, and looked his way. "There has to have been something in what you said, or else why say it?"

Adela clamped her jaws together, fierce tension in her face. He knew he was right. She'd spoken the truth, even though she hadn't meant to. And now that truth was making him a madman. He wanted to be ferocious with her, although not ever hurt her. He wanted to fuck her into submission, bind her and blind her with pleasure, so that she never again thought of another man.

"I don't wish to discuss this with you, Wilson. As I said before, it's none of your business and you have no rights over me." She turned away, reaching for her tiny coffee cup again, even though he could see from where he sat that it was empty. "Please go away. You're embarrassing me. People are starting to look."

"Let them look." He glared around at the curious faces turning toward them. Then forced a smile when he saw Mrs. Ruffington twisting her handkerchief anxiously. When he gave her a little wave, she smiled back at him, her entire demeanor signaling a sudden, intense relief.

What had he done now? Given the clucking mama some false hope? He didn't really care anymore.

"Della, who are these men? I need to know.... I'm concerned for you." It was only partially a lie. Who knew what she'd got herself into? She was a bold woman, though he'd never thought her foolhardy. But even the cleverest of either sex could be duped sometimes, especially when the urges of the flesh were concerned.

"I won't discuss it."

His desire surged. She was indefatigable. A warrior queen. His cock ached like the very devil and he wanted to toss her down onto the Aubusson carpet, fling up her skirts and mount her right now, regardless of the great and the good around them watching.

"You're a coward, Della. You're afraid to be honest with me." It was nonsense. She was the least cowardly person he'd ever encountered. But he had to get to her. "You ran from facing the truth with me before, and you're shrinking from it again."

Now he was the coward, almost ready to physically shrink from her. She didn't move, but in every other way seemed to reach out and strike him.

"I won't talk here. I have a headache and I'm going out into the garden to take some air." Snatching up her reticule, she rose abruptly in an elaborate swish of black taffeta, already walking away from him. "If you care to join me, that's your affair." She flung the words over her shoulder.

Not cowardly now. She was challenging him. He rose to his feet, walking behind her, his eyes on her slim waist and the proud line of her back.

"Mama, I have a little headache and I think a stroll in the garden will revive me," she said on reaching the group of ladies where her parent held court. Wilson waited for her to completely ignore his existence, standing behind her, but got a surprise. "Cousin Wilson has offered to escort me, to ensure I come to no harm."

He almost laughed out loud, but managed to curb it. What would Mrs. Ruffington think if she could read his churning thoughts and his animal urges? Clearly, she couldn't, though, for the plump blonde woman looked almost ecstatic. One of her goals for this house party achieved, no less. Her plain daughter courted by the "target" gentleman, an answer to so many problems.

"Oh, that's such a good idea, darling. The fresh air is sure to make you feel better." Mrs. Ruffington patted her daughter's hand, and beamed around her in Wilson's direction. "It's most kind of you, Wilson. I know you'll take good care of her." She slid a black shawl off her shoulders and handed it to Adela. "Slip this around you, Della sweetheart. Just in case."

"Thank you, Mama." Adela's voice was clipped and she almost grabbed the shawl, then stomped away. Wilson nodded to the matriarch and followed in her wake, smiling to himself. That little "act" must have stuck in Adela's throat like a fish bone, but she'd carried it off. Now she was in a clear hurry to get out of the room, and it wouldn't surprise him if she took to her heels once outside, so he quickened his pace, pausing only briefly at the French doors to salute her mother. Mrs. Ruffington favored him with another beam of approval, but Wilson noted a definite scowl from that solicitor, Blair Devine, adjacent to her.

What was all that about? He filed the datum away for perusal later. Adela was his prime concern now, and just as he'd suspected, she was stomping away in an impressively fleet fashion down the garden path, every step an expression of animosity.

You can run all you like, Della, I'll still catch you. You're mine and you can't get away from me.

Mine? *Mine?* The thought almost made him stop in his tracks...but not quite. Adela was getting away.

It was hopeless. She would never get away from him. Wilson was tall and long-legged, with a stride like a Thoroughbred's, and she was hampered by layer after layer of petticoats twisting around her calves and ankles. Wretched things.

Sweeping along the edge of the formal garden, away from the house and the lights, Adela flung herself down onto a bench, panting hard. But it was more tension and annoyance— and her accursed corset—that made her gasp for breath, not exertion.

Her cousin was but footsteps behind her, and before she had a chance to compose herself, he was there, too, sitting at her side, long lean legs once more stretched out in front of him. In the shadows, he looked threatening and mysterious.

"So? Aren't you going to interrogate me again? That is what you've come out here for, isn't it?"

His eyes gleamed in the low light as if they were polished, but he didn't speak, the contrary creature.

"Well, in that case..." Adela leaped to her feet again, but

Wilson whipped out his arm, faster than should have been possible, and grabbed her in a fierce, unyielding grip.

"Let me go!"

"No. Sit down. I want to hear about these men of yours."

She tried to shake loose, but it was like being in a shackle, on a very short chain.

"You're hurting me." It was a lie, but it worked. He released her instantly.

If I run to my room he'll only follow. If I lock the door, he'll either break in or sit outside until I yield.

With a sigh, Adela sat down again. "I suppose if I told you that I'd been exaggerating, you wouldn't believe me, would you?"

"No. When you first claimed what you claimed, it was spontaneous. A completely unfeigned and guileless statement. I know you weren't lying then, even if you'd like to do so now."

Heat flowed through her body, not only from what she had to tell him, but because perversely, the prospect of telling him excited her. And she'd called *him* a contrary beast. He was a simple, basic, masculine animal compared to the swirling muddle of fears and desires that she'd become.

"I'm not afraid of feeling desire for its own sake."

There was a long silence. The night air around them felt thick, like a blanket of deep thought pressing down on the pair of them.

"Nothing to say now, Wilson?"

Her cousin was staring out at the turf between his feet, as if some answer lay there.

"I'm trying to bring order to my thoughts. To reconcile my natural reactions with what I know, intellectually, to be correct." Apparently unaware of what he was doing, he assumed his inimitable position of pondering. Slumped back, he pressed his hands together and laid the tips of his forefingers against his lips. Adela could almost see the cogs of logic disengaging, spinning free, then locking again.

"Well, for those of us who aren't philosophers, have you arrived at any conclusions?"

He turned to her, eyes still on fire. "Why? Why would you seek out these gigolos? Wouldn't it have been better…safer… to pursue marriage to satisfy your carnal urges?"

Adela burst out laughing. She could barely believe it. Her free-thinking, progressive cousin…when had he turned into such a fossil? Such a throwback?

"I never realized you were so traditional. I thought you of all men would be a supporter of the rights and emancipation of women? Of equality in all matters. Political, economic and not least of all the freedom to dispose of one's body as one wishes?"

He looked horrified, but whether at her or himself, she couldn't tell.

"I am…but I hate the idea of you paying to be serviced by strangers. It's unsafe. You could get with child, catch some disease…." Shooting out a hand, lightning fast, he grabbed her arm again. "I can't bear to think of them touching you."

Ire burned like acid in Adela's chest. A dozen different kinds of anger. How dare he be so possessive now when in all like-lihood he'd barely spared a thought for her in seven years? How dare he think so little of her common sense, her intelli-gence? Against all the odds, she'd believed that he knew her, and knew her worth.

"What kind of featherbrained nincompoop do you think I am, Wilson?" She jerked her arm, trying to free it, but his hand was an iron clamp again. "I know there are ways to avoid pregnancy, and disease. I'm not one of these silly little chits who just succumb willy-nilly to the attentions of men."

Wilson snorted with laughter as Adela realized what she'd

said. Seven years ago she'd succumbed willy-nilly. Seven years ago, she'd opened her legs for Wilson without even the knowledge that there were "measures" to be taken, much less the idea of employing them. She could only thank the heavens that her cousin had been as virgin as she, and that by some trick of luck she hadn't conceived her first time.

"I've grown up a lot since then, Wilson. And learned a great, great deal. I might have been an idiot that once with you, but never since." She pulled again, and this time his grip seemed to loosen a little, but he still didn't release her. "At the establishment I attend, all precautions are taken. The gentlemen happily submit to regular examinations by a doctor…and, um, whenever congress occurs, French letters are employed."

A vile, profane oath seemed to split the very molecules of the night air. Adela was aware of the word Wilson used, but had never heard it spoken—shouted—in anger. Her cousin, the rarest and most handsome man she'd ever seen, looked almost ugly, like a ferocious beast, enraged and hurt.

"What? Would you prefer they not use a device? Don't be ridiculous."

Wilson released her. Did he think her polluted? She couldn't tell. But he looked as if he'd been poleaxed.

"I'm entitled to pleasure, Wilson. Like every woman," she said in a low, gritty voice. She wouldn't be cowed or shocked, or reveal any fear. "And as there have never been any admirers or suitors at my door, there's been no opportunity to obtain what I wanted through those more conventional means. So I took my chances…bartered a commodity I had in abundance, so I could experience what I lacked."

"You could have come to me."

What? What nonsense was he speaking? Adela glared at her cousin and matched his stubborn expression with one of her own.

"Don't be ridiculous! You didn't want me. You didn't want anything to do with me. You sought other women…" How could he not see how impossible this was? "Wilson, you just *weren't there!*"

"Well, I'm bloody well here now!"

Like a great cat from the jungles of Africa, he lunged forward, pushing her against the back of the seat, holding her with the weight of his body while he took her face between his hands and jammed his mouth against hers in a hard, savage kiss.

The urge to resist was pure instinct, and she thumped Wilson and pummeled at him even while her traitor mouth yielded. His tongue dived in, pushing against hers, teasing it and taunting it, his fingers around her face and head, digging into her hair and making it impossible to get away from him.

Animal!

Her eyes were wide-open, and on that thought, his shot wide, too, silver-blue and brilliant like metal fire. Dear God, he was laughing at her, though in silence. He was amused by her struggles and their lack of effect on him.

So, much as she refused to admit that she enjoyed the fierce kiss, and wanted more and more and more, Adela redoubled her efforts. And this time, she grabbed at Wilson's shaggy hair, tugging it until he yelped and let her loose.

"Ooh, you're a vicious witch, Della. You always fought unfairly."

"As do you, you towering hypocrite!"

His eyes were still wild, their centers black, pupils dilated. Pulling his hair had only incited him further. He gasped, and shook his head when she released him. "You'll not do that next time. I'll shave my head."

I should be terrified. He's bigger than me, wiry and athletic and strong, and he doesn't care about anything.

But it wasn't fear she felt now. Just a chaotic mix of anger and sudden, overpowering lust. Her body was on fire, every bit of it sensitized, every square inch of skin ready and demanding to be touched. By Wilson. Her breasts ached like fury, and in the pit of her belly, desire ground, a relentless mill wheel, inexorable. The division of her sex was molten, running with the silk that welcomed a man.

"No, you won't.... Now leave me alone, Wilson. Go away."

He laughed again, the sound lighter this time, like music in the night air.

"Now who's the hypocrite?" He reached for her again, with a softer touch, cradling her chin, but delicately. The hold secured her as surely as his fierce grip a moment or two ago had. "You don't want me to go away. You want me to stay and make love to you. Don't deny it. I can see it in everything about you. You're panting for me, cousin." He paused and licked his plush lower lip in a slow, lascivious stroke. "You're dying for it...ready for it." His eyes narrowed. "Is this how you feel when you haven't visited one of your gentlemen for a while? When your body is racked with lust? You claim that you're entitled to feel desire just like a man.... Well, if you are, why try to hide what it does to your body?"

Without warning, he plunged forward again. He didn't grab for her head, or tighten his grip. Adela could have broken free easily. But she didn't.

She yielded her mouth to his ferocity, let him plunder and taste, batter her tongue and make her jaw ache. All the while drinking in his darkness like the sweetest wine of life.

When he set her lips free again, she could have sworn she'd just swigged down a pint of brandy, soaring on a wave of delirious intoxication, but without the faintest hint of the less pleasant aspects of the grape.

And now she was literally panting. If not for him, from the force of his kiss.

"Do they kiss you like that, your gentlemen? Are they as good as me? Are you thinking about them, and their cocks, when I touch you?" His voice was hard, rough. A trial to answer.

The strange thing was, she'd barely thought about any of them at all while in the vicinity of Wilson. Yuri, Clarence and Lionel, the men who'd answered her needs, were all handsome, accomplished and finely versed in every erotic skill... but none of their caresses, nor their polished techniques, meant anything in the face of Wilson's raw, primitive force. They didn't actually kiss much on the lips, but it was difficult to remember any of their accomplishments when her cousin was raging around her like a physical storm and blotting out all thoughts of any other man on earth.

"Do they kiss you?" he demanded, making Adela realize she'd been drifting.

"Yes, they do, of course," she lied. "And they're all very good at it."

"Not as good as me, admit it.... You can't lie. I can tell."

He was right, and he knew she knew it. But she wasn't going to yield quite so easily, even if she wanted to.

"But you've barely done anything, Wilson. A little dalliance, a few rather rural kisses... Heavens, you haven't even fucked me in seven years, and that's a long, long time."

He gave her that slow, calculating, almost vulpine smile again, and through the satin of her glove, his fingertip slowly stroked the skin of her wrist. "Ah, but I will fuck you, Della, and I'll fuck you soon, mark my words." The finger moved, circling now, and Adela's clitoris leaped as if he were at work between the lips of her sex. "Maybe not tonight, or tomorrow, but soon…and you'll be hot and wet and begging for it when I do."

She was almost on the point of begging for it now.

"No, you won't, and no, I won't be." She wanted to curse because her voice shook a little bit, betraying her lie.

"Why do you talk such nonsense, cousin?" He seemed calmer now, not so wild and out of control. Adela shuddered, recognizing even greater danger. She knew she should rise from the bench, walk away, not look back. She knew Wilson wouldn't stop her.

But she still couldn't move, much less leave.

"What does it take to prove to you that you want me? Even if I am just a substitute for your precious gigolos."

Never that, never that…*they* were the substitutes.

"Let's get things out in the open, reveal your readiness…." Moving quickly, he plucked at the hem of her gown, and in a panic, Adela grabbed a hank of his hair again as he bent down.

"No, no, no…" Without any effort at all, he prized her fingers from his hair and quickly grasped both her hands in one of his. With his free hand, he deftly loosened his soft tie and flicked it from around his neck, then in a heartbeat, he had her two hands secured, the foulard fastened around her wrists.

"Wilson! You devil!" she cried. "What are you doing?" She flexed against the silk but it wouldn't yield.

His grin was more playful now, but still dark. Not friendly. "Hush! Do you want me to push my handkerchief into your mouth to shut you up?" He winked. "I have another one handy and I can assure you it's perfectly clean and fresh from the laundry."

"No! Don't do that!" The idea was appalling, and all the more so for the way it excited her. People played such games—binding, gagging…blindfolding—along with the spanking. Activities like that were among the most popular of all at Sofia's pleasure house, and Adela had sampled from the menu on occasion. But somehow, wearing a silk mask and receiving a few light and playful slaps on the rump from Clarence were a world away from this dangerous dance with Wilson.

Clarence and the other lads were there to serve only her wishes. But Wilson was here to serve Wilson. With a force of will that made even the simplest of games a thousand times more perilous.

"You'll have to keep quiet on your own, then…or risk summoning an audience when I make you scream with pleasure."

"Who says you can do that?" she said, knowing that he almost certainly could and would. She was so roused already that her vagina rippled; she could almost feel that long, elegant finger of his inside her again, adamantine while she clamped down upon it.

He gave her a narrow, superior look. "Do you think your paid men are the only ones who know a few tricks? You know what I'm capable of. Didn't I make you moan this afternoon? And I was barely even trying then." He held her bound hands in one of his, and cupped the swell of her breast, squeezing the gentle curve that rose from the edge of her corset. "Damned frock…I can't get to your tits in this. Unless I take my penknife to it. Shall I do that? Carve open your pretty dress and your stupid corset so I can suck your nipples until you can't sit still anymore?"

Adela shuddered. Her face was hot, despite the cool evening air, and there was sweat trickling in her armpits and between her constrained breasts. Oh, Lord, she wanted him to do exactly what he'd threatened. She wanted him to slice her clothes from her body and kiss her all over. Maybe spank her again, and do it hard, until her bottom was steaming and she was weeping, not from pain but from the gouging need to have his cock inside her. She could see the picture now, just as she might draw it, and how it might be engraved. Her naked white body, stripped, apart from her stockings and shoes. She was kneeling on the dark-painted bench, offering up her rosy rump and her juicy puss to Wilson, and he had his marvelous cock out and was presenting it to her entrance.

"Oh…"

"Do you really want that?" Abandoning her breast, Wilson fished one-handed into his pocket, and brought out the slender knife in its gleaming silver jacket. The blade was completely enclosed, safe in its mechanism, but inside it would be sharp as sharp could be. Wilson was a craftsman in all things and even as a youth had taken pride in having the finest of tools.

"No! This is my best gown…and I don't have all that many good ones."

Coward.

"I'll buy you a dozen gowns, Della. I've got plenty of money. Hell, I'll buy you a thousand dresses. I'll keep Monsieur Worth busy for a year just for you!" He let go of her hands and toyed with the knife, running his fingers along the casing. It had a fine silver chain and fob, attached to the base, as if it might be worn in the manner of a pocket watch.

"I don't want anything from you. Leave me alone."

"You don't mean that." He moved close, and even though she tried to push at him with her tied hands, he was unstoppable. "And you do want something from me, at least right now. You want release, Della…you want to spend. And you can't diddle yourself when your hands are tied, can you?" Slowly, he dangled the penknife between her breasts, in the dip of her dress, and let it slide in while he plunged his face into her décolletage and licked the trembling skin of first one upper slope, then the other.

The sensations were so unusual she gasped aloud. Wilson's hot tongue, wet against her skin; the silver coldness of the encased knife, dangling between her breasts, its menace resting on the upper edge of her corset where the garment hooked together. His mouth roved, kissing and licking every part of her bosom that was accessible to him. Laughing low in his throat, he bared his teeth, not biting, but drawing their sharp edges over her slight curves.

"You're aching to spend already, aren't you?" he whispered, then opened his mouth against a patch of skin just beneath her collarbone, and began to suck, suck hard, pulling, pulling, pulling....

Adela let her head fall back, so weak with lust she could hardly support it. Her body was betraying her completely. Her sex *was* aching. A heavy, grinding ache. Without thinking what she was doing, she sat down hard, pressing herself against the firm wood of the seat, trying to get some ease through the multiple layers of skirt and petticoats and drawers.

"Tut tut tut…not until I grant you pleasure," murmured Wilson, kissing where he'd sucked, gentling where he'd hurt.

Pitching forward, Adela struggled to see where he'd love-nibbled her. Damn him, there was a purple mark already. She'd have to cover it up with Mama's shawl.

She glared at Wilson, holding his gaze defiantly and surging against the seat, rocking her hips. It probably wasn't possible to get any kind of ease that way, but she wasn't going to stay still just because Wilson told her to.

"I never realized you were such a trollop, cousin. So carnal…. It's no wonder you need to seek out and pay men to service you, if you have an itch like that in your drawers all the time." Toying with the silver chain of his knife, which still dangled over the black taffeta of her bodice, he leaned forward and kissed her neck, right beneath her ear. "You don't need to sell your drawings to earn money for yourself, Della. If you sold your hot, lubricious puss, you'd be the one patronizing Worth. You'd make a fortune."

"You are despicable and disgusting." She spat out the words, but what Wilson had said almost made her swoon. Why did the idea of being insatiable make her...*more* insatiable? Being helpless with lust ought to be a shaming experience, but she adored it, and became all the more lubricious at the thought.

Inside her drawers her sex was running like a river. And when Wilson gripped her crotch, pressing on her neediest zone through all the layers of her clothing, she moaned out loud, and knew beyond doubt he comprehended her condition.

"Oh, yes, I've got to see the thing." *Squeeze.* "I've got to touch it." *Squeeze.* "I've got to taste it."

Adela whimpered, hovering at the very point of losing her senses.

"Yes, that's it, that's it." Wilson grinned like Satan himself. "Come on, let's get this confounded nonsense of petticoats out of the way."

Taking hold of her by the arm, he urged her up off the seat, then grabbed at the mass of her skirts, behind her, and began hauling them up. Stunned, half out of her mind with desire, Adela let him—even while a reasoned observer somewhere within her seemed to take note that beyond this moment, and ones like it, submission was not in her nature.

Wilson gathered the material of her skirts and petticoats in an almighty bundle at the small of her back. For someone simply gowned and unbustled like Adela, the process was far easier than for a fashionable lady, but it still seemed a strange, dark pantomime. Especially when Wilson wrenched at her drawers, parting the vent at the back and baring her bottom to the night air and the moonlight.

Almost beside herself, Adela buried her blushing face in his shoulder while he fondled her buttocks, one hand still holding her linen, the other roving free, fingering, touching, squeezing. She gulped when he dipped into her puss from behind, paddling in the heavy flow of moisture.

"So wanton," he purred in her ear. "So uncontrolled...so licentious..." His fingertips palpated her soft inner lips from the rear. "Did you know there are still some reactionary members of the medical profession who think this is an illness in women? A dangerous degeneration?" Wilson touched her entrance, and without any conscious thought, Adela pushed against his hand, her body trying to invite his digit back into her, into the hot channel it had entered earlier in the day.

But he didn't oblige her. The finger skirted around, not pushing in, not sliding farther. Denying contact with her clitoris. Adela moved again, trying to knock him toward the tiny aching organ, but he said, "No, no, not until I say so, wicked minx."

Dying of frustration, she thumped him with her bound hands.

"Now, now...don't be naughty," he chided. "You're out of control, Della...what these doctors would call a hysterical woman. Do you know what the fashionable treatment is for this supposed malady?" He flicked at her inner lips again, making her almost want to scream.

"No, I bloody well don't," she growled, "but it can't be worse than the treatment...or lack of it...that you're dishing out."

"Well, certain consultants employ various mechanical and electrical contraptions—devices that vibrate, and are applied to the clitty of the unfortunate hysteric, and then held there until she spends and becomes calm."

Adela laughed.

Oh, Mr. Clever, you think you know everything, don't you?

"What's so amusing?" he demanded, and as he did so, he pushed his fingertip into her a little way.

Adela panted, so close to pleasure now. But she knew he wouldn't give her satisfaction…not yet.

"The—the house I visit has one of those contraptions of yours." She fought for breath. "Some of the ladies have tried it. I haven't, though. I'm told it's rather noisy, and can, um, put one off. Although one or two of my friends claim it's the best thing ever!"

"Perhaps I'll design an improved version of this marvelous example of medical engineering. What power source does this miracle employ? Electricity? A wet cell or a dry cell battery? Is your friend's house supplied by a power company, or does she have her own generator?"

"How the devil should I know? You're the technological genius, not me." Adela suddenly wished she had the device here with her now, and could somehow whirl away from Wilson, use it and claim her own crisis, denying him the privilege of granting it. "And you really are the most aggravating lover!"

It was Wilson's turn to laugh. "It should be easy enough to construct. I have electrical power installed in my home and workshop, with many advanced refinements…and I could use you as my guinea pig." His eyes glittered in the dark. "Ah, yes, Della, that would be a very fine thing. To shackle you hand and foot to a bed, then treat you…and treat you and treat you and treat you…until you go insane from the pleasure of it or beg me to desist."

"I wish we had such a mechanism here, in some portable format." She pushed herself toward him, but he would not be tricked. "Then I could throw myself at it and not have to wait for you to oblige me!"

"Are you this strident and demanding with your gentlemen?" Wilson's fingertip withdrew, and dallied, so close to the area where she wanted it that she almost screamed. "They must find you an incredibly taxing customer."

She wasn't. She was only an occasional patroness of the establishment. But she wasn't going to tell him that. "Indeed. I'm voracious, as you well know. So if you're going to service me, please make haste and do so."

"Very well, then," he said in a low, hard voice. Was his opinion of her so poor? Had he been harboring boyish dreams of her remaining pure and reticent for him? That was ridiculous. She'd never been reticent seven years ago, so why now? Surely an enlightened man like Wilson didn't adhere to outmoded tenets of a "woman's place" and suchlike?

Grabbing hold of her buttocks beneath the mass of petticoats, he kissed her voraciously on the mouth again, then pushed her back down onto the seat, setting her in place, then withdrawing his hands. It was cold where he'd parted her drawers and bared her bum, the wood rough and a little damp against her skin.

Adela shuddered. How lewd did it feel to have her naked buttocks pressed down on the old wooden bench? And worse yet, her roused sex hot and dripping against it? Wilson barely gave her time to absorb the sensations before he was pushing aside her bound hands and hauling at her linen from the front. Up and up the bunched mass of cloth came, until she was exposed at the front, too, her dark *motte* a shocking contrast to the white skin of her belly and the even whiter froth of muslin and discreet lace framing it.

"As I have no French letters about my person, I shall have to improvise," said Wilson, dropping to his knees on the grass in front of her. "Dinner was indifferent, but I shall certainly enjoy *this* feast." He grabbed her by the buttocks again, this time from beneath, and edged her toward the edge of the seat, opening her for his delectation.

Ooh! Oh, no! Oh, yes!

Not pausing, barely even looking at what he was doing, he plunged his face in between her thighs, nudging her damp curls aside with one hand, while he clung on to one of the cheeks of her bottom with the other, his fingertips wickedly brushing her anal crease.

Not wasting time on the niceties of exploration, he lashed her clitoris with his tongue, then encircled it with his lips and sucked hard.

"Oh…oh, God! Oh, dear!"

Pleasure blossomed instantly in her puss, too sudden, too soon, almost painful. She'd been aching to spend, but this quick, almost violent completion was as shocking as it was delicious. As her channel clenched and clenched, and her legs kicked out, she grabbed hunks of Wilson's hair again with her bound hands. He grunted, but kept on sucking, making her orgasm into a fierce, relentless trial of the senses.

And just as he'd predicted, she had to bite her lips to keep in her ecstatic screams.

12

A Feast for the Senses

Something so intense could not endure long. And perhaps it was just as well, or she might have passed out. Within moments, Adela was descending again, not even sure whether she'd enjoyed the experience. She opened her eyes, unable to remember when she'd closed them. Amazingly—and disappointingly—she hadn't wrenched out hanks of Wilson's hair by the roots.

Had she hurt him? She *sincerely* hoped so. He'd given her pleasure, but he'd stolen it from her, too. Being compelled into a brief, hard, almost brutal release was a long way from being fully sated. "Unfasten this," she commanded, tempted to cuff him on the side of the head with her bound hands. Especially when he lifted his face from her loins and grinned up at her, his lips wet and shiny.

"Why should I?" He ran his tongue round his mouth in a slow, provocative circle. "And why would you want me to? In my experience, ladies find that fulfillment is all the more intense when they're constrained. Surely that's common knowledge at this pleasure house of yours?"

He was right, of course. It was. She'd indulged herself, once or twice, but very safely. There was a world of difference between fur-lined cuffs with Yuri or Clarence, both so trustworthy and paid never to exceed a lady's limits, and Wilson, who was not trustworthy and who dedicated his life to exploding limits in every sphere.

"Unfasten me, you clod!" She biffed him on the side of the face with the back of her hand.

He stared up at her, still smirking.

"I'll do it myself, then." Kicking at him with her heels, and tipping forward so he was compelled to shuffle back on his knees, Adela bit at the knot in the foulard. Trying to loosen the fabric with her teeth was an unpleasant experience, but after a few seconds of worrying at it like a terrier with a bone, she got some purchase and started to pull it free.

Only to have her hands drawn away from her face by Wilson. Gracefully, but with muddy trouser knees, he'd resumed his seat beside her, and now proceeded to unfasten the foulard and release her hands. Stuffing it into his pocket, he gently chafed her wrists as if they'd been cruelly bound with hemp rope instead of lightly constrained by a little piece of silk.

"Better?" he asked, bending to kiss each wrist.

Yes, better, but a perverse part of her still wished she was bound. This dark Adela *wanted* the danger only Wilson could offer, and low in her belly, desire still plagued her. She wanted to be tied to that bed while he tormented her yet again with his games. She didn't care about any fancy mechanical device, though; she knew full well Wilson was more than capable of driving her witless with just hands and mouth…and cock.

"Yes, thank you." She shook herself free, and tried to rise, but he retained his hold on one hand, folding his fingers around it, not forcefully, but in a light, sweet grasp. "Wilson, I should go now. This has been unwise. Surely you realize that?"

"I suppose so...." He raised her hand to his lips again, kissing it with exquisite delicacy on the back, then turning it over and doing the same on the palm, only lingering longer there. "And I haven't been kind, have I?"

Adela blinked. She didn't expect Wilson to be kind. Kindness belonged to their past relationship, way back beyond the time when they'd first lain together, when things were simple both between them and on the larger, familial scale. But he was being kind now, with his soft kiss still lingering against her skin.

She suspected a trick.

"You've dispatched the office of a lover. You've made me climax, which was the whole point of the exercise, I'd imagine, in order to show me how superior you are to my other... paramours."

The expression on Wilson's face tightened momentarily, but it was fascinating to observe the way he cleared it.

"I wasn't superior at all, though, was I? What I did was rough and crude, and not, I suspect, fully satisfying." He paused, then pressed a more open kiss to her palm. "Let me set the matter straight, and then if you wish it, I'll leave you alone and not trouble you further."

What? Did he mean to fuck her now? That was impossible. Unthinkable. But oh, how she wanted it.

Alas, there could be no intercourse without some preventative device, without a French letter. In her discussions with Sofia Chamfleur and her other close intimates of the Ladies' Sewing Circle, Adela had learned everything that Mama would never have thought it seemly to tell a woman without marriage prospects. Namely that even if a gentleman withdrew before completion, there was still a significant possibility that he could get you with child. Or worse.

"No, I can't lie with you, you must know that. I might be an old maid by most people's standards, but I'm still in my childbearing years."

Wilson reached up and set his free hand across her lips. "Don't be ridiculous, Della, you're not an old maid." His long lashes flickered. "And congress is not what I meant. My suggestion is to repeat what I just did…but do it better, and how it should be done."

She wanted to say no, but the area where his mouth had lingered fluttered so hard in anticipation that she gasped. How would a slower, more sensuous examination feel? She had no doubt that Wilson had skills as well developed as those of any of Sofia's boys. Demanding mistresses like *that woman,* and whoever he'd courted before her, would expect nothing less than manly excellence.

He seemed to sense Adela's hesitation, and moved closer, his mouth near her ear now. His breath made wayward strands of her coiffure, which had tumbled when she'd shaken her head, drift and tickle her skin. "Come on, cousin, let me impress you. Show me you're not afraid to indulge yourself. Make me believe that you're really a libertine, not just playing at it."

Out of the corner of her eye, she saw the sly challenge in his expression. The devil, he knew how to provoke her. She should get up and walk away now, but she was tempted, far too tempted. Why deny herself? Turning toward him, she took a kiss from his lips and enjoyed the surprise in his face as he drew away.

"Very well, then. Make recompense. But this doesn't mean

I permit unlimited liberties. Just this one occasion, then you must keep your word."

It wasn't that she trusted him. She was only using him. Wasn't she?

WILSON'S HEART LEAPED at her capitulation, conditional as he knew it was. Why was it so necessary to prove himself? What was it to him that she had other lovers, these men whose advanced lovemaking techniques she paid for?

And yet it *was* important. They might part tonight, never to have anything further to do with each other beyond dreary legal dealings, and he didn't want her to consign him to the status of just one man who'd brought her to orgasm, among many. It was a matter of pride.

He kissed her again, slowly and more beguilingly this time, teasing, tasting, his tongue flirting with hers while he craftily eased up her skirts. No mean feat with such a volume of fabric. The two halves of her drawers had closed again, and that frustrated him. He wanted to be able to run his hands freely over her sleek thighs and trim buttocks as he kissed her, then pleasured her. Caressing her through the last muslin layer, he glided his hand up her haunch, over her hip and to her waist, finding the fastenings. Thank the Lord, she still wore this more old-fashioned kind of undergarment, rather than the buttoned one-piece some women affected. As deftly as he could with all the obstructions, he undid the fastenings that kept her drawers up, and slowly but determinedly began to tug.

"What on earth are you doing?" she squeaked against his mouth. She was alarmed, but he could feel her excitement. That was the difference between an inexperienced miss and someone like Adela, who now so obviously knew the score. Not that he'd been with any inexperienced misses lately. She'd been the only one, ever.

"Clearing the field of play... Don't worry, I'll help you put them back on again afterward."

That seemed to mollify her, and she even helped him work the voluminous white garment off over her knees, her calves then her feet. As he set them aside, he noticed that despite their forlorn little trim of lace, the drawers had been meticulously mended in places.

This isn't right. You deserve beautiful things, Della. New things...

Whatever happened, he'd ensure that she received some fancy fripperies, as a gift. Not, perhaps, the black silk he'd mused upon earlier.... No, despite the fact he was currently in the process of debauching her, he fancied something exquisite, white and pure, for his cousin. And he wouldn't allow her to refuse them if she tried.

"Ah, that's so much better," he told her, sinking to his knees and resuming his position between hers.

Framed in the frou-frou of petticoats—also mended, he noticed, on closer inspection—her thighs, her puss and her belly were all adorable. Skin white, curls lush and a lighter brown than the hair on her head, every part divinely formed. The sweet arc of her abdomen was perfecton, and the slender yet curvaceous shape of her hips and thighs was almost heartbreaking. A man might die down there, whether kissing or fucking, and that prospect made Wilson feel wild and uncontrolled again. Wild to plunge in and wring savage pleasure out of her, just as he'd done before.

No! Contain yourself, man! Show some decorum. Take it slowly, give leisurely, measured pleasure. You promised....

Yet why should he? She was a voluptuary. She partook of carnal delight, and paid for it. Confused anger surged again at the thought of Adela pleasured by others. But he took a deep breath and steadied himself. Pushing aside her linen, clearing the decks, so to speak, he bent forward and pressed a gentle kiss to the flossy hair of her puss.

Even that slight caress made her move, shuffle forward on the bench, rise toward him. Was this her favorite act? Most ladies, after the first shock to their sensibilities, quickly took to it. Surely Adela, the experienced connoisseur, was no exception?

He kissed her belly. He kissed the edge of her *motte*. He kissed the area where her hip met her thigh, on either side. Each kiss made her move, more and more. Parting her thighs wider, she seemed to invite, and demand, that he get down to business. He could sense her longing to command him, yet remaining silent.

Still resisting in your own way, eh, Della? In that case…

Taking hold of her legs, he manhandled her into position, opening her thighs wider so he could edge right in. Fingers probing, he parted the hair of her puss and bared the moist, sweet area. Then, reaching up, he tugged on the silver chain still dangling down the front of her bodice. With a flick and a jerk, he popped the little cylinder containing his knife out of her cleavage.

The small tool was precision crafted to his own design. The fit of the casing was perfectly machined, and required a secret series of twists, which only he knew, to expose the blade.

It couldn't possibly hurt her.

"OH, NO, WILSON, NO!"

He wasn't going to do it, was he? No, it was too wicked, too obscene.

"Yes, Wilson, yes," he chanted back at her, and before she could stop him, or summon the breath to protest again, he swung the little cylinder on its chain, then caught it up and pressed it gently against her entrance. "Something to bear down on, my sweet, when you clench your flesh and spend."

The silver casing slid into her sex, shockingly cool even though it had rested in her cleavage. The small hard shape was alien inside her. Not like a man, or even the erotic toys she'd played with, yet infinitely plaguing in a way that made her moan.

It was as if the very essence and spirit of Wilson's dazzling intelligence was in her, mercurial and dangerous, a fine, bright thrill.

"There…isn't that nice," he murmured, his breath hot against her bare puss and exposed thighs. As she shifted uneasily, the little chain swung where it dangled from her body.

Furling his tongue to a point, Wilson dabbed it against her clit, then delivered one long stroke. A second later the chain swung again as he retreated and rearranged their position. With her legs slung over his shoulders, he dived back in.

This time the assault of his tongue was so, so different.

Before, Wilson had devoured her, attacked her puss almost cruelly and tormented her with pleasure. Now his laps were slow and sweet and tantalizing. Building up delightful layers of pleasure, he teased her with flicks and dabs. Only the way he lifted her, raising her bottom from the bench and opening her completely, was extreme. Like the feel of the knife.

He was feasting on her, yet like a fastidious gourmet, he seemed to savor and analyze ever nuance of her taste and form. His tongue glided over her inner lips, lapping and exploring. He teased her clit with slow little forays, then showed mercy with longer, more comprehensive slides.

Dazzling sensations built and built, as if energy was pooling in her belly, swelling in her sex and winding tight around the little silver casing. Wilson was being an agent provocateur again, but not in a cruel way now, only to enhance her experience. Rising to him, she reached behind her to grasp the back of the bench and brace herself, arching toward his hot, loving mouth. As he licked and suckled, her heels kicked and dragged against the back of his coat, the blows harder as his tongue swirled and tickled her flesh.

"You are delicious, Della," he breathed against her moist membranes. "A feast fit for a king. I've never tasted a banquet more sumptuous and savory." He plunged in again, this time sucking ever so lightly on her clit.

All thoughts of who he might be comparing her with, and how he was probably exaggerating and fibbing, dissolved almost before they could be formed. Her mind went empty, then filled with light as sublime waves assailed her sex and her belly.

She climaxed again, long and intensely, soaring to heaven, her thighs clamping Wilson's head while her heels bashed his back. Her body bent like a bow, pushing her puss even harder against his mouth. She dug her teeth into her lower lip, holding in a scream.

The pleasure went on and on, then suddenly, the high wave ebbed. She was spent. Completely. Her body went limp, bereft of energy and any remaining scrap of tension, and Adela subsided onto the bench as if wrung out. She almost slid sideways, but Wilson, between her thighs, prevented her collapse.

There was nothing to do but lie there and breathe. Thoughts would not come; awareness of her surroundings was vague, peripheral. A nocturnal bird hooted in a tree somewhere close by, and the odor of night-scented jasmine blended with other fragrances, some vegetal, some human yet also feral.

Adela's eyes snapped open as a tiny ripple of residual pleasure assailed her: Wilson drawing out the tiny penknife. As she struggled to sit, he pressed it to his lips, coiled up its little chain and tucked it in the pocket of his frock coat. Then, still kneeling before her, he straightened her stockings and helped her struggle back into her drawers, holding up her skirts while she rocked this way and that, negotiating the fastenings.

"There, all decent again," he said, his tone vaguely cool as he stood and flipped down her skirts and petticoats.

Still winded, Adela didn't know what to say. She supposed she should thank him, but hadn't he also got what he wanted from her? Her capitulation to her own desires and an admission that she was a wanton? Just moments ago, she'd been elevated to paradise, a transcendent being forged in ecstasy by his perverse skills. Now she felt again that she was simply a licentious creature of appetites, and low in his eyes. Roughly or with sophistication, it seemed he could render her helpless and a slave to her senses either way.

"I should go. Mama will be worried if I'm out here too long." This wasn't strictly true. Mama would be happier the longer they stayed, and by now she must be already hearing wedding bells.

"Of course. She must be concerned that I've debauched her pure virgin daughter." Wilson's tone seemed to suggest that he, too, comprehended her mother's thinking on the matter.

Adela stared at her cousin in the moonlight. He was frowning, and his curly hair was awry. His face was still wet from pleasuring her. Wiping his hand across his mouth, he apparently discovered this and reached into an upper pocket for his handkerchief.

When he turned to her, though, he sat down on the bench at her side, and instead of attending to his own face, cradled hers and dabbed at her lip with the square of pristine white linen. Taken aback, Adela allowed him to do so.

"You bit your lip. It was bleeding."

Sure enough, crimson stained the cloth, and as she saw it, Adela realized that she could taste a coppery tang. She'd dug her teeth so hard into her lip that she'd broken the skin...

and not even been aware of it. Running her tongue over the wound, she winced. It was actually quite sore.

Wilson's expression was complex. He was still watching her mouth as he stuffed his handkerchief into his pocket, and the close scrutiny made her nervously lick her lip again. A tremor of something fierce crossed Wilson's face as he followed the minute movement.

"Yes, you should go now, cousin," he said harshly, apropos of her earlier remark.

"I...I will." She searched around for her reticule and found it, feeling uneasy now. Something seemed wrong. Well, *more* wrong than the fact that, once again, she'd somehow allowed her cousin to make free with her. Now that he knew her secret, it would be better to have as little to do with him as possible. Yet still she couldn't make herself go.

And she knew why....

Always a proponent of fair play and reward for effort, she couldn't leave without ensuring Wilson's pleasure, too. And it didn't matter in the slightest that his *will* had been served by what he'd done to her. She'd feel beholden to him if he didn't also climax. And as a New Woman, she was entitled to serve her own will, too.

"What are you waiting for, Della? Rush off to Mama now, only slightly sullied." He paused. "Or should I say, slightly *more* sullied than you were before."

Ignoring the jibe, but storing it away for a time when she might remind him that he was the one who'd "sullied" her in the first place, she shuffled toward him. "Not yet, Wilson. There are unfinished matters to attend to." Taking a deep breath, she reached out and pressed her palm to his groin, savoring his sharp gasp of surprise.

When she squeezed slightly, he tried to push her hand away.

"Don't trouble yourself, cousin. My appetites are not so un-controlled that I can't contain them."

"Implying that mine are," she said silkily, not allowing him to dislodge her fingertips from the front of his trousers. Regardless of his apparent disdain, his cock was hard like a rock beneath the fine worsted, and seemed to swell even as she cradled him. "I *chose* to let you pleasure me, Wilson. You know that you would have let me walk away if I'd really wanted to go."

His eyes flashed. His expression of lust and admiration was delicious. "You have me there, Della," he said, then glanced down, laughing at the irony when she gave him another warning squeeze. "Will you need my handkerchief?" He tweaked at the white corner of it, still peeking from the pocket of his coat.

So confident. So sure of himself. Adela narrowed her eyes. She'd shock him if it was the last thing she ever did to him, or with him.

"No, that won't be necessary." Kicking out her skirts behind her, she sank to *her* knees this time, and before he could protest, attacked the fly buttons of his trousers.

"What the hell are you doing?" It was less a protest than an expression of excitement.

Still at work, and already rummaging in his linen, Adela looked up briefly. "What do you think I'm doing, Wilson? Surely such an experienced libertine as you has received fella-tio before?" Reaching in, she found his cock, huge and hard, and so familiar. Not just from this afternoon, but from seven years of imagining. "The scurrilous gossip says that apparently the great Coraline is an expert in the art…although I'm hoping my modest efforts will be acceptable."

His whole body stiffened now, not just his masculine part. "Get off, Della. Leave me alone." Ah, she'd struck an emotional nerve, not just a physical one.

In the midst of her determination, cold gripped Adela's heart. Ah, yes, the great Coraline, not to be spoken of... *That woman,* but sacred to him, and not to be mentioned by a lesser mortal, even if that mortal was about to supply carnal pleasure. With a grim resolve, Adela took a firm hold on Wilson's cock and drew it out of his drawers into the perfumed night air.

"No, I won't leave you alone," she said, beginning to slowly and meticulously pump him.

"Oh, God... Della... No..."

Regardless of her cousin's words, Adela knew she'd got him. He was pushing into her grip, his lean hips thrusting forward, seeking more. His token show of reluctance became a complete sham when he grabbed her by the shoulder with one hand and cradled her head with the other. Long fingers dived into the silky hanks of her coiled coiffure, and several pins loosened and fell to the ground.

"No?" she inquired, looking up at him. But he was gone now, his eyes blank, gazing into the middle distance. Thinking of Coraline? After all that had taken place today, was he fantasizing about the Parisienne? Had he been dreaming of her *all* the time?

Damned cur! I'll show you!

Parting her lips, Adela stuck out her tongue and swirled it around the plump tip of Wilson's cock. It was slick and wet, in anticipation of pleasure. So much for his reluctance. His flesh disregarded his higher mental functions.

"Yes!" he growled, pushing forward, trying to insert himself. But Adela gripped his shaft, holding him.

Were all men so greedy? Even the experienced lovers? Working at her own pace, she lapped at the head of Wilson's cock, caressing it and exploring it, but not yet taking it in. Pleasuring with the mouth was something Adela rather enjoyed, but she hadn't attempted it as often as she would have liked to. Sophia's establishment was a pleasure house *for* women, and the boys there were so deliciously skilled at touching, caressing, licking, that it was sinfully easy to just lie back and luxuriate in it all, rather than to get up on one's haunches and be the active protagonist.

But that didn't mean that Adela didn't know what she was doing, and now she was resolved. She'd get the better of him. She'd go all the way with this.

"Oh, Della, Della, please…" burbled Wilson, gripping her head and her shoulder. His fingers were digging in hard now. Thick strands of her hair had come loose from their casual acquaintance with styling, and hung coiled to her shoulders.

After one last daring lunge at his eye of love with her tongue, Adela enveloped the head of Wilson's cock with her lips. And sucked.

The foray wrung a harsh cry from her cousin, and his hips bucked forward, but still she controlled him. With the fingers of one hand wrapped around the length of him, she inveigled her other hand beneath him and gripped his firm bottom through his trousers with the other. She sucked, then flicked, sucked, then flicked, repeating the sequence while she squeezed hard on the muscular round of his left buttock, pushing her fingertips toward the central groove.

"Oh, my dear, dear girl," he groaned, panting as she worked him. Adela almost smiled around his flesh, that he should call her a girl when he was barely any older than she was, just a year, nothing more. "I never realized you could be such a temptress. Oh, this is too delicious…too delicious…." He gasped, his voice tight. "But you really must desist or I'll spend in your mouth."

Desist? Never! To defeat him, make him so helpless that he couldn't contain himself, that was the entire object of this particular exercise. Fierce with resolve, she redoubled her efforts. Sucking harder, diving at him with her tongue, seeking out ever more tender spots. Fondling his muscular male bottom with her fingertips, and probing the cleft as rudely as she could through his clothing.

"Oh, Della…Della…please. I can't hold on much longer. You must stop."

"No," she growled, the word muffled and made uncouth by the obstruction in her mouth. Digging with the tip of her tongue, she probed ferociously at the groove beneath the head of his penis, and at the same time pressed hard on the vent of his anus.

Wilson let out a choked cry, his hips hammering, and thrusting his cock roughly and without control into her mouth. As it leaped and leaped, salty fluid bathed her tongue, and triumph was a silent, roaring cry.

Got you, you devil! Got you!

His cock still leaping, Wilson swayed where he sat, then seemed to brace himself, the muscles of his thighs tense. He still sought support, though, his hand gripping her shoulder.

"You wicked siren, you…" He ground out the words, chest still heaving. "You did that on purpose, didn't you? You did it to best me."

Adela withdrew, ejecting him and licking her lips, not sure whether she was angry or jubilant. Perhaps it was a little, or a lot, of both. Shaking Wilson off, she rose to her feet, but not before whipping the white handkerchief from Wilson's pocket and dabbing her mouth with it. Men, they were such an ungrateful lot.

"Yes, I believe I did." She half flung the handkerchief back at him and he caught it neatly, but then crumpled it in his hand as if not sure what to do with it. "I'm tired of you thinking you can make free with me, Wilson. And then judging me, because even though you enjoy the fruits of my experience, you disapprove of the way I've acquired my knowledge. I've said it before and I'll say it again—you're a hypocrite."

He glared at her, his eyes raging and confused. He still seemed to be half out of his senses from the pleasure she'd given him, and when he lunged up and forward, she danced away lightly, sweeping up her reticule and turning to make off down the path to the house.

An iron hand grabbed her arm. "Clearly, you're an apt pupil, Della. I don't think I've ever had a better sucking. These men of yours, the ones you draw and fuck, they must be the most accomplished tutors." Wilson was shaking with anger, but what right did he have to judge? Did he think he should have been the one to educate her? If he'd not been such an arrogant beast seven years ago, he *could* have been that instructor. Or perhaps if she'd been a little more tolerant of the foibles of a randy young man?

"But I can show you more, cousin," he went on. She could feel him shaking, the intensity transmitted through his fingers on her arm. "Believe me, I can show you more than these bought-and-paid-for stallions ever could."

"Let me go, Wilson, and kindly put your cock back in your trousers." She kept her voice low and controlled, even though the wildness in his eyes made her shake, too. She was reminded once again of his enormous strength, so powerful in a man of relatively slender build. That was familiar, but this degree of passion was new, and it terrified her.

For a moment there was a standoff. Had Wilson even heard what she'd said? But then his fingers loosened and when she shook her arm, his hand dropped away and he set himself to rights.

"This isn't over, Adela," he said to her retreating back as she sped away.

It is if I can help it.

"It is. Leave me alone. Keep your distance," she said, not turning, still striding. She would have to be very careful, and lie low for the rest of the house party. Or remain in the safety of groups.

She must never be alone with Wilson, ever again.

SMOKING ALONE IN a shadowed corner of the kitchen garden, Blair Devine was well placed to watch a male figure approach him. He remained hidden until he recognized Edward Foster, a valet of his acquaintance, with whom he'd had profitable dealings with before. Devine had been pleased to see the man's employer among the house party guests.

"Evening, Mr. Devine. How's tricks?" Foster's grin was sharp and wily. "You wouldn't have a spare fag about your person, would you? I'm gasping."

Devine offered his cigarette case, filled with the fine Turkish cigarettes he purchased in Bond Street. Foster took one, and Blair gestured encouragingly, so the valet took a handful more and secreted them in his top pocket. Money oiled the wheels, but other little treats smoothed the way too.

"Anything interesting?" he asked the keen-eyed young man.

Foster took a long drag. "Well, Mrs. De Vesey is sneaking into the room of old Lord Rayworth himself every night, but that's nothing new. Common knowledge… The Honorable Mr. Souter is on his uppers, despite appearances to the contrary…. Might be in the market for a loan, if you know anybody?" He winked, pulled on his cigarette again.

Devine considered this, and filed it away for future reference. "What about any juicy little items of reading material? And anything more on the Ruffingtons? I know your boss knows the family slightly…"

Foster gave him a speculative look, but Devine wasn't worried. The young valet had done well out of him, and seemed to have a relish for the dealings they transacted.

"Well, I've been romancing an upstairs maid here, a willing young miss and a real fast worker, if you know what I mean? She thinks she might have seen something along those lines, just the very thing you're looking for…. That young Miss Sybil R. is careless thing, and Maisie, well, I've told her about certain…ahem…opportunities there are for sharp girls like her." He favored Devine with another slow wink.

Devine nodded. This was all very satisfactory. "And what about Wilson Ruffington? Anything on him?"

"Nah, afraid not, Mr. D. All the staff think he's a bit of a strange cove. Keeps himself to himself…can't see why he's here, to be honest. And his man's a weird one, too. Very protective of his master, he is. Threatened to knock me down when I made a remark… Only joking I was. Anyway, he looks after his master's room himself…nobody allowed in…. Maisie tried to get in to do the room, normallike, and the lock wouldn't turn. Reckon old Wilson had done something to it, though I can't imagine what. Bit of a mystery…"

That was frustrating, but not surprising, and Blair Devine didn't brood on it as he paid off Foster and bade him goodnight…and good hunting.

He smiled again in the darkness. He already had plenty of choice lines of inquiry where that arrogant prick of a scientist was concerned, and he'd soon have his hands on more goods.

There was no need to rush, though. He'd bide his time. All would be well…although certainly not well for Wilson Ruffington.

TO ADELA'S SURPRISE, Wilson did keep his distance for the rest of the weekend. He didn't seek her out, or approach her, and when the demands of sociability made conversation unavoidable, he was both blandly and rigorously polite.

It's a trick. All part of some devious ruse, or experiment. So typical of you.

Adela thought this over and over again, but by the time they were leaving, she wasn't so certain. Surely by now he should have sprung whatever trap he'd been devising? Either that or become overtly hostile?

Either way, she would have known where she stood.

13

Stolen Goods

Where is it? Where is it?

The journey home had been a nightmare. What with Blair Devine in their compartment like a burr beneath the saddle of a horse, his particular watchfulness a constant, minor irritation, and the never-ending stream of Sybil's chatter about Algernon, a couple of hours had turned into a millennium. And all this had been exacerbated by the constant necessity of parrying Mama's not so subtle probings about Wilson. By the time they reached their London home, in a carriage from Waterloo Station, the headache Adela had pleaded, to avoid interrogation, was real. But at least the jabbing pain in her temples had given her an excuse to retire to her room in peace, in order to leaf through the new drawings she'd done, and decide which ones would be suitable for *Divertissements*. There was a certain dark glee to the idea of distributing images of Wilson's cock to the magazine's many avid subscribers…even if there was no indication to whom said organ was attached.

But when Adela came to unlock her carpet bag, where the

portfolio had been safely stowed, the black leather binder was nowhere to be seen. How could that happen, when she always kept the key safe on her person?

Upending the bag and flinging everything on the floor, Adela went through her belongings again and again. It was an absolutely pointless exercise. There was no way the dashed portfolio could just materialize, but still she rummaged, as if a miracle might occur.

Adela sat on the bed, surveying the chaos of shawls and gloves and hairbrushes and other personal and toilet items around her, and seethed. She didn't have to upend her brain to know precisely who was responsible for the loss of her drawings.

Wilson, you blackguard. When did you take it? I'll wring your neck!

The portfolio had been securely locked in the bag all the time she'd not actually had it with her, but locks were no barrier to the one who'd taught *her* to conquer them. And there'd been plenty of occasions when her cousin might have slipped into her room, not to mention the fact that he was the only one who knew that the portfolio was worth stealing.

To confirm her suspicions, Adela took a magnifying glass from her drawer and perused the lock. At first glance it was immaculate, unsullied, with no sign of tampering. Just as she would expect it to be if Wilson had breached it. If some other miscreant had been at it, there would be scratches from the tools used. Only Wilson would be able to pick the lock without leaving a mark.

And yet, leaning in close and squinting hard, Adela did see something. One single tiny scratch, almost invisible.

You despicable devil! You're taunting me. You left this on purpose.

It was exactly what he'd do, and she'd have it out with him. She would visit her cousin, alone, whether Mama liked it or

not. Lack of propriety or otherwise. A note had been waiting upon their homecoming, alerting Adela to a meeting of
the Ladies' Sewing Circle tomorrow, and if Mama objected,
it would be a simple matter to use that as a cover for her activities. She'd done it often enough to disguise her trysts at
Sofia's house of pleasure.

And it would be useful to drop in at the circle, too. Her
closest friends there, Sofia and Beatrice, were both women of
the world and might have counsel to offer on the subject of
Wilson and his infuriating foibles.

"CALL ON WILSON? What do you mean, call on Wilson?"

Adela sighed inside. Her mother's face showed exactly the
reaction she'd expected. A little alarm. Puzzlement. A smidgen of hope…then a bit more hope.

"Just exactly that, Mama. I'd like to continue one or two
points of conversation that he and I explored at Rayworth
Court." Well, it was a form of the truth, and better that than
the actual truth, which might kill her mother—or alternatively, give her too much hope.

Mrs. Ruffington frowned, clearly perplexed. Adela couldn't
blame her. "You really are the most contrary young woman,
Della. I don't know where I am with you. One minute you
seem to be getting on well with Wilson, even going off together on walks, unseemly as that is. The next, you don't
seem to want anything whatsoever to do with each other,
and he doesn't even show his face to say goodbye when we
leave." Mama shook her head, clearly perplexed. "And now,
suddenly, you're wanting to visit him alone, in a way that's
completely unsuitable. It won't do, Della, it really won't do.
If you want to talk to Wilson, we must invite him to dinner,
or to tea. I won't have you visiting him on your own, and
that's the end of it."

"Very well. I won't go, then." So it would have to be by subterfuge. Adela didn't like deceiving her mother, but she'd become well used to it. This deception was her sole cause for guilt when she went to visit Sofia's boys from time to time. Mama only wanted the best for her, but that "best" mainly involved marriage to a nice, respectable and preferably titled man. Ideally Wilson. But that wasn't going to occur until hell froze over.

Mrs. Ruffington plucked at her shawl, still frowning, and out of the corner of her eye, Adela saw Marguerite cast them both a shrewd look. Her younger sister was sage beyond both of them, she suspected.

"Shall I invite him, then?" persisted Mama.

"No, don't bother. He won't come."

"How can you possibly know that, dear?"

Just an instinct. A deep feeling. He'd stolen the portfolio to bring her to him. "Because he's just as contrary as I am, Mama. I think it's better if we just forget the matter."

Her mother's face was a picture of disappointment, and Adela's heart turned over.

"Well, perhaps we *could* invite him to tea, or perhaps luncheon? In a week or two…" She patted Mama's arm, and leaned in confidentially. "I know you have hopes, Ma. I understand that. But I'm not sure he and I are suited, in the romantic sense…. Perhaps we could all try to be better friends with him, though, if you'd like that? I'll make an effort."

Mama's eyes narrowed a little, and Adela wondered if her parent had seen straight through her. Mama was sharper than a lot of people gave her credit for. It wouldn't do to be too confident that one could pull the wool over her eyes. One of these days, she might ask dangerous questions….

A clandestine visit it is, then.

Another meeting of the Sewing Circle that *wasn't* a meeting of the Sewing Circle.

"Thank you, darling," said Mama, beaming. "You're such a sensible girl, really...and I still think you'd make a perfect wife for Wilson. A steadying influence. He's twenty-six and it's time he settled down."

Adela took a sip of tea. Anything to stop her from laughing out loud. If Mama only knew what her plain, sensible, steady eldest daughter was really like.

"Where's Sybil? We must start making plans. We need to be ready. Her dear Algernon could be ready to propose at any moment and she needs to be prepared. There's so much to do!" Mrs. Ruffington rose to ring for their solitary parlor maid. She liked to observe the proprieties, even though they now only had the skimpiest establishment.

Before anyone could answer, the door burst open and Sybil came flying in.

"Oh, Mama! Mama! What am I going to do? The most terrible thing has happened!"

Having flung this out, Sybil burst into a wild flood of tears to rival Victoria Falls in volume and intensity, becoming incoherent and not making any sense at all.

Adela's heart sank. Embarrassing and difficult as Wilson could make it for her, the loss of her portfolio paled to a minor inconvenience. She'd seen hysterics like this from Sybil before and had a sickening feeling that the cause was the same again. Vacating the seat beside Mama, she settled her sister into it and sat down at the other side, grasping Sybil's hand and putting a handkerchief from her own pocket into it.

"What is it, my dear? Please...calm down and tell us." The expression on Mama's face suggested she harbored the same fears.

"Don't cry, Syb.... Tell us what's wrong. Nobody can help

you if you don't share what it is." Adela touched her sister's face. Sybil met her eyes, pleading.

"It's my shawl…my favorite shawl. I think I—I lost it at the house party," the younger girl stammered. "I can't find it anywhere."

"A shawl? All this for a shawl?" Mama laughed in relief. Adela watched the horror drain from her parent's face. "When you're Lady Framley, my sweet, you'll have dozens of beautiful shawls. Don't fret so! I'll order more tea. We have Madeira cake and it's rather good for a change."

"Yes, the cake is good, Syb…do try a slice." Adela squeezed her hand. "And don't worry, I'll find your shawl. I promise you."

Sybil grinned back, her eyes bright, full of trust…and hope, but as Adela ate her own cake, it tasted like dead cinders on her tongue. What could she do? She had no doubt that all Sybil's many shawls were present and accounted for, and that it was a quite different item that had suddenly gone missing.

"I shall write to Lady Rayworth now," announced Mama, sounding decisive, "asking if her staff can look for your shawl. I'm sure they'll find it. They seemed very efficient. Come along, Marguerite, you can help me compose the note."

As their parent bustled out, with their younger sister in her wake, Adela wondered if Mama suspected the truth. She fancied not, though, as Mama had still seemed pleased with herself, and with life.

A state which neither she, or her sister enjoyed, as Adela rounded on Sybil.

"It's letters, isn't it? Tell me, Sybil…tell the truth."

On the point of tears again, Sybil nodded, her smooth young face blotched with distress.

"Which ones? Old or new? You weren't carrying the old ones you exchanged with Johnny around with you, too, were you?" She knew her sister had a habit of carrying keepsakes in her carpet bag, regardless of all her fine talk about safe places.

"Both!" cried Sybil, dissolving into tears again.

Oh, no! Could this possibly get any worse?

"Tell me how it happened…if we know when they went missing, we might be able to narrow down the possibilities of who might have taken them." It seemed a vain hope, but she suddenly thought of Wilson, and how he'd once expounded the merits of logic and sequence to solve problems.

"I don't know… I don't know… I was reading them when we first arrived, and I was resting after the journey. I was… um…comparing the two, in order to decide which was the naughtiest…and which had made me most daring…" She bit her lip, and seemed about to offer an opinion as to relative merits, but Adela gave her a stern look. "A maid came with some tea, but I hid the letters in my bag then…and I'm sure I saw them a couple of times later, when I was looking for things.…"

Adela suppressed a sigh. She didn't want to get cross, but Sybil could be so vague. "Were they there when you left?"

"I don't know," wailed Sybil again. "It was all such a rush… I wanted to catch Algie for a few moments before we set off for the station. They might have been… I don't know. It wasn't until just now that I missed them when I looked for them."

But as Adela considered the problem, it presented a completely perplexing variety of possibilities. There had been servants all around, both the Rayworths' staff and personal servants of the many guests. Any one of them could have slipped into Sybil's room at a mealtime, or during an entertainment, and perhaps seen the traveling bag not properly fastened. Not all domestics were as loyal and trustworthy as their Lizzie and Minnie; some might always be on the lookout for things to steal, especially at big parties like the Rayworths' where it was easier to shake off the blame because nobody quite knew everybody.

It might even have been one of the guests themselves, and one possibility sprang to mind, even though in her heart, she thought it unlikely. Most unlikely.

Even if she was quite certain that Wilson had purloined her portfolio, why in heaven's name would he steal Sybil's old love letters?

BLAIR DEVINE TOYED with the pink ribbon on the little bundle of letters, preparing to untie it and sample the contents. Lord Rayworth's under house maid—Maisie, or Flossie, or Mary or whatever her name was—had assured him they were sprightly and very incautiously phrased, but one never could tell with housemaids. Sometimes they tried to pull a fast one, and the supposedly risqué and damaging correspondence they handed over was really perfectly innocuous and without value, but in this case he was fairly confident that he'd struck juicy gold.

As a solicitor Blair Devine had seen many incriminating documents in his time, and from the very first, his mind had run on ways he could leverage the sensitivity of such correspondence to his advantage. But it wasn't until he'd discovered such a bundle as this one, quite by accident, at a house party not unlike the Rayworths', that he'd turned his hand to the lucrative little matter of blackmail. It had been risibly easy to ever so diffidently suggest himself as a discreet and sympathetic intermediary, a conduit between the victim of the loss, and some completely fabricated villainous blackguard who'd come into possession of the item. And that first sum he'd managed to purloin had been so daring it had set him scheming as to how he might repeat the trick.

Slowly, and with what he thought was admirable guile, he'd built up a network, a secret web of supply and demand.

His trusted manservant had sounded out other gentlemen's gentlemen—men like Edward Foster—in pubs and in the kitchens and servants halls, at social events and house parties. Word was put about, and maids with indiscreet mistresses and little moral conscience were soon coming forward with be-ribboned bundles such as this one.

Other interesting opportunities had presented themselves too. It didn't have to be rambunctious love letters. Important legal, commercial, even political documents that weren't kept as safe as they should be started to fall into his hands. He was doing amazingly well for himself, far exceeding his modest income from the law, yet nobody suspected a thing...because nobody liked to admit they'd ever made themselves vulnerable.

And Blair Devine's reputation for discretion, and an ability to mediate successfully and avoid scandal, was impeccable.

He was perfectly confident that when the time came, that bird-brained nitwit Sybil Ruffington would think that it was all her own idea that he should help her navigate the shoals of her little difficulty regarding lost letters.

14

The Ladies' Sewing Circle

"And I'm afraid I didn't get to see the Persian etchings, after all. I never returned to the study after my little contretemps with Wilson."

It was a relief to be able to tell at least some of her story, and know that it would be received without judgment, and nothing but sympathy.

"Oh, don't worry about that, my dear," said Sofia Chamfleur, reaching over to give Adela's hand a reassuring pat. "Your drawings and sketches are perfect in their own right. You're an original…. You don't need to copy others."

Adela smiled at her friend. They were in the spacious salon of Lady Arabella Southern's London home, sitting a little way apart from the other members of the Ladies' Sewing Circle, who were clustered around Lady Arabella herself. As usual, the peeress was telling tall and extremely scandalous tales about her vigorous and somewhat unlikely love life. Among those listening avidly, only one lady, Mrs. Julia Winterbourne, was actually engaged in any needlework, although without much enthusiasm. None of the others were even paying lip service to the faux purpose of their assembly.

The Ladies' Sewing Circle really gathered to discuss men and scandal and all the juicy details of erotic amours, both their own and of high society in general.

"But I did promise…and some of the subscribers may have been looking forward to my interpretation." Adela toyed with her coffee cup, then set it aside, without any real interest.

"Think no more about it. Just make something up…. I doubt if anyone will know the difference." Sofia gave her a shrewd glance. "Now, tell us more about this run-in with your cousin. Do you really think he's taken your portfolio? Why would he do such a thing?"

Why indeed? Because he could? Because he would never take no for an answer? It was difficult to describe, even to close friends like Sofia, and Beatrice Ritchie, who sat at Adela's other side, what her relationship with her cousin was really like.

"Because I refused to show him my work. Because I refused to discuss my private life with him." Nervous, despite her resolve not to allow Wilson to vex her, she pleated a soft fold of her black gown. "Wilson is just one of those men who simply have to have their own way."

"But you like him very much, don't you?" said Beatrice Ritchie in a low voice, smiling. Her brilliant green eyes twinkled. Adela was very fond of Beatrice, and had to admit that her friend was fully conversant with the ways of men who had to have their own way. Before her marriage, Mrs. Ritchie had been courted in a highly unorthodox way by her husband… who had paid her a king's ransom to be his mistress.

"No! I don't like him at all. He's an arrogant monster."

Two sets of elegant eyebrows quirked, Sofia's dark ones and

Beatrice's, which were auburn like her hair. Adela realized she was obviously protesting too much.

"You desire him, though, don't you?" said Sofia. "That's obvious. The way your eyes flash when you talk about him, and a flush rises in your cheeks. I don't think I've ever seen that happen when you speak of any of my 'boys'…but every time we've discussed the subject of your cousin Wilson, you're all aflutter."

"Because he thoroughly annoys me."

"A man can be both annoying and deliciously desirable," observed Beatrice, "as I well know."

"Your husband adores you, Bea. He absolutely dotes on you…." This was true. Handsome Edmund Ellsworth Ritchie was well known for being the most devoted of husbands nowadays. "And Wilson simply despises me as a useless relative and a creature of inferior intellect…although in respect of the latter, that's his opinion of just about everybody."

"Well, he's a famously brilliant man, as we all know, and notably disparaging of society's foibles, but I'm sure he doesn't feel that way about you, Adela," said Sofia, pausing to sip her coffee. "How could anyone think someone as talented as you is useless? If he has your portfolio, surely he recognizes your extraordinary artistic gifts? Even if he *is* a genius…. The truly great acknowledge greatness in others, too."

If only it was that straightforward. Wilson did admire her work. He always had done. But the complex twining of their history and their familial relationship made everything that passed between them into a problem. How could cousins so very, very distant be wound up so tightly in complications?

"Oh, he's always valued my work. It's just that I don't think he values me much anymore."

She had not told her friends everything about her shared past with Wilson. They knew only that he was her cousin, that they didn't meet socially, except by accident. He was well known, too, as Lord Millingford's heir, and the beneficiary of his assets in totality because of her grandfather's hatred of her mother.

"Anymore? But you were once much closer weren't you?" Beatrice's eyes were intent. She'd spotted something Adela hadn't meant to reveal. Both ladies almost imperceptibly leaned in.

"Yes…we were. Occasionally, when we were children, our families met. And one summer, we both holidayed at the same time at Ruffington Hall." She paused, looking from one companion to the other, then beyond. Across the room, Lady Arabella had clearly said something quite outrageous, because Prudence Enderby was shrieking with laughter and the rest of the group were openmouthed and wide-eyed. Nobody would be interested in smaller revelations at the moment. "I…I did care for Wilson then. In fact, I was completely infatuated. He was—is—such a remarkable and spectacularly brilliant character…and I can't deny he's physically attractive."

"Did something occur?" probed Sofia gently. Her expression was kind, and not at all salacious, as if she sensed that there was sorrow in the tale.

Adela looked away, letting her eyes flit around the handsome room, with its decor both ostentatious and strangely cozy. Arabella Southern had a beautiful home, and this salon was far superior to the one Adela had sat with Wilson in at Rayworth Court. It made the parlor at her own home in Digby Street look like a broom cupboard. It was also far more luxurious than the library at Ruffington Hall, where she'd once cast sheep's eyes at Wilson, all those years ago.

"Yes, it did. Wilson and I were intimate. He was nineteen, and I was eighteen, and we were both willful and adept at escaping supervision. One day, one thing led to another...and we made love."

"Oh..."

"Oh, my..."

Both women were too wise, and too worldly, it seemed, to ask why she and Wilson did not immediately become engaged.

"And afterward...we argued, I fled...." Unable to stop herself, she rubbed the bridge of her nose. "And along the path I stood on a broken branch that shot up and hit me in the face."

"But that wasn't Wilson's fault...not really," said Beatrice, her expression still sympathetic.

"No, the blame was equally divided. I see that now. But at the time we were too young, too proud and too foolish to realize that." Adela dropped her hand, but somehow, her fingertip still itched to rub at the kink in her nose. "We parted without ever resolving the issue...and have continued not to resolve it to this day."

"I can see how that might make things uncomfortable for you at Rayworth Court, especially with this more recent difficulty over your grandfather and his bequests." Sofia gave Adela a level, sensible look. The other woman was not all that much older than Adela, but somehow she suddenly seemed infinitely sage and wise in the world. "But couldn't you two agree to discuss your situation? Talk like two adults? Come to some resolution...at least between yourselves, if not in respect of the familial difficulties?"

Adela laughed. Suddenly she felt almost giddy. How funny, the idea of her and Wilson sitting down for a rational discussion. The fatal pull of their bodies, and the madness of desire, made it impossible to "just talk" for very long.

"Talking isn't something that Wilson and I are very good at. When we're alone together...well, things tend to happen. Reasoned conversation almost never occurs between us."

"But surely…" began Beatrice, and then she giggled. "Oh, I see. You didn't get time to talk because…other things happened."

"Precisely." Adela shrugged. "I hadn't seen Wilson for several months, and it was seven years since we were intimate at Ruffington Hall…but within minutes of us finding ourselves alone together I was behaving like an absolute trollop, and Wilson was making the most of the situation. As is his wont." She thinned her mouth into a hard line, crosser with herself than she could ever be with him. "He was no doubt missing the beauteous Coraline, and the sensual pleasures she afforded him…and so when his cousin offered herself to him on a platter, ever the pragmatist, he sampled the goods as a form of consolation."

Sofia cocked her head and pursed her lips. "I have a feeling it wasn't like that at all, Adela. Perhaps his affair with Coraline, and any liaisons he might have enjoyed prior to her, were simply consolation for something…someone else that he'd lost?"

No! That could not be it. Wilson hadn't lost her, because he hadn't wanted her in the first place. Other than in the carnal sense, to satisfy his curiosity and to assuage his young man's lust.

And it had been the same at Rayworth Court. She'd been an answer to his physical frustrations, and perhaps an experiment. An empirical study…to measure whether the responses of the woman were as willing as the girl's had been.

"No, you're wrong, Sofia. I'm afraid that other than an occasional object of dalliance, I'm nothing to Wilson other than a trap to be avoided. He knows how much my mother wanted him to marry me, especially after our cousin Henry and his fiancée were killed, and he became heir. But he's the last man on earth who'd allow himself to be maneuvered like that—"

she shrugged "—and as a consequence, I'm the last woman on earth he'd ever want for more than a swift grope or a tumble."

Both Sofia and Beatrice gave her steady looks. They didn't believe her. But they didn't know Wilson as she did.

If only things could have been different. But they aren't. I'm me. Wilson is Wilson. We're both too stubborn, and unfortunate circumstances divide us far too much.

She opened her mouth to explain, to expatiate, and try and make them see, but just at that moment, in a swish of silk taffeta, Lady Arabella arrived and, pulling up a chair, leaned toward Adela, her face eager.

"So, what wonders does 'Isis' have for us today? Some wicked pastiches of the treasures in that old dog Rayworth's collection? Or some new, delicious delight, as yet unseen?" Mercifully, the peeress kept her voice hushed. There were newer members of the circle who were not yet quite aware of the depth of the group's true nature, let alone that one of their number was one of the most notorious erotic artists in the country.

"Nothing, alas…not today," Adela admitted, wishing she'd had time, and heart, to dash off a few new offerings, at least, with which to amuse her dear friends. "I'm afraid my portfolio was stolen over the weekend, with all my latest work in it."

Arabella's eyes widened, and she frowned. "Well, I wouldn't have thought a stuffy crowd like that would have had any interest in such things…. Surely you were the only liberal-minded guest in attendance?"

"Not the only one, obviously." Adela sighed.

The peeress reached out and took her hand, her handsome face concerned now. "If there's anything I can do, Adela, please say the word. There might be some influence one may bring to bear that could help retrieve it for you?"

"Bless you, Arabella. That's kind of you." She stiffened her spine, buoyed up by the support of her friends, even if there was not one thing they could do. "But I know exactly who took the portfolio, and when I leave here I intend to make another call and retrieve it. The person is well known to me, and I will not take no for an answer!"

Adela warmed at the chorus of "bravos" and smiles of encouragement. She *would* retrieve the portfolio, and this time she'd accept none of Wilson's nonsense.

But in that case did she still quiver, on the inside, at the prospect?

❦ 15 ❦

Into the Devil's Lair

A narrow-eyed manservant with a vaguely protective air led Adela through the ground floor of Wilson's spacious London home, a rather fine villa in Maltravers Road, in the nicer end of Chelsea. Whether the man disapproved of her or not, she really didn't care. She was on a mission. But she supposed if *that woman* had treated his master capriciously, the dour young man perhaps viewed all her sex with an air of suspicion.

It was an odd residence. Used to dwelling in a home full of furniture, knickknacks, photographs and all manner of collected mementos, Adela found the Spartan yet vaguely aesthetic quality of Wilson's house a surprise. The entrance hall was almost bare, apart from one spindly but elegant table and a narrow mirror, and there were but two simple Japanese prints on the wall. Passing what was clearly a series of electrical light fittings set into the wall, she followed the thin, dark-haired servant as he led her length of the airy hall, then along an equally plainly decorated corridor, to knock on a white painted door at the end of it.

"Come!" called out Wilson's familiar voice from beyond, and Adela was shown in.

The room she entered could not have been more different.

An immense, glass-ceilinged area, it was a palace of clutter, crammed with a cornucopia of "things" that defied her classification on first glance, and probably still would on closer inspection. It was hard to tell whether she was in a workroom, a study, a conservatory, a day room or a library, or some kind of general space where all the artifacts and possessions that might normally have been spread throughout a house were stored, along with those of a magician, an alchemist and an engineer. And it was all haphazard, scattered about, in a perfect jumble.

The single most apt description of it might well be a "lair."

And as it all belonged to Wilson, she suspected that despite the apparent disorder, he knew exactly where every last item resided, and could put his hand on each thing within a heartbeat.

The man himself was standing before a large blackboard on an easel, staring intently at a surface covered with so many equations it was more white than black, and for several seconds he didn't even turn around.

"Miss Adela Ruffington, sir," the manservant said, spare and solemn, and Wilson spun around, tossing a piece of chalk in the general direction of the groove where other pieces lay. It missed and went skittering and rolling into a corner of the room.

"Della, what a delightful surprise." Wilson surged forward energetically, the panels of yet another dressing gown fluttering about him. This one was rather drab for him, a dullish gray-brown the color of a mouse adorned by several dabs of chalk dust here and there. He took her gloved hand in his and drew it to his lips, kissing it assertively through the thin kid leather. In her mind's eye, Adela could see his servant's eyebrows lifting behind her.

"Hello, Wilson," she said coolly, on the point of wrenching back her hand when he finally released it. His pale eyes were dancing, already full of mischief, and she'd been in the room only a moment. His cool, detached demeanor from Rayworth Court seemed to have vaporized.

"Do sit down. Will you take tea?" He gestured toward a sofa, set by the longest window facing the garden. It was covered in newspapers, but he swept them aside and onto the floor, to join a variety of other papers and documents. His manservant swooped in, retrieved them and folded them, and set them on a nearby worktable. "Or perhaps coffee? I mostly take coffee." Wilson hovered, clearly waiting for her to sit.

Adela wasn't entirely sure she wanted to sit. Being off her feet in Wilson's presence made her feel vulnerable, and she was vulnerable enough to him already with her precious drawings in his possession. Finally, though, she subsided, arranging the black barathea skirt of her sensible walking costume carefully as she settled. "Coffee would be very pleasant, thank you."

"Teale, coffee, if you please."

Teale sped silently away, closing the door behind him and leaving Adela alone in a room full of arcane mystery and gilded light, faced with a Wilson who was smiling in triumph.

"I knew we'd see each other again soon. I told you it wasn't over."

Straight to business then? Well, after Wilson's fashion...

Adela knew she had to get a direct answer out of him, both in respect to the portfolio and maybe even the letters, but the glitter in his eyes and the overpowering sense of disgustingly male self-assurance that he exuded were already enough to make her want to punch him in the nose.

Either that or give in to the urge to hurl herself at him, to kiss him and touch him and a good deal more than that.

It was barely more than a day or so since she'd last seen him, yet to her chagrin she realized she'd also really missed him. Even in his dressing gown, with his shirt in dishabille and missing its collar, and yes, wearing his carpet slippers, he still looked so devilishly attractive he was almost edible.

His dark curls were slightly awry, as usual, as if he'd been running his fingers through them as he'd grappled with a knotty problem. Untidy as his hair was, it imbued him with an almost angelic quality, like Mercury from Botticelli's *Primavera,* or a Renaissance princeling come to life in the modern world. Adela could almost imagine Wilson posing for such a work, in the manner of classical statuary, wearing a laurel wreath in those black locks and not a lot else. He certainly had the body for artistic modeling, although certain portions of it were far too abundant to be contained by the standard fig leaf.

Good grief, Adela, what is the matter with you? You shouldn't be sitting here imagining Wilson naked. Get to business, woman. Retrieve what you came to retrieve, and effect your escape.

"Well, I don't know what you think *it* is, Wilson, but if there ever was anything, it is most certainly over now," she said, rushing out the words as she realized she'd been daydreaming and Wilson was eyeing her suspiciously. "I won't beat around the bush. I'm sure you know exactly why I'm here, and I'd like my belongings back immediately, if you don't mind. And then I won't trouble you any further."

"Whatever are you talking about, Della?" The devil! His expression was so provocative. He was playing with her again, like a sleek dark cat with a mouse, punishing her purely for entertainment. "And surely you're not going to leave without sampling Teale's coffee? He makes a rare brew, and he'll be hurt if you don't at least try one cup."

Despite Wilson's vexing and befuddling behavior, the prospect of good coffee was ridiculously tempting. Mama didn't often serve coffee, as she claimed it was too exciting to the senses of young ladies, and bad for the constitution, but Adela adored the powerful beverage. Sofia Chamfleur always had the most delicious French coffee on hand, and that was where Adela had gained her taste for it. The beverage Lady Southern served had also been adequate, and had only primed Adela's longing.

"One cup, then. And stop being evasive. Please give me my portfolio back. I know you purloined it somehow while we were at the Rayworths'. And I'd also like anything else belonging to my family that you might have lifted."

Wilson frowned and Adela's stomach dropped. She'd hoped against hope. They'd been such long odds, but she knew from his face he hadn't taken the letters.

"Well, you have me bang to rights, cousin, in respect of the portfolio. I broke into your room and your carpet bag and took it, I admit that." He shrugged. "But on my life, I didn't take anything else. I promise you, Della. Believe me. I had a hankering to take one of your shifts, as a fetish object to fondle when you're not near...but I managed to resist that temptation."

Heat flashed through Adela's body. She didn't need to be told what Wilson would have planned for her shift. Gentlemen's foibles and peccadilloes were the premier topic of conversation and amusement among the ladies of the Sewing Circle, and she could easily picture Wilson naked on his bed, rubbing her garment against his loins.

Enough of that! Sybil's letters!

"You swear that's all you took?"

"I do swear it, Della. Why, what else has gone missing? Something of yours? Something precious?" He laid his hand on her arm, his expression intent, but suddenly more serious. "Tell me, and I'll do what I can to help you retrieve it."

She believed him. He was a curious conundrum of a man, precocious and arrogant in some ways, but fundamentally worthy in others. If it were possible to tell him, she had no doubt he would help. But the fewer people who knew about Sybil's indiscretions, the better.

"It's nothing. Nothing of importance. One loses things all the time."

His silver-gray eyes narrowed, but he seemed to accept that. "So…" he murmured, sliding his palm down her arm, then taking her hand and removing her bag from her grip and setting it aside. That done, he plucked at her right glove, easing it off, then followed with the other, tossing them after the bag. Adela tried to shake him off, but somehow she couldn't resist when he enfolded both of her hands in his.

"Don't try to bamboozle me, Wilson. I came here for my portfolio, nothing else. What happened between us in the country was an aberration only. It won't happen again."

"Is that a fact?" Not looking at her face, Wilson examined her hands as if they were rare artifacts, tracing his fingers over one palm, then the other. "How do you propose to induce me to return your drawings to you, then? Have you suddenly become versed in safe-cracking in addition to all your other talents?" Still smiling, he nodded to something she hadn't noticed before—an enormous strongbox in the corner of the room. It was painted green, massive and impenetrable, with what looked like a numbered dial next to the keyhole. Some kind of advanced technological lock?

"Is that where you keep all the items you've stolen from ladies? If so, you must be a considerable robber." Indeed, it was an exceptionally large safe. She supposed he must keep the mechanical designs that he worked on for the government, and for wealthy clients, inside it.

"No, alas not. I have no provocative treasures in there, other than yours. But I do have other items of value. Certain blueprints and specifications. Secret projects for the government and for various captains of industry. All priceless if they get into the wrong hands."

Just as she'd expected.

"I don't doubt it. But I can't see why you would secrete my portfolio among such treasures. It isn't priceless at all, except to me."

His fingers tightened around hers. "It has great value to me…as trade goods." He conveyed her right hand to his lips and kissed the palm slowly, in that lascivious way he'd employed so effectively back at Rayworth Hall.

Adela fought against a shudder of desire. So that was his game? She didn't know whether she was appalled or excited. Probably both, and in equal parts. This close to Wilson, her body had a rebellious streak that defied all her qualms and her outrage. Already, everything was stirring, heating, hungering, growing desirous of the pleasures he'd provoked in it so recently…and for more, oh, dear, *so* much more.

No!

Adela stiffened her spine. Snatched back her hand from him.

"Why would you say something like that, Wilson? Can't you accept my decision?" She cast around for her gloves and bag, but somehow he'd kicked them away. She had to go, but how to get the portfolio before she went? "I'm not prepared to be some kind of perverse erotic experiment for you. You can keep the drawings. I don't care…. They don't incriminate me, and I doubt if the subjects themselves are concerned. They might even increase in popularity. Expand their clientele…"

Wilson pursed his lips, his face twisting as if he'd tasted

something unpleasant. Or as if he was compelled to do something he didn't want to.

"You do realize that this man brothel your friend runs is far from legal?" His glinting eyes narrowed. "I have friends in the judiciary, Della…and friends in low places, too. I've a shrewd idea of the parties involved, and it would be a simple matter to inform the appropriate authorities. My word would be taken, believe me. And with supporting evidence." He nodded toward the safe, and the pictures within.

Angry to start with, Adela boiled with red rage. Her hand flew up to strike him, but he snatched ahold of it again, his grip implacable.

"You are despicable and hideous, Wilson. How could you threaten such a thing? What have any of…of my friends ever done to you? Have you never heard of live and let live?"

"Indeed I have, Della, indeed I have." His hand tightened, containing her, and when she attempted to land a blow with the other, he grabbed that, too. "It's a maxim I normally espouse wholeheartedly." His fingers were locks on her wrists. "But not if it's a case of you preferring to take your pleasure with naked gigolos, such as the gentlemen you've drawn so magnificently, instead of me. In that event you drive me to the most extreme and ruthless of measures. I can't help myself."

Snagging both her wrists in one hand, he took her by the shoulder with the other and brought her face to his. "Let me touch you, Della, or let your friends suffer the consequences."

WHAT ON EARTH *is the matter with me? This is abominable. Why am I behaving like a monster?*

The look on Adela's face made Wilson want to enfold her in his arms and say that he was sorry and that he'd never dream of doing something so vile and reprehensible.

The whole situation was absurd, and he the most absurd

thing about it. He *did* care about Adela, as much as he believed himself capable of caring about anyone, and as a person who believed himself enlightened, he should have been
the last man to deny a woman the chance to fulfill herself in
whatsoever way she chose.

Yet, faced with her, he was primitive. A savage beating his
chest and roaring with defiance over his "possession."

Those drawings. Those men. They'd pleasured her. They'd
fulfilled her. Handsome faces and handsome bodies. Clever
hands that had touched her intimately, and with far more skill
than he'd ever wielded on their own first encounter, seven
years ago.

They'd made her cry out in ecstasy, made those eyes that
were spitting fire at him now go blank with lust, and the
thought of that made him boil up, incapable of rational, reasonable thought.

He *had* to make her forget them, and to do so he had to
blot them out by exceeding anything they'd done.

*Because you've blotted out Coraline for me, Della. One brief in-
terlude and you completely negated her, the woman I once thought I
might marry.*

That was another thorn in his primeval paw. Without even
trying, Adela had reduced what he'd idiotically believed was
the grand passion of his life to little more than a forgettable
folly.

"Very well, then, have me!" she all but growled at him, not
even blinking. She was panting, though. With anger? Or was
it desire? Her shapely lips were parted, the lower one moist.
She was so succulent he wanted to devour her.

Just as he pressed forward, so did she. Their mouths met
as if they were perfectly engineered to engage. He gasped
when her tongue pressed immediately between his lips and
his teeth, seeking his.

Goddamn, she'd ever been the pragmatist. Now she was going to wring the best out of him in the course of achieving her goal. If he hadn't already been kissing her, he'd have laughed out loud. *Bravissima!*

He let her master his tongue, loving the fight in her. She was caught in his hold, and fully aware of his greater strength and his particular skills in subduing an opponent, but still she defied him. Vanquished him, even though he was the one with her hands captured tight.

His cock was an iron bar, aching and agonized.

Right. Now. I can't wait.

But as he released her, and moved to take her in his arms to woo her rather than commandeer her, a sharp rap on the door made him curse into her mouth.

Goddamn the bloody coffee!

Adela froze. Oh, no, Teale was here with the coffee. It should have been a relief, the way that stopped Wilson completely in his tracks, but instead it was a frustration.

"Come!" called out Wilson again, and the door swung open. Teale took the tray from a small table in the corridor and strolled in, placing the fragrant coffeepot and all its accoutrements on a map chest just to Wilson's right.

"Will there be anything else, sir?" The servant's voice was silky. Did he suspect his master of having an assignation with this mysterious woman in black who'd never visited him before? There was no twinkle in Teale's bland eye, but who knew?

"No, nothing, thank you, Teale. I'll not need you or any of the other servants for the rest of the day. Simply tell cook to prepare cold cuts on a tray, and leave it in the dining room. You can all take a trip to the music hall, if you wish. Use the money from the household kitty and I'll reimburse it tomorrow."

"Thank you, sir." The servant did smile then, but as if with simple pleasure in the kindness of his master. His step seemed lighter as he left the room and closed the door.

What are you doing, Wilson? Emptying the house so we won't be disturbed.

Adela's belly trembled, not in alarm, but with excitement.

"So? Clearing the house so you can have your way with me?"

Wilson regarded her out of the corner of his eye while he attended to the coffee. "Yes, precisely that. Why, have you changed your mind?"

Had she? In her heart and soul, she really didn't think he'd do anything to threaten Sofia and her establishment, but still, there was a niggling suspicion inside her that he might have changed since his days as the provocative but high-minded youth she'd once adored. Life might have soured his principles over the years, so she had to give herself to him to be sure.

You're making excuses for yourself, Della. Why lie? You want him…you want pleasure, and you're entitled to take what you want for yourself. It might be a secret, but you're an emancipated woman.

"Not in the slightest. Shall I disrobe now?" She plucked at her hat, sliding out the pins and removing it, then stabbing them back in before flinging it in the general direction of an armchair. Not even bothering to see if it had found its target, she started on the buttons down the front of her bodice.

Wilson stayed her hand.

"Much as I'd like to see your delectable body, Della, do drink your coffee first. It's rather good and you'll find it invigorating."

Her fingers stilled, buttons unfastened to the lace-trimmed edge of her chemise beneath. She was trussed up today, corset and all. Mama always objected stridently if Adela attempted to leave the house in her rational apparel, despite tolerating it—under protest—in the confines of home.

"Why, is it loaded with exotic aphrodisiacs to make me pliant?"

Wilson laughed, handing her a small cup, then offering the cream jug. Adela nodded, accepting a little, but refusing sugar.

"No, but if you want a love potion, I can easily make one up for you," he replied. "There are a number of herbs and compounds most efficacious on that score."

"Is there anything you can't make, brew, design or imagine? It's as if you fancy yourself a modern da Vinci with your cornucopia of knowledge."

"I simply use the gifts bestowed on me, Della. Just as you do yours." He sipped his own beverage unadulterated, no cream or sugar. "The gift of drawing and the arts of sensuality."

"They're all I have," she said simply, tasting the dark rich coffee. It was so devastatingly strong that it almost made her eyes water, but also delicious, and as predicted, invigorating.

"Not so," countered Wilson. "Generosity, kindness, intelligence and loyalty. You have those qualities, and others, in abundance. And they're probably far more valuable, ultimately, than simply being too clever for one's own good."

Adela almost reared back, shocked by the unexpected sincerity, and self-deprecation, of Wilson's words. Did he mean it?

"You think I'm lying to you, don't you? Sweetening you up for the kill."

"It's crossing my mind." She sipped more of the robust coffee; it seemed more essential than ever to command her wits.

Wilson drained his cup and set it aside. "I want to fuck you, Della, obviously. And to do other things. But that doesn't mean I can't be honest about my general regard for you." In a swirl of silk dressing gown he rose and strode across to the safe.

Adela finished her coffee, set the cup aside and leaned out to watch Wilson's fingers dancing over the numbered dial. He spun it this way and that without even glancing at it, his head cocked to one side. It seemed as if he was listening to it, but that he didn't need to look. After barely a moment or two, he swung open the heavy door and drew out her portfolio.

"It seems superfluous to give it back now," Adela said as he strolled forward and put it into her hands. "You have other leverage to exert over me."

"Very true." Wilson's silvery eyes were sharp, assessing. "But I thought you'd like it back all the same. Will you check to see that all is present and untampered with?"

Adela's fingers shook as she negotiated the tapes that fastened the leather folder. Heat flooded her body as she thought of what she'd see. Wilson had seen them, too, and likely speculated and brooded, imagining her with the men she'd portrayed.

Lionel. Clarence. Handsome, mischievous Yuri. Why did she suddenly wish she'd never lain with them?

Anger boiled. She was *entitled* to her pleasure, entitled to frolic with her handsome, well-formed friends, and seek oblivion in their arms. Wilson had taken pleasure with women, and the sumptuous Coraline was not the only one.

I'm a New Woman. I can take what I want.

Adela flipped open the cover and this time she did rear back, despite trying to hide it.

The drawing at the top was superbly rendered, perfect in proportion and every detail of anatomy, as well as breathtakingly lewd and specific.

And it wasn't one of hers.

~ 16 ~

A Practical Arrangement

"You drew this." She didn't ask. She didn't have to. She was sitting beside the most accomplished draftsman she'd ever met.

"Yes. I was inspired by *your* work."

What she saw seemed to have more in common with the naughty drawings that had been done for the praxinoscope reel. A man was spanking a woman, his hand caught in flight, speeding down toward her vulnerable flesh, although in Wilson's world, both parties were participating in the game completely naked, and posed like a god and goddess from Greek mythology. The woman knelt on a couch—not unlike the one on which Adela and Wilson were sitting—with her sleek bottom offered to the gentleman behind her. The most delicate of cross-hatching indicated that he'd already been at her, and if the work had been tinted there would have been a patch of pink.

Adela leaned in closer. The detail was preternaturally fine, almost as if it had been drawn under a microscope. The spanked woman's hair was draped over one shoulder, to show her profile, her throat and her bosom, and on closer inspection, she wasn't completely naked. Around her throat was something readily familiar.

The Ruffington diamonds.

When Adela saw the necklace, she saw a lot of other things, too. The woman's hair was dark and thick, and her profile wasn't the pristine, harmonious line of an Aphrodite or a Helen of Troy. Her nose was slightly kinked. Only a little, though, not nearly so much as the real nose it was no doubt meant to depict. The artist's hand was kinder than a certain unforgiving tree branch.

The man, too, sported a familiar look when studied more closely. His hair was wild and dark, and his body exceptionally lean, though poetic in its power. Hazily sketched in behind his athletic form was a dressing gown, laid across a chair.

"Well, if the technological consultancy ever runs dry, and you ever run out of ideas and inventions to sell, Wilson, you could make your living drawing for a certain magazine I know called *Divertissements*." She cocked her head, still studying the drawing. "Although you might like to make everything just a little less perfect. People are flawed and have small quirks of appearance. They aren't immaculate constructions in alabaster."

"I'm used to drawing diagrams, not people, and adhering to very fine tolerances. But I suppose I could learn to be a bit more slapdash, if it were required."

"Oh, so you think my work slapdash, then?" Adela set the drawing aside and found a couple more examples of Wilson's work, variations on the same theme, only showing the couple posed in different parts of this very same room. In one, the man—Wilson, why avoid the obvious—was right behind his paramour, his erect cock almost touching her as she lay prone, facedown over the large map chest. His hand was raised to spank, but his member looked as if it was finding its way to a target of its own, although which orifice, it was impossible to determine.

"I never said your work was slapdash," said Wilson, reaching over and stacking his work to one side, to reveal Adela's. She blushed on seeing a very full-blooded and decidedly unslap-dash study of Yuri reclining on a daybed, fondling his cock, his eyes closed, near ecstatic. "Did you fuck him when you'd finished this?" Wilson added, flicking the study aside to expose another one, of Lionel this time, sitting on a chair, legs akimbo, member rampant. "And him?"

"No, of course not!" Adela snapped the portfolio shut and placed her hands flat upon it. "Work is work and…play is play. And I often draw entirely from memory, or even imagination, you know that."

Wilson reached over, slid the folder from beneath her hands with barely any effort at all. Was he going to insist on reviewing everything? It seemed not, though. He set the thing aside.

"If I were the one posing, would you be able to resist then?"

No! No, I wouldn't….

"You're too busy and industrious ever to have time to spend lolling around stark naked long enough to be drawn."

It was true. Adela had often wondered how he'd had the time to spend cavorting with Coraline, a famous sybarite and not known for any kind of productive or industrious activities. Had his scientific and technological consultations suffered from the liaison? Was that one of the reasons they'd parted, aside from the Italian duke?

"Ah, but even the most productive scientist or inventor needs to rest sometimes." Wilson slanted her a look, his pale eyes sultry. "Sometimes a short period of repose, followed by an orgasm, can be most energizing. Don't you find that,

Della? Do you do your best work when you've diddled your-self...or been fucked?"

"Don't be stupid, Wilson."

He had a point, though. Release did revivify. She always felt lighter in spirit and had more zest when she'd spent.

"I'm not being stupid. I'm being rational." He reached across suddenly and began unfastening the buttons of her bodice, taking up where she'd left off. "If you must continue to draw such esoterica for your paying customers, Della, I'm offering myself as a model, instead of these men. And I'll save you a considerable expense, too.... I'll fuck you for free."

Adela's mouth dropped open. In her mind's eye, she saw it. Herself doing drawing after drawing of Wilson's splendid body...then afterward, writhing in pleasure beneath that same body, naked, on this couch.

It was outrageous. But it was also, as he'd pointed out, com-pletely rational.

"Don't you see what a practical arrangement it is, Della?" he went on when she was unable to answer him. His fingers were still at work on her buttons, and a second later her bod-ice was fully open to reveal her underclothes. "We both get something we want. Nobody has to take risks. Nobody has to waste time doing the absurd courtship dance just to get the physical satisfaction they need." Plucking at her dress, he began to push it off over her shoulders, and without think-ing, Adela assisted him. It was like a dream.

"You make it all sound so clinical. So scientific."

But as Wilson worked on her underbodice, it was far from clinical. She shuddered finely, the tips of her breasts tingling as she anticipated the moment when he finally breached all her layers. She wanted to rend her clothing like a madwoman, expose herself to him and be free. Petticoats, corset, che-mise, the whole lot oppressed her. How delicious it would be to work in this room, sketching and drawing, wearing only loose, light, rational gowns...and nothing else. Then, when lust gripped her, she could simply fling the thing off, mount Wilson...and ride him.

"There's nothing clinical about this." His fingers drifted over the exposed skin of her chest, then dipped into the shallow cleft between her breasts, where they were pushed up by her corset. It was such a slight touch, but Adela almost growled, it stirred her so. Impatient, she knocked away his hands and attacked the next layer.

It was broad daylight in a room that was almost half windows, yet she wanted to be completely naked and unfettered. As she fumbled with buttons and hooks, Wilson slid to his knees and unfastened her boots. Within moments he was sliding his hands up her legs under her skirts, then tweaking down her garters and the stockings they held up.

"Yes...yes..." he said, his deep voice exultant as he ran his hands up and down her naked legs. Adela parted her thighs, hoping to entice his wanderings through the vent in her drawers, but instead, he stood up and pulled her to her feet. So he could attack the fastenings of her petticoats.

Within a moment, she was stepping out of them, only for Wilson to kick them away across the carpet.

"You look very bonny in your corset, Della...but I want to see you nude again. It's been so long." His nimble fingers flew to the hooks down the front of her corset, uncoupling a few. "Adorable," he said, inserting a hand beneath the boning, and inside the fine lawn shift beneath so he could cradle her breast.

It was another slight touch, but the heat in his fingers made her gasp. The nipple he laid his thumb against was already peaked, aching hard, and as he lightly flicked it, a delicious, voluptuous welling sensation between her legs bore witness to her wetness, her lusty flow. When he pinched her teat, her clitoris seemed to throb with a life all its own.

"Don't savage your lip again, Della. Groan if you need to…. You've never been silent in your pleasures. Please don't hold back now."

He beleaguered her nipple again and a sob broke from her lips. If only he would touch her between her legs now. If only…

Adela's eyes shot open. To the devil with "if only." Reaching down, she slid her own hand into the vent of her drawers, searching for her center.

"You're a wicked girl, Della." Wilson brought his face close to hers, and she smelled coffee and a spicy exotic shaving lotion. Probably yet another thing he'd concocted for himself. "If you touch yourself, I'll be forced to spank you, you know that, don't you?"

"But you want to spank me, anyway," countered Della. Why draw a spanking scene, and show her it, if he didn't want to enact one?

"You know me well, cousin." He kissed the side of her face and she could feel him smiling, even as she rummaged in her linen, impatient to find her clitoris.

"It's not difficult. You drew me a picture, you fool— Oh!"

As she pressed her most sensitive place, he tweaked her breast again.

"Oh! Oh! Oh!" Her sex rippled, not quite climaxing, but almost…almost…

Grabbing her wrist, Wilson wrenched her hand away quite forcefully. There was a silvery fire in his eyes. A thread of fear wound through Adela's desire. Full grown, Wilson was far wilder than the boy he'd once been, but the sense of risk made him ever more exciting.

"Enough with the prevarication." Holding her wrist firm

with one hand, he pinched her nipple again with the other. She could have hit him and wriggled away, but she didn't. And when he released her, she renewed their struggle with the fastenings of her corset.

"Here…wait a moment." Wilson produced his ubiquitous penknife from his pocket, opening the silver cylinder with an arcane twist. Then, reaching over and behind her, he sliced her corset laces in a swift movement. "Don't worry, I'll lend you some string if you must put the stupid thing on again afterward."

As the corset started to slip, he sliced again at the laces until it was completely free, then flung it toward the ever-growing heap of her discarded clothing. Then, with rough, jerky, impatient movements, he pulled off her chemise and unfastened her drawers, compelling her to step out of the latter.

He moved away and perused her. Eyes narrowed, he was both draughtsman and libertine, and Adela's skin was instantly awash with raging heat. Perspiration gathered in her armpits and her groin, and looking down, she could see a blush of pink across her chest.

Her fingers seemed to burn, too, alight with the urge to touch her sex again. But this time she resisted the compulsion. Fondling herself while naked would be far too lewd… and yet somehow, she knew Wilson would shortly ask her to do it, or perhaps *order* her sooner or later.

He stepped toward her again, standing so close that the silk of his dressing gown floated against her breasts, her belly and her thighs in a tantalizing infinitesimal caress. Slowly, he pressed a soft kiss to her lips, barely stroking their seam with the tip of his tongue. Then, as he probed for entrance, she felt his hands come up on either side of her, to her hair. Unfastening and unwinding it, then tossing away the pins, he let the thick, slippery weight slide over her shoulders like a cape.

Her own arms had no strength and she couldn't move them. They hung inert at her sides, constrained by his will.

Wilson dug his fingers into the thick tresses of her liberated hair, gripping her head and holding her while his mouth plundered hers far more voraciously now. Adela shuddered right down to her toes, drenched in the overpowering licentiousness of being completely naked in this high, sunlit room, locked in the power of this most beautiful, dangerous man.

As Wilson drew back, still holding her face, her sex overflowed and silky fluid slid down her leg. The way he breathed in, and then smiled, told her he'd smelled her.

"You're a very carnal woman, Della. A creature of the senses. I wonder how many men in society would believe you lead a secret life when they see you so prim and composed in your black gowns, and with your quiet manner?" He breathed in again, then slid his tongue around his lips as if tasting the air. "You hide your true self so well. You act the respectable, dutiful young woman and yet your appetites are as voluptuous as any courtesan's."

He slid a hand down her body and cupped her between the legs, squeezing. Adela gasped, and fought for composure. "Men in society don't often look at me, Wilson. Because of the sober dress I choose, and the fact I don't put myself forward, and because my looks are indifferent."

"Well, they're all fools, and I should beat *you* for being so willful and deliberately obtuse, you witch. Always persisting in this claim you're not beautiful. I swear you only do it to make me feel guilty because you ran from me." He gripped again, and Adela tossed her head, bearing down, riding his fingers. "And who needs common prettiness when they have a nature like yours?" His face was next to hers once more, and he held her close, by a hank of her hair. Still massaging her sex, he kissed her again, hard this time.

"You can't help yourself, can you?" he growled, almost into her mouth. "And yet you deny it…parade yourself as the grim, dried-up spinster, when really you're a lush and juicy libertine. I'll wager your paid-for boys think you're a beauty. I bet they can't believe their luck when you purchase their services."

Swiveling around behind her, still clasping her puss, he grabbed her by the shoulder and walked her over to a mirror that stood in the corner of the room. Adela tried to turn her head and not look. The shock of her own reflection was too much, the column of her white body blatantly displayed against Wilson's clothed form. She'd never been one for admiring herself in a glass before her nose was broken, and since then, she'd mostly avoided it unless absolutely essential.

"Look!" he ordered her, fingers under her chin, thumb cradling her jaw. "And don't try to hide yourself. Don't insult me by hiding yourself."

She snapped her eyes open, peered at herself framed by Wilson's hold on her chin and her sex. His thumb and fingers divided the dark cluster of her *motte,* and she could see the muscles of his hand flexing as he worked her. Even as she writhed, her belly in a tumult of gathering lust, the detached aesthetician in her admired the juxtaposition of him and her, and stored the image for future reference.

"You're magnificent, Della, magnificent." Wilson rubbed his face in her unbound hair, like a male animal nuzzling its mate, a wild beast compelled into some kind of faux display of affection before mounting her and copulating. "You said I can have you, and I shall, but I'd like to spank you first. You have the most divine bottom…." For emphasis, he circled his hips, rubbing himself against her buttocks, butting at her with his cock, so hard inside his trousers. "I know you'll never be one of these sniveling misses who grovel to please a flagellant…but at least I can fool myself for a little while that you might submit to me." His teeth caught her earlobe and he nipped it lightly. "Even if I know you've got a spirit no man can conquer."

Adela trembled from head to foot, almost spending, but whether from Wilson's grip or his thrilling words, she did not know. His finger was hard in the groove of her sex, right up against her clitoris, and she imagined it still here while he slapped her on her bottom. Pleasure and pain. Pain and pleasure, becoming one. Enjoying a few playful spanks from the boys at Sofia's house had never stirred her like this. But with Wilson, all was different. All was real.

His finger moved. Her crisis welled. She couldn't help it. The pleasure was stolen and she knew that he'd beat her for it.

"Wicked, wicked girl." Wilson laughed, rubbing her as she pulsed. It was as if he wanted to get the orgasm over quickly so they could move on directly to the spanking. Adela's knees weakened, but he held her against him, still holding her chin. "Greedy, lewd and licentious...."

I am. All three. Even the boys at Sofia's don't realize how much.

Wilson walked her across the room to the map chest. It was a deep wide structure, and just the right height to bend a woman over, whether to smack her bottom or to fuck her soundly from behind. He nuzzled her hair again for a second, then snatched a cushion from the settee and set it over the hard edge of the chest. "There you are," he said, settling his hand at the small of her back, to urge her forward.

The odd little moment of solicitude confused her. Wilson could be so unexpected. Arrogant, selfish and willful one minute, capable of sweet kindness and consideration the next. Adela's eyes prickled a little as she laid herself across the surface of the chest. So many years had been wasted because she'd kept herself away, unbending, and resisted the challenge of his complexity.

The intricately patterned inlaid wood was cool beneath her cheek, and her arms, where she circled them around her head. Against her breasts, though, it pressed hard, chafing the aching points of her nipples. The cushion protected her pubis, but she almost wished it wasn't there. The urge to grind herself against something hard was unbearable. Surreptitiously, she shifted her hips.

"Uh-oh… Naughty, naughty! I know what you're about." Wilson's palm pressed on the small of her back again. "Keep still, my randy madam, keep still."

Holding her firm with one hand, he began an exploration with the other, sliding his fingers over her thighs and buttocks, investigating both the curves and indentations. Adela's face flamed with embarrassment, even though she'd expected this trial and wanted it. When Wilson squeezed one cheek of her bottom and then pressed its soft contour sideways, opening the cleft, she moaned out loud.

"You like that, don't you?" He bent over her, his voice rough yet breathy in her ear. "Don't you?" he persisted more forcefully, as he put both hands to her rump to manipulate her. Pulling apart the lobes, he exposed the tiny vent, then leaned over it, blowing his warm breath on it and making her shudder wildly.

"One day I'll have you there, Della. I'll take you and I'll plow you, right up to my balls in your gorgeous backside." He dropped a kiss on first one cheek and then the other. "But not today, my sweet… Today is for spanking and servicing your cunt in the standard manner."

"Well, that's very civilized of you, Wilson." The robust words he'd used thrilled her, even while the threat of sodomy made her heart pound. That was something she'd never done, never wanted. But now a dark imp whispered, "What would it be like?" One or two of the more risqué ladies of the circle seemed rather keen on backdoor pleasure, and proclaimed it sovereign as a way to fuck and not conceive.

"Yes, I think so," Wilson replied jauntily, and as he straightened up, he shrugged out of his dressing gown as if stripping for action. Out of the corner of her eye, Adela saw it float away across the room. He really was the most untidy of men, and didn't seem to put anything anywhere if there was the slightest opportunity to throw it on the floor.

Straining, she followed his small movements of preparation. Rolling up his sleeves. Unfastening another button or two of his shirt. Even cracking his knuckles, the devil.

"Right, my dearest voluptuary…just a few licks to warm you up." His hands were on her rump again, measuring, testing.

"Don't you think I'm warm enough? I seem rather hot already." She did feel overheated and sweaty, her skin almost sticking to the smooth surface of the map chest.

"You are hot, beautiful, Della, a furnace of temptation, and I'm eager to burn."

As she opened her mouth to tell him he spoke nonsense, as usual, the first blow fell, a slow, lazy spank that landed hard against the underside of her bottom.

Heavens, how it stung, how it stirred her. One little tap and she *was* a furnace, the embers of her pleasure instantly rousing. He slapped again, and she yelped, moving helplessly, her body craving more, so much more. More of his touch, more of his energy, more of him.

Blows fell, burning, sizzling…and yet in a certain way, she barely felt them. They were but a precursor to the real act she craved. The act for which she'd been yearning for seven long years, despite all her caprices with Sofia's accommodating gentlemen.

Adela parted her thighs, lifting herself, flaunting herself.

Take me, Wilson. Possess my body. Make me yours, if only for today.

It was madness. This…this hysteria for him. He was a peril to her, to her heart…to her body, too. With a shock, she admitted the danger, yet knew she must embrace it.

"Enough, Wilson! I can't wait. Fuck me now."

"My, aren't we the impatient one? Shouting for service. Is this the way you conduct yourself at the man brothel?" Wilson's hand stilled on her bottom, fingertips pressing, stirring the ache there, and the other, inner ache.

"Damn you. Stop taunting me," she gasped, still rocking. "If you won't do the business, I'll leave. I'll put my clothes on, hail a carriage and take myself to the wretched 'man brothel' and get what I want. With what's in my portfolio, my credit will be good, an all-time high."

"No, you will not go." The words were hard, cold, like wrought iron. His hands were hard, too, holding her shoulder now, and her burning bum. He was indomitable, immovable. More thrilling than ever. "Stay exactly where you are." Then the pressure was gone, and he was stomping away across the room.

Adela trembled, in chaos, listening to the sound of him dragging open a drawer in a bureau, and searching within it. As he returned, she craned to look over her shoulder and saw he had a small tin in his hand. It was of a size and shape well known to her, and even though thought of its contents had slipped her mind, she almost gasped with relief and recognition.

"Yes, I use them, too. I always have. Except just once…but then, you were there, so you'd know that."

Had he really? Most men barely knew of the existence of prophylactics, and if they did, eschewed them for reasons of expense or inconvenience. After all, it was the woman who got with child…and as to *other* consequences, well, so many thought only with their cocks, not their brains.

But Wilson was ever different. No doubt he'd read a paper or a report somewhere, and decided scientifically on the most prudent course of action. He might be behaving like a wild man now, but with him, the intellect was always foremost.

"That's very forward thinking of you, cousin. Now please proceed."

He came up very close beside her, as if wishing to assure her he was going to use a device. Adela rolled onto her side, unable to look away as he unfastened his trousers, fumbled with his shirttail and drawers, and drew out his cock.

This was substance, not shadow. Faced with Wilson in all his glory, Adela found the energetic boys at Sofia's house paled to insignificance, even though she'd admired all their handsome organs at the time, and taken pleasure in them. As before, at Rayworth Court, when she was with Wilson, only *his* cock seemed to exist. Fanciful as it seemed, his member set the standard of excellence for all others, so thick and eager and rosy. The artist in her protested when he clothed the length in a coat of fine rubber. "My own formulation," he remarked, adjusting the fit. "I sold it to the manufacturer for shares in the company. It's bringing in a considerable profit and growing by the day. All the more satisfying for the knowledge that I'm promoting health, too.…"

Adela almost choked with laughter. Only Wilson could reason this way at the very moment before penetration.

"Where do you get yours?" His voice was low as he leaned over, pressing his rubber-coated cock against her tender haunch and making her hiss.

"My friend gets them from France, surprisingly enough."

Wilson swirled his hips, rubbing himself against her as if savoring the heat in her skin through the prophylactic. "Good…

that's excellent. The French-manufactured ones are generally far superior to the ordinary English product."

Rolling her onto her front again, he continued to massage himself against her. It was hard not to moan at the fires he stoked. Adela found herself biting her lip again, desperate to touch herself. She was just about to do it, Wilson be damned, when he reached around and beneath her, burying his fingers in her fleece and finding her center.

He rubbed her briefly, and a little roughly, but it was still wonderful, reigniting her pleasure. It seemed that, like the most experienced gigolo, he was devoted to ensuring his partner's delight as well as his own. Adela supposed that was one of the reasons Coraline had taken up with him, until the financial and titular benefits of her Italian nobleman had proved more tempting than simple physical pleasure.

"Oh, Della, Della," Wilson breathed against her hair, nuzzling it again as he readjusted their positions across the chest. Grasping her tingling thigh, he lifted it, opening her up, making her ready. Then, guiding his flesh with his fingers, he found her entrance.

Oh, Wilson! she wanted to cry, but the words wouldn't form. He was there, the thick head of his cock touching her, nudging, probing. With a hitch of his hips, he pushed in a little way.

"There, do you feel me? Do you welcome me home?" He pushed again, a bit more of him pressing in. Adela wanted to scream at him to drive in to the hilt. Strange as his harsh muttering might be, it did feel as if something beloved and familiar had come back to her.

"Yes…yes, of course I do, Wilson. You're not an insubstantial man, and you know that. So why ask?" Her own words were harsh, but had to be. Otherwise, she might reveal too much, to herself as well as to the man possessing her.

Another inch. It felt like a yard. Intellectually, she knew

that was nonsense, but her perceptions were with her heart and soul and flesh, not her brain.

"Good. I want you to feel me properly. To feel *me* and *know* it's me, and no other."

He forged in a little farther, but still not fully. He was taunting her, compelling her to comprehend every fraction as it entered, so that the slow introduction would expunge all memory of any other man.

She jerked her hips, pushing back against him, compelling him this time. With her inner musculature, she gripped him hard, squeezing his cock with her body to impose herself on him as he imposed on her.

"You witch…you witch! You'll unman me with those tricks."

She gripped again, feeling a faint ripple of response along the length inside her.

"Do you want me to come off before you do, Della? Is that really what you want? To make me your slave again as I was before, defenseless against you?"

Defenseless? He'd never been defenseless. It had always been the other way around.

"You, you're the one with tricks. Don't give me half measures. Stop taunting me, you beast," she muttered.

Wilson didn't answer. He just shoved. Hard. All the way in.

Adela howled. Lord be praised. At last. Grinding her hips, she pushed at him, then at the desk beneath her. The way he held her open, with one thigh up, meant her puss and her clitoris were bumped as she undulated…and he thrust.

And he did thrust. Again and again. Ferociously. Desperately. The cloth of his trousers and linen chafed cruelly against her punished bottom, but the simmering pain only seemed a different kind of pleasure. She surged and circled, rubbing and writhing, half…no, almost completely out of her wits.

This was Wilson. Her Wilson. At last. Pushing at her. Pounding her. Almost climbing inside her soul, as much as ravishing her body.

"Is that enough? Is that full enough measure for you?" His voice was angry, almost from another place. He thrust again, nearly sending her sliding across the top of the chest. She hung on to its edge, bracing herself, thrusting back at him.

"More," she groaned. "Give me it all. Give me everything."

He jerked, hurling himself into her. "Jezebel! I'll make you forget those men." His fingers gouged into her thigh. He pushed her wider, went in deeper, deeper. "You're mine, Della. You'll always be mine, even if you fuck a hundred thousand men. They'll never have you the way I do."

Still plunged into her, he adjusted their positions on the chest. Adela gripped harder, for dear life, her inner muscles already beginning to flutter, the bright pennants of orgasm unfurling as Wilson grabbed her by the haunch with his left hand, and with his other, reached beneath, twisting his wrist, to find her clitoris.

Adela squealed, racked by great wrenching waves of agonized pleasure, her spirit leaping from the highest place into a tumbling, ecstatic fall. Across her back, Wilson fell, too, collapsing upon her, assaulting the air with a string of oaths as his hips jerked and hammered.

"*Now* you're mine," he cried, his voice cracking and barely recognizable.

Losing her senses, Adela didn't have the strength or wits to argue. In that instant, being his was all she wanted.

17

Wilson's Fait Accompli

"Don't come in. I don't feel equipped to explain your presence to Mama right now. She'll want to know how I came to arrive home in a carriage with you, when I set off for a meeting of the Ladies' Sewing Circle."

It seemed cruel, brushing him off like this, but it would be too uncomfortable to explain him to her mother. Especially as Adela wasn't sure she could explain what she'd been about even to herself.

"If you wish." Wilson's low voice was sober, but the way he played with the brim of his top hat betrayed his inner tension. The fact that he had one with him seemed to indicate something amiss in itself. He looked entirely ill at ease so conventionally dressed, even though his fine frock coat, surprisingly subdued waistcoat and small, neat bow tie became him well.

"I'm sorry, Wilson. But you know Mama. Even if there was a reason for you to be delivering me home at this hour, she'd still make far too much of it." It was Adela's turn to fidget, fingering the handle of the small carpetbag that contained her precious portfolio.

After they'd coupled, Wilson had held out the portfolio to her, free and clear, while she was still naked, crouched on the sofa in a large red blanket he'd draped around her in a strangely tender gesture.

In fact, he'd been solicitous in the extreme, swathing her in the blanket, bringing her brandy, smoothing her hair back from her face as if she'd suffered some terrible shock or been rescued from a disaster at sea. He'd even winced when she'd grimaced from the lingering soreness in her buttocks. And he'd done all this while strolling round his spacious work-room stark naked himself.

Afterward, he'd retrieved her clothing and escorted her to an impressively modern and well-appointed bathroom and lav-atory. Everything in Wilson's home employed the latest tech-nological development, and some features, she suspected, did not exist elsewhere. He'd run hot water from a miraculously efficient system for her bath, providing a full tub of heavenly soothing heat in which to wallow. Then, when she'd returned to the workroom to take her leave, he'd plied her with orange pekoe tea and an excellent seed cake, this reviver presumably prepared by his own hand, if his servants had all taken advan-tage of their unexpected liberty. At least she sincerely hoped that was the case, because the idea that some lingering servant, especially the smoothly efficient Teale, might have heard all the screaming and shouting and carrying on she'd done was simply unthinkable.

"Perhaps you're right," Wilson said more gently now, fa-voring her with a slight, crooked smile. "A visit from me will only complicate matters."

But as they drew up before her house, perhaps it was too late, anyway. Mama was bound to be in a state of high anxiety, and looking out of the window for her. It was six o'clock and Adela had gone out at half past one.

"Don't get out. Let the coachman help me down. Mama's going to be on watch for my return."

"Very well."

It seemed strange that they could hardly speak to each other, but no words could encapsulate Adela's feelings, and even Wilson, who could segregate his emotions with glacial ease, seemed affected much the same. She'd never traveled, and had never experienced a tropical cyclone or other fierce wonder of the weather, but in the aftermath of such a phenomenon, one must experience the same state of stunned incomprehension she was in now, Adela decided.

It's like I've been to heaven—and hell—and back again.

If only Wilson had never been at the Rayworths' house party. How much simpler life would be now.

And how boring and insipid, too, caprices at Sofia's house of pleasure notwithstanding. Adela couldn't seem to remember a single thing that had ever taken place there...while her mind had recorded every word, every gesture, every breath that Wilson had taken back in his workroom.

His caresses and the feel of his cock were indelible brands, imprinted on her far more deeply even than the heat of that spanking.

But now she must return to her normal life. Normal but changed. Even if she never fucked Wilson again, she still wouldn't turn to Yuri or Clarence in his stead. Sweet as they were, virile as they were, they could no longer satisfy her heart.

"Shall we see each other again?"

The tentative quality of Wilson's voice was unsettling. For a capricious, arrogant, domineering man, it echoed oddly, like the plea of a lost and lonely boy.

"I'm not sure that's wise." She had the portfolio now. There was no reason.

"A letter, then? I'll send you a letter." More confident now, more her familiar Wilson.

Adela swallowed, at a loss to imagine what he'd write. It would probably be some lascivious screed to rival, or surpass, anything in *Divertissements*. Or alternatively, a treatise on the more esoteric properties of steel, with a few words of light regard appended as an afterthought. Wilson simply couldn't be normal. "Um...yes. Yes, of course. That would be pleasant."

This stilted conversation was too painful. She rapped on the door and the coachman let her out. Wilson ran his hand down the back of her arm, but true to his word, didn't follow her from the carriage. And Adela didn't look back as she ran to the front door of her home and let herself in, not even waiting to hear the noise of the coachman resuming his seat and the carriage pulling away.

Inside, there was no time to even draw breath. As Adela removed her hat and handed her gloves to Minnie, the parlor maid, her mother swirled into the entrance hall to meet her, all aflutter, swathed in several shawls and clutching her handkerchief.

"Della! Good heavens, where have you been all this time? I've been worried to the point of prostration." Mama's eyes looked red, as if she'd been crying, and Adela felt a spear of guilt pierce her. Her mother *did* care for her, and worry about her, despite her apparent preference for Sybil. It was just that the love was quieter, and more shadowed.

"I sent round to Mrs. Ritchie's, and to Mrs. Brigstock's, but they hadn't seen you at all. I even sent a note round to Mme Chamfleur...even though you know I think that woman isn't quite respectable." Mama stood, mangling her handkerchief, compounding Adela's guilt.

"Now, now, Mama, Sofia is a splendid woman and very kind, and her house in Cheveley Street is perfectly respectable." Which was completely true…because the man brothel was situated in a large and rather fine house in Hampstead that actually belonged to her husband, Monsieur Ambrose Chamfleur. "Come along, let's take some tea. You must settle down and not worry so about me, you know. I'm twenty-five, Mama, not a silly romantic chit like Sybil, bless her heart. I simply decided to pay a call on a different friend while I was out. I'm sorry, I know I should have sent round a note with a servant."

"What friend? What friend, Della?" demanded Mama, as Adela hustled her into the parlor, having requested Minnie bring them tea.

What friend indeed? Was Wilson even her friend? Yes, he was her distant cousin, and a man who'd possessed her body twice in her life now, but *friend* was such a small, inadequate word for what he was.

"Yes, what friend?" inquired Sybil, looking up from a copy of the *Young Ladies' Journal*. Even Marguerite looked interested for a moment, although she returned almost immediately to her book.

"Not someone you know…but very, um, very respectable. Someone interested in art and anxious to show me a new acquisition."

Lies and avoidance. How was she going to talk herself out of this one? The guilt piled up. And not for what she'd done with Wilson. No, that seemed beyond all consideration of desire or respectability, of right or wrong. It was the fibbing to Mama and to Sybil that made Adela feel hot and uncomfortable. Not to mention the fact that she suddenly realized she'd never even asked Wilson specifically about the letters. She hadn't really considered it possible that he'd taken those, as well, but with his powers of observation, and insatiable curiosity, he might have been able to offer some theory as to their whereabouts. Moreover, his deductive skills would have been useful in solving the dilemma.

Both Mama and Sybil opened their mouths to continue the inquisition, but there was a rap at the door. Surely not the tea already? Minnie was quick and efficient, but nobody could get down to the kitchen, assemble the tea things, brew the pot and get back up to the parlor in barely moments.

Minnie entered the room again, sans tea and looking flustered.

"Mr. Wilson Ruffington to see you, ma'am." She held out a card on her little silver salver, but it was immediately made redundant when Wilson strode into the room, right on her heels.

"Wilson, how delightful to see you again so soon! To what do we owe the pleasure of this visit?" Suddenly beaming, Mama held out her hand.

Adela was glad she was sitting down, because if it were otherwise, she would have had to flop into a chair. What was Wilson doing here? Had the carriage moved even one inch from the pavement outside the house?

You scheming devil, what are you up to now? What deviousness is this?

Wilson had dispensed with his hat and gloves and cane, leaving him still looking extraordinarily sartorial. His lean form in his dark and sober suit was drawing admiring glances from both Sybil and Marguerite, and Mama looked as if she was about to leap up and shower him in kisses.

Adela just wanted him to go. As soon as possible. She knew him, and this could only end in some kind of disaster.

"I won't prevaricate, Mrs. Ruffington. I'll get straight to the heart of my intentions." Like some continental courtier, he swept up Mama's proffered hand and dusted a kiss upon it.

Then he turned to Adela, with a melee of dangerous emotions in his eyes. Humor. A strange excitement. Masculine triumph.

No! Please no!

She suddenly knew exactly what he was going to say, and silently exhorted him not to. It was incomprehensible, but she knew, she knew....

But it was too late; he was reaching for her hand now.

"I should like to ask for Adela's hand in marriage. It would make me the happiest man in the world if you'd give us your blessing, Mrs. Ruffington."

The room instantly became a chaos of excited voices. Mama almost shrieked and bounced up from her chair like a spring lamb. "My dear Wilson, this is such a surprise. But a wonderful one. I'm quite overcome!" Overcome or not, she wrapped her newly prospective son-in-law in a hug that was considerably more uninhibited than ladylike. "Of course you have my blessing, dear boy, of course."

But what about my blessing, Wilson? You've presented me with a fait accompli.

Adela sat in silence. It was like being immobilized in the eye of a vortex. Mama, Sybil, and even Marguerite—who'd dropped her book in surprise—were all chattering to each other and to Wilson, but to Adela the words were jumbled noise, making no sense whatsoever. The only thing that did make sense was Wilson's gaze upon her, his silver-gray eyes focused on her alone, even though he was surrounded by, and conversing with, three other females.

"Della, Della, Della...I never realized. This is the most wonderful news!" It was Adela's turn to be hugged by her parent now, as if Mama had finally remembered her presence in the room. "You are such a sly one, my darling, so clever. But believe me, you've made me happier than you can possibly imagine."

In the midst of her elation, Mrs. Ruffington suddenly looked deadly serious for about half a second, and Adela's heart plummeted as she recognized the clang of the shutting gate. *This,* this ruse or whatever it was of Wilson's, was the answer to all Mama's prayers. A greater prize even than a potentially noble marriage for Sybil. A solid alliance with Wilson would mean the end of fear of poverty and being cast out in the cold. The happy return to the female Ruffington line of all that had seemed lost by Mama's inability to produce a male heir.

Mama's dream had come true, and thus, there was no escape. And even though Adela had no idea of Wilson's real motivation for wanting to marry her, she prayed, for Mama's sake, that it wasn't just some capricious trick on his part. It would certainly crush her parent for good and all if he was merely playing out some cold experiment in human response and behavior, and planning to snatch back the proposal as suddenly as it had been proffered.

But even if his request was bona fide, and exactly what it seemed, the enormity of what lay ahead made Adela's blood sink from her head, and giddiness engulf her.

"Dearest, are you all right?"

It was Wilson's voice that brought back her wits. As if part of some elaborate dance, Mama had vacated her place on the sofa, and surrendered it to Wilson, so he could take his place as the dominant male of their small pack, seated at his chosen mate's side.

His hands felt hot as fire around hers, and Adela realized that was because her skin was ice-cold, from genuine shock.

"Yes, thank you, *dearest,*" she said pointedly, rallying herself. This was no time to turn into Mama or Sybil, and succumb to the vapors. She needed all her faculties about her now. In fact, she'd need all her faculties around her for the rest of her life if she was to deal with a creature like Wilson on a daily basis.

"I'm quite well. Just a little taken aback…I thought that we weren't going to reveal our happy news for a little while yet."

Wilson chafed her hands in his, clearly knowing she was not precisely well. His eyes were smiling, but a little narrowed. He nodded as if he were acknowledging and applauding her quick uptake and the way she'd resisted the urge to protest, make a scene, or possibly even strike him.

"Ah, you know me, darling Della. I'm ever impatient." His eyes glittered like pale blue steel fresh from the furnace, still sparking. "I just can't wait to have you for my own."

The word *again* seemed to sound between them like a bell.

Mama was still burbling at them, but Adela wasn't taking any of it in; she could register only the touch of Wilson's fingers, and the look in his eyes. He appeared so confident, so assured of what he was doing, and yet somehow, despite the fire, did she detect the merest hint of shock in his expression, too?

At Mama's summons, champagne was brought. Probably one of the last bottles in the cellar, Adela guessed, hoping that there was still at least one left for the announcement they were anticipating for Sybil. Was her sibling a little miffed to be pipped to the post by such a rank outsider in the marriage stakes? It didn't seem so. Sybil appeared to be at least as excited as Mama, possibly more so. Perhaps already planning a grand double wedding?

Wilson, however, would not be pressed on details.

"I'll visit again tomorrow, Mrs. Ruffington, and then we'll discuss the formalities. I think Adela is a little tired now, after all the excitement. Let's just enjoy the moment and this excellent champagne, eh?"

Mama looked a little worried. Was she frightened that this bright new happiness was about to be snatched away? But Adela watched her parent squash the doubt and cover it with a fond smile.

"It's a beautiful evening. Why don't you take Wilson for a walk in the garden, Della? Show him the gazebo. Now that you're formally betrothed, a few moments alone won't harm anybody."

Adela was almost compelled to bite her knuckle. Mama's face was perfectly straight, but was it possible she suspected that improper things, in abundance, had already occurred? Her own marriage had been a very fond one. In fact, though her parent never spoke of it, Adela knew that Mama's engagement had been scandalously short, and her own birth credited as premature.

"Yes, of course." She sprang to her feet. Fresh air would be a blessing, even if she had to share it with Wilson. The parlor was beginning to feel like a steam room, it was so suffocating. "Come along, dearest." Grabbing him by the hand, and digging in her nails out of sight of Mama, she hustled him from the room without further ado. At a swift march, they sped through the house and out of the back door into the garden, Adela keeping her lips tightly shut and her face resolutely forward. Wilson followed her lead, mercifully silent.

Because their house was small, their garden was pocket-size, too. A few paces brought them to the wrought-iron garden seat beneath an ornamental trellis. Adela wished the garden half a mile long, so the walk would have given her time to frame her thoughts. As it was, she sat down with a mind still blank from shock.

"Nothing to say, wife-to-be?"

That urge to punch Wilson on the nose surged up again, and her hand curled into a fist. But he caught her in time, effortless as usual.

"Well, that's not exactly the response I was expecting. Joy and gratitude seem to be more appropriate reactions, wouldn't you think?"

Snatching back her hand, she shuffled away on the seat, then grimaced when the heat in her bottom reminded her of what she and her "fiancé" had done such a short time ago.

"I'm completely at a loss for words, Wilson. I don't know what to say.... What on earth are you thinking?" She scowled. "I know this isn't because you respect and admire and adore me...so why are you doing this?"

Wilson looked as if she had indeed landed the intended blow. Or at least something had shocked him. But the expression faded in a moment, replaced by a grin.

"Logic, dear Della. Logic. It suddenly occurred to me that a marriage between us would actually be a perfectly rational act. It would solve a lot of problems and make some people, if not everybody, happy."

A little bit of that was right. Mama was clearly ecstatic.

"How shiningly altruistic of you, Wilson." Adela stared at him, wondering anew what he was up to and aware that confusion, and suspicion, were making her ungracious. "But if this is some kind of devious trick, and you up and renege at any minute... Well, I swear I'll kill you with my bare hands. I *will* do it. You've elevated Mama's hopes now, and if you crush them it will cruel beyond imagining."

Wilson gave her a steady look. A serious look, oddly unnuanced for him. "Your opinion of me is very low, isn't it? Do you really think I would be so despicable as that? Well, I swear, too.... I swear to you that my intention to see this through is sincere and steadfast, Della. I want us to marry, for a number of reasons. Financial in particular."

Adela frowned. What did he mean?

"Well, I don't see any particular fiscal advantage to you in marrying me. Quite the reverse. You famously pointed out that the four of us are a quartet of parasites who expect to be supplied a luxurious living for having done very little."

Wilson let out a sigh and stared up into the foliage above. "I've already told you that was a random, incorrect statement on my part, and that I didn't really mean it. Why won't you believe me?"

But he had spoken words to that effect. And they couldn't simply be erased from her memory. Although it was looking as if he expected her to, now.

"Very well, I accept that. Now outline these advantages for me."

"The fiscal advantage is to you, your mother and your sisters." Without warning, he reached for her hand and folded it in both of his, almost in the way the sincerest of prospective husbands might. "I believe your grandfather, Lord Millingford, is being grossly unfair to you all. I have attempted to explain that to him in a number of letters, but even though he's named me his financial heir in addition to me being the heir to his title, he still won't see me in person, and persists in behaving like a recluse."

Wilson had done that? Neither she nor her mother had been aware of it.

"So, in marrying you, I'm able to legitimately support you all and ensure that you enjoy a pleasant standard of life free of all financial cares." His thumb moved over her knuckles in a caress she wasn't sure he even registered. "It's no burden to me. I'm independently wealthy with my consultancy, my patents and my investments, not to mention a generous bequest from an aunt on my mother's side."

"But you don't owe us anything."

"Yes, I feel I do. Since the untimely death of cousin Henry, the Old Curmudgeon seems to have fixated on me, to the exclusion of his moral responsibility to his closer family. It's not your mother's fault she didn't give him a grandson, and it's not her fault that your father died relatively young. It's just fate, if you believe in such things, and none of you should be punished for it." He shrugged. "And then, when the old monster kicks the bucket and I inherit, I can ensure that you all get your full share of the Ruffington assets…and I won't feel guilty anymore."

Adela had the sensation of being crushed. Diminished by emotions she didn't dare inspect too closely, and hopes she'd extinguished a long time ago. "Ah, so I'm to be shackled to you in matrimony just to prevent you from feeling guilty?"

Another sigh, and his fingers tightened a bit around hers. "Not just for that…and I don't intend you to feel shackled in any way." Was there a glint in his eye then, a touch of humor? "No, there are other reasons, practical ones, advantageous to us both."

"Pray tell."

"Well, as I've recently discovered, you and I are both people of enthusiastic carnal appetites. And though we don't always see eye to eye in some matters, we're well suited in the bodily sense. It seems to me that we both have physical needs at this point in our lives, and rather than seek satisfaction elsewhere…and take risks—" his eyes narrowed "—it seems more prudent, and more rational, to place ourselves in a situation where we can legally, morally and conveniently satisfy our needs and desires without recourse to other parties."

How long had he been formulating this rational solution of his? They'd barely seen each other at all in recent months and years. It wasn't until the Rayworths' house party that he'd even seemed to take the slightest interest in her again, as a woman, since their encounter all those years ago.

Was all this just to stop her going to Sofia's house of pleasure?

"Put like that, how can I argue? Although I would at least have liked to have had some choice in the matter. I was happy with my own arrangement. At least that way I didn't have to take on wifely duties and responsibilities to…to satisfy my urges."

"I'm not expecting you to take on duties and responsibilities, Della!" he cried, sounding exasperated. "I won't expect any duties of you. You can do exactly what you want…pursue your artistic career, or whatever you choose. All I ask is that you don't seek out other men, and preferably don't view them unclothed, either, in order to draw them! You're the one who's pointed out that you draw from memory…and dash it, woman, if you need a new model, I'll pose for you myself as long as you don't show my face too clearly!"

Adela started to laugh. She couldn't contain herself. The profound absurdity of what he suggested, coupled with its equally eminent practicality, was a complete paradox, both ludicrous and perfectly sane at the same time. Her giggles became uncontrollable. She got the hiccups. She couldn't breathe.

Wilson slapped her back. Chafed her hands. Sprang to his feet.

"I'll get you some water."

"No! No! I will be all right. Don't trouble yourself." As quickly and shockingly as it had begun, the fit of laughter subsided. But she clasped her hand to her chest, just in case, to calm her heart.

"So, this practical arrangement of money and lust and—and art? It continues for the rest of our lives, presumably? A marriage convenient to both." She pursed her lips. "But what of the more conventional aspects? What…what of children? Most married couples have them. Isn't it God's purpose for marriage, after all? I don't think He gave us the institution simply to provide an outlet for carnal appetites and the disposition of wealth and assets."

"Children? No, not really… I'm not sure I'm at all interested in being a father." Wilson's eyes suddenly looked glacial, almost dismissive. "And if you were to start producing babies, you're most likely to lose interest in your carnal appetites… except as a means to obtain more babies."

How could he suddenly be so cold? Not that she'd ever considered the chance that she'd be a mother. Nor even wanted it. Until now, perversely.

"You really are quite disgusting, Wilson."

"You've never complained that I disgust you when I'm touching you. Or fucking you…or even licking you."

Adela shot to her feet. This was a return to the usual Wilson, and for the moment, too much to take. It was all too much a shock to the senses, especially after this afternoon. And worse, his sudden, crude words seemed to stir instant fires and distract her.

"No, no running." His hand locked around her arm and he pulled her inexorably down again. "You know you can't say no to this, now that your mother's hopes have been raised." He paused, an odd look of uncertainty on his face. "But I…I wasn't planning to tie you to me forever, Della. I don't want to constrain you in that way. I thought we might ensure your financial security…and slake our appetite for each other… then perhaps come to some mutually convenient parting in the fullness of time. Either live separate lives, or a civilized divorce, certainly, if we were to fall in love elsewhere. I don't care about conventions. I'd make it easy for you, and make you appear the blameless party. Then, as a wealthy woman, you'd be able to have your pick of men for your next husband."

Divorce? Her *next* husband?

How could she ever forget that Wilson had the cool, dispassionate mind of a scientist and logician? If she hadn't been on the receiving end of his ferocious physical attentions, she could swear the man was a living icicle sometimes.

And yet the clarity of his proposal had a strange, detached appeal. Perhaps she was as much a logician as he? And wasn't it better to know the true state of affairs, rather than fool herself with silly romantic notions and the belief that a man might love her, when he patently didn't?

Wilson's hand loosened, but she didn't fly away. The cold rationale stunned her, even though she could see its merit. She just wanted to sit quietly, by herself, and contemplate all Wilson had said, even if he'd already made it impossible to go against his wishes.

"There's a lot to think about, isn't there?" he said more gently, getting to his feet. "I'll leave now, and give you time to yourself. Then I'll come back tomorrow, so we can discuss the arrangements."

Had he read her mind again? It seemed so. She waited for him to leave, almost as if she were watching a play, and outside the action.

But just when he seemed on the point of walking away, he bent down to her, cradling her face and kissing her on the lips. It was soft at first, but in an instant, he seemed to come alive…and Adela did, too.

Before she knew it, she was reaching up, holding him as he held her, her tongue pressing against his as it thrust into her mouth.

Carnal passions. They were undeniable. Even if temporary.

❧ 18 ❧

To Sleep, Perchance to Dream

Wilson stared at the ceiling. A little thin moonlight was filtering in through the window, peeking between the partially drawn curtains and making stark, clear lines on the white stucco.

It's a good idea. It makes sense.

His decision to propose to Adela had come as a shock to him, even as he'd formulated it, but he'd not given himself time to turn back once he'd leaped out of the carriage. Adela's reaction wasn't quite the rational one he'd expected, but she'd seemed to come around with that kiss. And she was a pragmatist, just as he was. A woman of sense.

Since boyhood, Wilson had never planned to marry. His parents weren't well suited, and though he hadn't understood the undercurrents of distrust at the time, it had been plain his mother and father weren't happy. Especially his mother, a strange woman, complex, secretive yet stiflingly possessive.

Aware of the predatory instincts of mothers with daughters, notably Mrs. Ruffington, he'd sworn to avoid matrimony, but then one day, not so long ago, he'd proposed it to Coraline. And she'd refused him. He'd thought at the time it was his age, a decade short of hers, but now he knew that her Italian duke had already hove into view, and she'd already been planning their parting.

So Wilson had sworn, once again, never to marry, only to perform a volte-face within days of meeting Adela again.

He frowned. What was this sparkling new idiocy of his, proposing to women who only really wanted him for sex? Coraline had apparently consorted with him because he was an eager and inventive bed partner, and Adela didn't seem to like him very much at all, except when he was touching her. And perhaps not even then.

And what of himself? What were his feelings?

He'd believed he'd loved Coraline, or come as close to it as was possible for him. But now Adela had effectively erased that, and made him feel as fickle and easily swayed as a flighty piece like cousin Sybil. Worse, in fact, as he was supposed to be a logician and a rational thinker.

"Women!" he growled into the night. Then laughed. It wasn't women who were at fault. It was *him*. Why had it taken him so long to realize that he was as in thrall to his cock as the next man?

The damn thing was hard now, too. Reaching down to hold himself through his nightshirt, he imagined Adela's narrow, exquisite hand doing the honors. She was graceful and deft, as befitted an artist. She could wield his flesh with all the skill that she did a pencil or a piece of charcoal, or no doubt a brush. Drawing her gigolos.

He smiled, grimly satisfied. Well, at least he'd put paid to that. Now he'd be the one to satisfy her, and no more gigolos. Was he up to the job? Beneath the sober black gowns, and attitude of reserve and restraint, she was a firecracker. He'd thought Coraline to be the ultimate voluptuous woman, but beside his clever—and yes, deceitful—cousin, his Parisian ex-mistress almost seemed like a nun.

For a moment, a pang of sorrow wrenched at him. Not for Coraline, but for the lost years. For the youthful falling-out that had turned into lingering enmity and avoidance.

We could have been so happy, Della....

Damn it, lying here aroused but unfulfilled was making him maudlin. And there was nothing to be maudlin about now. He'd no idea what might come in the years ahead, but at least the months of the shorter term were promising.

His cock throbbed in his grasp, as if recalling the fierce embrace of Adela's puss. How she'd gripped him and massaged him. The thought of her cries of pleasure, so uninhibited, made him tremble. He wanted to plunge into her now, but his hand would have to suffice. Whipping up the hem of his nightshirt, he grabbed hold of his rigid length and began to pump.

Soon you'll be here with me every night, to do this for me. This, and a lot more.

Would they share a room? A part of him yearned for that intimacy. How sweet to have someone beside him if he woke in the night. Especially when he had a headache from the thrash of thoughts and schemes and theorems in his mind. Sometimes it seemed the machine in his brain would not turn off, and that it ran even when he was asleep. That state of constant tension took its toll. Adela could be as gentle as she was fiery, and he imagined how she might stroke his brow, or even cradle his aching head on her breast.

Wilson laughed, giving his cock a squeeze to bring him back to his senses. Adela might be a loyal and dutiful woman, and no doubt she'd perform admirably in bed, to the satisfaction of them both. But she wasn't marrying him to dispense gentleness, nurturing and companionship. She was probably even less of a caring female figure than his mother had been, and than Coraline, too, for that matter.

If we rub along together well enough, maybe a gentler side will come? Maybe if I try a little harder myself?

But if it was only carnality, they'd still manage. Despite her own mistaken beliefs about her looks, Adela was powerfully attractive to him. Her body was lithe and exquisite, and her face full of character. She had the finest eyes he'd ever seen, and a full, lush mouth. Even her supposed flaws only made her piquant, and not run-of-the-mill. She was a rough diamond whose very imperfections made her glitter all the more.

Yet she was also radical, intelligent and cultured—and well-read, if she'd continued the habits she'd once kept. She was the one who'd begged him to help her gain access to the Old Curmudgeon's rare books that summer. She was the one who'd pleaded to be shown how to pick a lock.

Wilson's thoughts were straying down disquieting paths now. He was beginning to think about things that probably could not be. Time to return to the matter at hand. In the most literal of senses.

Working his cock fiercely, he imagined Adela in this bed with him, but not comforting his fevered brow this time. Now he saw her on her back, her slender legs spread wide and revealed by a nightgown pushed right up to her neck. Her narrow wrists were tied to the brass bedstead behind her head. She was constrained and vulnerable to him, her luscious dark *motte* laid bare, offering a tantalizing glimpse of her juicy, gleaming pudenda as she struggled.

And yes, she *was* struggling, but her dark eyes were alight with mischief and excitement. There was a pink glow to her cheeks, and she was gasping, her lips parted. Her sex gleamed yet more, awash with silky arousal as she wiggled and wriggled on the crisp sheet beneath her bottom, undulating her lithe limbs to enchant and inflame him.

Oh, what to do with you, beautiful Della?

She was a feast, a cornucopia of temptation.

Should he plunge his face between her legs and sup her nectar? Driving her to a distraction of lust with his tongue, as he licked her? Or should he simply eschew all preliminaries and thrust his rigid, tormented penis straight into her slick, welcoming heat?

She was tied…so he could loop his hand beneath one of her knees and raise up a leg. Perhaps slap her for a while on thigh and buttock, until she simmered there. Lord, how he knew she loved that. A little pain seemed to turn her into a maenad. He could spank her there, then press his cock against the heat, maybe come all over the warm silky skin?

Then afterward, while he recovered his hardness, he could gently stroke her puss, again and again, bringing her to crisis after crisis while she was still bound.

Finally, he'd free her, and possess her, hugging her to him while she reciprocated, clasping his back, rising to him, murmuring and moaning his name as their bodies finally convulsed together.

I love you, Wilson. I love you.

Hearing the imagined words, he finally exploded, his cock pulsing hard in his hand, his seed spurting out onto the sheet.

Afterward, he lay still and shattered, no nearer to sleep and dreams than before.

Bloody hell, where the devil had *that* come from?

NEVER BEFORE HAD it been so difficult to sleep. Always in the past, Adela had been able to find solace in the arms of Morpheus even in the most anxious situations. The death of her father, the seeming callousness of her grandfather, the strain on her mother over these matters and others. Adela had always been able to sleep, and wake refreshed afterward, revived and able to think clearly and see the best way to tackle difficulties.

But now, in the small hours, she was as wide-awake as if she'd been plunged into the brine in the course of sea bathing.

Wilson! Why on earth have you asked me to marry you? You don't want a bride, and if you did, why on earth would you ever pick me?

Of course, it *was* the most expedient match, in a normal, simple world. It solved so many difficulties. But nothing to do with Wilson Ruffington—or Adela Ruffington—had ever been simple or normal.

And yet she wanted it. For all the shock. For all the complexity of their circumstances. For all she knew that Wilson didn't love her, never had, never would.

Shaking her head, Adela flung off the covers and leaped out of bed. There was no sleep possible. She donned her old shawl, much darned but warm and comforting, draping it around her shoulders over her nightgown.

She'd draw. That always distracted her mind.

With the lamp turned up high, she sat at her bureau. Prizing the key from the crack in the woodwork she'd created to hide it, she unlocked the drawer and drew out her art materials. The portfolio was in there, too, but she let it remain. Too inflammatory to her thoughts at the moment.

Setting her pencil to a fresh page in her sketchbook, she attempted to clear her mind, and fill it with an image that would soothe. Within moments, she was drawing a flower, one of the beautiful roses she'd recently admired in the gardens of Rayworth Court. She worked hard to interpret the lushness, the velvet quality of the petals, and as she did, her thoughts returned to a more manageable form.

Marriage to Wilson. Perhaps it wouldn't be a bad thing. In fact, it could be a very good thing, for all its unconventional origins. Mama at least would be the happiest woman in the world, even if the bride wasn't. Everything would be restored to her that could be restored, through her daughter.

The pencil glided on, etching the stem, the thorns.

And for her own part? Would it be so horrible to spend her days with Wilson, even though they might be of a limited number? He was a brilliant man, fascinating and learned, and a thinker of the most original kind. Nobody could ever be bored with him.

She wouldn't be bored at night, either. With Wilson, she'd never lack for carnal pleasures, and knowing her own nature, a lusty husband was a great asset. He could satisfy all the needs she'd ever have in that respect. In the space of a few days he'd exceeded everything she'd experienced in the years since they'd first been together.

Yes, even if this wasn't the heart-fluttering romantic love match that a dreamer like Sybil aspired to, there was much to recommend it. A few years of interesting company and regular sensual pleasure were far more than many women settled for. And afterward, with any luck Adela would be a rich and scandalous divorcée. Perhaps there would be some quieter, more settled man then, someone who would overlook her less-than-perfect appearance for the sake of a reasonable fortune?

And if not, there were always Sofia's boys.

Adela laid down her pencil, blinking in the flickering lamplight, then peering closely at the very center of the rose. Then she blinked again, her mouth open in wonder at the strangeness of her own gift, and what it had wrought.

Without even realizing what she was doing, she'd drawn a tiny human face right in the heart of the flower.

Wilson, in miniature, gazed up at her. And despite the

smallness of the image, she'd caught his familiar smile, narrow and challenging.

A shudder of fear gripped her heart, but she quelled it. Turning the page, she began another drawing.

❦ 19 ❦

The Second Miss Ruffington
Gets Engaged

Never one for shopping, Adela found the experience exhausting. Which was unfortunate for a forthcoming bride with
a truncated engagement, because there was a great deal of
shopping to do in a very short space of time. Accustomed to
arguing with Wilson, she'd been pleasantly surprised when
he'd agreed with her over the arrangements for the wedding.

A grand affair, maybe in one of London's great houses of
worship, seemed hypocritical for a match such as theirs, so
they both settled on Saint Agatha's, the small but pretty church
just around the corner, where the Ruffington women were
regular attendees. Mama had protested vehemently at first,
but quickly became resigned. Her mother was so happy there
was a marriage at all, especially one she'd wanted so long and
believed so unlikely, that she was content to acquiesce to her
daughter's stubborn nature and, to her mind, irrational desire
for the simplest possible nuptials.

The wedding breakfast would take place in a private room

at the discreet and luxurious Hunters' Hotel, with a modest guest list. Lord Millingford had declined to attend on grounds of ill health, but to the surprise of all had sent a brief, dictated letter offering his approval and congratulations on the match.

"We don't need either his approval or his congratulations," Adela had pointed out, insulted by such condescension. "I'm of age and so is Wilson…and the old devil hasn't cared two pins about the welfare of either of us up until now, apart from bequeathing his millions to Wilson, who still claims he doesn't even want them."

Mama seemed delighted to have the Old Curmudgeon's sanction, though, despite his less-than-kind treatment. She curtailed her own invitations to a few of her cronies from various charitable organizations, some of whom she didn't really like, but to whom she was anxious to flaunt her eldest daughter's excellent marriage. Adela's guests were just her friends from the Ladies' Sewing Circle, many of whom were—in public—prominent members of society, especially Lady Arabella, and also Beatrice Ritchie, whose husband, Edmund, despite a lack of title, was one of the richest and most influential industrialists and financiers in the country.

Wilson's guests were few, but of sufficient reputation to thrill Mama with the quality, if not the quantity. Several eminent scientists, two members of parliament—one a cabinet minister—a senior policeman, a bishop and even a minor royal, attending semi incognito.

The invitations had been sent, the cake ordered, even Adela's wedding dress was almost finished. Not from Worth, to Mama's chagrin, as there simply wasn't time. But Adela was more than happy with a couturiere beloved of the Sewing Circle ladies, Mme Mirielle. To please her mother, Adela had agreed to a conventional design rather than Rational attire, but she'd put her foot down about the color.

Silver-gray silk.

"Out of respect for Papa, I think a more sober costume is appropriate and apt for a smaller, quiet wedding."

"If you say so, my darling. You are a very good daughter." Had there been a sly look in Mama's eyes? Did she strongly suspect her eldest was not quite as pure as a white-clad bride should be?

Still, if the wedding gown was not as lavish as Mrs. Ruffington would have liked, at least she had the comfort of knowing her daughter was correctly corseted for the occasion. She was less pleased, Adela knew, with the rest of the trousseau.

Mme Mirielle was a great exponent of the Rational and Aesthetic couture, and Adela had decided that as Wilson was no great fan of the corseted woman, she would from now on dress for comfort in reformed clothing.

Finally free of financial constraints as well as the whalebone variety, Adela looked forward to a life spent in lush fabrics, and looser gowns that skimmed the natural form rather than the ferociously corseted and far from healthy shape. Worn with radical new undergarments that clung gently and comfortably to her slight curves, enhancing rather than conquering her silhouette. Madame had a deft hand with imported patterns from France and from the U.S.A., adapting them with her own refinements. Carefully darted and seamed bust bodices with featherlight boning; loose, less heavy petticoats; a little satin belt with dangling suspender clips to hold up her stockings without the need for nasty garters and the red marks they produced. She also had a variety of very slimly shaped chemises and drawers, the latter clinging close to her thighs. Some even had buttons rather than an open vent. Adela wasn't sure how Wilson would react to having those to negotiate, fond as he was of sliding his fingers into the more convenient old design.

I'm sure you'll find a way, husband-to-be.

Adela patted the large pink dressmaker's box containing a selection of the contentious new undergarments as her carriage drew to a halt outside the house. Wilson's generosity now ensured that they had their own carriage again, and several new servants, all from a highly regarded agency. Despite all that was unusual and perhaps problematical about their coming union, to see Mama so happy, and living the comfortable debt-free life she'd so longed for, was enough to make everything worth it. At least for the moment.

After their new footman assisted her from the carriage, then set out arranging for the many boxes and parcels to be brought in, Adela strode into the hall, abandoning her outdoor jacket, her hat and her gloves to Minnie, who also looked exceptionally cheery now that her load of household chores had been considerably lightened. Trying on garments all morning at Madame's had been far more exhausting than it had a right to be, and all Adela wanted now was a cup of tea, and some solitude with her pencils and her sketch pad. A little oasis of quiet in the turmoil of bridal preparations.

But before she could make for the parlor, her mother appeared and grabbed her by the arm. Mama was even more happily agitated than she'd been for the past two weeks, if that were possible.

"Oh, Della, it's so exciting! Come along to the morning room…. Sybil's in the parlor. We mustn't disturb them."

"Disturb who?"

"Sybil, of course…and Algernon! He's proposing—at least that's what I hope!"

Relief washed through Adela. This was what she'd been hoping for, too. Although she'd clearly tried to rejoice in her sister's wedding preparations, Sybil had been a little downcast that it was Adela's forthcoming marriage causing all the excitement and not her own. Adela had been praying that her younger sister would soon have an announcement, too. Both for Sybil's sake and because a betrothal to the son of a marquis for the younger Ruffington girl would draw interest away from the marriage of the elder to the as-yet-untitled Mr. Ruffington.

"Oh, that's wonderful, wonderful," Adela said, shepherding her mother to the morning room. Mama had been showing a distinct inclination to go and listen at the door of the parlor.

It didn't take long. Adela barely had time to sip half a cup of oolong and nibble a fortifying madeleine when Sybil burst into the morning room dragging a pink-faced Algernon in her wake. Sybil's face was rosy, too, and her hair slightly disarrayed. Adela hid a grin, knowing her sister shared her own predisposition for sensuality, although perhaps not to the same extreme degree.

"Mama! Adela! Marguerite!" Sybil was dancing from foot to foot. "Algie's asked me to marry him and I've said yes!" She gave a little frown, but it didn't stand much of a chance, because an eyeblink later she was grinning again. "Please say that that's all right, Mama. Please say you give your consent!"

The room dissolved into joyous chaos again, much as it had done not all that long ago over Adela. In the midst of all the hugging and congratulating, she smiled wryly. This time all was as it seemed. Sybil adored Algernon in the simplest, happiest and most romantic fashion, and it was clear from the doting look on the young man's face that he returned her feelings completely.

Not a deal, a bargain or an arrangement of convenience. It's true love, this, not like Wilson and me.

For a moment, Adela shivered, despite the warmth of the day. For the thousandth time, her mind flitted to different circumstances, to a state of affairs that might have existed if the course of events had not gone so disastrously wrong that afternoon seven years ago.

Fiddlesticks, Adela, life is what it is. One must make the best of the hand one is dealt, and your hand certainly has…possibilities.

She stiffened her spine, smiled brilliantly and redoubled the fervor with which she hugged her sister. Sybil was sweet, uncomplicated and loving. Silly, sometimes, but basically good-hearted. And she deserved this happiness, as did Mama, who was both laughing and crying, barely able to believe this new bouquet of good fortune that had been heaped upon her and her girls, even though she'd anxiously anticipated it.

While their parent began a good-natured cross questioning of the second prospective bridegroom in less than a month, and Marguerite slipped away to read, as usual, Sybil drew Adela aside.

"Algie and I have talked this over. We won't announce our engagement officially until you and Wilson are married. I…I don't want to draw the limelight from you, Della. I want you to have your day in the sun, at the center of attention. I don't want people to be paying attention to me on your day."

Unlike Mama, Adela's joy for her sister hadn't expressed itself in tears, but now her eyes grew bleary. She hugged her again, harder than before. "That's a very sweet gesture, Syb, but it's not necessary. I know I can speak for Wilson when I say we'd actually *prefer* less limelight. So don't hold back on our account. I know you want the whole world to know, really, don't you?"

Sybil gave a watery grin. "Oh, Della, you know me so well. Are you sure you don't mind?"

Adela nodded, but later in the day she wondered. Would she have preferred to have her own day free of sisterly distractions, with her at its dazzling center? For once in her life, what would it have been like to project at least the illusion of perfect beauty that the bridal aura always bestowed?

She squashed the questions. Things were better as they were. More honest.

But there was still one significant flaw in today's general happiness, all so dramatically wrought by the new announcement.

Despite the sisters' thorough and unhopeful search of every possible place where they might have been misplaced among clothes, shoes, handkerchiefs and gloves, Sybil's incriminating bundle of letters was still missing.

∂♥♡ 20 ♡♥∂

A Wedded Couple

I have a wife. I'm a married man. How very odd.

They were back at Maltravers Road, after a very long day. Adela and himself. Man and wife. A wedded couple.

A fact, but he could still barely believe it, or how it had come about.

Wilson had offered to arrange a honeymoon on the Continent because such things were customary, but Adela had declined, insisting it wasn't necessary. A decision leaving him both grateful and a little disappointed.

Grateful, because he simply didn't have the time. His work on the submarine plans for the War Office was at a critical state, with ministers and other functionaries anxious to see results in short order.

But he was disappointed because the idea of traveling with Adela was strangely alluring. The more he saw of her, the more he had a yen to show her off, and the dining rooms of glamorous European restaurants, or the great opera houses or theaters on the Continent would make perfect settings for her. It was the most bizarre yearning, for a man who'd always preferred the quiet life, but still he wanted it. He longed to share a whole variety of experiences with her, and gift her with pleasures other than those of the bedroom. So that one day, she might…

Might what, you blithering idiot? Fall in love with you? She might have harbored a tendre for you once, long ago, but not now, not anymore. Her feelings for you now are as pragmatic as yours are for her… supposedly.

Adela *had* loved him seven years ago, he knew that. But she didn't anymore. She tolerated him now. Liked him well enough sometimes, and found him carnally compatible. There were plenty of other men who could have met those criteria for marriage…but he was simply the expedient choice, being the Ruffington heir, and thus a source of security for her, and her mama, and her younger sister.

And yet, as she'd approached him down the short aisle at Saint Agatha's, he'd been dazzled, and not only by the sublime diamonds around her throat. No virgin bride, she'd eschewed unsullied white, yet there had still been something as pure and untouchable as the gems themselves about her as she'd seemed to float toward him, her indomitable spirit capturing his mind as well as his body.

Picturing her slender, silver-clad form, he wanted her fiercely. All day she'd charmed her wedding guests and projected the perfect image of the glowing bride happily anticipating her wedding night, but propriety had decreed him unable to touch her, allowing nothing more than a few chaste kisses and a little hand holding. Now he wanted to plunge into her and claim his prize. Opportunities for intimacy had been achingly sparse during their short engagement, with barely more than a few moments of stolen fondling and a hungry kiss or two to show for their troth.

Hurry up, Della!

He lounged on her bed, in the room he'd had quickly prepared for her. Luckily, his house was spacious, so there was a suitable-size chamber for Adela's personal use. Even more luckily, he and Coraline had always met in hotels and at house parties, so there were no awkward echoes of his former paramour to make his wife feel uncomfortable.

But perhaps she didn't even give a damn? Wilson shifted uneasily against the pillows, naked apart from a new dressing gown of blue figured silk, a gift from his bride. A small suspicious devil in his mind goaded him about that, too. Had she purchased it with her small allowance from the Old Curmudgeon? Or from her earnings drawing naked men for the bored matrons of Belgravia? The silk itself was heavy, dense and gleaming. When he closed his eyes, its texture seemed to mimic the very texture of Della's secret flesh. His cock throbbed, as he imagined exploring her with his fingers. Any minute now he'd be touching her, stroking her…but only if the dratted woman ever emerged from her dressing room.

Just when he was considering taking himself in hand, the door swung open and there she was.

Wilson had never seen Adela in her wrapper before, and the sight brought a lump to his throat. How in the name of reason could she not believe she was lovely? The lace-and-silk garment was a soft shade, somewhere between the color of country cream and the bloom on a ripe apricot, and it flattered and illuminated her skin to perfection. With the lamps turned low, and a small fire burning in the grate against an unseasonable chill, the light was mutable and flickering, and it cast an ethereal glow over his bride, imbuing her thick, luxuriant hair with living lights, and making her fine eyes almost supernaturally luminescent.

"You look very lovely, Della," he said, rising from the bed, acutely aware of, and also strangely embarrassed by the fact that she must be able to see the jut of his erection through the fabric of his robe. He'd never been bashful about his maleness before. Dash it, she was making a crazy boy out of him again, an idiot in lust.

Her dark brows arched, and he expected her usual rebuttal of a compliment. But instead she gave a small smile, a pleased little quirk, as if accepting for a change. Unless she simply didn't want to be argumentative on her wedding night?

"You look rather dashing yourself, husband." The smile widened, her gaze glancing toward his nether regions. "That blue looks very well on you."

"As does that…whatever is that shade?" Why was she hovering over there by the door? With her robe, handsome as it was, fastened up to the neck and concealing all?

"Mme Mirielle calls it 'apricot parfait.'"

"Sounds perfectly edible, but I'd rather savor what lies beneath, if you don't mind."

She moved toward him, her gait a smooth glide, her hand at the lace collar of her robe, keeping it closed. When she reached the side of the bed, she paused, looking intently at him. For a moment a little frown pleated her brow, then she shrugged. Wilson almost sighed at the way the slight movement made her sleek hair ripple in the firelight. What would those thick, silken strands feel like wrapped around his cock? Maybe by the end of the night, he'd know.

"Why don't you take off your wrapper?" He tried to sound leisurely, but he was so wound up that the words came out rougher than he'd intended.

"Anxious to see the goods again, eh?" The words were combative, but her voice was soft, bordering on laughter. Wilson wondered if he was going to start shaking any second, he craved her so much.

"I am. I don't deny it. Come on, Della. Have mercy on me."

"Oh, very well, then." She spoke as if she were an indul-
gent governess conceding a treat to a naughty little boy. For
a moment Wilson imagined a risqué scenario, not a preference he'd ever experienced before, and it was almost his turn
to laugh. Adela might not love him, but she could inspire the
most bizarre thoughts and peccadilloes. Expand his horizons
in unexpected ways.

But for now, enough of her teasing. He made to move toward her and hurry the silk off her body, but she skipped back,
out of reach. Mercifully, though, she pulled on the apricot
satin ribbons that fastened the garment.

Then, slowly, she drew the panels apart, and eased off the
deliciously colored, frothy confection, rolling one shoulder
after the other and allowing the whole thing to slide into a
bundle on the carpet around her feet.

"Dear heavens…Della!"

She was naked and magnificent. Infinitely more radiant
than she'd been at eighteen, by the river, or even just weeks
ago, sunlit in his workroom. Her skin gleamed like milk, a
stunning contrast to her dark hair where it streamed over her
bare shoulders, a match for the tempting grove between her
legs. Around her neck she wore the only fitting tribute to her
goddesslike splendor—the Ruffington diamonds, as precious
and incandescent as a rainbow.

"Well, you did tell me recently that you'd like to see me
wearing only the diamonds, so here they are." She touched
the gems at her throat, stirring their fire. "They belong to
me now," she added, squaring her shoulders and giving him
a firm look. "Mama gave them to me as my wedding gift because that was what Papa always wanted."

The slight action made their iridescence ripple and flash,
and her breasts lift. The tiny movement was a provocation all

out of proportion to its dynamics, and Wilson felt like a wild beast, goaded and straining against its leash. "Exactly as it should be. You're the Ruffington woman most fit to do them justice." He paused, twisting the sash of his robe. "But doesn't young Sybil have eyes for the diamonds? She wore them at the Rayworths' shindig."

Adela moved ever forward, and to Wilson's surprise, climbed onto the bed with an unexpected ease and naturalness, and sat down facing him, legs tucked to one side. It was as if she belonged there. Which of course, she did; where else would a wife sit? But it was her complete lack of any apparent embarrassment that took him aback.

You're used to being naked with men, though, aren't you, wife? How in hell could I ever forget that?

He tried to quell the jealousy. She was with *him* now, wasn't she? And the days of her paid stallions were over. Why dwell on the past? He almost laughed at how quickly he'd shaken off his own caprices. Especially the absurd notion of wedding Coraline. That had seemed such a logical idea at the time, and he'd wanted it…but now the Parisienne was as unreal to him as the awkward flickering figures in Lord Rayworth's squeaky old praxinoscope.

Only Adela was real. Alive. Greater than life.

"Sybil isn't as acquisitive as you'd think. She's an innocent, really, and just likes pretty things. She knew these were promised to me." Adela touched the diamonds again, stroking their hard surface with delicate fingertips and making Wilson wish she'd touch *his* hardness soon. "All she wanted was to wear them once. She knows Algie will buy her a dozen necklaces, even prettier and more costly ones than this…if he gets the chance."

A look of profound distress flashed across Adela's face. Real pain, and sharply intense. Wilson couldn't bear it. He reached out and laid a hand on her slim shoulder, aroused by its smooth, silky warmth, even in the grip of other, more puzzling feelings.

"What's wrong, Della? What is it?"

She shook her head, making her thick hair fly.

"I won't say it's nothing...because it isn't." Her fingers settled over his, squeezing. "But now's not the moment to discuss it. I'll tell you some other time." She prized his fingers from her arm, and with an arch look, settled them on her breast. "Now we have other matters to attend to. We agreed to satisfy each other's appetites, didn't we?" Her tongue slid out and delicately circled her lips. "Well, I don't know about you, but I'm hungry now."

"As am I! As am I...." His fingers flexed. The beautiful curve they cradled was so sweet, so warm. "But when you wish it...whatever it is, I'll help you. I'm your husband now, and even though our marriage hasn't come about in the most regular fashion, I'll not shirk my responsibilities, Della, believe me."

As he caressed her, a look of such wonder spread across her face that she became, beyond a shadow of a doubt, truly beautiful. His heart surged. As aroused as he was, those other, more perplexing emotions welled up, too. He wanted to protect, to nurture...and much, much more.

THE NAGGING, STABBING sense of anxiety faded. There was nothing to be done tonight, fretting and panicking could not help, and to dwell on her fears for Sybil would be to deny Wilson the pleasures he'd been anticipating. The pleasures that he deserved, for the universal kindness he'd shown since their engagement.

He was correct about their marriage. It was irregular. But nobody could possibly know that from the way Wilson had conducted himself. He'd played the adoring fiancé to perfection, and been generous to a fault, lavishing upon herself and Mama and her sisters all the good things they'd not really been able to afford for quite some time.

For that at least, she owed him a delicious night and her undivided attention. No difficulty or hardship for her, either, given the rhythmic movement of his fingers, and the stroke of his thumb. His erotic accomplishments offered an oblivion, albeit temporary, but still welcome. Subsiding onto her back, she squeezed his hand, inviting more.

"Do you want to spank me, husband?"

He seemed to like that very much, and it excited her, too. The pain was piquant, but his hand was light, inducing heat more than suffering. She imagined its glow now, in her bottom, and the anticipation made her wriggle.

"I don't know…." His hand gripped her breast harder, finger and thumb settling on nipple and tweaking. "I think perhaps I just want to fuck you…but I can manage a slap or two, if that's what stirs your passion?"

"I don't want to be any trouble to you," she murmured. She had the strangest urge to tease him and provoke him, to goad him into some new and deeper excess. "If you're feeling fatigued, why not just climb on board and poke around a bit until you spend. I'll not insist on anything fancy if you can't manage it."

"Insolent minx." He leaned in closer, his mouth against her ear as he tugged at her nipple. Jolts of sensation shot from his fingers right down to her puss. "I'll show you. I've got more stamina between the sheets that even you know what to do with." For a heartbeat, Adela regretted every tryst with the boys at Sofia's, just because they rankled Wilson's pride. Even in this time of closeness and intimacy, he probably couldn't forget. Perhaps more so now than at other times.…

But then he laughed softly against her skin and nibbled her earlobe, catching it between his teeth, tweaking it in time to the work of his fingers. "I'll pleasure you until you can't see straight, my randy wife."

"Good. I look forward to it," Adela breathed, struggling to still her hips. It was as if a demon had climbed into her body, making it move and sway and jerk beyond her control. She grabbed at Wilson, trying to pull him close so she could rub herself against him.

"Tut-tut, be patient." Releasing her breast, he caught her by the wrists and pushed her arms back, against the pillows, fixing her there while he surged forward and kissed her on the mouth. As his tongue thrust, she could feel the hard length of his cock through his dressing gown, rocking against her belly as he subdued her.

Yes! Oh, yes! She wiggled faster, trying to work that hardness to the apex of her thighs, so she could massage herself on it, as a fulcrum, to pleasure her sex. For a few moments, Wilson seemed to allow it, even facilitating with movements of his own. Then he made a low, rough sound in his throat and stilled her with his whole weight upon her.

"Not so fast, wanton! Behave yourself." The grip on her wrists tightened, and his tongue went in deep, almost making her jaw ache. His sex was like a rock against her, but she could not move, held more by the force of his will than by his not inconsiderable strength.

"Will you be still and quiet and do as you're bidden?" he demanded against her lips as he broke the kiss. "Will you obey your husband and accept his dominion?"

It was a game of pleasure, but still she shuddered wildly. "I don't know if I can. You know my nature—I'm too sensual, and too willful, to be passive."

His grunt of triumph told her it was the answer he wanted.

"In that case, I'll have to bind you, and make you submit to my whims."

The sense of slight fear, and amusement, was intoxicating. She knew that if he'd had a mustache, he'd be twirling it now, playing Bluebeard for her. As it was, his silvery-blue eyes were glittering, and when he lifted his body away from her, he unfastened the sash of his robe and whipped it through the loops. With barely the breath to protest, and too riveted by the sight of Wilson's swinging erection to bother, anyway, Adela found herself secured to the brass rails at the head of the bed in a flash.

He'd fastened her quickly, but with complex knots, and the idea that he'd played games like these all the time with Coraline flashed through Adela's mind. The Parisienne was a sophisticate who made Adela's own sensual forays seem amateurish; the woman probably knew every carnal trick in the book and more besides.

But Adela banished her predecessor, as she sensed Wilson had managed to banish his for the moment. What did those others matter? What was past was past. Whether it was her amours or his, they meant nothing now.

The binding had plenty of give, and was comfortable, but firm. Each wrist was secured by an end of the sash, but the length was just passed behind two rails. She could easily turn over if she wanted to. Or Wilson could turn her. To get at her bottom, or her sex from the rear.

Her husband loomed over her, his member hugely erect between the silk panels of his dressing gown. Adela's mouth watered as he fondled himself in a slow, lascivious action. She licked her lips, hoping he'd allow her to suck him.

"Oh, no, not yet, Mrs. Ruffington. Perhaps I'll let you have a lick of the lollipop later. For the moment it's my turn to play with you. Your body is my toy...mine to do with what I want, now that you can't push me away."

Adela gasped when he moved forward and let the tip of his sex rest against her belly. When he drew it across her skin, it was hot as flame, moist and silky. She churned her hips and rubbed her thighs together, roused to distraction and craving his length between her legs.

"Oh, no, no, no..." His hands settled on her thighs, one on each, exerting pressure. "Spread your legs, Della...and keep them spread, or I'll fasten your ankles, too, as wide apart as they'll go, and then leave you like that while I read a book."

With difficulty, Adela fell still. The thought of what he described was a far greater torment than having her bottom spanked. It would be unbearable, although she sincerely doubted that Wilson would be able to concentrate on a book, tumescent as he was. But then, he *was* Wilson, supremely clever and perverse and a master of self-control. He could put parts of his mind and intellect into completely separate boxes...most of the time.

Their eyes met and he gave her a little smile that told her, without speaking, that his bold claims about book reading were without substance.

Adela spread her legs, just as he'd instructed.

"There, that's better. Your puss is delightful, Della, too pretty by far to hide."

In a move that was almost leisurely, he cupped his hand over her sex and gave it a slow squeeze. Adela bit her lip, fighting not to buck and writhe and drag her heels against the bedcovers. A second later he released her, and slid the flat of his hand over her inner thigh. "So smooth, so tender... Shall I smack you here and stoke the fires in your cunt?"

"If you're going to do so, kindly proceed and stop dawdling." She held his gaze, flaunting her hips at him. Why should she hide her desire? Wilson hadn't married her for her prim modesty. It was her sensual appetite for which he seemed to like her best, despite everything.

"Oh, you're such a delicious slut, Della…so randy. I should have known you'd turn out to be a supreme bed partner. If only—"

He stopped short, almost seemed to shake himself, yet made no move. Adela silently screamed for him to continue his sentence, but she knew he wouldn't. And indeed, the moment was gone as suddenly as it had appeared, lost in Wilson's narrow, lascivious grin.

Do you feel as I do? Do you wish that life might have taken that other path?

She smiled back at him. What was done was done…and they were married now.

"So, slap your thighs until they're pink? Or stick my cock in you? Which is it to be?" He ran his hand up and down her thigh, fingers curving on the upstroke, moving inward, flirting with her curls, tickling the underslope of her bottom.

"Both!" she challenged. "But not even you could manage both at the same time…no matter how flexible you are."

Wilson's eyes narrowed. "There might be a way…with a small substitution. Well, perhaps not that small."

Whatever did he mean? And then she comprehended it. At the same moment that Wilson leaned over and drew open a drawer in the chest beside the bed.

A *godemiché*. Not all that dissimilar to the one she possessed herself, a select item procured by Sofia for several of the more liberal-minded ladies of the Sewing Circle. But how did Wilson come to own one? Unless it wasn't his?

Her suspicions must have been written across her face, because he gave her an old-fashioned look. "Credit me with not being as crass as all that, Della." He twirled the ivory cylinder between his fingers, caressing it as if it were his own cock—which stood just as stiff and proud, barely inches away. "I purchased this especially for you as a private wedding gift, dear wife, knowing your adventurous and somewhat voracious nature. I was concerned that you should have something to satisfy you while I was recovering my powers."

"How thoughtful." Adela swallowed. It really was a rather sizable example. Certainly bigger than the one secreted away in the bottom of her trousseau trunk. She flicked her glance from the toy to Wilson's living equivalent, and back again. Bigger than him? Maybe a little, but not by much.

"Is it bigger than all the ones you're familiar with?"

This time he was testing her. Adela looked him in the eye. Better to face than to evade. "There have not been that many, Wilson, believe me. And none of them were as big as *that*—" She nodded at the *godemiché*. "Or *that*." She nodded at his cock.

It was the truth, but men were so concerned with their organs. Sometimes it was politic to exaggerate out of concern for their self-belief.

Wilson laughed. "There could well be a place for you in the diplomatic service, Della." He moved close beside her, his uncovered thigh pressing against hers, his cock almost touching her. Setting the *godemiché* on her belly, he slid his fingers into her sex, testing her readiness, and the intense sensations made her gasp, and the toy roll precariously.

"Mmm, very juicy…" He smiled in approval and raised his fingers to his lips to taste her. "I thought you might require a little oil in order to accommodate your new toy. But you're lush and flowing. I don't think you'll need it."

Snatching up the ivory phallus, he set it lightly between the lips of her sex and rubbed it up and down against her clitoris. The little organ was so sensitive that Adela tossed her head, her hair flying about. She clamped her teeth together to stop herself from moaning.

"Good?"

She nodded, her whole body tight with tension.

He rubbed some more and a ripple of reaction made her grunt, almost on the very point of spending.

"Oh, no, no, not yet!" Wilson whisked the phallus away and held it before her eyes. "See how wet it is, my luscious, wanton wife? It's big, but it will slip in nicely. Are you ready?"

Adela nodded again, not trusting her voice.

With a slight nod of his own, Wilson set about his task, businesslike now. Adela compressed her lips again to keep in all sound as he presented the solid tip at the entrance to her channel.

It was huge as he pushed it in. Far larger in perception than appearance. Even as wet as she was, it tasked her as if she was the tightest of untouched maidens. Yet her urge was to bear down on it, down on it, wanting its bulk.

"Too big?" Wilson's voice was low, not quite steady, almost as if he, too, were experiencing the pressure.

"Never!" she growled, pushing against the cool intrusion.

"A little oil, perhaps?"

"Yes…just a little. I think so…yes."

Setting the *godemiché* between her thighs, still touching her, Wilson reached into the drawer, bringing out a little vial of pale, almost colorless fluid and a piece of folded linen cloth. Taking away the toy for a moment, he folded the linen and placed it beneath her buttocks, obviously to avoid a nasty oily spot in the bed, afterward.

Next, he uncapped the vial and, placing the *godemiché* against her body again, poured a thin stream of it between her labia as he pushed in, in, in.

Adela grunted. The sensation of the dribbling oil was so

lewd and so alien, flowing over her clitoris and her inner folds and pooling where the bulbous head of the device stretched her. Still keeping up the pressure, Wilson set the oil aside, then rolled his thumb in circles over her clitoris, as if it were a crystal bead or a pearl, as precious in its own way as one of the diamonds around her throat.

It was too much. Adela shouted, her body rippling and yielding to the intruder as she spent. The *godemiché* rode home on the fluttering wave of her feminine pleasure.

"Good girl...my precious girl...my clever girl," crooned Wilson, still circling his thumb. He was gentle yet relentless with the erotic toy, compelling her to take as much of its length as she could, while also compelling her to endure a release so intense she could barely think or breathe. Then he kissed her hard on the lips, flicking her tongue with his own.

When he broke the kiss, Adela was gasping for breath, her head light, her senses befuddled by pleasure. It was a state both sublime and perplexing. He could control her so easily.

"Were you not going to slap my thighs, Mr. Ruffington?" she panted, moving her legs uneasily, intensely aware of the pale cylinder protruding from her sex.

Wilson's eyes were aflame. It was hard not to look away, but she held firm.

"You're a perverse one, Della.... You still want pain?"

"Yes, you devil! Give me a few hard whacks...anything to restore my wits to me."

He frowned back at her, and yet still smiled. In admiration.

"You are the most truly astonishing woman."

Adela stared back at him. Was he really so impressed? Was she really such a sensualist to him? He, who'd sampled the skills of the legendary Coraline, who was not quite, but almost, a courtesan?

"Yes, obviously I am. Now are you going to entertain me with your skills as a disciplinarian?"

"By George I am, you hoyden! You're a lewd and wicked madam with no decorum. You deserve everything that's coming to you."

With that he laid a stinging slap on the inside of her thigh.

Heat flared, as intense as the diamonds' luster, flowing through her skin and muscle, instantly gathering in her puss. She strained not to cry out.

Another slap landed, on her other thigh, the sensations complementing, cresting like waves that met at the very center of her pleasure where the *godemiché* stretched her. This time she did cry out, wriggling against her bonds, churning her hips. Wilson smacked her again, quick and fierce, two in fast succession, one on each thigh. The flames built, her need to spend gathered again. She moaned, long and brokenly.

As if heated himself by the exertion, Wilson flung off his robe, revealing his splendid body, another goad to her arousal. His smooth, pale skin gleamed in the lamplight; his muscles flexed as he raised his arm and slapped, raised his arm and slapped. His cock was so rigid and so rosy that surely that was a source of pain, too, as it swung in an agony of tumescence.

"Look what you do to me!" He paused in his efforts and folded his hand around his flesh, baring his teeth as he punished his own flesh with the heat in his skin. "It's always like this when I think of you…and these days I can't stop thinking of you. I need to have you near me, wife, so I can fuck you whenever I need to…. If I don't, I'll never be able to work."

"You could use your own hand," she gasped, watching the way his fingers gripped and moved, wishing that living length would soon replace the inert ivory inside her. She flexed herself around the *godemiché,* and gasped, almost climaxing.

"It's not the same…not the same at all." He leaned over

her, kissing her throat, right next to the diamond necklace, while pressing the tip of his cock against the burning heat in her thigh. "I want to fuck you now, Della. I need to fuck you. Are you willing?"

What a bizarre request! Surely he knew she was dying for him? He seemed to be able to read her every thought and desire, so he must be aware of her condition?

Perhaps some strange chivalric urge still compelled him to seek her leave to push himself into her?

"Yes. Please. I want you desperately, Wilson.... Please fuck me. Now."

In a swift, ruthless action, he wrenched the ivory toy out of her. Adela pumped her hips, wanting, wanting....

Still gripping his sex, Wilson gave her a searching glance, his own face suddenly a chiaroscuro of emotion. Questioning. Even confused.

"Do you want a child? I have French letters a-plenty, and I'll use them if you wish.... I don't want to compel you into something you might not want. At least not want yet..."

Adela's mind seemed to split, becoming both the lusty woman yearning to be fucked, and cooler dispassionate observer, considering the future and the consequences of their actions. If this sudden marriage was to be brief, and to end in a way as convenient as possible when the time came, it wouldn't be fair on a child, or children. In the very pit of her soul, she knew that she would love and adore and nurture any infant of Wilson's, but even though she knew him perhaps better than anybody, she wasn't sure he'd feel the same. Fatherhood required responsibility, and she wasn't convinced that was in his basic nature.

Yet she didn't want to hurt him by rejecting his seed.

She opened her mouth to form an answer, but he anticipated her.

"Shall we wait awhile? Not rush? We have choices and a condition of freedom here that many husbands and wives don't even consider. Let's use our enlightenment to our advantage, and choose the right time."

He looked calm, at least superficially at ease with his suggestion. Or as at ease as any male could be, sporting such a stupendous erection.

"I agree, husband, I agree." The question had arisen, and was now dealt with. Adela let the little portal to reason and debate in her mind close. All that remained was her desire, the requirements of her body, and yes, a wish to grant Wilson all the pleasure he'd given her. "Now come along! I want you. Kindly enrobe that magnificent staff you've been waving about for goodness knows how long, and put it to use."

Wilson laughed, reached into the drawer and drew out the tin of French letters that had been awaiting her decision. Within seconds, he was appropriately clad.

Leaning over her, he whispered, "Would you believe that I was thinking about this moment as we stood before the altar? It's a wonder the Lord didn't strike me with a bolt of thunder for disrespecting Him in His house."

It was Adela's turn to laugh. Certain thoughts had passed through her mind, too, and she'd welcomed them. They helped to banish others, ones about her and Wilson, and also other people. They threatened to rear up now, but the sensation of her husband's warm, skillful hands running up and down her flanks made them retreat. There would be another time for vexing questions, and perhaps she'd seek his counsel about them.

"I'm sure the Lord will forgive you. After all, you were only anticipating the act of 'worshipping my body' as specified in the ceremony." She glanced down at his cock, in its ingenious coat of rubber. "But didn't our friend there cause you some, um, difficulties?"

"Indeed he did, for a moment or two." Rocking his hips, Wilson pressed his friend against her inner thigh, right up against her *motte*. "But I was able to distract my mind by considering Fermat's great theorem until he subsided somewhat." Wilson nudged again, pressing harder. "But I doubt that anyone would have been looking at such a poor shade as me standing beside the brilliant beauty of my new wife."

Adela opened her mouth, but Wilson laid his hand across it. "I'll hear no protestations to the contrary. One thing we must agree on from now forward, if we are to live together amenably. There must be no denials of your beauty, do you understand me?"

Could it be true? *Was* she beautiful? She'd told herself for so long that her nose and her complexion were flaws in the eyes of all observers, but Wilson's words and the testament of his rampant cock were persuasive.

Perhaps not a classic beauty…but beauty of a different kind, maybe?

"I'm right, aren't I?" said Wilson, his mouth against her ear. As ever, it was as if he'd heard her very thoughts.

Adela nodded.

"Finally! Now let me get on with fucking you, will you?"

Her lips moving against his hand, she said, "What on earth is stopping you then?"

With a grunt of satisfaction, Wilson set about his task, settling himself between her thighs and greeting her sex with the tip of his cock. Resting on one elbow, he reached down and positioned himself more accurately, pausing in his efforts only to circle his thumb over her clitoris again.

"Oh, yes, Wilson, please… Please, I want you."

"Then have me, Della. Have me." He pushed in deep, the progress sleek and smooth and measured.

Adela rattled the bedstead, straining against the sash. "Release me! Let me hold you! I can't bear not to hold you!"

Wilson's eyes widened, his expression wild and unfocused, but he reached up and freed her, manipulating his clever knots in a trice. Could he read her mind, even now? Feel the great need in her, the unstoppable urge to be closer than close, even while they were joined?

Oh, Wilson, Wilson, Wilson…it's no good. I can't deny it.

Flinging her liberated arms around him, she buried her face in his neck, kissing him, kissing him furiously, tasting him and nipping at him, even as his strong hips pumped and his cock plunged into her.

I love you, Wilson. I love you. I know you're a strange, unusual, perverse man, and even if you like me, you don't really love me. But I still love you.

His hands slid beneath her body, gripping her bottom, clasping her ever closer, as if he were trying to climb inside her soul even as she yearned to climb inside his. She tilted her hips, trying to help him, bringing her knees right up and looping her ankles at the small of his back, arching against him.

They thrust and thrust against each other. Adela matched her ferocity with his, beating herself upon the rocks of his passion, taking all and giving all. If this physical union was the closest they could ever be, she would accept that, and revel in it as a rare gift not even always given to those that loved.

"Yes, oh, yes, sweet Jesu, yes!" she cried, gripped by a crisis so intense, her senses wavered. With her body pulsing and clenching around him, she ground her teeth, angry with herself all of a sudden for not being able to hold off and spend at the very same instant as him.

"Yes, my dear wife, yes…take your pleasure, take it!" Wilson growled, his voice muffled by her hair where he buried his mouth in it, kissing as hungrily as she'd kissed him.

Adela's heart turned over, even as she soared again. Despite all their differences, in this he was unselfish and caring. He seemed to give a far higher priority to her pleasure than his own.

Frenzied, she flexed against him again, squeezing him within as she embraced and clutched at him without. And he rewarded her with a great cry and a furious hammering of his hips.

In a great chaos of movement, and of tears, and heavenly bliss, they did this time, in the very same instant, spend together.

∽ 21 ∽

A Lucrative Little Matter

Blair Devine's mouth thinned as he toyed with the pink ribbon that tied the plump bundle of letters together. He hated pink. A young lady who he'd once courted had been very fond of pink. And she'd looked very fine in it on the day she'd informed him she did not wish to see him anymore, having heard that the bequest he'd been hoping for had eluded him.

But this could still be a lucrative little matter, and he deserved some recompense. He'd wasted enough hours with those tedious Ruffington women already, and his grand scheme for them was now scuppered, alas. Thanks to an alliance that he simply hadn't seen coming.

He wrenched at the pink ribbon, and it flew free, sending the little envelopes scattering over his desk.

Fucking hell, this affair could have been so much more than just a handy bit of blackmail. With certain other items in the safe behind him, he could have had millions in his grasp, and no further need for leveraging people over a few rude letters.

Although he might have done that just the same, for entertainment.

He clenched his fist. It was either that or tear the valuable letters to bits in exasperation. Damn that upstart Wilson Ruffington. That arrogant clever devil had thrown a spanner in the works of Blair's grander scheme, by marrying his crook-nosed "cousin" Adela.

He'd had it all worked out. He'd discredit Wilson Ruffington as the legitimate heir of Lord Millingford—he had the means to do it now—and then, in the absence of another living male heir, the old miser would have to settle his millions on his eldest granddaughter, whom Blair would have married in the meantime. Millingford wasn't keen on women—he was famous for that—but he'd rather leave his pile to a Ruffington woman than to no Ruffington at all.

But of course, all that was out the window now, before he'd even had the chance to start romancing Adela. Wilson Ruffington, arrogant, eccentric and wealthy in his own right, would get his paws on Lord Millingford's vast fortune now, anyway, because *he* was suddenly and very conveniently married to its most likely recipient.

Spotting a few choice phrases in the letter in front of him, Blair Devine smiled again. He'd never been a man to sulk over lost opportunities. Some other rich plum would drop into his lap, he was sure of it. He was already eyeing another prospect, the wealthy widow of a northern rail baron this time, whose money was all her own, dependent on no one. Well, it would be until Blair married her and relieved her of control of it.

His smile widened and he felt much better about the whole Ruffington business. The big prize there had slipped out of reach, but there was still a nice little income to be got from them to tide him over. And this first letter was proving most tasty. That girl Sybil had a rare, lickerish tongue on her, and writing in this cast to some less than scholarly swain, her language was quite basic. "Ooh, it was lovely when you touched my puss," indeed? What would her family pay to ensure that that choice sentiment didn't get into the hands of her fiancé's notoriously unbending patrician father?

Some Ruffington or other would have to shell out for these, and the funds would ultimately come from Wilson, Blair supposed. Or maybe there was some other prize his imaginary "client" might ask for?

The diamonds, perhaps? He had to admit they'd looked very fine on Adela at her wedding. They'd almost made her look beautiful. Almost made him think that a marriage to her might have been much more amenable than just a bounteous source of income, and a few quick fucks to get her with child.

Why couldn't *she* have written some letters? Given him some leverage to compel her to marry him?

Blair had often wondered if Adela had a secret. Sometimes, just sometimes there'd been a look in her eye, a hint of something that stirred his cock, despite her scrawny silhouette, her broken nose and her imperfect skin.

But now it turned out that she'd always been just exactly what she seemed, a respectable and less than pretty spinster who'd spent her time in drawing, and chattering at her Sewing Circle, and who'd disdained even the very few males who bothered to make advances…because all the time, she'd been in love with her strange, arrogant cousin.

Well, enjoy him, Mrs. Ruffington, enjoy him. I hope you still dote on him as much when you discover that his mother was a bigamist and a liar, who tricked a gullible man into believing your beloved was his son.

Yes, according to the documents in Blair's sturdy, impregnable safe, Wilson so-called Ruffington was illegitimate and not a Ruffington at all.

22

Honeymoon at Home

Adela decided that she rather liked married life. Even if the circumstances of her marriage were not those of most new brides, even if she missed her mother, her sisters, the familiar servants and the cat, dear Mr. Kipper, she was still surprisingly content.

There was no honeymoon. Wilson had offered a trip, even seemed enthusiastic, waxing lyrical about not only great cities like Paris and Rome, but also famous seats of learning he longed to share with her: Heidelberg, Gottingen and Montpellier, where he'd pursued his many scientific interests. But though she'd been tempted, Adela had declined the tour. She was too worried about Sybil and her missing letters, and couldn't shake an ominous sense of foreboding on that score. It seemed callous to go swanning off to the Continent, playing the real blushing bride, when that was far from the truth, and furthermore, her vulnerable sister needed her.

Expecting a protest from Wilson, she was surprised at his response.

"Please don't worry, my dear, we can travel at anther time. Next spring, perhaps, we could take a tour on the Continent. Explore at length…and perhaps visit Greece and Italy together and view all the greatest classical treasures of architecture and art." He squeezed her hand, his touch strangely tentative. "And perhaps it's for the best. I'm engaged on a project of critical importance for the War Office and it's at quite a delicate stage. I wish I could tell you more about my work— I trust your discretion, Della, truly I do—but I've signed a document of secrecy and I consider that binding, even though you're my wife."

"I don't mind. I certainly wouldn't expect you to reveal state secrets, Wilson." She laid her hand over his, touched by the fact he'd even want to tell her his secrets. "And yes, the Continent in spring would be wonderful."

If we're still together.

Had Wilson forgotten about the expediency of their marital arrangement? Sometimes it almost seemed that way, although perhaps he was simply making an effort to be nice Wilson instead of the usual cool, cantankerous Wilson, in order that the act of living together be pleasant.

It was certainly a logical approach, this companionability. Especially because his place of work was also their residence. So, in purely spatial terms, he was almost always near, and it wouldn't do to keep snipping at each other and making a nasty atmosphere.

What if this lasts? Would I mind that? He doesn't love me, and probably never will…but how would it be if we could stay together as friends?

Might there be a quiet pleasure to be had, working together, yet following their separate pursuits? Especially when, astonishingly, Wilson gradually began to share things with her. He asked her opinion on nonsecret matters, explaining scientific theories and practicalities to her. He went to great lengths to outline the wonders of their home's electric lighting, and its many modern amenities. He showed her how he used electrical power in the large workshop he maintained at the end of the garden, and all the functions of the many tools he'd designed. Clearly an electrical enthusiast, he even escorted her to visit the small generating station of the local power company, on whose board he served and whose construction and development he'd supervised. She clung to him throughout, slightly alarmed by the peculiar charge in the atmosphere that made her scalp prickle, and the roar of the boilers, and the heavy hum of the dynamos that seemed to vibrate in her bones. Yet to see her husband's passion for the subject, almost taste it, made her apprehension worthwhile, and she resolved to learn all she could from him about the work of Mr. Tesla and Mr. Ferranti of whom he spoke so highly, praising their generating systems over the prevailing preference for "direct current," with which he didn't seem overly impressed.

"Perhaps I should have gone more single-mindedly into electrical engineering myself?" Wilson mused as they walked home, his hand still over hers where it rested on his arm. She didn't seem to want to remove it, and as he didn't seem to mind… "But there are so many different branches of science and technology, and pure knowledge itself, that interest me…" He sighed and gave her a crooked little smile. "I can't seem to be satisfied in one particular area. I have to know all. Sometimes my brain seems to whirl with too many ideas at once…." His hand tightened, fingers strangely tender. "So many ideas and concepts that I forget about people…"

If they'd been lying in bed, she would have hugged him, and drawn him to her. Offered him a distraction from that desperate tyranny of his own intellect, an escape in the form of simple, straightforward physical pleasure. At least she could do that, even if she could never match the dazzle of his mental powers.

But they were walking along a public thoroughfare, superficially at least a conventional husband and wife of some status, and thus subject to propriety. So she just squeezed the strong arm beneath her fingers and answered his smile with her own.

"Well, don't worry about me, Wilson. I'm happy left to my own devices." She lowered her voice to a bare whisper, and looked briefly around before dropping him a wink. "As long as you attend my bed at night, I'll not consider myself neglected."

"You're a splendid and most accommodating woman, Della," he replied, winking back at her, but in his gleaming eyes, was there still a hint of shadow?

Was the rationally devised perimeter of their relationship blurring for him, too?

ADELA CONTINUED TO execute her own talents, too.

Freed from the necessity of drawing for money, she found it became an even greater pleasure. Not that she planned to let down Sofia and her friends, or her many other patrons. They'd supported her, purchasing her work in times of difficulty; it seemed uncharitable to desert them all now. So she continued, but drew only notional heroes from her imagination, characters from the classics and mythology, men who were composites, not any actual living male. Luckily, some of her most generally popular compositions had always been sold as prints, the original copied by the same engraver who prepared the illustrations for *Divertissements*. And now that she had the support of an independently wealthy husband, she asked that the similarly well-heeled aficionados of Isis's special talent donate an appropriate sum to the Saint Agatha's Church fund for disadvantaged women and children.

And her new artistic liberty allowed her to explore other

subjects. Wilson had a surprisingly beautiful garden, and even though he didn't dig and trowel it himself, he'd designed its layout and he supervised the purchase of plants and their disposition. Soothed by the gentle calm out beneath the willows, by the lily pond, Adela took to drawing there sometimes, and launched into a series of somewhat fanciful images of tiny but robust fairies, cavorting among the grasses and shrubs. She wasn't sure she actually believed in the little creatures, but she saw them in her mind's eye at least, and her Oberon bore a startling resemblance to her husband.

Wilson said nothing further about her visits to Sofia's pleasure house, and she never mentioned *that woman,* Coraline. Both were topics now closed, irrelevant, over. It was important to make the best of their new arrangement, and raking over the coals of their past amours would only make their chances of a true rapprochement difficult.

But still Adela wondered…and she had a feeling that Wilson wondered, too.

His passion, though, remained voracious, which was both convenient and delightful, because the more she lay with him, and touched him, and kissed him, and fucked him, the more voracious in turn Adela became.

Regular sex was a wonder, and different, and new. And not only for all the daring experimentation…but also the sense that she never had to yearn in the back of her mind for someone else. Now she could lie with that "someone else" every night of the week, and be thoroughly and deliciously serviced by him.

She couldn't get enough of Wilson's sleek, powerful body and his narrow, precise hands. She couldn't get enough of gazing into his pale, beautiful eyes as he fucked her. They coupled in every position known to her through her reading of esoterica, and a few that were luscious and new. Wilson had a fine collection of pillow books of his own.

They always used French letters. Another unspoken agreement.

There was only one thing that Adela would really have liked to change. Wilson's insistence on maintaining separate bedrooms. But Adela accepted her husband's rationalization for the sake of marital harmony, and he was right, in some ways. She knew his whirling, inventive mind often woke him in the night, so crashing with ideas that he'd spring out of bed to record them at the desk in his room. She'd frequently heard him get up and go bounding down the stairs to his workshop, when simply writing in his notebooks wasn't enough. All this coming and going was sure to wake her, so it was better for the health and welfare of both of them if they each had their own bedchamber. Surely?

It makes sense. It makes perfect sense.

It was all definitely much more than she'd been given to believe that most married couples enjoyed, probably even the ones who shared a mutual love.

One morning, Teale announced a visitor. It was something of a novelty, as even though her friends from the Circle had sent charming notes keeping her up to date, nobody had called in person since the wedding, clearly respecting the Ruffingtons' "honeymoon at home." The weather was gorgeous, mild and sunny, and Adela had chosen a spot under the gazebo in which to work today. It was rapidly becoming one of her favorite places—out of Wilson's way while he muttered and gnawed his lip over his "secret" work for the government, yet still allowing her to see his dark curls as he sat at his desk in his workroom. Somehow having him in sight lent a greater vibrancy to her work, even when she wasn't drawing him.

"Miss Sybil Ruffington, ma'am."

Happy for a change of routine, Adela set aside her drawing— a sketch of Wilson's austere yet harmonious profile. But her heart sank at the sight of her sister's flurried and pale face as she dashed past Teale across the lawn.

"Hello, darling." She rose and hugged her sister, alarmed that Sybil was shaking quite hard. "Come and sit down here and we'll have a chat." She glanced toward Teale, hovering discreetly, waiting for the logical instruction—to bring tea.

Up close, Sybil was as white as milk and her eyes were red. She'd been crying, and for an extended period, judging by the state of her.

"Teale, I know it's a little early, but do you think you could possibly bring us some sweet sherry? I'm feeling a little daring this morning, and I've a hankering for something a touch more exciting than tea."

"Of course, ma'am." He sped away.

"Now, sweetheart, I know what you're here about, but let's wait until we have our sherry, and you can tell me all."

Sybil nodded woefully. Then attempted a smile, her eyes roving over Adela's appearance. "You…you look very well, Della. In fact, you look *really* pretty…. Married life must be agreeing with you, even if you haven't had a proper honeymoon." Her attention settled on Adela's waist, not so clearly defined now in her loose emerald-green gown. True to her intention, it was of rational design, and skimmed only gently over her corset-free form. Wilson was delighted with her trousseau, too. Unfitted gowns, and light, nonconstricting undergarments were ideal for impromptu caresses.

"You're not, um… You're not enceinte already, are you?" Sybil inquired.

"No, I'm not." Again the new yearnings stirred, but Adela firmly put them aside. Sybil's difficulties were her priority now, not her own. "It's just that I can please myself what I wear all the time, now that I have my own establishment, and I don't have to worry about upsetting Mama with my lack of corsets. You should include some rational clothing in your own trousseau. I'm sure Algie would approve. There are certain, shall we say, advantages."

Sybil's eyes widened and she opened her mouth to pursue the subject, but just then Teale arrived with the sherry decanter and glasses on his silver tray.

When he was gone, Adela took a sip of the sweet and deliciously syrupy wine, then fixed her sister with a firm look. "So, have you received a communication about your missing letters? Has there finally been a demand?"

Sybil took a long swig from her own glass, in a way that made Adela half suspect that her sibling was quite familiar with the wine. Then, starkly, she named a sum.

"Good Lord, Sybil, I wonder where this person believes you might get an amount as large as that? One might almost think they've been biding their time until we were back in funds again, thanks to Wilson." Adela's fingers tightened on the stem of her glass. Anxiety swirled. Wilson would happily pay up. Money of itself meant nothing to him. But the thought of a blackmailing predator out there, taking advantage of the unwariness of young girls, and women in love, was disquieting and made her shudder in disgust. "Is there any indication who sent it? Any instructions about how to pay?"

Sybil's face crumpled. "Yes…the payment's to be delivered to a private *poste restante* at the Farage Hotel in Coop Street. I believe it's somewhat seedy, not a nice place at all… but that's not the worst of it…" She paused, twisting her fingers so tightly around the sherry glass stem that Adela feared she might break it. "I think I may have made the situation even worse…"

Worse? What could be worse? Adela ached for her sister, waiting for her to expound.

"In what way, sweetheart?"

"I confided in Mr. Devine. I didn't mean to…I wanted to tell you first. But Mama invited him to dine, and when I went out into the garden, to take the air and clear my head from all the whirling and worrying, he was out there, taking a cigarette. You know how tobacco smoke in the house makes Mama sneeze. He saw my abstraction, and remarked that I seemed pale…and…well…I found myself telling all. I don't know how…or why. He just seemed so very sympathetic."

Adela's heart sank at her sister's words. Devine *would* be sympathetic; it was his stock in trade.

"I don't even like him, Della," Sybil continued, "I never have done. I just tried to like him because of Mama. It seemed unkind not to be civil to a friend she seemed so fond of."

Adela frowned. Not at Sybil, but at herself. Once again, she'd underestimated her sibling. Warm, pleasure-loving Sybil did see the truth in people. Her only failing was that most of the time, she preferred to see the *best* in them instead. She wanted to be nice.

"I know, my dear, we've all be trying. You, and I, and Marguerite… So, what else transpired?"

"He offered to help. With his services as an intermediary, as he didn't think a gently bred young woman should have to… to negotiate with the blackmailing classes. He said he'd deliver and collect any correspondence from the *poste restante,* advise me what to write…so he could perhaps ameliorate the terms."

Sybil rubbed her eyes and drank more sherry. "But that isn't the very worst thing of all."

Suddenly Adela knew what that was, too, the very worst thing. In her heart and her gut she knew. She'd always known…well, something. But instead of protecting and advising her vulnerable sister and her vulnerable mother, she'd connived, by default, with a predator; preferring to devote her time and energy to her friends of the Sewing Circle, her drawing…and her sexual appetite.

Adela resisted the urge to toss back her own sherry and pour a second glass. "Go on, Sybil."

Sybil took a deep breath, straightened her spine and took another fortifying sip. "I've a feeling that Mr. Devine is more than an intermediary, Della. I think…I believe that he's the one with the letters. The blackmailer. It's just something I heard when I attended an exhibit with Daisy Drummond and Agnes Wentworth yesterday, trying to distract my mind. We fell to discussing a mutual friend who none of us has seen for a while…and a story came out."

Adela laid a hand on her sister's arm. "Can you tell me?"

Haltingly at first, then with a growing confidence and a new grit that Adela admired in her flighty sister, Sybil laid out what she knew.

The disappeared friend, Viola Champney, had also had letters stolen from a house party. Mr. Blair Devine had been a friend of that family, too, and offered his help. But later it had transpired that someone had seen a maid suspected of taking the letters in clandestine conversation with the young solicitor…and something, something that might be a small bundle had been seen to be passed across.

Adela didn't ask how that all might be verified, but she could believe it. It was common knowledge that servants talked to servants, and even if it was not meant in a bad way at all, secrets and ruinous information could travel like wildfire.

If only it had traveled in the direction of the Ruffington women before Devine had pinned them as a possible target.

"That horrible snake! I can't think why he would believe we had any money to give him. At least not before I married

Wilson. Why he would be interested in us at all? He must have known we had very little redress against the Old Curmudgeon, and his blessed will…and yet suddenly he's Mama's dearest confidant." Adela wondered again if she dare top up her glass without seeming a terrible example to her sister.

Sybil gave her a despondent look. "You've always been so very self-sufficient, Della. I suppose you decided when your nose got broken, and you had chicken pox, that you'd learn to live without hope of getting a husband." Despite the gravity of their talk, Adela had to hide a smile. Sybil was shrewder than she looked sometimes. "But Mama isn't like you. She adored Papa, but she's a woman who needs company, who needs admiration. I think she was flattered by Mr. Devine, and was probably indiscreet." Sybil drew in a great breath. "I think Mama was so cross about Wilson getting all the money as well as the title, that she really made herself believe that Mr. Devine might be able to obtain legal recompense for us. For you."

Adela saw it all now. Indignation welled up like a fulminating chemical. It wasn't just Sybil's letters, it was more…so much more. What a sly devil that man was! Once or twice, she'd sensed him on the point of making overtures to her, but he'd made no blatantly obvious move. She'd been repelled by his oily nature and perhaps he'd sensed that, and chosen to bide his time. Presumably his longer plan had been to romance her, and failing that, romance Mama herself, in order to gain access to the Ruffington wealth when the prospect of it was returned to them, rather than Wilson.

"So, that was his plan—help Mama overturn Grandfather's will, then marry me, or failing that, her, to get his paws on our money." Gritting her teeth, she topped her glass, and Sybil's, from the decanter. "But why on earth did he think he could succeed? Wilson *is* the old beast's closest male relative. He *is* the next Lord Millingford, and if Grandfather chooses to bequeath all his money along with the title, that's his prerogative."

Sybil pursed her lips and played with the strap of her small beaded bag. "Yes…but there's something. Something Mama hinted at, but wouldn't say more. I believe there was—is—some question about Wilson. Something concerning his parentage… I think Mr. Devine must have obtained some papers…or something."

"What?" Adela clenched her teeth to stop herself adding an oath, not sure who she was more surprised and vexed with.

Mama could be such a schemer, and it seemed her dear parent had tried to plan for two eventualities. Either she managed to marry her daughter off to Lord Millingford's heir, or if that wasn't possible, prove that the heir wasn't the heir, after all, so that, hopefully, the money, if not the title, would still come to that daughter.

"Ah, Mama. I know you mean well…." Steadying her breathing, Adela took a sip of sherry. Who cared about slight inebriation now? This was enough to drive anyone to the bottle. "But you're not a very good judge of character…. You should have chosen a better conspirator to share your grandiose schemes."

"She just wanted the best for you, Della, really."

"I know that, Syb. I know…." It was true. Mama loved them all, but sometimes her decisions were far from wise. It seemed they might have made an enemy now.

Adela drew in a calming breath. Spiteful enemies were made to be vanquished. Wrongs were placed in the world to be put right. She would not let this viper Devine hurt Sybil or Mama, or anybody else for that matter, if it was in her power to prevent him doing so. But she needed a plan and she needed help…from Wilson.

As she thought of him, the back of her neck prickled, and

as if summoned magically like a djinn, her husband appeared in the doorway leading to the house. He was clad in his usual working garb of silk dressing gown, trousers and loose collarless shirt, but to Adela he was a valiant knight in shining armor. As he strode toward them, he seemed almost mythical, his robe turned to a floating cloak of chivalry.

"Hello, Sybil, how are you? How kind of you to call. I'm sure Della has been missing you and Mrs. Ruffington and Marguerite…." He picked up the sherry decanter and poured himself a measure into a glass that he produced from his pocket like a conjurer. "May I pour you both some more?"

When they declined, he took a seat in the wrought-iron garden chair facing them, and stretched out his legs. "Very well, then, tell me immediately what's wrong and how I can help. I can see from both your faces that something less than pleasant has occurred."

Adela smiled at him. He was so clever, so observant. He could detect the subtlest signs in a person's face. Not that anyone would need arcane skills to read the faces in this instance. From the way Sybil glanced nervously and imploringly at her, even the densest of dolts would have been able to deduce a serious dilemma.

"Don't be scared, Syb. You can put your complete trust in Wilson. If anyone can fathom the correct solution to this wicked business, he can."

Haltingly, Sybil repeated her tale of woe, but for the first few moments, Adela hardly heard her. She was dazzled, made almost faint by the way Wilson glanced at her from time to time. He was listening intently, and paying attention to Sybil, but at the same time there was a silent aura about him focused solely on her, Adela. It was as if the fact that she had trusted him, brought him instantly into their circle of concern, touched him, and touched him deeply. He effected a little nod in Adela's direction, favoring her with a tiny but infinitely telling smile.

When the younger woman fell silent, Wilson seemed to contemplate for a moment, fingertips pressed together, touching his lips. His eyebrows had risen when Sybil had touched on his own status, but Adela could see from his face that the revelation wasn't a complete shock from the wild blue yonder. Had he suspected something akin to it all along?

"What should we do, Wilson?" she prompted.

"Well, naturally, if you wish to pay this creature off, I'll put all the funds you need at your disposal, Sybil. Regardless of what he's found out about me, you're still a cherished member of my family because Adela and I are married. I'll aid you in any way you need."

"Oh, thank you, cousin Wilson, thank you!" cried Sybil, her eyes shiny with tears and relief. "I didn't know what to do, or how I could pay. And I don't want Mama to know, because she's so desperately happy about my engagement—" she paused, and glanced between the two of them "—and your marriage. I don't want to spoil it all for her. And make her feel a fool for trusting that horrible man. And Algie's parents must *never* hear of the letters. Algie doesn't mind that I wrote to a sweetheart before him…he's a darling like that. But some of his family are terribly straitlaced about things like decorum and respectability."

Wilson sat back in his chair, his fingers still a steeple, his eyes intent on the point where they met. His thinking pose. He was working out something much more than the most discreet way to pay up. Something far grander in scope, and despite her worry for Sybil—and for him, if there were damaging documents about his parentage—Adela's heart fluttered with excitement. Wilson was brilliant and innovative, and he was afraid of nothing.

"Now then, Sybil…" He gave the younger woman a firm, almost schoolmasterly look. "This taking risks with letters has to end. Now. It isn't worth putting yourself in jeopardy just for a few pretty words. If you've written more letters to Algie, and he to you, you must both destroy them immediately. You must watch him burn yours before your eyes, and vice versa. Do you understand me?"

Sybil nodded, her eyes wide. Adela hid a smile. Wilson, the man of decision, had struck awe in her sibling. And, she'd be the first to admit it, in his wife, too.

"And I need you to give me a full list of what's missing. I think that before we're forced to the last resort, that is, paying this blackguard, we should first try to recover the letters by other means and then guarantee their destruction so they no longer represent a risk."

"But how can we do that?" Adela asked.

"'We'?" Wilson smiled.

"Yes, of course…I plan to assist you in this. Sybil is my sister, and I'm determined to help resolve her difficulty. With all respect to her, I don't think she's in a position to participate, but *I* certainly am." She held Wilson's gaze. "And I feel a degree of responsibility. I told Sybil to burn those letters, but I never ensured that she'd done it. If I'd insisted, and watched her do so, she wouldn't be in this predicament."

Again, he dazzled her with that radiant look. Again, her heart wanted to fly. Wilson's respect was infinitely precious to her. Even more, perhaps, than his desire. Desire would fade eventually, with the inevitable march of age, but respect could go on forever.

His scrutiny created another long pause, and Adela felt dizzy inside.

Speak, you devil, speak!

At last, he nodded. "Very well, I understand how you might

feel that way, Della, and I respect it. If there's any part of this enterprise that you can safely perform without risk of harm, I'll be glad of your help."

Sybil had been quiet for a few moments, as if sensing matrimonial undercurrents, but now she almost bounced in her seat. "Oh, thank you, thank you, both of you. I knew I was right to come to you. Mama would just have got into a flap, and I can't risk Algie getting into a bother with his family.... You're the only ones who can help." She sprang forward and gave Adela an enthusiastic hug, then darted around the garden table to embrace Wilson, too.

"Now, to the practicalities," he announced, when Adela's sibling had settled again and tea had been brought at Wilson's request. Adela smiled into her teacup, recognizing his caution. A giggly and intoxicated Sybil might give the game away before it was even afoot. "What specific threat has been made? How much time has been allotted for you to obtain and hand over the money?"

Sybil swallowed. "If I don't deliver the money by the date of our engagement ball, the letters will be sent to the Marquess of Spencerleigh." Her lip wobbled. "And if *that* happens, there'll be no engagement ball because there won't be any engagement."

Wilson tapped his finger against his teacup, and seemed to look inward for a few moments. More deep thought. "Now then, Sybil. I don't want you to do anything for the moment, do you understand me? And say nothing to anyone." His voice was steady, not domineering but intense, and Adela knew that not even *she* would argue with Wilson in this mode. "I shall visit Devine as your concerned brother-in-law and suggest that he negotiate more time for you, acting as your representative. I have a ruse in mind that will ensure no demand until after the engagement ball, and all I need you to do is ensure that

Devine is invited to the event. Are he and your mother still on good terms?"

Sybil looked horrified at the prospect of inviting the man who was now her worst enemy to the greatest event of her life so far, but to her credit she nodded. "Yes, as far as I know. He's not called on her quite as much lately, since your marriage, but I don't believe they've argued or anything. Just a cooling, now that he's…well, now he's changed his plans."

Adela imagined Devine's face. He'd probably love to be at the ball to see his victim's discomfiture. She could imagine him as just the nasty kind of bully who'd enjoy seeing his prey squirm.

Businesslike, Wilson went on. "Good. We need to know where he is at a very specific time. I could arrange to have him followed, but if he were to be seen at the ball, by many, his location would be fixed for certain."

"Why do we need to know where he is, Wilson?" Adela asked after Sybil had departed with her instructions. She had half an inkling that she knew what her husband was up to, but she'd quizzed him, anyway.

"Because if I know where he isn't, *I* can be there…retrieving those letters."

23

A Nefarious Scheme

"You mean you're going to steal the letters back from him?"

Adela stared at her husband, nonplussed despite her suspicions. This was exactly the sort of bold, nefarious scheme she'd expected of him.

"Precisely, my dear." He beamed. "Well, perhaps not steal them. Depending on the amount of time I have, I may burn them in situ, along with any other incriminating letters I find, from other impetuous young men or women. I might as well relieve the anxieties of as many correspondents as I possibly can, because I suspect Sybil is far from Devine's only victim. This kind of parasite gets a taste for such ruses rather quickly."

"But how will you gain access? And where?"

Wilson tipped his head to one side and shrugged. "I would deduce that he doesn't keep such items at his place of work or this accommodation address of his either. They're precious to him. A prime source of income… He'll keep them close, probably in a strongbox at his home. Do you know where that is?"

"Yes, he has a villa in Upper Norwood. A rather nice one,

but larger than one might expect for such a young man, alone. He invited us all to tea once….” She shuddered, remembering an uncomfortable experience. “It was dismal. He did nothing but keep steering the conversation around to his own accomplishments. Of course, Mama lapped it all up like cream.”

“Did you see much of the house? Could you describe the general layout? The disposition of the rooms?” Wilson’s eyes were sharp. She could almost see the cogs of his rational mind whirling, calculating.

“Not really. We saw only the parlor and the entrance hall.” She racked her brain, trying to recall tedious details that she’d dismissed from her mind. “I believe he might have an office or a small library on the ground floor, at the side of the house, facing the garden. He went to fetch a photograph album to show us, and was out of the room for barely a moment.”

Wilson’s eyes were almost triumphantly bright now. “An office on the ground floor, eh? That would make things so much easier….”

“In what way?”

“If his office is on the ground floor, it should be a relatively simple matter to…well, break into it and crack his safe.”

“A simple matter?” The man was astounding. He never ceased to amaze her, and yet she had to admire his stunning boldness. “Breaking open a strongbox is a good deal more of an enterprise than simply picking a door lock, Wilson.”

“Have faith, woman!” he said with a laugh, catching her by the arm and planting a kiss on her cheek. “I’ve made a most detailed study of safes and strongboxes. I can’t tell you the precise circumstances, but I was called by a manufacturer to consult when they were creating a new safe for, shall we say, our premier London bank.” He leaned forward and whispered the name, and Adela gasped. “Given what I know, I could probably break in there, too, if I wanted to.”

"Well, I'm glad you don't want to! I—I've rather got used to your company now and I don't want you to be thrown into prison." The idea of being parted from him made her shudder. It would probably have to happen eventually, but she prayed for just a little while longer. Long enough for their European trip, perhaps, and maybe also to conceive a child. "But what if you get caught at Devine's house? You'll be prosecuted just as surely for that, won't you?"

Wilson's expression was almost serene, and his fingers were gentle as thistledown as he cradled her cheek. "Ah, but I have one sovereign advantage on that score, my darling." He kissed her again, just as gently. "Remember the work I'm doing for the government? The critically important work?" She nodded, dazzled by the glint in his eyes. "Well, it means that I have friends in high places…perhaps the highest places one can aspire to. It doesn't mean I'm completely above the law, but I might be able to get away with bending it a little bit." He quirked his dark brows playfully.

Despite her concern for Sybil, despite her concern for Wilson himself, Adela almost gasped. He was dazzling in his magnificent, bright self-confidence. He shone like a god. She longed to kiss him in return. Really kiss him. And drag him to her bed.

He looked at her searchingly, his fingers against her face. "I know, I feel the same, but there's much to do. I have to go out now, first to pay a call on Devine at his chambers in that guise of a concerned family member, anxious to discuss Sybil's difficulties. And then perhaps I'll pay some other calls and see some people who can help and advise me on certain points." He nodded in sudden satisfaction. "Norwood, you say? That's opportune…a friend I need to consult lives there. Now, there's not much time. The ball is almost upon us. We've only a few days."

"Can I come with you?" Suddenly, she didn't want to be parted from him. "At least to see Devine."

Wilson pressed his forehead to hers for a moment, then pushed away. "No, my sweet, I suspect that a conversation with him might be better man to man, and any discussions I have afterward with my consulting friend will be too frank for refined ears. And after that I may have to visit some other, far less salubrious venues to find out what I need to know. Probably places I'd hesitate to take a lady...even a strong-charactered Athena like you." He grabbed her hand and squeezed it. "But I'll report all when I come back. The plan is ours, and I'll need your opinion."

Her heart soared, making her bold. "But when you go and...break in, I want to come with you. I can help."

"But, Della, it might be dangerous. Even if all my planning is perfect, there's always some random event that can occur and tip it all up." His words were doubtful, but something in his eyes told her she might win.

"I'll exercise every caution. I'll follow your lead. You know I can be stealthy."

Wilson grinned. "Indeed I do...indeed I do." He pursed his lips, effecting profound thought, but she could see she'd got him. Almost. "And I might need someone to hand me my tools, and to hold the dark lantern."

Adela gazed at her husband, willing him with all the force at her disposal to yield. She knew he had the power to persuade and compel like this, almost by mystical means...so why couldn't she do it, too?

"Very well, then. Depending on what I discover today, I'll consider it. But you *must* obey every instruction, and if I tell you to retreat, you do so, and run like the wind back to safety, do you hear me?"

She nodded, trying to suppress her smile and ignore the

huge pounding of her heart that she was almost sure Wilson would be able to hear. The nod was a lie. Whatever happened, she'd stand with her husband to the end.

"And you'll have to wear masculine dress, you know. Even your rational attire will be useless if we have to wriggle under fences or climb over walls and maybe shin up drainpipes if his strongbox turns out to be in an upper room. Can you shin up a drainpipe?"

The smile broke out. "Well, I can certainly climb trees, and it must be similar. I'll practice."

Wilson reached out and very gently touched her nose. "Beware of trees, my sweet. I wouldn't want another one to hurt you."

Adela smiled to herself as he leaned in and dusted a fleeting kiss where his fingers had rested. To her astonishment, she realized she'd forgotten about her flaws, her perceived blemishes. They were nothing to her now, and she never thought of them. And even when she did, they no longer had power over her. Living with Wilson, and flourishing in his manifest desire for her, had made her invulnerable to those old fears. "Don't worry, I'll be careful," she said.

"Very well, then. I'll survey the lay of the land, and if it seems reasonably accessible, I'll consider taking you on as an accomplice." He took her hand, raised it to his lips and kissed that, too.

How am I going to follow his lead and break into a house if I've come to a state where even his lightest touch makes me want to swoon?

It was a conundrum, but she could overcome it. Wilson was prepared to trust her to be his partner in crime, and that seemed to be a critical new step along their path as a couple.

"Now, I must change and be off. Maybe you can practice climbing while I'm out?" He laughed softly, but then his face changed, grew more serious. "I do trust you, Della, believe me. There's nobody I'd rather have by my side in a tight spot. Now, can you remember the name of the road where this blackguard lives?"

Adela reeled off the address, then Wilson squeezed her hand, kissed it again and strode to the door. He seemed to have already begun his mission, and put her behind him. But when he reached the door, he turned to wink at her roguishly, before pounding off along the passage and up the stairs.

Adela stared at the empty space where he'd been, and then moved into it.

I love you, Wilson, but if you don't love me, it doesn't matter. If you trust me, that's enough. I can live on that.

HE WAS GONE for hours. But Adela had expected that. When he was working, he was often sequestered for hours, too, absorbed and oblivious to the passage of time.

Determined not to fret and worry and generally act the powerless little woman waiting at home, she entered Wilson's dressing room and reviewed his clothing, searching for a suitable attire for breaking and entering. Picking the odd lock at a country house party was a world away from entering a residence under false pretenses, and as Wilson had pointed out, she had to have the right clothes for the job.

For all his bohemian pretentions, Wilson's clothes were kept in perfect order by Teale, who was his valet as well as his butler. All hung neatly on their hangers, and though the wardrobes all smelled of camphor to protect cloth from moths, the provocative odor of Wilson's own spicy shaving lotion still seemed to haunt each garment. Grinning, she tried on a few of his dressing gowns, aware that she was deviating from her objective, but she couldn't resist whirling about in them, imagining she was he, the great eccentric genius.

She pressed her face against his shirts, breathing in his scent, suddenly longing for him in the most visceral way. Her body heated, hungering for him, and she considered touching herself, right here in his room, surrounded by the scent of him, and clothing that had touched his body. But she resisted. Wilson was out and about, possibly getting into danger for the sake of her sister and her mother. The least she could do was act constructively toward their shared goal.

Though most of Wilson's clothes were "town," she discovered a few items at one end of a wardrobe that seemed more fitted to country wear, and a couple suits of clothes seemed most promising. Both comprised an Argyll jacket and knee breeches, and each was made from a handsome but fairly dark tweed. One had a grayish-blue hue and the other was more brownish, but either would be perfect for creeping around in the shadows and undergrowth.

Adela selected the brown suit, purely for the fact that her hair was brown, and the blue-gray suit would go better with Wilson's beautiful eyes. She giggled at the silliness of her reasoning.

But what to wear on one's head with such an ensemble? Wilson rarely wore hats, but he seemed to have one or two, and she picked out a flat cap in a similar tweed to her chosen suit. She would have to wear the simplest of coiffures to the ball if she were to get her hair into the cap's confines, but it looked as if it might be possible. Gathering up her spoils, she made her way to her bedroom. Who knew what valet's task Teale might choose to engage in at any moment? And it wouldn't do for him to find the mistress of the house dressed only in her underpinnings.

Wearing Rational dress style made changing clothes to try on her disguise an easy task. It wasn't only carnal play that simple clothing facilitated. Stripped to her drawers and her lightly supporting bust bodice, Adela began to wiggle into

the breeches. They were a bit of a squeeze, from a combination of the fullness of her drawers and her womanly hips. But
at least here was one advantage to being on the scrawny side:
it allowed her to get into the breeches at all. And there was
some generosity in the seams. She could let them out a little to accommodate her slight curves, and wear a pair of the
newer, more slimly cut drawers she'd purchased from Mme
Mirielle beneath.

Excellent. Unpinning her hair from its loose knot, Adela
gathered it up in hanks and stuffed it beneath the cap as she
crammed it on her head. It was a struggle, because her hair was
so thick, but with a bit of pushing and poking it all went in.

What a strange boy.

Her reflection looked terribly odd to her, but somehow also
attractive. What would Wilson think of her in this ensemble?
Would he still desire her? Wicked thoughts of seducing him
while she was dressed in his country suit flitted through her
mind. Perhaps presenting herself to him as a youth, baring
her buttocks not for spanking, but for…for other activities.
Lady Southern at the Sewing Circle, for one, had described
in the most hair-raising terms how one of her lovers always
preferred to plow her that way. And how deliciously and perversely pleasurable it was….

Adela shuddered, trying to imagine it. Would she enjoy it?
When Wilson stroked her between the buttocks while they
were playing or fucking, it always excited her. But the full
act was a very different kettle of fish. She'd never sampled
that particular activity during her frolics with Sofia's boys,
although Clarence had once asked her if she wanted to try it,
she and Wilson had not yet ventured that way.

What would it be like?

Still in her suit and cap, she laid herself facedown on the
bed, her legs dangling over the edge. Closing her eyes, she

pictured Wilson coming up behind her, his face fierce with lust, his eyes burning.

"Show me your arse, lad," she imagined him commanding roughly. "Let's have a look at it."

She would obey, unbuttoning trousers and drawers and pushing them down. She could almost feel his hands manipulating the cheeks of her rear, pushing, pulling. Pulling more, exposing the pouting little vent. Such a little vent…for such a large cock as her husband's to enter.

Would he pleasure her? Of course he would. This might be a little dramatic performance she was fantasizing about, but it would still be Wilson. Her husband who was even more scrupulous about her pleasure than any gigolo had ever been. While he admired her bare rear and fancied himself sheathed in it, he'd have his hand under her belly, his fingers plying her clitoris in the clever way only he could.

With a little moan, Adela made at least part of the fantasy real. She unbuttoned her trousers and unfastened her drawers and worked her hand inside, finding her center with clumsy haste. She was already wet and ready from her imaginings.

Yes, Wilson would finger her roughly, muttering delicious profanities in her ear, something else he excelled at. She'd wriggle against the bed, as she was now, encouraging him.

"I'm going to fuck your arse, you sumptuous little pansy," he'd say, his fingers moving, probing the little hole, making her grunt. "You're going to take me there…you're going to take all of me. My big hot cock. I'm going to fill you up and make you squeal like a little pig."

Rocking against the bed now, Adela rubbed herself with furious, inaccurate haste. She was desperate to spend, her sex aching. The desire for fulfillment was agonizing, and though she wished Wilson was really there behind her, her own hand would suffice for the moment. As she shuffled and wriggled, pounding herself, she laughed. Perhaps she'd tell him about this, for his entertainment, when he returned. He loved to see her bring herself off, and always encouraged it, whether he was present to view it or not.

Back in her fantasy, her husband opened his trousers and drew out his cock, huge and rampant. Adela trembled. It was very big and her bottom was very tight. Surely he'd need something to ease the way. Her imagination supplied the oil he used to grease the *godemiché,* and in her mind's eye, he poured a stream of it between her bum cheeks.

And then he pushed himself into her.

Adela tried to imagine the sensation, but could not with any clarity. But the idea of it, just the thought of it, was enough.

Rubbing her clitoris madly and imagining buggery, she spent and spent with her husband's name upon her lips.

24

Wilson Reconnoiters

Concealed behind a laburnum bush, against the wall in the garden of Blair Devine's Norwood villa, Wilson imagined Adela crouching beside him.

What would she look like in man's dress? He tried to picture her sleek thighs in trousers or breeches, and had to put down his miniature pair of field glasses for a moment, overcome by a sudden gouge of lust. Despite her innate femininity, she'd make a handsome boy with her thick, lustrous hair contained in a cap, and her pert bosom concealed by a loose, untailored jacket. Waiting for Devine—who was framed in the square of flickering yellow light that was his library window—to move from his desk and hopefully reveal the location of his strong-box, Wilson entertained the notion of kissing his wife while she was dressed as a man. Kissing her, and then doing other things. Things an invert man might do to a pretty boy if he had him in his clutches. Or simply daring games that a man, and a woman who trusted him, might play.

This is not the time to get a raging erection, you imbecile.

But still Wilson couldn't help himself, or control his flesh. Visions of Adela bent over the back of that nearby rustic garden seat taunted him. Her masculine trousers would be around her ankles, along with her drawers, and her creamy bottom present to the moonlight, for his pleasure. He pressed his hand to the front of his own trousers, although there wasn't much likelihood of stilling the ache now his imagination had got ahold of him. Would he spank her beautiful behind? Possibly...and then, oh, then, which of her lusciously exposed portals would he enter?

She was masquerading as a boy, after all. Why not possess her as a boy, and fuck her perfect arse?

Would she wriggle and struggle and mock resist him? Or would she be stoic, attempting to hide her anxiety—and desire—boldly reaching around to hold apart her own buttocks to ease his entry?

Oh, that would be his daring, fearless Adela. She'd gasp, strain against him, almost compel him to proceed in the dark possession. And she'd be tight, oh, so tight. Her sex was sublimely snug, a perfect embracing fit, but her arse would grip him harder, fiercely holding him as he plumbed her depths and made her groan.

Oh, for pity's sake, Wilson, you'll be a poor excuse for a thief if you allow yourself to be distracted by your wife's arse, right at a critical moment!

He couldn't laugh aloud, but he grinned at his own foolishness. It might actually be more prudent to have Adela with him, after all. She was all good sense, and her cool disapproving glare would quell his idiocy until the appropriate time.

Still hard, but not distracted by it, he returned his attention to the window, and felt a jolt of attention when Devine rose from his desk.

The man was both smooth and despicable. Wilson had

fought a good fight to remain as smooth in return as he'd faced Devine in his office earlier that day. What a hypocrite the fellow was. Feigning concern and sympathy for Sybil's plight, and yet radiating malice and resentment and a gloating confidence beneath.

Devine had barely been able to suppress his glee when Wilson had suggested that they might present a counter offer to the mysterious blackmailer.

"My sister-in-law isn't wealthy in her own right, as you know. As a concerned brother-in-law, I want to help in any way I can, but my wife and I, too, are of modest means until the death of her grandfather. The only significant assets we have between us are the Ruffington diamonds." Oh, how those weasel eyes had sharpened. Did he know that Wilson could pay the purchase price, and barely notice the deficit? Or was it the mention of the gems that had piqued his interest? "My dear wife is fully prepared to sacrifice them, in order to purchase back the…items in question. But I wanted your opinion as to whether just one concession might be wrung from the party involved?"

"I couldn't say.… It's possible. These types are sometimes prepared to horse trade if the circumstances are advantageous. It all depends on whether they've been strung along in the past, in which case the possessor of the item may be inclined to stand firm."

Wilson wanted to spring across the desk and beat the man to a pulp. "I'd ask for only a few days…simply to allow my dear wife one last opportunity to wear the diamonds in public at her sister's engagement ball. Then she'd put them up for sale, discreetly, at a gem dealer of the greatest discretion, and the funds would be readily available."

Greed and triumph shone in Devine's pale eyes. "That's one course of action. Or perhaps we could offer to hand over the diamonds directly? I could draw up a note to that effect and have it sent round to the *poste restante* if you like? Either way, if the party is a reasonable man, a charitable man—" the solicitor licked his lips "—I'm sure he wouldn't deny Mrs. Ruffington one last opportunity to dazzle."

How magnanimous.

When the interview was over, and the formalities settled, Wilson had experienced difficulty in quelling his urge to run from the room and hire a hansom to take him immediately to his favorite Turkish baths. Anything to wash—or steam—away the repugnant sense of grubbiness that seemed to coat him after spending time near Blair Devine.

He felt dirtied by the man even now. Although some of that sensation was probably actual dirt, from lurking around in the bushes, watching him.

Wilson held his breath. What was the odious creature doing? Did he know he was being observed, and was behaving in a way that was deliberately taunting?

Focusing his glasses to their maximum acuity, Wilson watched as his quarry ran his fingers down the edge of a particularly ugly painting of a horse, and abracadabra, the frame swung forward to reveal the heavy iron front of a safe. It was too far away to see the make of the lock as Devine manipulated it, and there was no indication as to whether he kept the key on his person, or secreted somewhere in the room, but Wilson wasn't daunted. He was sure he could crack most strongboxes in England today, perhaps even in the empire or the whole world…and failing that, he had other avenues of attack. Certain acidic compounds he'd developed could be carefully utilized.

Yes, he could do it! He was confident.

Wilson smiled as he waited for the safe to be closed, the

picture to swing back and eventually, the light to go out as Devine finally quit his library.

All Wilson wanted to do now was to get back home to Adela.

❧ 25 ❧

After Midnight

It was after midnight, and still no sign of Wilson. Adela had heard sounds in the house a little while ago, but there was no way of knowing if it was him, back from his long day of studying the lay of the land, and other preparations, or just one of the servants going about their normal nighttime tasks.

Come and tell me about it all, my love. I'm awake. I need to see you, even if you don't stay and make love to me.

The plea was silent, but as the clock ticked quietly and the low lamp flickered a little, indicating a minor fluctuation in the supply of electrical power, a clearer sound made her heart leap in anticipation.

The door handle was turning slowly and stealthily.

"Adela? Are you awake?" called a low voice quietly from the shadows. Then Wilson stepped into the room.

It was an effort not to fly upright in bed, grinning like a fool. Wilson probably wouldn't appreciate that. A measured response was better, even if she was elated that he'd finally appeared.

"Yes, I'm awake." Propping herself up, she reached out for her shawl and drew it around her shoulders. "Have you eaten, Wilson? Shall I ring for Mrs. Rogers to prepare you something?"

"Don't fret, Della. I'm perfectly all right," said her husband, moving into the pool of light. His voice was mild and friendly despite the words, and he smiled at her as he stood beside the bed, looming a little as he almost always did. "I'm quite proud of myself. I stole into the kitchen and purloined some bread and ham and milk from the cold box, and now I'm well fed."

Adela longed to reach out and grab him. He looked so enticing, so lean and powerful in his thin silk robe, and with his dark hair gleaming, as if damp from recent ablutions. "Excellent." She smiled back at him. "Stealing from the kitchen is good practice for our forthcoming endeavors."

Wilson seemed to hesitate, still hovering beside the bed. Was he shivering? It was unusually cool for this time of year and the splendid system for heating the entire house that he'd shown her, his own design, was not yet in operation. He certainly appeared weary, too, now she had a chance to look closer. "Would you mind if I slipped into bed for a little while, just to tell you about my progress today?" he said. "It's very late, and you must be tired, as am I, so I won't trouble you...."

It's no trouble, my love. Never...

Adela lifted the covers, shuffled over and patted the place beside her.

"Thank you, my dear.... It's chilly." Slipping off his blue robe, Wilson climbed into bed. He was naked, as she presumed was his custom for sleep, and his long limbs were pale in the soft light. She tried not to glance at his cock. This wasn't a time for carnal matters; he'd said as much. But she still couldn't prevent herself from stealing a peek.

He was unaroused, and yet somehow, she didn't feel disappointed. In fact, his quiescence moved her. In this instance, at least, he wanted something other than lovemaking from her, and that seemed more important for the moment than the flesh.

"So, how did you fare? What did you see? Did you speak to Devine?" She shrugged out of her shawl and snuggled beneath the bedclothes, flinging the shawl over Wilson's side.

He shuddered, clearly with distaste, not cold now. "I did, and that worthy graciously agreed with me that it might be possible to persuade the blackmailer to wait until after the engagement ball for his payment. The gall of the man! I almost got the impression that he knew I knew it was him…. Either way, he seems to like the idea of taking the diamonds in return for the letters, goddamn him."

"Did you meet at his office? Or his home?"

"His office. It was during business hours, and I think it's better not to remind him that we're familiar with where he lives. That way he'll not suspect there's a game afoot."

Adela smiled at Wilson's relishing the idea of an adventure. He would think this plan out to the very last detail, but that didn't in any way quash his boyish enthusiasm for it.

"Very good. Sensible thinking."

"Yes, I thought so." Wilson beamed, stirring in the bed. Adela held herself still, trying not to reveal how the sensation of his firm bare thigh rubbing against hers through her nightgown excited her. This was not the time, this was not the time.

"Tell me more. What else did you achieve?"

"A very great deal, Della, a very great deal. I do believe we'll be able to pull off this scrape magnificently." Edging a little closer, he laid an arm across her, the gesture companionable, almost brotherly, but still welcome.

Speaking low and soft, but with an air of excitement, Wilson briefly and succinctly outlined his progress. After his interview at Blair Devine's chambers, he'd hailed a cab and ridden to the house of an old friend of his, who, as luck would have it, had recently moved to a house not all that far away from Devine's Norwood residence.

And he'd sought advice.

"What is he? A criminal? A policeman? A judge?"

"No, none of those… He's a doctor and a writer, actually, but he has the most original and imaginative mind, with, well…a flair for the devious and the study of crime." Wilson's eyes glittered, as if he admired this clever man as a peer and equal. "He was able to make some useful suggestions for our enterprise, and confirm some of my own ideas on how to proceed. He said he'd love to come along…but alas, he has an engagement that evening."

Adela was glad. Paragon or no paragon, she wanted to effect the escapade with Wilson alone, not accompanied.

After his visit to his clever friend, Wilson had made his way, on that friend's instruction, to a public house in the vicinity of Devine's home, and made casual inquiries, saying he was interested in purchasing a house locally and had heard Devine's might be for sale. After initially drawing a blank, Wilson was preparing to leave when a stroke of good fortune had occurred.

He had encountered a local plumber and handyman in his cups with much to say about Blair Devine, and all of it disparaging. "He's not well liked by locals, by tradesmen or even by his own servants," Wilson told Adela. "Fred is quite friendly with Devine's footman and he sent a note round, with a boy, to fetch him."

"Won't that make Devine suspicious, if he finds out about it?"

"That would have been true…if he'd been well regarded. But as he isn't, I found not only Fred but the landlord also anxious to help. Especially when I was acting in the manner of a private detective looking into Devine's affairs for a client. And the footman, Earnest, was thrilled to be of assistance in my surveillance."

"Oh, Wilson, you're outrageous! A detective, whatever next?" Adela chuckled, even more aware of his body as he hugged her and waggled his brows devilishly.

"Don't laugh! I think I would have a flair for it. Crafty thinking and all that... And I'm sure Arthur would give me plenty of tips."

"No doubt he would.... So, what else did you discover?"

Adela listened, rapt, as Wilson described all that he'd learned from the footman, and then how he'd lain low outside Devine's house for an hour or so, watching.

"No wonder you're chilled and tired," she exclaimed, imagining her husband crouched in the cold, watching and waiting. "I hope you haven't caught a cold."

"Don't worry." Wilson inclined toward her and kissed her on the forehead. "I might look like a skinny, pasty-faced scholar, but you know I'm tough, Della. I'm perfectly well, and I had a hot bath when I got in." He slid his arms around her and drew her to him. Still gently, still chastely...or almost chastely. Against her thigh, Adela detected something herself. "And Earnest was able to tell me something of the layout of the house, and the best points of access. Our luck is in, my dear. Devine's study *is* on the ground floor and has a convenient window...and I was even able to see him open his safe."

"Goodness...a safe? Doesn't that make things more difficult?"

"Not in the slightest!" Wilson sounded so confident, and it was difficult not to be swept along. "Remember, my dear, I'm quite an expert on safes, and have even designed several. And this one did not look too difficult. I should be able to crack it quite easily…or failing that, compromise the lock with a spot of acid."

"Acid?"

"Never fear, you know me better than to think I'd take risks with chemicals. It will be safely transported in a vial of my own design, and I shall wear gloves when handling it."

"If you say so."

"That I do. Trust me, Della. I'm thinking all this out most carefully, and we'll be especially cautious as we proceed."

We. How good that sounded. To be part of this bold scheme to save Sybil's engagement. To be considered a worthy "partner in crime" by perhaps one of the most brilliant minds in the entire British Empire. Edging closer, she murmured, "I do trust you, Wilson…but I almost feel guilty."

"Why?" His mouth was against her brow, and she felt his hand come up and his fingers delve into her hair. He loved to do that to sample its texture and thickness.

"Because it's all so exciting, and I'm really looking forward to it…and I shouldn't because it's serious and Sybil's so upset."

He shrugged slightly. "It's a challenge to the intellect and to the spirit, Della. No wonder you're excited. Of course, we're both worried about Sybil…but we can still enjoy our little adventure, too."

They lay in silence for a little while. Adela tried to relax, but she still felt tense. Every part of her was yearning, aching in hope that just this once, Wilson might actually stay instead of returning to his own room. But she wouldn't ask and she certainly wouldn't beg. No matter how affectionate he seemed sometimes, and how astonishingly more amenable he was being these days, she must never forget the deal between them. The arrangement. They were both being sensible and adult, and making the best of things…weren't they?

"Can you not rest?" Wilson's words made her jump, but

immediately, almost as he were doing it purely on instinct, he stroked her hair again.

"I suppose I'm just thinking over our little endeavor and how it might progress. My mind is turning over. You must know how *that* is. Yours never seems to stop."

"That's very true, Della...." Was he pressing closer? Was his cock hardening? She'd thought it was wishful thinking, but now it seemed it wasn't. He was most definitely stiff. "I...I was wondering...as you're not ready for sleep just yet, perhaps I might, um, trouble you, after all?" He rocked his lean hips, pressing the evidence of his desire to *trouble* her against her belly now.

Adela pursed her lips, once again trying not to grin like a fool. "It's no trouble at all, Wilson. In fact, it might help us both to sleep, and you obviously need rest after such a taxing day."

"Yes, that's what I thought, too." She could hear the puckish little smile in his voice, even though she couldn't exactly see his face as he cradled her head against his shoulder. "You're a very wise woman, dear wife. You always know the correct thing to do in any given situation."

Long, clever fingertips started plucking at her nightgown, easing it upward. In a flash it was bundled around her waist, then onward and upward until it was pushed right up to her chest. Wilson curved his hand around one of her breasts, the hold light yet assertive, and so familiar now, that his fingers seemed to be saying hello to her skin.

Reaching for him, too, she buried her fingers in his dark curls, and slid her other hand around his lean hips, drawing him to her. With a sigh, she pressed her lips to his, opening hers to invite his tongue inside.

Yes! His mouth tasted fresh, minty from tooth powder as he accepted her invitation, invading and playing, darting and teasing. All the time, he squeezed her breast in a light, provoking rhythm, stroking her nipple with his thumb and making her wriggle. Wriggle and rub her pelvis against his, and against the only part of him that was not slender and wiry, but thick and imposingly solid.

"Ah yes…ah yes…" His voice was low, even more husky than its normal note as he smothered her face with kisses, and slid his hand down her torso and her belly to the juncture of her thighs. Adela leaped against him, hungry for his squeezing touch as he cupped her puss in a tender grip. "I thought of you as I lay in the undergrowth, standing surveillance. I wished you were beside me. I knew it would be absurd to make love to you there, but I just wanted your company. Your presence…"

Behind tightly closed lids, Adela's eyes watered. He sounded so affectionate, so devoted. Yet she knew he thought of her only in the most pragmatic terms. A pleasant, intelligent enough companion; an eager bed partner, willing to experiment. She wasn't sure Wilson could love, and she still plagued herself, wondering what his feelings for Coraline had been.

Gasping as his long, flexible finger accurately located her clitoris, she embraced the delicious pleasure, but also stood apart a bit, in her mind. Sternly, she told herself not to be silly, and a ninny. So many women were doomed to less than ideal marriages, and often a lifetime of disillusionment. At least she knew where she stood with Wilson, and there were many, many compensations to offset any lack of the most delicate feelings. Even if their time together was finite, it would be a good time, an excellent time, if she could forget about her annoying urge to want more.

Enjoy what you have. Because it's so very good!

More than good, it was wonderful as Wilson cleverly circled the pad of his fingertip, rolling the sensitive bead of her pleasure in exactly the rhythm, and with exactly the pressure, that she adored. Her sex fluttered wildly, brought almost to crisis in just moments by his splendid precision. Heels dragging against the mattress, she arched up into the caress, her own fingers clutching hard at the firm muscles of his bottom.

"Wonderful… Always so ready…" purred Wilson, still circling, more slowly now, more tantalizingly. "I love that you're always so wet for me. I've always loved that…. Even when you were barely more than a girl, you were still a woman." He kissed her again, his mouth gliding over her face.

And then he stopped and reared up, looking down at her in the low light, the shadows beneath his high cheekbones pronounced. "I—I always wish things had been different, you know. I was a clod and a gauche boy…with no sensitivity. I never wanted to hurt you, in any way, and I ended up hurting you in many ways."

Were his eyes gleaming? Normally so pale, they were darker now, in arousal, but they shone, how they shone. Adela could barely speak, for any number of reasons, but she managed a whisper.

"What's done is done, Wilson. No use living in regret. We must enjoy the moment, husband, no use fretting about the past."

Wilson smiled, eyes twinkling now, his moment of ennui gone as fast as it had arrived. "Again, you're so full of good sense, Della. I know I can always rely on you for that." He swirled his hips, rubbing his erection against her, as if for the pure joy of it. "And I can't think of a moment more enjoyable than this one." He paused, withdrawing his hand and pushing his cock in the general direction of where it had been. "Apart from the moment when I actually possess you, dear wife."

For a moment, Adela was right on the point of reaching down, taking hold of him and guiding him inside her body… unsheathed. But then she hesitated. That way lay possible total commitment, and she wasn't sure he wanted that. He seemed to confirm her hesitation by pressing a swift kiss on the end of her nose, then rocking away from her and reaching toward the top drawer in the chest by the bed.

For a French letter. She knew he kept a plentiful supply of the things somewhere, and always made sure that the small stock in her drawer was replenished, no matter how carnally active they'd been.

"Shall I?" She reached for the fine rubber sheath.

"Please do…. I always find your touch most deft."

As she enrobed him, she wondered, as she often did, if he was thinking about her experience in these matters. Was he imagining her putting the device on Yuri, or Clarence? She didn't regret the pleasures she'd purchased for herself. What she'd learned at Sofia's house had certainly made her a better lover for Wilson, but sometimes, she wished in a small corner of her heart that he'd been her only man.

But then, she would never be his only woman. There was Coraline, who he'd probably loved as much as he was able. And others, he'd admitted to her, while assuring her that he'd always taken care. As she'd assured him…

They could not expunge the past. The past made them what they were. And now she must follow her own advice.

"There, nicely clad," she said, reaching across to kiss him on the nose, as he'd kissed her. "Shall we put it to good use and enjoy the efficacious, relaxing benefits of a good fuck?"

"Indeed!" Wilson chuckled, reaching down to position himself. "Nothing too fancy, I think. As you say, just a good fuck. I'm a little too fatigued to manage anything elaborate tonight."

Adela shuffled into a better position, tilting her hips to help him, and spreading her legs wide to invite him into the cradle of her sex. Adjusting his weight, and moving fully over her, Wilson pushed home, sliding to the hilt with a long, happy gasp.

With a gasp of her own, Adela wound herself around him, arms, legs, her very being. There was nothing like the sensation of his solid presence inside her body, a delight in itself, even when still, before the action. Flexing against him, she gripped and held him from within.

"Oh, Della, Della…you are a wonder." He pushed yet deeper, rubbing his face joyously against hers like an affectionate cat. "How good you feel."

For a few moments they lay inert, and joined, as if that were enough. Then Wilson gave her a fierce kiss on the soft skin of her throat, and began to swing his narrow, powerful hips in a slow, solid rhythm. Adela matched him, rising reciprocally, arching hard.

It didn't last long. She wanted him too much, and the angle he fucked her at was so perfect that a part of her wondered if at some time he'd sat down and calculated the best way to knock against her clitoris and stimulate her with each stroke. She wouldn't put such a thing past him, and the thought made her giggle even as she hit her crisis and her channel clenched and gripped him even harder. She was half laughing, half moaning through her orgasm, and when she looked up into Wilson's eyes, and he waggled his dark eyebrows playfully in the very instant before his pale face contorted in ecstasy, she soared again, crying his name and scoring his back with her nails.

A little while later, he asked, his voice blurred with sleep, "What was so funny? When you were spending?"

Her limbs still tangled with his, and her nightgown still bunched beneath her arms, Adela stirred, and wondered if she dare speak the truth.

"I sometimes fancy you're calculating the angle at which you thrust, for maximum effect, when you're tupping me. And

I thought of it right at that moment and it made me laugh at the same time as my pleasure."

Wilson eased his weight off her, and Adela tensed, fighting the urge to hold on tight and prevent him. Any moment now, she'd get a kiss on the brow and he'd be out of bed, in his dressing gown, and on his way to the solitude of his own room. Sometimes, she knew, he even returned to his workshop after lovemaking.

But not tonight, it seemed. Wilson flopped onto his back, with his arm still draped across her belly. "Well, actually, I have done some anatomical studies…and I *have* deduced the optimum angle…." His hand moved slowly, in a light, almost unconscious caress.

"Well, I must admit I'm heartily grateful for that, husband. I commend your scholarship." She tried to make her voice light, her tone casual, but she was half afraid Wilson would hear the pounding of her heart.

Was he staying? He seemed to be showing no signs of moving. His dark head looked settled and at peace on her pillow. She hardly dared breathe, in case it disturbed him and he sat up, searching for his robe.

Then his eyes snapped open, as if he'd felt her watching him. Which he probably had, with his unusually acute senses. "Aren't you sleepy?" He came up on one elbow, his silver-blue gaze sharpening. "Would you prefer me to leave?"

Adela could hardly respond. She tugged ineffectually at her tangled nightgown, grappling with it.

"Here, let me…. Lift up your bottom." As she complied, Wilson deftly whipped the voluminous garment down beneath her, then smoothed the front of it, too, before arranging the bedcovers neatly over her. Then he gazed down at her again, his eyes intense, as if he were asking his question again, and many more besides.

"Can I stay, Della?" he said at last. "I think I'll sleep bet-ter…and perhaps you will, too. But the decision is solely yours, my dearest."

Dearest?

Feeling as if she were going to explode, somehow, Adela fabricated an easy smile and patted the pillow at her side. "Of course. Do stay. I think you're right. We're both tired and I'm sure we'll be able to sleep well together. It's a wide bed and we're both quite slender, aren't we?"

"Indeed we are…indeed we are." Wilson settled back, still looking at her, still the perfect enigma. Rolling onto his side, he smoothed her hair where some of it had strayed across her cheek. "I'll turn out the light. Now rest, Della, go to sleep… and try not to fret about Sybil and her letters. We'll soon have them retrieved and all will be well."

He rolled away for a moment, and then the light went out, but Adela could still see his silhouette. He seemed to hesitate a second, then kissed her on the brow and lay down again beside her.

A few moments ago, sleep had seemed a thousand miles away, but now, suddenly, exhaustion claimed her. She smiled to herself, realizing as she did that for the past half hour or so, she'd not spared a single thought for Sybil's letters. All she'd had in her mind was Wilson, and his delicious lovemaking, and after that, their future together.

Turning her head on the pillow, she focused what remained of her senses on her husband's noble profile, accepting the even sound of his breathing as a good sign, and the very embodi-ment of "possibilities."

And hope.

❧ 26 ❧

The Game's Afoot

The next few days were a whirl of preparation for the engagement ball, and Wilson divided his time between work on his secret, mysterious projects for the War Office, and devising a careful plan for the assault on the house of Blair Devine.

He grinned with approval at Adela's choice of the heather-brown tweed knickerbocker suit, and darted over, kissed her hard and squeezed her bottom when she tried it on for him. "If I weren't so pressed for time, I would be compelled to do something about you, you naughty handsome lad. My mind runs on the most wicked perversions, seeing you with those trim breeches clinging to your delightful buttocks."

"I must own that similar thoughts have passed through my mind, too," replied Adela, gasping. The pressure of Wilson's fingertips was tantalizingly close to her sex as he gripped her. Was he actually shaking?

"I might have known. You have a wicked mind to match your tempting body, Della, and I promise you, when all this business is over, we shall explore those delightful avenues."

The press of his fingers into her rear groove left her in no doubt of the orientation of said avenues.

And now that they were sleeping together, there were more opportunities for play.

After that first night, when he'd not only stayed until morning, but woken her in the small hours for more lovemaking, he'd said nothing more about the situation. But every night he'd come to her room, bare under his robe, then slid into bed beside her. Moments later, they were kissing, exploring each other's bodies then very soon fucking. Adela was thrilled by these new sleeping arrangements, but sensing Wilson preferred not to make a to-do about it, she remained silent and hugged her contentment to herself.

As well as the heather suit, there was another costume to be tried on, too—her gown for the ball. Mme Mirielle had excelled herself and produced a magnificent confection of midnight-blue velvet, trimmed with tissue of silver-and-gold embroidery. The clever couturière had put the garment together at extremely short notice, and even though the rational styling was very simple—a loose-flowing Empire line—the ornamentation must have taken much painstaking work. Adela had gasped at the final price, but when forced to approach Wilson for an addendum to her allowance, he'd pooh-poohed the cost and announced the results of Madame's labors to be magnificent, and worth twice the price. He'd also suggested that Adela have more gowns made up in a similar style and degree of embellishment.

"You look very beautiful, Della." His voice had been strangely rough as he'd surveyed her in the gown. It was necessary he approve it from a technical standpoint, too, for if she were to climb into it quickly after their benevolent but nefarious endeavor, he would have to help her don the gown while they traveled in their coach to the Spencerleigh mansion from Norwood. Luckily in most ways, the two venues were conveniently close by carriage, with fast horses, but it would mean a harum-scarum flurry of disrobing and dressing again in close quarters. A closely confined space that would be rocking from the motion of the horses' gait.

"That color is perfect on you. It complements your hair and your eyes. You'll outshine every other woman in the room." He twirled her around. "And these simple buttons down the back should be easy to negotiate." Because the gown was un-fitted, there were just a few fastenings at the back. The whole thing could actually be put on over her head, such was the convenience of so modern and sensible a garment. "What shall we do with your hair?" Her husband stroked his fingers over the crown of her head, lingering a little. "Something simple, I think… Loose, with a few strands caught back. And a feather or two, perhaps? Or flowers? No, some kind of clip or comb, I think."

Adela suppressed a smile. Who would ever have thought that Wilson would be so well versed in the finer details of a woman's toilette? Or maybe it was just *her* toilette? She couldn't imagine a queen of fashion like Coraline ever letting a man influence her choice of gowns or the arrangement of her hair.

Or taking the opportunity to accompany her lover on a blatantly illegal escapade.

He may not love me, but at least he seems to trust me more than she.

AT LAST, AFTER what seemed like an eternity of time spent in meticulous preparation, in reality barely more than a week, the fateful night arrived. As was hardly surprising, another communication had arrived from the "blackmailer" consent-ing, with some subtle menaces, to the delay and the alterna-tive offer, so all was set fair for Wilson's scheme.

"Better not tell Sybil anything about this endeavor of ours. It's enough to know that we have the matter in hand. If she knew specifics, she might speak unwisely in a state of anxiousness or anticipation," said Wilson, as he overlooked the tweed suit set out on her bed, and the dress box containing her blue gown, a wrap, her small evening bag and her dancing slippers. Tucked away beneath the layers of velvet and tissue was the jewelry case containing the Ruffington diamonds.

Adela agreed. She'd refrained from telling Sybil any details, only assuring her that all would be well. "Quite right, although I believe Marguerite might be trusted, if need be. She's the most sensible of all the Ruffington women."

"Perhaps you're right...." Wilson sounded thoughtful. "Although I'm sure on the surface, most people have always thought you the sensible one. Yet here you are, about to embark on this mission of high derring-do with me."

Don't you realize that I'd go anywhere with you, my love? Surely, if you're so clever, you've perceived that? And yet, you do nothing to discourage me. I could almost imagine...

Imagine what? Adela banished her wishful thoughts and focused on Wilson, who was fishing in the pocket of his dressing gown. As she watched, he drew out another blue velvet-covered box, slightly smaller than the one packed with her gown, but still obviously the vessel for some mysterious item of jewelry. It certainly wasn't any of the very few modest pieces that Adela had brought with her on her marriage.

"I never purchased you a ring to mark our engagement... and I feel I should have done." He glanced at her left hand, where she wore only a very simple golden band. "So here is a token of my esteem in its place." He pursed his lips, tapped the box with his fingers. Was he nervous? "I know you've tried out other pins or combs for your hair tonight...but I'd like you to wear these, if they're suitable for the purpose. They have a very clever fastening, which I devised myself, I might add. We can use them to swiftly fasten back a few tresses in a pleasing style." Still clutching the box, he reached out again, catching a strand and smoothing it back.

"Oh, Wilson, that's thoughtful. May I see it?"

With a little smile, he flipped open the lid…and Adela gasped.

Beautiful diamonds glittered on their velvet bed, all set in a pair of simple but elegant curlicues, and each stone more than a match for the family gems she would be wearing.

"Oh, Wilson…" she sighed, at a complete loss for anything else.

"Do you like them?" He still sounded anxious, lifting out the ornaments and tossing the box aside. "Here, see how the clip works…" He demonstrated one the ingenious fastenings. "Shall we try them?"

"Um…yes, I think we should." Adela reached for her comb and neatly caught back sections of her hair, holding them in place while Wilson affixed first one of the diamond clips, then the other. It seemed odd for her husband alone to be attending to her toilette on the night of a grand ball, and Adela's new maid had been mystified and a little crestfallen when told her services weren't required. But the young woman had brightened again immediately on receipt of a generous bonus and extra day off to visit her family.

It wouldn't have done for her to see her mistress donning not her beautiful blue-and-silver-gold gown…but instead one of the master's country suits!

Still taken aback by the beauty of Wilson's gift, Adela found her hands shook when she attempted to make an adjustment to her hair. But gently lowering her fingers, Wilson took over and performed the task perfectly, teasing a few soft, fetching shorter fronds around her face.

"There," he said, clearly pleased with his efforts.

Adela laughed, smiling at her own reflection. Crooked nose and chicken pox marks notwithstanding, she acknowledged freely and without any qualm that she looked a picture.

Was it living with Wilson and being the recipient of his frequent and inventive lovemaking that had given her such a glow? Or was it because, even in the absence of spoken avowals of love, his obvious respect, companionship and affection had transformed into her a beauty? Perhaps it was simply the new confidence she felt inside herself that had initiated the change?

"Is there not one skill or task at which you don't excel, husband dear?" she asked brightly, to hide the way her own radiant appearance shook her. "There's a future for you as a ladies' hairdresser should the government and the captains of industry ever dispense with your services."

"I could call myself Monsieur Wilsonetti." He waggled his dark brows playfully at her, and ran his fingertips down the smooth fall of her hair, where it hung down her back. "So, do you like the clips? I think they should perform their purpose admirably."

"Wilson, they're exquisite! Beyond beautiful…" Adela turned, reached around for the stroking hand and drew it to her lips, impressing a passionate kiss upon it. "It's the most beautiful gift I've ever been given…." She kissed his fingers again, acknowledging a lie. His regard for her, which seemed to grow despite the unusual nature of their marriage, was a greater gift by far.

He dipped down slightly, and with his face beside hers, turned her to the mirror again, so his reflection could grin at her. "Good. I'm glad you like it…but you're going to have to earn it tonight, my dear. We've got an adventure ahead of us, and alas, these pretty baubles must go in the box with everything else, and we'll have to tie up your hair or plait it, ready for the cap."

With a brisk kiss to her cheek, he straightened up, instantly businesslike again as he unlatched the clips, then stowed them away in the box, ready for transit in their carriage to Spencerleigh House.

In an upper bedroom window of the handsome south London villa, an oil lamp flickered.

"There. That's the sign." Wilson pointed toward it with a long, black gloved finger. His voice was low, and his pale eyes gleamed in a way that was almost unearthly behind the dark silk mask he was wearing, a match to the one that covered the upper part of Adela's face.

"So the coast will be clear?" she whispered back to him. They were crouched behind abundant bushes in the corner of the garden of Blair Devine's house, after having climbed the wall, Wilson having given her a leg up before shimmying over himself, his height giving him a distinct advantage as a climber.

"Yes. My new young friend, his footman—soon to be a footman of ours—was instructed to light the lamp once Devine has left for the ball."

"What of his other servants?" Adela adjusted her position. She'd worn the borrowed trousers before, and others in her youth, but it still felt extremely odd to have so much cloth between her legs—the sturdy breeches and the narrow cut drawers she'd selected especially for the occasion. It wasn't an unpleasant sensation. In fact, it was vaguely exciting in a perverse way, and she had to school her concentration so as not to give in to the lascivious thoughts that she'd had while first trying on the heather suit. It didn't help that Wilson looked so mysterious and downright devastatingly attractive in his devilish silk mask.

"Don't worry…a couple bottles of brandy, courtesy of my friend the local innkeeper, judiciously dosed with a little laudanum by Earnest, our footman friend, will have them snoozing by now…while he keeps watch at the other end of the lane."

"So we appear to have all angles covered then, with Teale and the carriage around the corner at the other end?" She reached up to adjust her cap. Her hair was in a plait beneath it, and she'd jammed hat pins through the tweed for security, but it still felt precarious, and she kept having to push shorter strands back out of view.

"Quite so. And with luck, we should remain undisturbed and have more than sufficient time to get in, breach the safe and peruse the documents within." He reached out and tapped her shoulder reassuringly. "Now come along, my dear…the game is on now. We're about to break the law, and the sooner we're about our task, the sooner we can be back in the carriage and on the way to Sybil's grand event, just as if nothing had ever happened." He winked. "And who wouldn't believe I hadn't been detained making love to my glorious wife? The perfect reason to be late to the affair."

"Wilson, behave," she mouthed to him, grinning despite the tension of the situation as she braced herself to move forward. They both wore black rubber-soled shoes, designed for sporting activity, in order to be silent and fleet of foot, if required.

Wilson took her gloved hand in his, then led her forward, skirting the edge of the garden, then scuttling to the next bit of cover afforded by bushes. Pausing for a moment, he whispered, "I might even be compelled to actually ravish you in the carriage, my dear, if we have time. The sight of you in those breeches is having quite an effect on me."

"I hope you'll be able to concentrate on the task in hand."

"I'll manage, never fear." With that he urged her forward again, and they ran at a crouch until they reached the window to the room that Wilson had determined was Devine's study.

First, her husband popped up his head and peered in, then he scanned the garden behind them, his sharp gaze darting hither and thither, checking all aspects. Cautiously edging to his side, Adela peeked into the room, too. It was unlit, but the remains of a small fire shed some radiance, creating ominous shadows and deep, dark corners.

"I think we may proceed," Wilson whispered, then reached into the canvas satchel he had slung over his shoulder, the mate of which Adela carried.

She watched, entranced, as he employed a device that was a combination of a large rubber suction cup and a pair of protractors, ingeniously carving out a circle of the window glass, removing it in one piece, then reaching in through the aperture to open the window snib.

The room lay accessible before them, and first Wilson climbed nimbly over the sill, then he assisted Adela's entrance, reaching though, gripping her strongly and lifting her to the sill, too, so he could help her down onto the carpet. With purpose, Wilson strode to an incredibly ugly and badly rendered painting of a horse, then ran his fingertips down the edge of the frame. With a barely audible click it yielded to him, too, and when he swung it back out of the way, a green painted safe was revealed, squat and heavy and impressively defiant.

"Now for the more difficult task, my sweet." His eyes glittered in the gloom, and Adela had to smile. Oh, how he relished this. Challenges. Difficulties. They were all meat and drink to her husband. He thrived on pitting his fine intellect and instincts against obstacles.

I wonder if that's why he's come to hold me in a better regard? Because I'm certainly not the easiest person to get along with?

But that was a question for another time. Now she had to help him. She drew a small dark lantern from her satchel, lit it carefully then set it on an adjacent chest of drawers to one side. Wilson handed her a leather pouch from his satchel, and she unrolled it, revealing not his usual set of tools, but those of a cracksman. As if stripping for action, he removed his black gloves and his mask, pushing them into his pocket. Adela removed mask and gloves, too.

For a moment or two, Wilson just stood there, his narrow hands pressed together in front of him, forefingers just touching his lips, thinking, assessing. To Adela he looked more than anything like a genie or mystic summoning a trancelike state of concentration, and she suspected that was more or less exactly what he was doing.

In a low, intense voice, he requested the first tool.

Adela wasn't sure what she'd expected. Perhaps that the safe would spring open in short order for Wilson, because his skills were so much more refined than hers, and his equipment was far superior to the stiff hairpins she'd resorted to when she'd broken into Lord Rayworth's secret library, and on the few other occasions she'd employed what Wilson had taught her. It seemed like a hundred years since the house party now, and as if it had been another world. How much had changed since she and Wilson had been thrown back into close orbit around each other, like two celestial bodies who'd swung away for a few years, but circled back under the power of a strange gravity.

Ten minutes passed, then another ten, punctuated by Wilson's terse demands for items from the roll. The torsion wrench. The offset diamond pick. The short hook. She'd learned all their names and functions in preparation.

Eventually, though, when Adela's nerves were almost shredded, there came a fearsomely ringing clunk, a noise that seemed infinitely louder than it actually was, and Wilson's jubilant but quiet, "Excellent!"

A twist of the handle and the safe door swung open in a heavy arc.

Documents filled one entire shelf—small bundles and individual envelopes. Many looked like personal letters, some poignantly fastened with ribbons, as if they were keepsakes of love affairs, much like Sybil's. Others appeared more formal, perhaps business documents and papers.

"You skim the love letters, Della. I'll peruse these." Wilson lifted out the far less romantic items, a frown creasing his brow. "Lord alone knows what the blackguard has been up to. I suspect far more than personal threats against incautious sweethearts are involved here."

They took everything to the rug in front of the fire, where the best light was, and began to study them. Adela blessed her ability to rapidly scan and absorb the content of any given thing, her invaluable gift as an artist. But speedy as she was, her talent was rudimentary compared to Wilson's amazing powers of comprehension. He was reading and assessing documents ten or twenty times as fast as she was, and she suspected his recall was far more detailed than hers.

Quickly, she found Sybil's letters, tied with a familiar rose-pink ribbon, one Adela herself had given her as a birthday gift when they were girls. Her sister's name was printed on a small slip of paper tucked into the bundle, and she noticed other names affixed to other bundles. With a pang, she prized off the ribbon and slipped it into her pocket. She didn't intend to read the words. It seemed an invasion. Gingerly, she reached for one of the fire irons and poked the coals as quietly as she could.

"I'm sorry, my dear," she whispered to her absent sister, then threw the envelopes into the flames, pressing them in with poker and watching until every scrap was consumed. Obliterating the letters was the only way to be sure. If she returned them to Sybil, she would keep them out of sentiment, and someday in the future, her marriage might be shattered because of them. Another heinous blackmailer and another traitorous maid would come along and the whole horrid business would start all over again.

What to do with the other bundles? Adela knew she'd made the correct choice for Sybil, but did she have the right to do the same for these other correspondents, these other lovers? Surely they should be left to decide for themselves? Gathering up all the bundles, she began stowing them into her satchel. It would be necessary to make discreet appointments, and visit their rightful owners.

"Good God!" It was a low exclamation, barely more than a let-out breath, but with the last of the letters in her hand, Adela turned toward Wilson. He'd clearly found, read and evaluated something momentous. "He has business letters, details of secret transactions…and yes, I do declare, political papers here. Where does he get all this? He must have a secret low life and connections that nobody in polite circles is aware of…." Wilson turned to her, frowning. "I suspect the man's a filthy spy as well as some kind of master blackmailer."

"Well, he always did boast to Mama about his influential friends. Seems he must have connections with the servants, and maybe the disgruntled clerks and secretaries of these people, too."

"I agree," said Wilson, still sifting through documents. "Ironic, isn't it, though? He seems to have a profitable working relationship with underlings of all kinds, and yet by the sound of it he treats his own servants extremely shabbily. Come his downfall, which will be inevitable if I have anything to do with it, I must see that they all find decent places."

Adela eyed her husband with ever-gathering respect. The more she had close dealings with him, the more she admired his principles. The wild, heedless boy had become a man of great integrity.

"Now, what have we here?" he went on, opening a last slim file, having stowed away the crucial documents in his satchel. He tilted it her way, and Adela saw Wilson's own name inscribed on the manila.

He read in silence, taking what seemed an age for him, scanning and comparing several sheets, and then staring blankly.

"What is it? What's wrong?"

He handed them to her, and Adela read quickly, scanning the words with growing shock.

The first document was a sworn affidavit, a statement by one Henry Rowson, groom to Mr. Arthur Edward Ruffington, describing how Rowson's mistress, Mrs. Berta Ruffington, had already been secretly married to him when she'd wed Mr. Ruffington. Along with it there was their marriage certificate, and a second affidavit from a maid, detailing a conversion with Mrs. Ruffington in which she admitted that her only child, her son, Wilson, was fathered by Rowson.

The papers shook in Adela's hand. How must Wilson be feeling? She reached out and rested her hand on his arm. "I'm sorry, Wilson. This must be a horrible shock for you."

He turned to her, his face a curious amalgam of a slight smile and blankness, a jolted state. Then he shrugged in the firelight. "No, my dear, not a complete surprise. I always felt there was some secret my mother kept, but we didn't converse much…. She didn't seem to care for my company."

"Oh, Wilson…" How sorry Adela felt for him. Her own

mother was a silly woman sometimes, but she loved her girls, pretty or otherwise.

Wilson pursed his lips, tapping one long forefinger against them. "This explains much. My father, bless him, was always the best and kindest of parents, as if lavishing his love on me was a way of compensating, and assuring me that I wasn't second best to him, and that he didn't resent me for my birth. He must have known, but he didn't want me to suffer for it."

"And what of…of this other man?" asked Adela, surprised. What a rare and tolerant man Wilson's father must have been.

Wilson's expression grew more bitter. Well, perhaps not bitter; he appeared more sad than anything, on closer inspection. "Would you believe that I barely noticed him? When I was home from school, I saw the lack of love between my parents. But…but, my God, Adela, Rowson was a servant. We exchanged the usual words. He seemed a decent man while he worked for us. He came with my mother from her previous household. She was a young widow…." Wilson heaved a sigh. This emotional conundrum was somehow beyond his cool brain. "I cannot imagine why she would marry him, and then not acknowledge it…not acknowledge me as the product of their union."

Adela didn't know what to say. She slid her arm around her husband's shoulder, his comforter in this valley of the shadow of memories…and of present felony.

"I think I was a constant reminder of her mistake, who knows? And she certainly resented my father, too, perhaps for his easy tolerance." Wilson gave Adela a perplexed look. "I'm not an expert on the human heart, my dear, but I could certainly tell from an early age that my mother didn't really like either of us very much."

How sad for him, denied a mother's love. Denied knowledge of his true sire. The only compensation was that his faux father had given him affection.

"It could be fraudulent. It might all be lies." Adela shook the papers.

"We'll never know. Unless there are other documents or letters...other people my mother might have told. Witnesses... All the parties involved are deceased now, however." Wilson waggled his fingers, indicating she should give him the affidavits. "I'd better show these to the Old Curmudgeon's solicitors. It makes a good deal of difference to us, Adela." He quirked his dark brows. "If I'm not my...my father's son, I'm no longer Lord Millingford's legitimate heir...at least I don't think I am. I'll be out of the frame like a shot once your grandfather discovers I'm not of his blood." A crooked little grin formed on Wilson's lips, real humor this time. "He'll be forced to relent and bequeath his millions to you, my sweet, in the absence of somebody with a cock. Even if the title itself dies out..."

The papers shook again, this time involuntarily. The world shook, too. Adela saw her mother's elation, her joy at securing the title for her daughter that she'd been denied by fate herself, turning to ashes.

27

The Future Lady Millingford?

Adela gazed into the fire, where Sybil's incriminating letters were reduced to hot flakes of disintegrating dust. She flexed her fingers, wishing to toss the affidavits and the marriage lines after them.

But she couldn't act so impulsively. She turned to Wilson, fixed her eyes on his, willing him to pay attention.

"Wilson, I know you've never wanted the title or the money, but…" She bit her lip. "Let me destroy these documents. Let things be as they were…please." He was frowning. "Ever since Papa died, one of Mama's dearest wishes, perhaps her dearest wish of all, has been to see me as Lady Millingford, because she never held the title herself. I know it's not possible in my own right…. It would require litigation, legislation, I don't know what…. Chances are it could never happen. But we both know what Mama's always hoped for—that I'd marry you and acquire the title that way." Adela shook her head. It sounded all wrong and jumbled. "Please don't deny her that dream. I don't want any of it for myself, and I know it might be, well, temporary…but at least give her the chance of basking in her wish fulfilled for a little while. Please, Wilson."

Time seemed to halt while he stared at her, his expression inscrutable in the uncertain light. Seconds and minutes were ticking by, seconds and minutes in which something could go horribly wrong and they might be caught in their act of lawbreaking. But still she knew she had to wait until Wilson was ready to answer.

Her heart lifted when he smiled at her and touched her arm.

"You're a loving and dutiful daughter, Della. My dear mother-in-law should be proud of you, and I'm sure she is." His pale eyes shone. Was he proud, too? "So I think I should try and make some effort toward acting the loving and dutiful son-in-law." He nodded at the papers, then looked toward the fire and the destroying heat, and nodded again.

Adela flung them on the coals, and Wilson took up the poker and pressed them down, prodding and stirring until they caught and began to blaze.

"Don't worry, my sweet, I'm sure I can endure the title when the time comes…. It's not as if I'll be a duke or anything, and Ruffington Hall is a fine old pile. Lots of excellent outbuildings for experiments." He paused and his smile widened to a distinctly lascivious smirk. "Some very amenable walks by the river, too…although I think we might have to do some path clearing and careful management of low-hanging tree branches, don't you?"

Adela's fingers twitched, as if preparing for the usual protective gesture across the bridge of her nose, but she resisted. Nothing to be ashamed of. Her appearance might be less than perfect by the standards of a Professional Beauty, but that didn't seem to cool Wilson's carnal ardor, so who cared about a little bump out of shape here and there?

"And it might be fun to make a bit of mischief in the House of Lords, don't you think? Stir them up a bit, eh?"

"Oh, they'll be delighted to have you among them, I'm sure." Adela grinned, imagining Wilson in the House, his long form lounging on one of the famous benches, not a speck of respect for the august institution in him. But one never knew, perhaps he'd do some good? He was probably more intelligent than all the rest of the peers put together, twice over, and he was certainly of a humanitarian bent.

The chime of a small clock on the mantel shattered her fancy, and seemed to galvanize Wilson, too. "I think we'd better get a move on, Della. Time's a-passing and we have a fair drive to Spencerleigh House. Your mother will be fretting over where the future Lady Millingford has got to."

"Sadly, you're right. She'll be fussing, wanting us all to present a united front. I believe we're done here, though, aren't we? We have both the personal letters and all the critical documents. We must decide how to return them when we're safe and home."

Wilson nodded approvingly, and rose to scan the strongbox one last time. When he'd rummaged through everything, and ensured that only Devine's personal papers and some rather large bundles of money were left, he swung closed the heavy door. "I wish I knew who he intimidated to get all this cash, and then we could return that, too. But I suspect we'll never know." Wilson turned the handle back to where it had been, then inserted a pick into the lock and gave a few swift, decisive jiggles and jerks until it clicked again. Reversing his successful crack somehow, Adela assumed.

With all stowed carefully in their satchels, and the ashes double-checked to ensure all was burned beyond retrieval, they set masks and gloves aright, and looked around to ensure everything in the room was just as it'd been when they arrived. Then it was out over the windowsill and into the garden.

Carefully closing the window by reaching through the circular aperture, Wilson then took a syringe from a small box that he'd had stowed in his satchel. Adela watched, rapt, as he squeezed a thin stream of some sticky, colorless substance around the edge of the circle, then around the matching piece of glass that he'd removed and, using the suction cup, fitted it back into place. When he released the suction, the glass stayed put, and it remained so when he tapped it lightly.

"A new adhesive I developed especially for this job. I think I'll patent it." Grinning, he put the last of his tools in his bag, then took her by the hand and led her back along the path they'd arrived by, skirting the bushes before helping her back over the wall.

"Now, to the carriage. I need to assure Earnest that all's gone well."

Adela obeyed, looking back when she reached the corner, to see the small figure of a very young footman emerge from his observation spot in the shadows. Wilson took something from his inner pocket—banknotes, she suspected—and passed them to the lad, before offering his hand, which was shaken with enthusiasm. The two exchanged a few inaudible words, then Wilson saluted and turned, sprinting toward her.

"Look sharp. No loitering. This countrified area seems to be unpoliced, but you never know, a constable might come ambling along any moment." He grabbed her hand and hauled her after him. Adela clutched her cap with her free hand, feeling the weight of her plait slide inside it.

At the end of the lane, around the corner in the lee of a line of copper beeches, stood their carriage. The tiny glow of a cigarette tip indicated that Teale was savoring a smoke to pass the time, and the two-in-hand horses were enjoying their break, too, with a nose bag apiece. As Adela and Wilson approached, Teale extinguished his gasper and leaped lightly down, to attend to them.

Wilson drew out his pocket watch and checked the time. "Eight-thirty. Do you think these two beauties can get us there in half an hour, John?" Snapping shut the watch case, he gave the nearest horse a pat on the neck.

"Shouldn't be a problem, sir. It might be a bit of rock and rattle inside, but I'll do my best to keep them smooth."

"Good man." Flinging open the carriage door, Wilson bundled Adela inside, pushing her up by her bottom, then following close on her tail, and settling down beside her on the velveteen seat. "Let's go," he called softly up to Teale, then latched the door, enclosing them in the intimate, well-padded interior of their conveyance.

Immediately, Teale got them under way, the well-matched pair moving at a steady walk at first, until they were out of the lane and onto the nearest road.

As the motion of the carriage settled into a smooth fast clip, Wilson reached up and removed his mask, then pulled off Adela's, too, followed by her hat.

"So, my dear Cinderella, you shall go to the ball," he said in a low, excited voice. "Now let's get you out of those tweeds and give me a chance to admire you in your frillies before you have to get dressed again."

Grabbing her by the shoulders, he leaned in close and kissed her hard. Adela couldn't help but respond, even though she knew there was much to do in a limited time, and none of it easy in the rocking carriage. Wilson's mouth was irresistible. It always had been. She slid her arms around him as his tongue darted and thrust. Her skin felt hot in its carapace of tweed. She wanted to be naked against him, whether he took his own clothes off or not.

Still kissing her, Wilson pressed her back against the seat, his nimble hands attacking her jacket, almost ripping it open and then finding and cradling her breast within, squeezing and caressing through the layers of her light woolen shirt and the filmier, lacier things beneath.

"Oh, Della, Della," he gasped, cupping her bosom with a rough enthusiasm, "you make the most adorable safecracker's assistant a felon could ever wish for. Although I could probably have breached that box in half the time if I hadn't been distracted by thoughts of flinging you down on the carpet, ripping off your breeches and having you there and then." He laughed against her lips. "Just think how amusing it would be to look at Devine when we encounter him, and know that we'd fucked in his office while we were robbing him."

Adela giggled, too, but it cracked into a groan as Wilson's thumb and finger tweaked her nipple through her clothing. Squirming, she pressed her pelvis against him, unable to resist the urge to excite herself.

He pushed her down to lie on the seat, and with his hands on the buttons of his trousers now, he seemed just about to climb on top and ravish her when suddenly he threw back his head.

"What the devil are we doing?" He laughed and sat back, reaching out to pull Adela up to a sitting position, too. "Aren't we incorrigible, eh?"

In a turmoil of lust, she still saw the funny side, too. She still wanted to be ravished, or even to climb atop Wilson and ravish *him,* but it was perfectly absurd when in not more than twenty minutes they'd be pulling up at the august residence of Sybil's fiancé's family, and would need to appear presentable, stately and respectable.

"Yes, we're terrible. Like a pair of rutting weasels." She reached out and laid a gentle finger on Wilson's lips. They looked rather red where he'd kissed so hard. "We really must save our ardor for later, and behave ourselves."

He shrugged, wickedly licked her fingertips then put her hand from him. "Quite right, dear wife, quite right." He waggled his dark brows. "But we have an appointment later for carnal intercourse, so please make a note of that."

"Duly noted," said Adela, and began the awkward process of changing herself from a breeches-clad tomboy into an elegant, if somewhat idiosyncratic, lady of quality attired for a gala ball.

The transformation was nowhere near as straightforward as they'd hoped. Two people taking off their garments and replacing them with others, in a confined space that was jerking and rocking as it moved at high speed, was no easy feat. Adela cursed and grappled with stockings and the little satin belt to hold them up, and her petticoats, the latter having seemed to triple in volume since she'd last tried them on.

"A curse on this frightful palaver!" she cried, batting down the layers of lace and cambric. "Heaven alone knows how I'd manage if I was like all those other poor creatures who still wear corsets. It would be impossible."

"Here, let me help." With his long, firm hands, Wilson smoothed down the masses of cloth. "There, that's better.... But I must admit I'm having trouble with this shirtfront, and my studs. Usually in this situation, Teale is helping me to dress, rather than driving a carriage."

"Come here, let me." Adela attacked the studs, but found them difficult and fiddly. "Devilish things...they're dashed hard to manipulate, aren't they?"

She struggled and struggled, but her fingers fumbled and the studs ended up rolling about on the floor of the carriage. Wilson bent to retrieve them just as Adela did, and they cried out as their heads knocked together with a bump.

Rubbing their skulls, they collapsed into helpless mirth at their plight.

"This is hopeless. We'll have to stop," said Wilson, nodding to himself. "I'll ask Teale to pull up somewhere secluded if he can find a place, and we'll get out and arrange our apparel while on solid ground and standing still. It's the only way." Reaching up, he rapped on the roof of the carriage, and as it slowed and stopped, he lowered the lamp, raised the shutter and looked out. Adela huddled in a corner, drawing her evening cloak around her, while Wilson leaped out, in shirtsleeves, to converse with Teale.

"He knows a place," announced Wilson as he climbed back in and the carriage quickly got under way. "We're not too far off now, and there's a small lane leading to a side entrance to Spencerleigh House...the tradesmen's entrance." Wilson grinned. "Perfect for a pair of lowlifes such as we." Rummaging in Adela's dress box, he pulled out the last petticoat and shook out the creases. "Now let's do the best we can in the meantime, eh, my dear?"

28

The Belle of the Ball

Three quarters of an hour later, they stood at the top of the steps, looking down on the ballroom at Spencerleigh House, waiting to be announced. Adela reached out and straightened Wilson's white tie, even though it didn't need it, her nerves jangling. Wilson in turn nudged the Ruffington diamonds until they were set just so around her throat. She could almost see him calculating the fine measurements so the magnificent drop lay exactly centered. His eyes flicked to her hair, and she turned to show him the disposition of the new clips, too, their elegant glitter holding thick brown tresses away from her face.

"You look like a goddess, Della. Quite stunning. I hope Sybil doesn't take umbrage with you for outshining her on her big night."

"Oh, don't worry, she'll probably think my dress is peculiar and my choice of coiffure downright bizarre for a married woman. And Mama will have a fit of the vapors and accuse me of turning up looking like something out of the circus." Adela laid her hand on Wilson's immaculately tailored arm.

"But they'll both be delighted with you." She brushed away an imaginary speck of lint. "I don't believe I've ever seen you look so sartorial."

It was true, Wilson looked breathtaking, and apart from his wedding suit, was dressed in probably the most conventional attire she'd ever seen him wear. Tails, white tie, white gloves, the perfect gentleman. Only his slightly unruly hair, which refused to be tamed, remained defiantly Wilson.

"I feel as if I'm being throttled." He ran a gloved finger round the edge of his collar. "I wish I was wearing my dressing gown and a comfortable shirt. Perhaps I should have retained my tweeds?" He gave her a sly, sideways glance. "We both should have, sublime as you look in that dress."

"Don't be absurd, Wilson. People are staring enough already."

It was true. As they waited behind several other pairs to be announced, curious eyes were scanning them. Adela's loosely flowing gown with its lightly defined waist was drawing disapproving—or maybe envious—stares from women laced into the tightest corsets. What discomfort they were enduring for fashion. Adela drew in a deep breath, enjoying the simple ability to do so, and lifted her head proudly. Even if they didn't care for her choice in modes, they were certainly covetous to a woman of her legendary diamonds…and her beautiful man.

At that moment, a gap opened before them. They stepped to the top of the staircase. It was their turn to be announced. Even more curious sets of eyes were turning in their direction from the dance floor below. Music played on, something bright and cheerful, but in her state of nerves Adela heard only an ominous silence.

"Mr. and Mrs. Wilson Ruffington," rang out in the master of ceremonies' sonorous tones.

There seemed to be an empty space in Adela's stomach.

She'd never been so anxious—even when she and Wilson had been breaking the law and burgling Blair Devine's house— and she didn't know why she was. She didn't care what people thought of her. She cared only what Wilson thought. But conventional as it seemed, she wanted to be a credit to him, to be seen as much a jewel on his arm as the diamonds were around her throat. She wanted to be the belle of the ball, and as much a desirable and admired woman as Coraline would have been at such an event.

It was like being frozen in a block of ice, a block of time.

Then she turned to Wilson and his smile was like the sun, thawing her fear and warming her heart. He tucked her hand under his arm and put his own palm firmly over it, the sensation of his sure hold on her shoring her up and making her soar.

"Shall we?" he said softly, but then, just before the first step, he leaned in close, his lips right against her ear, and whispered, "You do know that I love you, don't you?"

The top step seemed to shudder under Adela's feet, but Wilson held her steady and she seemed to float down the grand staircase, almost oblivious now to the fellow guests who might be watching their descent. To her there were no other people in the grand room, nothing but the pounding in her heart and joy bubbling up like vintage champagne, making her giddy.

When they reached the foot of the stairs, she turned and said to him, under her breath, "Wilson, you really do pick your moments, don't you? I could have gone arse over tip down the staircase! Making an announcement like that when I was teetering at the top…"

"I'm sorry, my darling." He was grinning and unrepentant. "But I thought it bore mentioning at that juncture." He patted her arm and urged her into motion. "I thought a declaration of my feelings might boost your confidence. I know I'm not the most romantic of men as a rule, but I've deduced that women always feel more assured when they receive pretty compliments and protestations of affection."

Weaving through the throng, nodding to acquaintances as they went, Adela was in a state of shock. She'd hoped... She'd sensed... But hopes and inklings weren't the same as confirmation. She grinned brilliantly at a rather disapproving dowager as they passed, and was rewarded by a sudden softening in the other woman's demeanor, as if the power of such obvious happiness had touched her.

The Spencerleighs were in possession of a tremendously imposing mansion, and the ballroom was vast. Adela and Wilson's progress was slow, as many people stopped them to exchange courtesies. Her husband was a highly regarded man in political, academic and even business circles, for his brilliance, but titled ladies and fashionable women who normally wouldn't have wanted to pass the time of day with Adela were suddenly amenable and gracious.

"My dear, how lovely to see you. How well you're looking," gushed a politician's wife who Adela couldn't remember for the life of her ever speaking to before.

"Do let me congratulate you on your marriage. You're so lucky. Your husband clearly dotes on you," murmured a noted Professional Beauty, rumored to be a conquest of the Prince of Wales himself. "Do come to tea one day next week. I would so love to chat."

A footman proffered champagne, and despite her interior effervescence, Adela accepted a glass gratefully. Drawing her to one side, Wilson clinked his glass to hers.

"To us, Della. Partners in crime...and partners in life." He gave a little shrug, a hopeful little gesture, as if he were momentarily unsure of himself. "Look...don't trouble your mind if you can't fully reciprocate my sentiment. I believe if you

can simply like me a little…well, sufficiently to put up with
me for at least a portion of each day, we have the basis for a
viable and quite pleasurable marriage." He paused, something
almost imploring in his eyes. "At least for a while."

What did he mean, "for a while"? Did he love her or didn't
he? Surely if he did, the pleasurable marriage should last indefinitely? She opened her mouth to question him, then heard
her own name called out, in Mama's familiar tones.

"Adela! Wilson! You're here at last. Where have you been?"

Her head filled with her own questions, Adela spun round
to find Mama and Marguerite bearing down on them. A shudder of distaste rippled through her at the sight of Blair Devine,
so smug and smooth, in their wake.

"Sorry, Mama, something cropped up at the very last moment. We came as soon as we were able."

As she hugged her mother, she caught sight of Marguerite
smiling. Their parent, however, remained blissfully in igno-
rance of the true nature of their tardiness, and as Adela stepped
back, Mama rounded on her. "Oh, Della, what are you thinking of? What will the marquess and marchioness think of you,
turning up in a tea gown? And with your hair all awry?"

Wilson stepped forward, took his mother-in-law's offered
hand and dusted a chivalric kiss on her gloved fingertips.

"Look at Wilson…even he's made an effort," Mama ranted.
"Dressed the perfect gentleman, while you look like a gypsy."

"Please don't scold Adela, Mrs. Ruffington," Wilson said
as he gave Marguerite a brotherly kiss on the cheek. "I ap-
proved her gown and I think she looks exceptionally fine in
it. She has superb taste and her choice in all things is both elegant and modern."

"If you say so, Wilson, if you say so." Mama didn't seem
convinced, even though she obviously had a soft spot for her
son-in-law now that was what he was. All ideas of removing

him as the Old Curmudgeon's heir seemed never to have existed, and cousin Wilson was the apple of Mama's eye now.

But he's not my cousin. Not really.

It was all so perplexing. But now wasn't the time to ruminate on the repercussions of what they'd discovered. Especially as Blair Devine was pushing forward and grinning unctuously. As he opened his mouth to speak, Adela wanted to punch him right in it.

"Mrs. Ruffington, may I say how beautiful you look this evening." He aped Wilson's graceful gesture, raising her gloved hand to his lips. Adela had to exert supreme control in order not to cringe. Especially when his eyes roved to her throat and cleavage. "The famous diamonds look most becoming on you. You should wear them on every possible occasion."

Beast! She wondered precisely what Wilson had said to him when they'd faced off against each other. Did he realize that she knew everything her husband did? Or was he just aiming his barbed remarks at Wilson?

Those dear, blue eyes were like chips of ice and narrowed as they fixed on the smooth solicitor. Adela could almost imagine psychic daggers emanating from them and hurtling toward their foe.

"Thank you, Mr. Devine. That's just what I plan to do." She looked at Blair Devine levelly, aware of Wilson having moved up right beside her, and placing his hand on the small of her back in a protective gesture. "Until such time as I have a daughter, or a daughter-in-law, to whom I can give them as a betrothal gift." There may well not be a child if she and Wilson were to be together for only a short while, but that horrid wretch Devine wasn't to know that, was he? She felt Wilson's fingers curve against her spine as if in approval of her bravado.

"Yes, indeed," her husband said, giving her a fiery, slanted smile. "The Ruffington diamonds will be a treasured heirloom. It seems only right and fitting that they should always be passed down to beautiful Ruffington brides." He paused, and Adela noted the slight tension in his lips. Like a quirk of challenge or triumph, as if he'd taken off one of his immaculate white gloves and smacked Blair Devine across the cheek with it. "Always," he finished, with a vaguely pugnacious emphasis.

Devine's face was a picture. He looked flummoxed. Unsure. Perplexed. There'd been no mistaking the timbre of Wilson's voice. The intent and the message. Blair Devine knew something was awry now, but not exactly what. It was like watching him twisting in the wind, desperate for an explanation but unable to ask, because he couldn't reveal himself.

"Um...yes, of course," Devine said, frowning. His face was flushed, and he appeared slightly angry, as well as puzzled. "Might we have a word, Ruffington?" He touched Wilson on the arm, as if to urge him away from the group.

"I'm afraid not," Wilson responded, cool and imperious. "My dear wife and I are just about to go across and congratulate the guests of honor at this happy occasion. Come along, Della, time to wish Sybil and Algernon all the best." Tucking Adela's hand under his arm yet again, he drew her along, sure and unstoppable, nodding briefly to her mother as they went.

"Oh, dear, he doesn't look very happy, Wilson, does he?"

Wilson squeezed his hand over hers where it rested on his forearm. "Don't you worry, my love. Let him stew. He'll be a lot less happy when I acquaint him with what might happen when certain parties take delivery of their stolen papers, and how they might exact retribution if word should come to their ears about just how those papers came to be missing."

"But *we* broke into *his* house," Adela pointed out in the softest voice.

Wilson winked at her, and replied, equally sotto voce, "And

we got away, remember. There's no proof we were ever there, and don't forget, there are those in high places willing to allow me a very great deal of latitude, even if we were suspected." He leaned across and pecked her quickly on the cheek. "Now let's put Sybil out of her state of anxiousness so she can enjoy the rest of her party free of worries."

"Oh, yes, let's!" Adela looked toward her sister, standing receiving guests, with Algernon alongside her. Sybil looked dazzlingly pretty and adorable, and Algie was positively splendid in evening dress, but to the careful observer they both bore signs of strain and tension, in their eyes and in their stance.

"Darling, what a wonderful affair this is." Adela embraced her sibling. It *was* a splendid affair. The mansion house was breathtakingly decorated and filled with examples of fine art. What young woman wouldn't be thrilled beyond measure to know that one day she would be its mistress, with a doting husband at her side? Well, most young women, corrected Adela instantly. It was too ornate a place for her. She preferred her new home in Chelsea, and even Ruffington Hall was less palatial, suiting her better…but only if there was the prospect of sharing both residences indefinitely with the tall lean figure at her side.

"You look very beautiful, Sybil. Pretty as a picture," opined said tall figure, greeting his sister-in-law, kissing her cheek before shaking hands with Algie. "Evening, Framley."

There seemed to be a little lull around them, and Sybil grabbed Adela's hand. "Any news? You said you might be able to, um, do something," she said, her sparkling smile slipping completely and revealing her anxiety.

Adela touched her sister's cheek gently, smiling in reassurance. "I've got a gift for you, Sybil." She unfastened the clip of her little evening bag, and drew out a familiar ribbon, holding up its length before pressing it into Sybil's palm. For a second she exchanged sideways glances with Wilson, and saw a grin on his face. A job well done.

"Oh, Della…Della…" Sybil's pretty mouth opened and shut, much like a pet goldfish, for a moment. "And…and the other things?"

"I'm afraid they accidentally fell into the fire, Syb."

For a moment, the intimation of a pout appeared on Sybil's lips, but then she pursed them, squared her shoulders and seemed to straighten up in a way Adela had never seen before. Her little sister was an adult at last.

"Yes. The best place for them." Sybil turned to her fiancé. "Don't you think so, Algie?"

"Absolutely," the young man agreed, his own face almost alight with relief, too. He thrust his hand into Wilson's and pumped it. Clearly, neither of the younger pair knew exactly what had occurred to free them from threat and doubt, but they were both shrewd enough to deduce that their saviors had taken some kind of risk to ensure a happy outcome.

"Oh, Della, I love you!"

That's the second declaration in the space of half an hour.

But this one was so much easier to deal with, as Adela found herself wrapped in a veritable bear hug of sisterly gratitude. No complications here.

"What's he staring at?" demanded Sybil as they drew apart, glaring over Adela's shoulder.

It was no surprise, on turning, to see Blair Devine staring. Staring at the little length of rose-pink satin ribbon still dangling from Sybil's white-gloved fingers. All trace of his sleek, smug expression was gone now, replace by total confusion and horror. Not to mention frustration. There was nothing he could do. He was shackled by his supposed role as family advisor. He couldn't even claim to have ever seen the ribbon, much less the letters they had once secured.

Adela glanced at Wilson, who was staring at Devine, too. His head was up, his mouth curved just a little. Not gloating, but bearing a look of satisfaction.

Yes, indeed. A job well done.

Her husband turned to her and nodded. The look in his eyes was unmistakable. He *did* love her. That was no untruth.

But did he want to spend the rest of his life with her? That seemed to be a different matter altogether.

THE BALL PASSED in a whirl. Music. Dancing. Smiling faces. Chatter, chatter, chatter.

The joy of Sybil and Algernon seemed to spread out like a sweet, sparkling blanket of good humor that embraced everybody, making the entire event an outstanding success. Even Adela found herself forgetting her questions about her future with Wilson, and succumbing to the general aura of celebration and high-spirited optimism.

No questions, Della. Just enjoy the moment. You've got the most handsome, unusual and brilliant man at your side. You never hoped to ever be able to attend a ball under such circumstances, so relish every moment and savor it to the full.

And Wilson could even dance. Which was unexpected, and yet on reflection shouldn't have come as a surprise to her. He ran and boxed and practiced an Eastern martial art for exercise, which made him light on his feet and agile. He was lean, athletic and graceful. He'd probably made a study of the repeating patterns and the physical mechanics of the waltz, the gavotte and all the other figures, and was able to reproduce the steps perfectly from memory. Adela was a modest dancer herself, but she seemed to glide and fly over the ballroom floor like a virtuosa with Wilson to guide her.

It wasn't normally her way, and she wouldn't have admitted to it if he'd caught her, but every now and again she found herself staring at him adoringly, when he wasn't looking.

What other husband or partner would have countenanced such a daring scheme to come to the aid of Sybil, and all the other victims of blackmail? Anyone else would have simply scurried around, desperately trying to amass sufficient funds, and then, even if they could get the sum together, the victims would still be left at the mercy of Devine, if he'd chosen to retain a choice letter or two as a security.

But Wilson's solution was unequivocal. And not only for Sybil, but for others enduring a similar plight. Adela had had time to note only a few of the names on the labels from the bundles of letters, but she saw at least two of those who were in jeopardy among the guests. She didn't know them as personal friends, so there was no way she could race up to them and tell them the news that would take the haunted expressions off their faces. But in the next few days, a visit would bring them relief and make them smile again.

It certainly made her heart glad to see Sybil and Algie in a seventh heaven of happiness, but there was one person who certainly didn't look happy anymore. Blair Devine had disappeared not long after the incident with the pink ribbon.

"I hope he doesn't take his wrath out on his servants when he discovers what's happened," Adela remarked to Wilson. "It's not their fault he's been foiled, but he's such an unpleasant piece of work I'm sure he'll lash out."

"Don't worry, Della," replied Wilson. They were at the buffet now, and despite everything, Adela received a wicked little thrill watching her husband eat a dish of ice cream pudding. His tongue was so mobile, and he was thoroughly enjoying the sweet confection. When he ran his tongue around his lips it did astonishing things to her imagination and made her shudder, as if that tongue were plying elsewhere.

"I left a sum of money with Earnest in case of that contingency," continued her husband, licking his spoon with scant regard for the august personages in attendance at the ball. "If he cuts up rough, I've instructed Earnest to distribute it, and find lodgings for himself and the other staff, and then tell them all to call on us in a day or two, either for a place or a recommendation. I don't intend that anybody suffer further at the hands of Blair Devine, whatever their station in life."

"Thank you, Wilson. You think of everything."

"One tries." He wiggled his dark eyebrows. "And speaking of stations in life, do you think the marquess and marchioness would think me a yokel if I took another dish of ice cream? It's really rather good."

"I'm sure they wouldn't. They've really taken a shine to you, and that's even without knowing how you've saved their family from a horrid scandal."

"How *we've* saved them," said Wilson firmly. "You were my trusty right hand, Della. You deserve equal credit…as well as every other good thing that's owed to you." He looked serious for a moment, and yes, inscrutable as always. "And speaking of shines… The marchioness seemed very taken with you, and your frock. Perhaps you've created a new convert to rational, aesthetic clothing?"

It was true. The marchioness had been among many unexpected admirers of her unconventional attire, and she had also promised Mme Mirielle's address to several ladies. It might be because most were so dazzled by the Ruffington diamonds that they looked on any gown they adorned with favor, but it was nice to be on the receiving end of such a great deal of admiration and approval, after years of feeling like the odd one out, or an ugly duckling.

As the evening wore on into night, and the small hours, Adela found it difficult to hide a growing fatigue. She had to purse her lips now and again to stifle her yawns, and she knew Wilson had noticed, even if nobody else had.

"Do you think Teale's returned by now?" she asked when, to her chagrin, a yawn escaped her control completely. There was consolation in the fact that other guests were also beginning to fade, but still it was a bit galling to be seen yawning one's head off in polite company.

"I believe so. He's had plenty of time. Shall we say our goodbyes and depart?"

Wilson had been concerned about the strongbox where they'd stored the letters and documents being left unattended in the Spencerleighs' mews. It was unfair to expect Teale to stand guard for every second of the time they were at the ball, so Wilson had dispatched the valet home, to put the precious box in safekeeping, have his supper and then, making sure that their residence was far more secure than Blair Devine's had ever been, return for them. Wilson had charged their two footmen, loyal and brawny lads both, to keep watch all night, lest Devine turn up there on some misguided quest for retribution himself.

After many hugs, and social kisses and promises of visits and of invitations forthcoming, eventually they climbed into the carriage and settled themselves as Teale got the horses under way.

Sleep still pawed at Adela's mind, wanting to claim her, yet at the same time, she was on edge. The interior of the coach was a different place now. Last time she and Wilson had ridden in here, it had been *before*. Before his sudden declaration of love that had seemed to shift the whole universe on its axis. She wanted to throw herself at him, and kiss him and embrace him and tell him that, yes, she loved him, too, and probably always had done, even throughout all the years of their estrangement and at the height of their most savage conflict.

Yet her eyes drooped, and her tongue felt so heavy. "Wilson…what you said…I…" Blinking, she was just on the point of framing the words and getting them out when he laid a long fingertip lightly over her lips.

"Hush, sweetheart, there's plenty of time to discuss all that when you're rested. I can see you're desperate to sleep now." His pale eyes were gentle and kind. Sometimes those eyes could be sharp and fierce and coldly dismissive of all those who didn't meet his exacting standards of intelligence, but that particular Wilson seemed to be off duty now, replaced by the solicitous husband, sensitive to her fatigue after a long, strange night. "Why don't you rest your head on my shoulder and see if you can doze for a while? It's been a most eventful evening, and I must admit I feel sleepy myself."

The offer was so tempting. Her eyes were so heavy. Maybe if she just closed them for a while, she'd feel more alert…and then she could properly tackle Wilson and the issue of her loving him to distraction.

Resting her cheek against his shoulder, she found the smooth cloth of his overcoat felt like the softest pillow, and his arms winding around her were the warmest, snuggest blanket. Even the spicy tang of his shaving lotion was a soporific vapor. She snuggled up, loving the place she was in, and loving the man.

As her eyes closed, and the embrace of Lethe claimed her, she fancied she heard him tell her again that he loved her.

❦ 29 ❦

Do You Love Me?

Wilson stared down at his wife where she lay on the bed, wishing he could invent some mechanism to see inside the mysteries of her heart and mind.

Do you love me, Della? Have you finally forgiven me for all my shortcomings?

He wanted to touch her. He ached to touch her. She had become the only thing that made him feel complete. Yet she was sleeping so soundly now, after all the excitements and triumphs of the evening. She deserved her rest, and she'd barely even stirred when he'd divested her of her cloak and gown, and her petticoats and stockings and shoes.

There was solace in just standing watch, though. In repose, her face was exquisite to him. Everything about it. His heart swelled with a little pride, knowing that with his help, she'd finally accepted that the shape of her nose and the tiny pink scars of chicken pox were not flaws. They were simply Adela, the kink distinctive and the scars the marks of fairy kisses on her skin.

Wilson had to bite his lip in order not to laugh at his own ridiculousness. Was this what love did to a man? It must be, but he didn't care. He could be both whimsical *and* analytical now, in the best of both worlds.

Whether she loved him or not. If she did, he was a king, an emperor, raised up by her. If not, he would make it a priority to ensure that he supplied love enough for two and didn't harm or annoy her in any way. Well, that he wouldn't annoy her *too* much. He was no paragon, and he could be beyond disagreeable even when he didn't mean to. But he'd try. Oh, how he'd try.

"Do you love me, Della?" he asked again, framing the words inaudibly.

The signs were good, and she certainly liked him quite a bit now, at least. She'd gone along enthusiastically with his scheme to retrieve the letters, one that would have been deemed outrageous by most other women of his acquaintance. His mouth twitching wryly, he tried to imagine Coraline subjecting herself to creeping around in the bushes of Devine's garden wearing a tweed suit and no corset. She'd have told him he was ridiculous, and looked at him with disdain. Whereas Adela had plunged into the scheme with gusto and proved to be a valuable assistant. With a delicious flare for the nefarious and the dangerous.

But that wasn't Adela's only enthusiasm. She was a willing and imaginative bedmate, too. Had some of that vigor come from her experiences with the gigolos? He had to face that fact, so he brought it out of its box to examine it.

In the main, contemporary society was hypocritical with respect to women's erotic desires. For many, still, it was as if they weren't supposed to have them at all. But he knew Adela did have those desires. She'd had them in abundance that very first time, their first, and no doubt before. Despite their virginity, she'd enjoyed the experience as much as he had, that had been evident. And it was absurd and unfair that she be asked to expunge those natural physical feelings because his own thoughtlessness had spoiled everything, and other men had been too short-sighted to see her desirability since.

Yes, Adela was entitled to have everything she wanted and needed, and if that had included carnal satisfaction in his absence…well, good for her! He wished he could have been those men, teaching her, and enjoying her…but what had happened could never be reversed, and the only rational thing to do was to accept it, and focus on the positive aspects.

And it was certainly very positive that Adela knew what she was doing in bed, and knew how to please him.

Oh, yes, indeed…

Randy beast, Wilson Ruffington.

He laid his hand over his crotch. He was rigid again, and the sight of Adela's lush hair fanned over the pillow, and her smooth white throat, and her gorgeous pert little breasts beneath her pretty bodice, only hardened him more and more.

She'd been the belle of the ball, no matter how blonde and pretty her sister was. Wilson had seen the men eyeing Adela, heat in their expressions, roused by the free, unfettered sensuality of her beauty, and the way her warm glow fired the cool glitter of the Ruffington diamonds into even greater brilliance.

He'd noted their envy, not of the gems, but of the fact she was on his arm. The fact that they knew he was the one to possess her, and pleasure her, and be pleasured by her.

The fact that he was the one she'd chosen to abide with, in fondness, in friendship, in companionability and in sensuality.

And even in the absence of actual love, that was a precious gift indeed.

ADELA'S EYES SNAPPED open. She wasn't sure what had awoken her, but when she looked around, she saw the familiar furniture and surroundings of her bedroom. The lamps were turned down low, but through a crack in the curtains, dawn light was showing pearly from outside. The clock on the mantel showed that the hour was now six-thirty.

Wilson!

The sound of even breathing, the sense of a warm, benevolent presence next to her, and a glance to her side revealed him lying stretched out on top of the coverlet, fast asleep. His dark curls were a tousled disorder; his waistcoat was undone and so was his dress shirt. There were studs scattered on the bed and presumably on the floor at his side of the bed, along with his shoes, because his feet wore only socks.

Adela stirred, searching her own form with her fingertips, beneath the blankets. She wore only undergarments—bodice and drawers—and the rest of her clothing was strewn over the end of the bed. The Ruffington diamonds lay on the beside chest, gleaming in the low light: necklace, earrings and her divine new clips, all present and correct.

Sitting up, Adela watched her husband closely. He didn't move. He slept on, his lean face almost angelic in repose. She reached out to shake him, then snatched back her hand. She'd slept in her frillies. Her hair was a tangled mess. Her body felt far less than fresh, after a night of dancing, and before that creeping around in the undergrowth and being a burglar. Slipping from the bed as silently and with as little fuss as possible, she crept across the room, snatching up her wrapper as she went, and sought the refuge and modern plumbing of her private bathroom.

Some while later, she peered around the door, and found Wilson sitting propped up against the pillows, writing in one of his many notebooks. He was wearing his dressing gown and his hair looked a little damp, as if he, too, had performed his ablutions.

"Did you sleep well, Della?" He laid aside his book and pen, a tentative, almost boyish look in his pale, gleaming eyes. Wilson was the most confident man she'd ever known, but now he looked far from it. She wanted to race across and hug him and reassure him.

"Yes, thank you. Well, just for an hour or two." She joined him on the bed, kneeling at his side, reaching for his hand. "Look, Wilson, about what you said at the top of the staircase—"

"It's all right, Della. It's all right. You don't have to love me. I don't expect it." His hand curved around hers, tightly. "Over the years, I've behaved abominably toward you. I've tried to do better lately, but I've still been an idiotic ass sometimes." He raised her hand and kissed it, with a kind of desperate ferocity. "I know you want us to stay married so your mother can see you as Lady Millingford. I want to stay married, but if you don't, we can divorce at some later date. Or live separately. Whatever you choose. I won't make life difficult for you."

Adela sighed. Sometimes men could be such dimwits, even the most brilliant ones.

"Wilson Ruffington, for a man who's a genius, you are the most towering imbecile sometimes! If you'd let me get a word in edgeways, I'd tell you that *of course* I want to stay married, and *of course* I want a proper marriage. One that lasts as long as possible." She drew his hand to her mouth this time, and kissed it with just as much passion as he'd done hers. "I love you, you blithering idiot, isn't that obvious? I have done since we were together back at Ruffington Hall."

Wilson grinned. Grinned like the famous Cheshire cat, his head raised in triumph. "I knew it! I knew it!" Lunging at her, he rolled her over onto her back, pinning her down, his eyes ablaze. "Minx! I knew you loved me, I was just waiting for you to admit it. But good God, woman, you've a damned peculiar way of showing it sometimes."

His mouth came down on hers, hard, yet tender. He seemed to be laughing as he kissed her, elated. The emotion was infectious and as Adela giggled, too, the kiss fell apart again. "You are such a smug creature, Wilson—and you're a liar. You looked apprehensive just now.... *I'm* not sure that *you* were sure."

Wilson kissed her again, more in control this time, his tongue moving boldly. "Maybe I was, I don't know," he gasped, lifting up momentarily. "All I care is that now we *both* know, and we're in accord at last, Jesu be praised for that!" Moving farther over her, he resumed the kiss, hungry and intent, rocking his body against hers, letting her know that, sweet and sacred though the sentiments were, delicious carnality, and his virile member, were on the rise, too.

Adela wasn't going to argue. Wilson's hot mouth plundered hers, his strong body was pressed to hers and his cock was pushing against her, rigid and insistent.

All was right in the world, because he was driven by love now, not simply lust alone. Wiggling beneath him, she opened her thighs, inviting him to do something about the situation.

"Mrs. Ruffington, are you inviting me to make passionate love to you?" Wilson's low voice was thrilling in her ear, and even more exciting was the way he nipped and nuzzled at her neck, while pushing his cock at her through their clothing. Thin layers of silk didn't do much to mask its heat and solid intent.

"If it's not too much trouble."

"Dear God, you are such a saucy madam. It's fortunate I'm such a modern man. A traditionalist might discipline his wife for such disrespect and impertinence." Reaching beneath her, Wilson cupped the cheek of her bottom, squeezing it through her robe. Oh, how fond of caressing her there he was. And she loved it, too. She couldn't help but wriggle harder, enticing him. "And you're a lewd wench, dear wife. You always become enthusiastic in the most unseemly way when I play with your delicious bottom."

Unseemly? I'll show you unseemly, you rogue.

Sliding her hand between them, Adela reached inside her robe, finding the pit of her belly and the curls of her *motte*… then her clitoris. With her eyes boldly challenging Wilson's, she began to pleasure herself, while undulating beneath him and rubbing her bottom against his hand.

"Wicked woman!" he growled, half laughing, gripping her bottom cheek harder, his fingertips digging in, and dipping into the cleft, to stimulate her sensitive vent. "I'll spank you for that."

"Oh, yes. Oh, do that. I'd love you to." Adela squirmed harder, rocking her hips and rubbing her clit. She was possessed by desire, full of daring. She could do anything now. Knowing she was loved made her bold and full of relish for her own hungers and Wilson's.

He reared up, wrenching at the silk of her negligee, half tearing it off her, even while she still worked her own flesh. Pulling her hand away from her sex, he kissed her fingers and licked them, cleaning them of her essence, before returning to his task of stripping her. For a moment he held her hand again, preventing her from touching herself, but she fought him, staring up into his blazing silver eyes, and finally making him yield his grip.

After a lick of her own fingertips, she applied herself to her task again, writhing and undulating against her abandoned robe, opening her legs wide so he could see every detail of her actions.

"If you steal an orgasm, there'll be retribution, madam."

His voice was so low, it almost seemed to vibrate, the thrum of it stirring her just where her fingers did.

"I don't have to steal what's mine," she purred back at him, redoubling her efforts, letting her fingers rove to her nipple, too, tweaking and twisting. The little pain seemed to fly to her clitty, enhancing the sensations, and fly to Wilson's eyes, too, making their pale irises shrink and the pupils expand into black orbs of lust.

"Wicked. Wicked. Wicked." Cupping her cheek, thumb beneath her chin, he made her keep looking at him while he reached down, slid his hand close to hers and, hooking a long finger, pushed it into her vagina while she still pleasured herself. A heartbeat later, he pushed in a second digit, parting them to stretch her, and to ply the most sensitive areas inside.

"Well, then, Mrs. Ruffington, finish what you've started. What are you waiting for?"

Uttering a noise that came out part gasp, part moan, part grunt, Adela rubbed herself furiously, staring into Wilson's eyes, forcing herself to keep her own eyes open. His hand around her face was unyielding, his fingers inside her demonic and just as taxing.

It took but seconds for the crisis to bloom. As her channel clenched and the divine pulsations racked her sex, Wilson slid his thumb into her mouth, subduing her groans with a wicked pressure on her tongue. His fingers flexed inside her and the pleasure soared.

Shattered by her climax, Adela wilted, but Wilson wouldn't allow her respite. Withdrawing his hands, he flung off his robe, then, kneeling on the bed, draped her facedown half across his knees, half on the mattress. Her limbs were limp and her body still singing. Wilson's rampant cock was like a burning brand against her hip.

"Delicious, beautiful, decadent woman," he intoned, punctuating each word with a lazy slap across her buttocks. There was no great force in the blows, but the heat of them reignited her, reenergized her. She squirmed, rubbing her puss against his thigh and using her whole body as a means to rock against his erection. "Insatiable siren," he breathed, leaning over her, landing more slaps with one long hand, while with the other he dug around beneath her and into her cleft, to find her clitoris.

As Adela braced herself against the mattress, he rubbed her with the side of his hand, then flicked the little button of her anus with a fingertip.

Adela squealed, spending again, her legs flailing.

"Yes! Yes!" she cried. "I love you, Wilson.… Yes!"

This time he soothed her through the chaos, murmuring gentle nonsense words as she crested, hit the peak and then drifted down. Rolling her over, he folded her into his arms, then slid his hand down to her bottom again, to cradle the glowing, heated areas.

Strange, there was no real pain in it, just the delicious warmth. A miraculous warmth that seemed to charge her sex with new energy despite her feast of orgasms. Reaching up to touch Wilson's face, she told him with her eyes that she wanted more, the ultimate joining, his cock inside her.

"Shall we join?" His voice was husky. She fancied it was shaking with emotion. His eyes were still both dark and light, lambent with desire.

"Yes. I want you, Wilson. I want to feel your pleasure."

Those magic eyes widened, as if comprehending her meaning before she understood it herself. She wanted to feel him, share the most intimate contact again, in a way she'd never shared herself with a man since one day, by a river, in that summer of youth.

She pressed her lips to his, and whispered against his mouth.

"Never once, since then, untrammeled. I was always cautious." Cautious, yes, but perhaps all along wanting to save that one thing for him, in case they were united. Flesh on flesh.

"The same for me." In his eyes she saw the same message, both the spoken and unspoken versions. He, too, had held back from that ultimate intimacy, perhaps for the same reason, perhaps because he was a scientist and an astute observer of life and its perils. She did not care which.

"You could have a child." The words were so soft she could barely tell whether he'd made an observation or asked a question.

"Indeed I could. Would you want me to?"

A shadow danced in his eyes for an instant. Was he cut out to be a father? Would the demands of parenthood be difficult for one sometimes so unworldly and detached, devoted to his scientific and philosophical pursuits? She rubbed her thumb over his lip, to prompt him without actually doing so...and as she did, a new thought occurred.

Had he wanted a child with Coraline? Adela wouldn't ask now; the moment was too delicate. Maybe another time? Whatever had happened, either he'd not cared enough for the Frenchwoman or she'd not cared enough for him, so it no longer mattered.

"Yes!" His pale face glowed, and beneath her thumb, his beautiful mouth curved into a wide smile that was totally unalloyed with doubt. "Yes, I would." He hesitated, his eyes reading her now, looking for truth. "And you, would you like to be a mother? I know it changes a woman's life completely, perhaps limits her.... But I can help, and provide, ensure other help. We're wealthy enough."

Adela laughed, patting his cheek. It was smooth. He must have quickly shaved while she was about her toilette. "Don't worry, Wilson, I think I can manage to prevent my brain from turning to mush when I have a child. I shall endeavor to improve my mind with reading while the babe sleeps, and to continue my artistic efforts." She winked at him. "Although it might be wise to broaden my range of subjects."

"Indeed," said Wilson, moving his body insistently against hers, now that it seemed the various points of possible debate had been dealt with. "Although if you should wish to continue your more…risqué studies in private, you may always draw me, for your own pleasure." He jerked his hips, indicating the item in question.

Reaching down, she fondled the magnificent totem. It was indeed a subject of which she would never tire.

"Well, then, we seem to have dealt with everything. Shall we proceed?" She slid her thumb beneath the head of his cock and circled it.

Wilson groaned like a dying man, and his eyelids fluttered. "Oh, dear Lord, Mrs. Ruffington, yes…let's proceed. Let's proceed or I shall anoint your beautiful hand."

He moved over her. She parted her thighs. With a touch of his hand, he positioned himself.

"My dear, I love you," he gasped, pushing in, pushing home.

"And I you," she answered, tilting her hips, pushing back, taking him in.

30

Diamonds in the Rough

"Wilson, please keep still. It's difficult to draw you when you keep twitching like that."

"I'll try," Wilson muttered between clenched teeth. "But it's very difficult to keep still. I don't always have total control over that portion of my anatomy."

"Very true," observed Adela, tapping her teeth with the tip of her pencil and considering her latest artistic endeavor.

Which was a sketch of Wilson's erect penis with the Ruffington diamonds draped around its base and partially nestled in the dark hair at his groin. They'd made love on returning from a soiree, fired up with giddy excitement and jubilation, and Wilson had insisted on rogering her while she wore the beautiful gems. Afterward, Adela had suggested it was only fair that he should don the diamonds for a change…and when she'd arranged them, an inevitable reaction had occurred.

"How much longer, dearest?" Wilson shuffled against the mattress, making the brilliants slide and glitter. "It's not that

I'm exactly bored, but it seems a shame not to put this phenomenon to good use."

Yes, it was a shame, and Adela's own anatomy was already roused and ready for a second round of pleasure. But she was determined to finish the study.

"I might ask you the same—how much longer?" she replied, licking her lips and wondering how much stiffer and more rampant her husband could get. Her fingers slipped, distracted by him, and she had to reach for her India rubber eraser to make a correction. "Only a minute or two, Wilson. I don't want to make a mess of it. It'll be perfect for *Divertissements*."

"Oh, so you're going to put my cock on display for the delectation of all the randy gentlewomen of London, are you?" His protest didn't fool her. She could tell he was actually inordinately amused by the idea. He didn't mind a bit being drawn for the magazine these days, as long as she never showed his face, and like any man, he enjoyed showing off his virility.

"We have subscribers in the country, too. And some on the Continent. Your magnificent appendage could become a worldwide favorite." Finally satisfied with her efforts, she signed "Isis" in the corner with a flourish, then held up the sketch pad so Wilson could see it.

"Not bad…not bad at all." He moved closer, head cocked to one side to study her work. The necklace slid onto the sheet at his hip, and as Wilson took the pad, Adela reached for it and fastened it around her own neck again. She always felt well dressed and glamorous when wearing the Ruff diamonds… even when she was stark naked, as she was now.

"You really are remarkably talented, Della. It's not easy to reproduce the iridescence of a diamond in this medium, but you've done a pretty fair job, I must admit."

"I'm glad you think so." Adela grinned, amused that Wilson could be so objective about her drawing technique, when faced with an image of his own erect penis.

"Although I should imagine it's not the necklace that your women friends will be appraising, but the form and angle of your husband's erection."

"Don't fret, dear," said Adela, beginning to investigate said form and angle, as it was now so conveniently placed. "Only Sofia, Beatrice and trusted members of the Ladies' Sewing Circle know that I'm 'Isis.' To anyone else reading the journal, it's just a cock, albeit a very nice one."

"Well, that's a relief." Wilson's normally low voice had become thrillingly husky, and he was moving his hips a little, pushing into her grip. "I think we've had enough brushes with scandal recently, without it being touted high and low that there are pictures of my masculine equipment available in a woman's journal of dubious provenance."

It was two weeks now since the events of Sybil's engagement ball, and this morning, Adela had visited the last of Blair Devine's potential blackmail victims. Another woman had sobbed with relief on having all her lost letters put into her hand again. Another woman had promised eternal gratitude, when her offer of recompense was dismissed. This evening's glittering musical soiree had been one of many invitations extended to the Wilson Ruffingtons by way of saying thank-you.

The retrieval of the other documents, and their safe return to various offices and personages, had set other wheels in motion. Because the secrets and precious information had come back to rights by such an unconventional manner, it was difficult to punish Devine for his misdemeanors. But pressure had been brought to bear, heavy hints dropped, emanating from the highest of high places, and the solicitor had been advised in no uncertain terms that it might be in his best interests to emigrate. Somewhere. Anywhere. And by all accounts, he was already on his way, traveling with a rich widow who one hoped had the measure of him. Adela's mother had expressed disappointment at the departure, but Wilson had counseled waiting some months before it was prudent to reveal the truth to her. He'd also introduced his mother-in-law to a distinguished friend of his at a soirée; a retired judge, a widower somewhat older than Mama, but a gentleman of vigorous bearing, with a merry twinkle in his eye. Mrs. Ruffington's eyes had twinkled in return.

"It's not dubious. *Divertissements* is artistic and informative," Adela observed now, plying him with her fingertips. "Although I can reliably predict that the circle ladies who do know whose cock is portrayed will be quite envious of me."

Gnawing at his lower lip, Wilson gasped. "Of course they're envious, woman! You're married to an eminent genius with pots of money, and sooner or later, you're going to be Lady Millingford."

Indeed, she had every good thing to be thankful for. A husband who loved her, and a perfect lover. Total honesty reigned between them now, encompassing all, and the path that had brought them to it was brilliantly illuminated, with no blame, no recriminations, no doubts. More comfortable with Wilson than she'd ever been in her life, Adela edged over to his side, then flung a thigh across his narrow pelvis. Rearing up, she took hold of him by his tip, positioned herself carefully...then released him and sank down and down and down.

"Heaven save me," breathed Wilson, and for a moment, Adela couldn't even say anything. The delicious impact of this feeling was always new.

"No, it's the cock they'll be envious of," she panted, after dragging in a few deep breaths. "Definitely the cock."

"If you say so." Wilson grasped her by the hips, holding her down while he thrust upward. "If you say so..." He seemed to be fighting for breath, too. "I wonder if these women have any idea what a daring and adventurous creature you are, too? Committing acts of burglary with this massively blessed husband yours?"

"I've no idea…but they must think it's an adventure just to live with you. Because of the…blessing…" Summoning her composure, she gripped him fiercely with her inner muscles, smothering her grin when his beautiful silver-blue eyes nearly crossed. "And your dazzling scholarship and your notorious eccentricities."

Wilson came up on one elbow and slung his free arm around her, pulling her down to him. "I'm the one who's dazzled, Della," he whispered, pressing small kisses at the corner of her mouth, then nipping her lower lip.

Slipping her hands behind her neck, fiddling with the necklace's catch, Adela imagined that she and Wilson were diamonds, too. Rough diamonds, not without flaws, but each perfectly matched to the other. "Shall I take them off? They are rather bright," she said, but he caught her wrists and conveyed first one hand, then the other to his lips.

"I'd still be dazzled, my love. You know that, don't you?" Subsiding back against the pillows, Wilson drew her hands down to his chest, then rocked his hips up again, encouraging and provoking, his face bright and handsome with love. "And I always will be."

"Me, too," whispered Adela, dazzled in return.

★ ★ ★ ★ ★